Pip Fox lives in south London with a husband and a cat. Pip likes swimming, nature, getting freckles and throwing fictional characters into sticky situations. This is Pip's first book.

I KNEW YOU WERE TROUBLE

PIP FOX

One More Chapter
a division of HarperCollins*Publishers*
1 London Bridge Street
London SE1 9GF
www.harpercollins.co.uk
HarperCollins*Publishers*
Macken House, 39/40 Mayor Street Upper,
Dublin 1, D01 C9W8, Ireland

This paperback edition 2023
First published in Great Britain in ebook format
by HarperCollins*Publishers* 2023
1

A catalogue record of this book is available from the British Library

ISBN: 978-0-00-859713-9

This novel is entirely a work of fiction. The names, characters and incidents portrayed in it are the work of the author's imagination. Any resemblance to actual persons, living or dead, events or localities is entirely coincidental.

Printed and bound in the UK using 100% Renewable Electricity
by CPI Group (UK) Ltd

To my mum, Sue

ONE

A Terrible Day – A Father's Help

S tart at the river. Let's say on Waterloo Bridge. Put your back to the north and march on to your nearest bus stop. Catch one, or perhaps two, buses (make a note: buses are useful) into south London, over a hellish roundabout and along a seemingly interminable road (highlights: a huge Chinese restaurant, an apothecary established in 1844, an Afghani restaurant-hotel-massage parlour, a Nigerian nightclub and a new library), and go further, up a hill and down again into Zone 3 suburbia. Go past a park, a fire station, restaurants and DIY stores. Disembark at a pawnbroker's, turn the corner by the ghost sign for a 1940s radio components shop, and you'll just make it in time to see Charlie B Hughes emerging from the front door of a block of flats and standing there, open-mouthed, and rather lost-looking.

Perhaps we should take a moment to look at Charlie. She is twenty-seven years old, not terribly tall, and a definite pear-shape (Conference); she tends to sport a slick of scarlet lipstick and matching nails, the polish on her thumbs often flaking away due to being gnawed at when nervous. Today, her short black corkscrew curls are tied in a messy top-knot. She is pale and copiously freckled, a complexion owed to the double-whammy of a pale redheaded mother from Nottinghamshire and a pale, freckled father from County Cork. She is sometimes prone to a speckling of tiny spots across her chin if she drinks too much coffee, has a small mole below the left side of her bottom lip, and another on her right cheekbone. She is almost always impeccably dressed.

However, she is looking a little less than impeccable at this moment. She is gazing distractedly along the pavement, where a woman with toned arms walks at Olympic speed with three small dogs, a small child passes on a scooter with her hair in two bunches and a bus approaches from the south. Charlie blinks as if waking up and runs towards it, looking five times (right, left, right, left, right once more) despite the zebra crossing, and climbing aboard just before the doors close. You'll have to follow her (buses really *are* going to be useful).

This bus heads back towards the park. Note Charlie's body language – temple pressed against the window, phone clutched in her hand, the expression of someone who has recently had a blow to the skull. Follow her as she hops off the bus, past the double bass shop, past the secondhand furniture place, the Jamaican vegan café and the sustainable fashion store. Turn up a side street and follow Charlie as she walks, heavily now, down the steps to a three-storey terraced house and unlocks the door.

'Hello?' she shouts, into the ether.

There's a bump and the muffled sound of a sleepy, annoyed person shouting back. 'What?'

Charlie throws down her keys. 'This day is literally the worst day of my entire life,' she shouts.

• • •

Charlie was a little prone to exaggeration, but even a neutral observer would agree that Monday 16th of September 2015 had not been her best. It began with her alarm taking the highly independent decision not to go off. Her boyfriend hadn't stirred, but he was a very intellectual Masters student studying Digital Media in the 21st Century and he had to get nine and a half hours otherwise he wouldn't function at full capacity. Therefore Charlie had woken with a start at 9.14am, fourteen minutes after she was supposed to be at her desk, didn't shower, and got to work seventy minutes late, not entirely helped by a breakdown (bus) and signal failures (tube), smelling disgusting and with her hair looking distinctly unkempt.

She had been immediately summoned to her boss' office.

'I am so, so sorry,' she said, waving her phone, hand on heart for extra honesty. 'Our boiler burst, and I would've called, but my phone's playing up.'

'Hmm,' said her boss, Andreas. Andreas's hums signified different things, from anointed approval, to indifference, to downright disappointment. This sounded rather more like the latter. 'Take a seat, Charlene.'

'Um,' Charlie had said, sitting down, and accidentally swivelling round ninety degrees on the office chair. 'It's actually Charlie.' She swivelled back round, realising that she was still in her trainers, having left her heels by the porch in their flat, and that she hadn't brushed her teeth and seemed to smell of aniseed. 'If that's OK.'

No one, apart from Andreas, called her Charlene. Even her parents had become rather embarrassed about having christened their daughter after the nation's darling Australian soap character, circa 1989.

'Hmm,' said Andreas, noncommittally. He had an array of

pristinely ironed shirts in pastel shades, and today was sporting the mint green. 'It's not about the lateness. It's about last night.'

There was a small ringing sound – not unlike the alarm that should have gone off at 7.25am – in Charlie's brain, faint but distinct. 'Last night, cool,' she said, sitting a little straighter. Her stomach grumbled.

'How did it go, in your opinion, hmm?' Andreas clasped his hands on his torso.

Charlie tried to arrange her face into a pensive expression. In truth, last night was a little hazy. She'd been charged with taking clients out for dinner, hoping to make a company selling data analytics products seem wildly entertaining. They'd gone to a posh Japanese restaurant, the food assembled expertly in front of them, the sake poured. Quite a lot of sake.

'Great,' she said, with a fabulously bright smile. 'Mr. Rodríguez was very excited about today's meeting. He said he was looking forward to further developments.' Best to keep it vague, when she couldn't entirely remember. God, she was hungover.

'On the contrary,' Andreas said, stretching. He went to the gym at 6am every morning, and always arrived drinking a protein shake in a reusable container and cricking his neck. 'He called me last night to tell me the deal was off.'

Charlie stared at Andreas. Her throat tasted rather acrid.

'In fact, he told me all about the evening, and how you seemed to drink rather more than everyone else, before raising a toast with a shot of flaming sambuca. Remember? Hmm?' He cocked his head.

Yes. Of course she did. The gin and tonics, the sake, the increasing confidence, the encouraging smiles of the Spanish visitors round the table, the feeling of being good at something and the chance of being promoted, of having a job that didn't have the words 'junior' and 'executive' in the title. Then the toast. Charlie had stood up to gather the attention of the table, stumbled in her heel and, as her ankle twisted sideways, so too did the hand holding the shot glass, and if she really thought hard about it, she could picture the glass tumbling out of her grip and flying to a tier of drinks on the trolley next to them before going up in an impressively theatrical fireball.

'Someone could have been very seriously hurt,' Andreas said.

'It went a bit wrong,' said Charlie, with a marginally less fabulous smile. 'It really *was* meant well.' She always meant well.

'Hmm,' said Andreas. 'The thing is, Charlene, you've had two warnings already. When you booked the Korean visitors on the flight to Portland, Oregon rather than Portland, Maine, which cost this company much more than had been budgeted. When you replied-all to the entire company talking about my deputy in less-than-complimentary terms and then replied-all *again* with the words "shit shit shit sorry". And when you first started, I should have given you a warning for using the photocopier to print out the details of flats for rent.'

'Yeah, I know, I'm so—'

He steamrolled right over her. 'And we both know that you've not always been on time.'

'The buses,' Charlie said, weakly.

'Yes, the buses.' Andreas shook his head, as if buses themselves were a fiction of Charlie's imagination. He lived out in East London, very close to a tube line. 'If the buses really are so bad, you could get up earlier, as I've said on several occasions. Or cycle.'

Charlie went to agree, and realised she felt strongly that she didn't want to do either of those things.

'I don't see much evidence that you're committed to this position.'

'Hmm,' said Charlie, who had absolutely nothing to counter at this point. 'I see what you're saying.'

'You are still within your probation period, as you know.'

Five and a half months into her six-month probation period, she thought with a dull pang of dread, knowing very well what must be coming.

'I think we should look into parting ways.'

A breath. There it was. She knew that she should be defending herself, but found that she simply didn't have the heart.

'Good,' said Andreas, standing up, his chest muscles tight against his shirt. 'HR will deal with everything else. Take the last two weeks off. It's been *interesting* working with you.'

Charlie had quietly packed up her things – a pencil tin that she'd never used, glasses case, framed photo of her and her boyfriend outside that yurt in Cornwall two summers ago – feeling utterly dejected. She'd looked at the photo – Alex's adorable, goofy smile and thumbs-up – and knew that he would make her feel better.

Until she got hold of him, and he told her that he was breaking up with her.

'Literally the worst day of my life,' she was saying for the fifth time whilst her younger sister Casey gazed at her, stoically eating a Toffee Crisp. 'Fired. By my boss. And by my boyfriend.'

Exaggeration again. The actual worst day of her life had occurred long ago, aged six, the day their big sister Jools went to visit her friend and never came back. However bad this was, it could never beat that.

But still. It was only 1pm.

'Your boyfriend,' said Casey, crunching into her chocolate bar, 'is a douchebag.'

'*Was* a douchebag,' Charlie said, or attempted to say, because her teeth were glued together by the components of the Lion Bar Casey handed to her as she lay on her back on the sofa. 'Because he is no longer my boyfriend.'

After leaving the office, she'd texted him, knowing he'd be busy with his library research. She left him a voicemail. And another. Texted him. She'd decided to head home to their flat when finally Alex had called back. Not to follow up on her hysterical messages with boyfriendly reassurance but to tell her, in his relaxed yet highly erudite way, that he'd been having a good think and had decided that they shouldn't be together anymore. Because he needed someone more motivated. More together.

'But I've just lost my job,' she'd said.

'Exactly, babes,' he'd said.

'But—'

'That's what I'm saying. I'm in a place where I need to be really focused, you know? Nothing too dramatic.'

'*Dramatic* is breaking up with me. That's dramatic. We *live* together.'

'Yeah,' he'd said. 'About that.'

. . .

'I mean, I could have told you that. I *did* tell you that.'

Casey, aged twenty-two, was not the most sympathetic of sorts. She was usually too busy having her head in the clouds – almost literally, what with being a third year astrophysics student with little interest beyond thermodynamics and stellar evolution.

'You would have said that no matter who he was, or what he was like,' said Charlie.

'Exactly.'

Charlie sighed. 'What am I going to do, though, Case?'

Homeless. Actually homeless. Alex had informed her that he needed to live on his own for a while in order to finish his dissertation on Ecosophical Praxis of New Media Space Design and therefore she needed to move out. Immediately. He'd even offered to get storage boxes from IKEA. 'You can keep my Mighty Mouse T-shirt,' he said. 'As a leaving gift.'

'I'll have one month's salary and then… ' Charlie put down her Lion Bar and stared at the ceiling. 'And nowhere to live.'

'Obviously Mum and Dad are going to say you can stay here. Though it's not going to be in my room. I'm making that clear right now.'

Charlie sighed, for the fiftieth time. She knew Casey wasn't the right person to talk to about this, but her very best friend in the world had just moved to New Zealand with her boyfriend and it was after midnight there. 'I can't believe he's just—' Two years and four months with Alex, curled up next to him on the sofa or in their bed, even if half the time he was, to be honest, reading a book on the intersection of new technology and storytelling and not listening to her. But then he'd put down the book, roll over and start singing Taylor Swift songs in her ear (he loved Taylor Swift). Or take her to Dulwich Park where they'd do circuits in one of the two-seater recumbent bikes whilst swigging cans of gin and tonic, followed by a drunken go on the green gym equipment. Or they'd head up to Kensal Rise for Saturday night dinners at his family's house, with his Chinese mum feeding her Henan braised noodle soup, heavy on the ginger and star anise. 'It's like the rug's been pulled from under me. And there's not floor underneath, just a big gaping canyon of nothingness. I don't know where I am. *Who* I am.'

'Well, that is lame,' said Casey. 'You're Charlie. End of.'

But Charlie had never known what that had meant. Not since Jools's accident. Some people defined themselves by their jobs, but hers had always simply been a means to an end. The end being the payment of rent on the one-bed flat she shared with Alex, bills, council tax, food, London transport, MAC make-up, weekend brunches with Alex, holidays with Alex and the odd excellent piece of statement clothing. That's what she did – she looked for someone else to define her, because she didn't know how to define herself. 'I'm not good at anything.'

'If you're fishing for compliments, you're not going to get them.'

It wasn't true, of course. Charlie *did* excel at some things: she always bought a cake for people's birthdays, had an ear for singing harmonies, an impressively high tolerance for chillies (which is how she won over Alex's mum), made superlative breakfast smoothies – though their virtuousness was often diminished by the amount of salted caramel chocolate she ate in the afternoons – possessed a Mastermind-level knowledge of South London bus routes and had the ability to fall asleep in seconds (including on South London buses).

'Just start over,' said Casey, who'd never had to do any such thing, being a super-brain. 'Not a big deal.'

'Urgh,' said Charlie, still picturing herself floating in a starless vacuum, like an abandoned astronaut. 'I need to be more independent. Once I have some money.'

Casey blew out her cheeks, as if glad this conversation seemed to be drawing to a close. But then she looked over with a modicum of interest, or perhaps even sympathy, and Charlie waited for her soothing, sisterly affection to finally emerge.

'Can I finish your Lion Bar?' Casey said.

Charlie had grown up on the edge of Brixton that merged gently into Herne Hill's suburban streets. It hadn't always been gentle, and there were memories of raucously drunken singing outside, broken bottles, the odd police car. All of those things still happened, sometimes, but largely the streets were pretty sedate. Too sedate. Every so often a new inappropriately posh wine bar would open up, and just as often close down again, to be replaced with another. Charlie liked the places that had been there forever, felt part of the community. The jerk chicken place on the corner and the shop where drivers got their cars kitted out with window-rattling bass-bins were still going strong, for now at least.

The family residence, a stone's throw from the low hills, lido and pond of Brockwell Park, sat on one of a collection of roads named after great English poets and playwrights. It was a slim three-floor terraced house bought for next to nothing in the 1980s and now, due to the preposterousness of London house prices, worth a great deal more.

Casey had gone to a seminar, so Charlie took a quick nap

on her parents' bed and woke up three hours later to the sound of very loud grime emanating from downstairs. Which only meant one thing.

In the kitchen, Charlie's dad was chopping up peppers and swaying his not-insubstantial rear very much in time. His mother called him *a great big lump* and he didn't seem to mind one bit.

When he saw Charlie, his face lit up. 'Well, sweetheart,' he said, leaning his cheek down so it could be kissed. 'What a nice surprise.'

'Hey, Dad.' Charlie dragged out a bar stool from under the counter and rubbed her eyes.

'How was your day? Finished early?'

'Work has sort of ended.'

'Wonderful,' he said, over the clattering beats. 'Good to have a boss who gives his employees some downtime.' An emphatic final chop, and the peppers were added to the hillocks of finely-diced spring onions and slivers of ginger.

Aidan was the deputy head of a primary school round the corner. He had been known to set up parallel playground tournaments for World Cups (putting all the strongest players in the Republic of Ireland team, whether they had qualified for the real thing or not) and take his charges to old people's homes for tea parties. In 1986, he had led Charlie's mother to the Ritzy Cinema Club and pointed upwards, where the lettering had been arranged to say: NELLIE, WILL YOU MARRY ME?

'No,' said Charlie, putting her elbow on the kitchen counter and dumping her head on her hand. 'I mean, *really* ended.'

Aidan stopped his expert chopping and looked at her. He always thought the best of her, and it made it so much harder to own up.

Charlie moved her eyes up to him. 'A couple of things have ended, actually.'

Aidan put on the kettle as Charlie filled him in.

'I'm sorry, kitten,' he said. 'I thought Alex was a good one.' He would often genially slap her boyfriend on the back so hard that he almost fell over, and engage him in loud, profound discussions about the morality of mobile phone adverts or the downturn in Taylor Swift's songwriting since she moved from country to pop.

'Yeah. So I am jobless, boyfriendless and homeless.' She stretched. 'Yay.'

He looked sternly at her. 'You are never homeless. You know that.'

'But what about Bryn?'

Bryn was their lodger, an eerily quiet photo archivist and the current occupant of Charlie's old bedroom, following a succession of equally odd tenants. He tended to eat in his room and play morose ambient music at a high volume. He'd lived there a year, and Charlie had glimpsed his retreating back exactly twice.

Aidan gave an easy shrug. 'We can put the camp bed in Casey's room for you. Until you get somewhere else, that is.'

Charlie sighed into her mug. 'Yeah. OK. Thanks, Dad.' As expected, and fair enough. They couldn't just chuck Bryn out just because she was an utter failure at life. She knew she was lucky, really – plenty of people genuinely wouldn't have anywhere to go in her situation.

'So what now?' Aidan said, leaning back on the counter and folding his arms. 'What's the plan?'

'Oh, you know.' She felt shattered. Shaky. 'Job. New room somewhere.' She didn't say boyfriend. There would be no boyfriending, or dating, or hook-ups, for a long while. They were bad for her health.

'You can do it,' he said, as he always did. The utter confidence of a devoted father, the one who had told her she could go down the big slide (she did, only after getting stuck and having to be forcibly pushed by the kid behind), join the debating club (the other team won) and score five goals in her Under 11s football final (she scored the first, before getting sent off for punching the goalkeeper). He'd been Charlie's ultimate cheerleader, and after what they'd all been through, she'd needed it. 'Come here and give your bossman dad a hug.'

'That's not how you use bossman, Dad.' He partly listened to the radio station to keep up to date with any slang that the older kids at school might say, except he tended to get it wrong.

'Never mind all that.' Aidan's hugs were all-encompassing, the embrace of a very benign grizzly bear. Charlie let herself get engulfed, and felt a tear or two come.

A different grime track came to a rattling close, the DJ giving shout-outs. 'Props to my man Aidan in Brixton, making some tasty noodle soup tonight. Yes, bruv! I'll be coming round later to taste it, yeah?'

'You are classic,' Charlie said, the words muffled by her mouth being pressed against his shirt.

'You love your peng dad,' he said.

'Hmm.' She did, though. 'Um, Dad?' she said.

'Yes?'

Her sweetest, most compliant voice. 'Please could I borrow some money?'

''Course you can.' He let her go and reached over for his wallet, delving into it to bring out a twenty-pound note. 'Here you go.'

Charlie looked at it. 'Um… I was hoping for a bit more.'

'How much?' His face was open and uncomplicated.

She felt very, very small. 'Maybe, um, a grand?'

His eyebrows came down and he put his wallet on the counter. 'Charlie. If I had that sort of money floating about I'd have taken your mother on that cruise around the fjords by now. Do you really not have any?'

'I'm so sorry. I've been a bit behind with things, and I'll need a deposit for a room.' Alex was staying in the flat, and said he'd give her half the deposit back, but it wouldn't be enough.

He gave a large sigh. 'We named you for a reason.'

'Because Mum was obsessed with *Neighbours*.'

'Not your first name. Your middle name.'

Charlie drew in a breath and let him give her the gentle lecture he did approximately once a year. Her parents had seen fit to give her and her sisters the middle names of three Irish war goddesses and it was frankly hard to live up to.

'You know we wanted our daughters to be strong women. Independent women, who don't take any nonsense. I don't want you going all wasteman on us.'

'I won't go all wasteman,' Charlie said, too tired to correct him.

'Good.' He proffered the twenty-pound note again. 'You can start off with this, and we'll see how you go.'

TWO

Job-seeking – A Generous Man

The city in September. It can be a mixed month, the rains bringing the leaves down early to clog up the gutters, or the summer hanging steadfastly on. School children pour onto the buses, the diminutive Year 7s among them, their blazers too big; by the end of the year, they'll be pushing to the back seats like the older kids. People sit on the picnic benches outside the pubs of Herne Hill after work, and talk about office politics and last night's TV. Charlie walks past them, avoiding – as she has done for twenty-one years – looking at the sign for Shakespeare Road. If you listen very closely as she crosses (having first checked for cars five times), you might hear her breath catch and be held until she is on the pavement again. For it was halfway up this road that Jools had burst cheerfully out of her friend Josie's house, and slipped between two parked cars, turning round to shout to Josie that liquorice *was* and always would be disgusting and that was the end of it. Charlie turns onto Spenser Road, a heaviness in her chest that is partly the memory of that time, and partly because she is far too old to be lifting the lock on her parents' gate for another night.

———

'Casey.'

The room was giving off a dullish lime-green glow. There was a light, irregularly rhythmic tapping sound.

'Mmm.'

'*Case.*'

'Yeah?'

'Please, please, *please* can you turn that off now? I can't sleep with the glow from the screen and you typing all the time.'

'I'm working.'

'It's half-midnight.'

Casey, sitting up in bed, tapped some more, and finally closed the lid of her laptop. 'Fine.' She blew a deliberately unsubtle gust of air through her lips. 'You always have to be the boss.' She leant over to put the laptop on her desk and lay down.

Charlie shifted over to her other side, her left hip already aching from the flimsy camp-bed Aidan had set up. A twenty-seven-year-old staying on her little sister's floor. Absolute class.

She'd never really known how to be a big sister. Only a younger one. For the first six years of Charlie's life, Jools had told her what to do – helped her stir chocolate chip cookie dough, encouraged her down the slide in the park, reminded her to water the left-hand sunflower in the garden. Even now Charlie often felt like the baffled little girl she was in the weeks and months following Jools's death, and not an adult at all.

There was another intense sigh from near her head, the sort that clarified the resentment at being told to stop working, because Casey's brain needed constant activity. She was the undisputed genius of the family, stomping to the top of the class, determinedly the swottiest of swots. She'd been drawing planets and solar systems since the age of three, and her obsession with all things astronomical had never gone away. In her last year studying Physics with Astrophysics and Cosmology at King's, she had professors at several universities clamouring for her to take up an MSc. No doubt she would be heading up some NASA space programme and discovering a new solar system by the time she was Charlie's age.

'You should get yourself a better job,' Casey said stroppily, into the darkness. 'I still don't know what you actually did in this one.'

Me neither, thought Charlie. 'Easier said than done.'

'What do you want to do? Like, for an actual career?'

Career was the grand word for those becoming lawyers and doctors and astrophysicists. Not for the girl who'd picked her A-Levels, and indeed her degree course, by closing her eyes and jabbing a finger onto a piece of paper. Charlie's twenties had seen a succession of short-term positions whose titles would make up the contents of a very dull set of fridge magnet poetry. Telesales assistant, administrative assistant, receptionist, data entry administrator, administrative assistant again.

She absent-mindedly thumbed the faded pastel beads of her friendship bracelet. Jools had made it for Charlie two weeks before she died, and Charlie had never removed it, except to occasionally rethread the beads onto new cotton. 'I'm not like you, Case,' she said. 'I don't have a vocation. Or as much brain mass.'

Another weighty sigh. 'Why do you have to play the idiot all the time? Just get a better job.' She rolled over and her next words came from under the duvet, though they were still obvious enough. 'So I can have my bloody room back.'

———————

'Jobs,' said Charlie. 'Jobs, jobs, jobs.'

Today was a fresh, sparkling thing. Today was the beginning of the new, improved, man-ignoring Charlie. If she just said the word enough times, something astonishing would leap out from the app she'd downloaded this morning and she wouldn't revert to thinking gloomily about Alex and stalking his Instagram feed, which hadn't been updated. She'd texted him to say she was back at her family house and would pick up her stuff later; he'd responded with a single, blasé thumbs-up, leaving her feeling emptier than ever. The more she thought about it, the more she realised how indifferent he'd been in the last few months. Perhaps this hadn't been a sudden decision by him, but had been brewing for a while.

The café at the southern end of Herne Hill had recently reopened, stocked with retro wooden school chairs and mismatched tables. It had once been a tailor's and there were brutish antique sewing machines on high shelves as well as two *wunderkammers* – cabinets of curiosities – with yellowed tape measures, thimbles and other paraphernalia. Apart from the army of gym mums and their tank-like pushchairs, just one youngish white guy sat reading a book in the corner, his head propped on his fist.

Charlie kept scrolling through the adverts. *A job tailor-made for me*, she thought and managed not to say aloud, as the soulless list of vacant positions continued to blur past.

Marketing. HR. Graduate. Central London. They all meant the same thing: getting up, eating a breakfast bar as you ran to the Underground, squeezing onto a carriage with your nose underneath the armpit of a large, un-deodorised man, your high heels in your bag, buying lunch in too much plastic packaging from a chain sandwich bar, counting down the hours until home time by flicking furtively between various social media sites. It would be nice to have a job with purpose.

The coffee machine behind the counter started up its drilling sound again, adding to the violent protests of at least three babies and their determinedly oblivious mums. Charlie leant towards her phone on the table. One more jobs category.

ADMINISTRATOR, CITY FARM,

she read, and clicked on the link.

POINT OF CONTACT FOR ENQUIRIES AND GENERAL PROJECT ADMINISTRATION. FUNDRAISING, MANAGING VOLUNTEERS AND ARRANGING WORKSHOPS.

Well, that sounded all right. It wasn't even that far away. She'd been faintly aware of the corner of a new site up at Ruskin Park; they'd had diggers there for ages. Working in a little office with a *baa*-ing lamb on her lap (she assumed) felt more tempting. She did have a lot of admin experience, albeit rather less in the way of farmyard knowledge. But how hard could it be? The job didn't actually require dealing with the animals as far as she could tell. She rather liked the idea of people's eyes not glazing over at parties when they asked what she did, though she couldn't imagine what a city farm might possibly look like. Would there be cows? She had a thing against cows, having once been chased down a sloping field after a festival by a marauding pack of them – no, pack didn't sound right. What was the collective noun for cows and would they ask this if she somehow got an interview?

The salary was on the slim side. The size *zero* side. Barely enough to cover the ridiculous amount she needed to rent a room. Really, she should only look at office jobs in the city, serving the needs of shouty, striped-shirted moneymen.

But then there was a sudden unbidden memory of Jools staying silent for a whole day, even when her little sister was tickling her. Jools had enjoyed a sponsorship craze, raising money for Comic Relief and Children in Need. There'd been a sponsored fast, a sponsored skip, a sponsored three-legged walk, tying her and Charlie's legs together with their dad's dressing gown belt and not letting her escape until they had remained bound for five hours. Not that Charlie had wanted to.

She looked at the ad again. Maybe this was what she needed to do. Give something back.

'Are you going soon?' A woman with two very red-faced, squalling children in a double pushchair was hovering with an unsubtle glance at Charlie's almost-empty mug.

'Yep, sure thing.' Charlie took a screenshot of the page, drained the cold dregs of her latte and went to the counter to pay.

'£2.90, please,' said the rather dead-eyed girl at the till.

Charlie did a swift add-up of her change, lining it up on the wooden counter. Two pounds eighty exactly. 'Damn. Can I pay by card?'

'It's £5 minimum.'

Arse. She was supposed to be saving her pennies. She shouldn't really have come in here. Five quid for a coffee was very bad on principal. Charlie gave a sweet smile. 'Can I give you the 10p next time? I'll be in again; I live round the corner. I'm just short.'

A dead-eyed shake of the head. 'Sorry. You can buy something to take away and then you can use your card.'

Charlie gave a small sigh of frustration. 'I promise I'll be in again. I'll come tomorrow. First thing.'

'Sorry. If I did it for you, I'd have to do it for everyone.'

Charlie's shoulders sagged and she did her very best not to loudly swear.

'I have 10p,' said a voice at her side. The sandy-haired man who'd been reading in the corner was standing there, cupping some silver coins in his hand.

'Oh no, you don't have to do that,' she said. That wasn't the point at all. It was literally 10p, and they were charging ridiculous amounts for a small mug of what was essentially flavoured milk and water.

He glanced at Charlie, and passed it over the counter. 'It's no problem,' he said. His accent sounded German, or Polish maybe.

She felt a rush of embarrassment. 'Fine,' she said, to both him and the sullen coffee girl. 'Fine. Thank you. You really didn't need to.' She gave the briefest of smiles before putting her bag strap over her shoulder, and walking out.

It had started raining, the especially dirty, polluted kind of rain. Charlie stood under the awning of the next shop along for a moment, to see if it might lessen. She tried not to sulk, but she couldn't help feeling put out. She had other options back there – she *could* have bought a £4 brownie, rather than having been shamed into looking petty, poor, or both of the above. She turned round to check her appearance in the reflection of the newsagent's. She should have brought a brolly; now her hair would frizz.

'Herd,' she said suddenly, the correct word for a group of cows popping into her head.

'Excuse me?'

'Huh?' She turned to see the 10p guy standing there, holding out her favourite scarf, the one with roaring tigers' heads on it.

'You dropped this.' He pronounced it *dis*, with the subtlest *d*.

'Oh. I totally did. Thanks.' Everything was leaving her – employment, boyfriend, small change, wardrobe.

She took the scarf from him and he gave a small, uncomplicated smile. He was tall, quite tanned, with hazel eyes and the slightest curl to his short hair. Late twenties, probably. *Quite cute*, said one half of her brain. *Shut up*, said the other half.

'Definitely need it in this weather,' she said, wrapping it around her neck, just for something to say, and to not seem ungrateful. She'd been rude by the till. *My girl's got tiger-pride*, her dad would say, if Charlie had argued about something. *She rears her head and roars.*

He squinted upwards. 'Yeah. I guess the summer is over.' He was holding the book he'd been reading in the café. It had a very evil-looking pig on the front.

'*Állatfarm*,' she read, craning her head. George Orwell.

He looked down, a little self-consciously. 'Oh. Yeah. It's the Hungarian version. Do you know it?'

'I haven't read it,' she said. Though maybe she would, as research for that job. The book seemed like a good sign, even if she was fairly sure it didn't end well for everyone. She glanced up again. 'I guess it's not stopping.' Time to face the frizz. 'I'm going to take off. Are you waiting for the bus?'

'No,' he said, taking a step backwards. 'I have my bike.'

'OK. Well… thanks very much for saving my neck. Literally and figuratively.' She gave a semi-wave, and as she made off, she saw him give a semi-wave back, and shrug his rucksack round to his chest to put the book away.

Charlie dashed down the road, picturing the porcine gothic watercolour on the book's cover again.

A piggy omen. Yes. She would bloody well go for that job, and she would bloody well get it.

THREE

A Sign – An Interview – A Cottage

'Rooms,' said Charlie. 'Rooms, rooms, rooms.'

It had been a week since she'd applied for the city farm job, and several other jobs besides; a week of staying on her sister's floor listening to a wealth of booming sighs and having to wait eons for the bathroom – the near-invisible Bryn spent mysteriously long amounts of time in there.

She was back in the Old Tailor's café, this time with three room-renting websites open on her phone, each promoting horrible rooms for horrible amounts of money. The ideal advert would be a light, airy double bedroom with white-painted floorboards in a huge loft conversion with very quiet, rich housemates of diverse backgrounds who mostly worked abroad, held the occasional civilised party and charged £200pcm, including bills.

Charlie had endured a ghastly half-day of packing up her stuff from the old flat. Alex hadn't been in, but his new housemate – a suspiciously gorgeous, sallow-skinned French girl he'd recently made friends with, who was apparently staying on the living room's sofa-bed – had hovered politely by the bedroom door the whole time, as if unsubtly trying to check that Charlie wasn't stealing anything. She even put her hand out for the keys when Charlie left.

'Men are horrific,' she said to her mum, Nellie, who was waiting outside to put the final boxes into the boot of their old estate car, following her shift at the hospital in Tooting where she was a nurse. She'd wanted to sound brave and dismissive, but it ended up coming out in a cracked, pathetic tone.

'Oh, sweetheart,' said Nellie.

Charlie got into the car and stared at the windshield. 'I kind of thought he might be the one, Mum.' Even as she uttered the words, she wasn't sure that she believed them, but she'd certainly hurtled into the relationship with determination.

Charlie had always tried to live for the moment. But it wasn't done in the chilled, mindfully-appreciating-every-leaf manner, but rather with her head down and a faint sense of panic. The hare, not the tortoise. You never knew when you or anyone close to you might get mown down by a bus, or have a heart attack, or choke on a peanut without anyone in the vicinity who knew the Heimlich Manoeuvre. 'Let's live together!' she'd said, after only three months of dating cute, dreamy Alex Zhou. ''K,' he'd said. She suspected, having now removed her Alex-tinted glasses, that he'd only agreed so that he could share the rent on a nicer place.

'You don't need to be looking for the one yet, darling,' said Nellie, shutting the driver's door. 'If there is such a thing.'

'Don't you think there is?'

'Not really,' said Nellie, with her usual frank cheer. 'Your dad and I just got lucky.' She put her hand over her daughter's. 'It wasn't to be. Onwards and upwards.'

Onwards. Charlie had already spent three days visiting houses and flats, trying to convey her best and most capable self. It was necessary to go through personal ads rather than estate agents, seeing as she didn't have a job. That way she could lie through her teeth and use the words *temping* and *short-term contracts* and *maternity leave cover*. But in every case, she'd had a polite and apologetic phone call later that day saying they'd gone with someone else, probably a journalist or entrepreneur or criminal lawyer with more self-esteem, a fat wallet and martini-making skills. The only positive response had been from a basement flat with three hirsute guys who'd been playing a computer game featuring thick-thighed women with swords of fire, their curtains shut and the Overground line clattering right outside, and it was she who'd politely declined.

Charlie had come back to the café to start another round of room-seeking, seeing as she'd spotted the job advert while there. Perhaps luck was in the air. Today, there was a soundtrack of old blues songs, and a rather gentler atmosphere. She'd even brought enough change.

She bent her nose down so that it was almost touching her phone on the table. 'Give me a dream room,' she said, in her best hypnotic murmur, and swiped at the screen.

Half an hour and a distinct lack of dream rooms later, she had paid and was heading out of the door, feeling morose.

'Hello.' The Hungarian guy was standing by the noticeboard, holding a local newspaper and a millionaire's shortbread in a clear bag.

'Oh. Hey. How are you?'

'I'm fine.'

Charlie glanced at his paper. 'Finished Animal Farm? What's it in Hungarian again?'

'*Allátfarm*,' he said. 'Yeah. Pretty powerful at the end.' There was a blunt, slightly bruised quality to his accent.

'No spoilers. I haven't read it.'

'Well, they don't all live happily ever after.' He had a bit more stubble than last time. And possibly, she thought, the slightest blush high up on his cheeks.

'Bad pigs.'

He smiled at the notices. 'But in real life I can beat them.'

'How d'you mean?'

'I'm a butcher.' He told her that he and his friend had taken over a railway arch in Peckham last year and had been slowly building up their business, selling other local deli produce alongside the meat.

He didn't really look like a butcher, Charlie thought, but perhaps butchers didn't sport their blood-spattered aprons outside the shop, or all look like the rotund, sweaty men of cartoons. 'Bacon sandwiches all round, then,' she said.

When he smiled, the corners of his eyes creased into three delicate lines.

She was trying to imagine him hurling a massive cleaver into the belly of a cow when her phone buzzed with an email alert. 'Oh my God,' she said, as she read it. 'Wow.'

'Are you all right?' The guy was looking at her.

'Oh my God.' Another blink. 'Yes. Totally. I am awesome.'

He gave a slightly surprised grin and nodded. 'Cool.'

Charlie held up her phone. 'Job,' she said. It had been true. She just had to say it enough times, and someone would offer her an interview for a position she actually half wanted, as long as she was able to stand the smell of sheep shit and wasn't going to be terrorised by cows. 'Gotta go. Research.'

He turned as she put on her coat. 'What will you research?'

'Pigs,' she said.

Walk from Denmark Hill train station with the NHS staff – detectable by their lanyards and determined, exhausted expressions – overtaking you with takeaway coffees in their hands as they rush towards the ever-expanding King's College Hospital or the Maudsley opposite. Go straight ahead, through a black metal gate and you're in the corner of one of the area's smaller parks, spreading between suburban roads and the railway line.

Named after eminent Victorian art critic, writer and thinker, John Ruskin, the park is a squashed oblong whose features include tennis courts, a large paddling pool and playground, the most rudimentary of skate parks (two small ramps), a bandstand, a pond, and a labyrinth garden. If you stand at the highest point, you can see the Shard's severe blade-tip and the City's increasing collection of oddly shaped skyscrapers. If you stand at the lowest point, nearest the hospital, you'll see Charlie, standing outside a large sign and a mosaic of tiles painted by children, taking a deep breath and lifting the wooden latch.

South London's newest city farm had been funded by the council, a collection of charitable trusts and corporate sponsors. Following the successes of others dotted around the capital, there had been several years of hard campaigning before the council had agreed to turn a neglected corner of the park into a community farm. Construction had begun by the railway line eighteen months ago, and the farm had opened at the beginning of the year to a muted fanfare and in the presence of the local MP and mayor.

It was still early days. There was a dedicated plot for growing vegetables, salads and herbs, a shop selling produce, a café, a classroom for educational visits and a range of pens and enclosures for the animals. But compared to other rather more established farms, it felt a little rough and ready.

'So, have you done this sort of work before?'

Charlie sat up and blinked. She had already been given a brief tour, and had nodded authoritatively throughout, although cooing at the goats may have let her down. There appeared to be no cows, thankfully. She wondered if the smell – distinctly hay and animal faeces, even here in the classroom – would stay in her hair, and what shoes would be appropriate yet still make her ankles appear slimmer.

She was definitely overdressed. Her last interview had been at a chrome table in a tall glass building with three men in suits. Now she was perched on a child's chair in the farm's classroom with her knees somewhere near her ears, clutching a mug of very strong tea and finishing a slice of carrot cake. Her A-line leopard print skirt, red kitten heels and white pussy-bow blouse felt rather ridiculous.

'Not exactly,' she said, with what she thoroughly hoped was a winning beam. 'But I'm super-experienced, as you'll see from my CV, in quite a range of administrative roles.' She prayed they wouldn't ask why she had left her last job. She'd put down her dad as one of her referees, with a different surname. 'Jack of all trades,' she added, leaving out the very truthful 'master of none' bit.

'OK,' said one of her interviewers, a man in his fifties with chin-length twists who'd introduced himself as Adebayo ('call me Ade'), the Chief Executive. The sleeves of his checked shirt were rolled halfway up his brown arms and he had an energetic, slightly harassed air. 'Well, have you worked for a charity before?'

'No.' She smiled brightly. 'But I am very charitable.'

There was a muffled snort from her second interviewer. Jan, the farmyard manager, was a stout, extremely healthy-looking woman in a dark-green polo shirt with the farm's yellow logo on it, cargo shorts and hiking boots. She had the hair of a 1940s fighter pilot, the newly-razored sides displaying a whiter rim beyond her pink-toned skin, and her arms were festooned with the sorts of tattoos eighteenth-century sailors and East London hipsters wore.

'I worked at a nursery for a while,' said Charlie, trying to make up for her idiocy. 'I love working with kids.' She'd been the administrator on a short-term contract and had hardly anything to do with the children, but they didn't need to know that.

Jan sat up, put the heel of one boot on the opposite knee and leant forward. Frankly, she looked a little terrifying. 'You'd be doing a bit of everything here. Workshops, advertising classes, recruiting and managing the volunteers, fundraising. Basically everything except animal husbandry.'

'I'm staying well away from husbands at the moment,' Charlie said, automatically.

Jan gave another quiet snort. Ade looked mildly at Charlie.

'No. Yes,' Charlie said. 'Animal husbandry.' She gave a thumbs-up. She would Google that word as soon as she was out of here.

'I'm saying it's going to keep you busy,' said Jan. 'You've got to be committed.'

'Absolutely.' She straightened and strong-armed herself into efficient admin mode. She *did* have it in her. 'I've got experience in various fields of communication, customer service and client management,' she said. Not a lie. 'I feel confident that they're transferable skills.' Not exactly the truth.

'And you've just left your last job because…?' There was a glint in Jan's eye.

Ade glanced down at her covering letter.

Visions of fireballs and the faint sting of sambuca. 'I wasn't committed enough,' she said. 'I'm aiming to change that.'

Ade was still eyeing her with an ambiguous expression. 'Why do you want to work here, Charlie?'

She took a deep breath and held it. There was the stuttering sound of a sheep, or maybe a goat. 'I just really want a job. One I care about, I mean. I don't want to work in an office anymore. Not the usual kind, anyway.' She stopped smiling for the first time during the whole interview, felt something between desperation and determination. She was going to do better – for her parents, for Jools, for herself. 'I'll throw myself into this. I'll be here early and leave late. I'll give it everything. I'll amaze you all,' she said.

There was a short silence. That had probably been too much, she thought.

Ade stood up and put out his hand. 'Nice to meet you, Charlie,' he said. 'We'll be in touch.'

'How did it go?' A young white woman of about twenty was shouting over whilst shovelling manure towards the corner of a pigpen.

'Oh, hi,' said Charlie, wondering how to answer that. 'Probably not great.' She felt her right heel sink between the woodchips on the path.

The young woman was wandering over, dragging the large spade behind her: a robust girl in tight jeans and the same polo shirt as Jan's. Her straight brown hair bore a semblance of a French plait, though most of it had feathered away either side of her head. She had fantastically ruddy cheeks. 'Think positive!' she said, in an exceptionally broad Dorset accent. 'Normally the stuff you think went brilliantly went shite and the stuff you think went shite went brilliantly so you're probably well in there.'

'Fingers crossed,' said Charlie, feeling extremely unpositive, and leaning down to hook out her heel. 'See you.'

'Laters!' shouted the girl, even though Charlie was only a few feet away.

Charlie loitered at the entrance to the farm's café, a sweet place with checked tablecloths and reggae playing from corner speakers. A small child tottered out holding what was left of a chocolate ice cream.

She'd messed it up. The farm was… not exactly lovely – in fact, a little down-at-heel – but there was something endearing about it. She sighed in front of the noticeboard, which had leaflets for activities at various farms, local yoga classes, adverts for removal men – and one small handwritten advert, big letters on pink paper:

ROOM FOR RENT IN REALLY CUTE COTTAGE,
BRIXTON/STREATHAM
DIRT CHEAP TO THE RIGHT PERSON!
Email Lydia at lyddie1994@yahoo.com

Charlie glumly took a photo of it. If she didn't get the job, she could at least try this.

• • •

'No. Way!' said the young woman at the door, the same Dorset-accented one who'd greeted her at the farm. She was now wearing a T-shirt saying DUE TO UNFORTUNATE CIRCUMSTANCES I AM AWAKE and fluffy pink boot slippers.

'Oh,' said Charlie, slightly flummoxed. 'Hey. Um, Lydia?'

'Nice one,' Lydia said, beaming. 'I didn't realise it was you who called.' She turned. 'Come in, I'll show you my manor.'

Really cute cottage had been a remarkably adept description. Charlie could hardly believe that such a place could exist just off the main thoroughfare where Brixton Hill became Streatham. Most of the kids outside the strip-lit grocery store drinking energy drinks and smoking weed would have absolutely no clue that around the corner and past a security gate lay a gravel lane leading to four white-walled houses at least two hundred years old. It was as if they had been stolen from a chocolate-boxy village, the Middle England sort usually populated only by people with Lib Dem posters in the windows. The furthest cottage, tucked in a corner, had wonky paving stones, with honeysuckle and ivy trailing up the walls.

Lydia didn't stop for breath as she showed Charlie around. She'd already enthusiastically explained that she had recently upgraded from the farm's most dedicated volunteer to highly underpaid intern, bolstering her time on her Business Management degree course at Westminster. 'I only just put the advert up and all. You're the first to look round. It's my great-gran's place, she's had it forever, came up to London when she was in her twenties 'cause she was a right goer, and she's like literally ninety-seven now, the women in my family start having their babs young, though I'm hoping to break the trend because it is the twenty-first century and anyway, she likes me living here now that I'm working so close, well, interning anyway, she's pleased I'm in London – I love it, it's mad, totally different from home, literally my clubbing mates were two Shorthorn cows and a horse – and anyway, she said I can live here for free as long as I get a housemate who can pay rent, but she doesn't know how much to charge so it's cheap as chips, and my mate's just moved to Cardiff so I need a new one.'

'Wow,' said Charlie, both to Lydia's monologue and the main room. There was a working fireplace, lopsided beams, and a wooden stairway leading up to two bedrooms. The room for rent wasn't tiny, looked out onto a wormy apple tree and seemed quiet. Outside, there was a dank bench and a large cauldron used as a firepit. The shelves in the living room were stuffed with large books, their spines faded, and some crystals in an array of different colours.

'Most of this stuff's my great-gran's. She's in a home now but she's still got it all up here'—Lydia tapped her temples—'and she made me promise not to get rid of anything until she's croaked. Her words.'

The cottage was peaceful, even if Lydia was not. Charlie tried to imagine living here with her slightly overwhelming youthful energy. 'It's lovely,' she said.

'Where are you living right now, then?'

Charlie told her, and briefly explained about the break-up with Alex.

'Boys. Can't live with them, can't live without them,' Lydia said merrily. 'They drive me up the wall. But I love them, the little bastards!'

'I'm going to try living without them for a while,' said Charlie. Alex had finally put something up on Instagram: a photo of him and the French housemate, sucking on the straws

34

of their iced lattes on the South Bank. They looked very *companiable*.

'Yeah, give yourself a break, why not?' Lydia held her hand up for a high-five, which Charlie met, slightly less fervently. 'So, what do you think?'

'Don't you want to see a few other people first?'

Lydia shrugged. 'Go with your gut, my mum always said. You seem like a good egg. I suppose I should interview you.' She frowned at the ceiling for a moment. 'Do you like romcoms?'

'Um. Some?' Better that than *Call of Duty VIII* on repeat.

'Girls' nights in?'

'Maybe. Yes.'

'Big power ballads?'

'Whitney Houston is my pop queen.'

'Dancing?'

'Definitely.'

'You've got the job. By which I mean room.' Lydia winked. 'Oh, what *is* your job, by the way? I mean, I know you've gone for the farm administrator and everything, but at the moment? My mum did say I should make sure they had a proper job.'

Charlie did the only thing she could, and gently lied.

FOUR

Success - An Accident - A Proposal

Thwack. Grunt. Thwack.

'That is an incredibly annoying sound.' Charlie was on the sofa in her parents' living room, staring at her phone, back on the jobs pages. Three days, and she hadn't heard anything from the farm people. Obviously her interview had been disastrous. Lydia had messaged her again asking if she wanted the room, and she'd not replied. She'd decided to only take it if she got the farm job, when the cheaper rent would be extremely necessary. Though, rom-coms and slumber parties sounded quite fun compared to watching her sister stoically work out.

Thwack. Grunt.

'Casey.'

Thwack. 'I'm exercising.' *Thwack*. Casey was playing an interactive tennis game on the TV against Venus Williams, a sweatband around her ginger curls, and had developed a distinctive, breathy grunt. She only seemed to leave the house to go to classes and otherwise seemed to spend her time exhaling theatrically in whichever room Charlie had gone to avoid her.

'Why don't you go outside?' Charlie said. 'Play proper tennis? With actual live human beings?'

'It's raining.' *Thwack.* 'Anyway, I don't play proper tennis.' Polite applause emanated from the TV.

Casey had never made it easy for Charlie to be an older sister. She had, even as a child, actively elected to be a pole apart; you could trace the history of their relationship through their opposing views. Strawberry ice cream was the best flavour, not mint choc chip. Swings were better than slides. Walking boots, not hi-top trainers. Mahler, not Mary J. Blige. Museums, not art galleries, which apparently served no demonstrable use. She argued in favour of the Conservatives from time to time, which just made their dad laugh, slap his thigh, and tell her to stop being so Mary, Mary, Quite Contrary. Unlike Charlie, who might end up shouting and storming out, or at the very least be as wound-up as she was right now.

'I can't concentrate,' she said.

Jools would have said that Alex and her boss didn't deserve her. They would have lived together, partied together, curled up on the sofa together watching reruns of the *Twilight* movies.

'There's an answer to that.'

Charlie glanced up from her job search. 'You can't beat Venus Williams. That would be impossible, seeing as she's a twenty-times world champion.'

Grunt. 'Not on this,' Casey said, thwacking. 'It's fantasy, innit.'

Fantasy. Exactly, thought Charlie. The idea of having a job and possibly a room she wanted. Total, ludicrous fantasy. PR,

HR, spreadsheets, tube-hell and living with three nocturnal gaming nerds was her future.

Louder applause from the TV. '*Yesss*,' said Casey. 'I broke her serve.'

Charlie got up. 'Fine,' she said. 'I'm going out.'

'Bring us back a Coke,' Casey shouted, as Charlie left the room.

Charlie wandered down the street under her umbrella, wearing her cherry-red rain mac and missing Alex. He would sit on the sofa with his arm around her in front of a film that she'd never heard of, explaining the symbolic meaning behind a particular shot. He looked very sweet first thing in the morning when his dark eyelashes were just fluttering open, the pillow leaving a crease on his cheek. He wore T-shirts featuring classic cartoon characters that showed off his lovely biceps, and had the sides of his head shaved every week to 'fix up, look sharp, babes.' He loved cookery programmes and concocted fancy meals for her, like poached salmon with samphire and tarragon butter, or squid ink pasta. He spoke French, and she loved listening to him on the phone conversing with his student friend-cum-new-housemate, who – now that she came to think about it – had been round quite a lot in the last couple of months, and they were often found having earnest heart-to-hearts in a corner. *French* heart-to-hearts. God, she hated Alex. And rain. Everything was greyer, grimmer, more pessimistic.

She glanced into the window of the Old Tailor's. The windows were steamed up and it was rammed full of people escaping the weather. Fine. She'd go a bit further, walk off her melancholy, buy herself a millefeuille from one of the newish artisan bakers in West Norwood, or more frugally and possibly more satisfyingly, get a massive slice of bulla cake from the Jamaican place.

A buzz in her pocket. Charlie stopped, juggled her umbrella and phone, and managed to say hello before dropping it.

'Agh, fuck.' She picked it up and swiped at the moistened screen. It wasn't a number she recognised. 'Hello?' No answer. 'Fuck,' she said. 'Argh.'

There was a man's voice on the other end of the line. 'Hello? Is that Charlie?'

'Sorry, yes, hello,' said Charlie. 'Is this about the room in Crystal Palace? I'm free to look at it anytime, really.'

'No, this is Ade. From Ruskin Park Farm. Are you good to talk?'

'Yes,' said Charlie, accidentally dropping her umbrella and scrambling for it, this time managing not to swear. 'Yes, I am.'

'We'd like to take you on,' said Ade. 'For the admin job, if you're still up for it?'

As he spoke, the rain seemed to grow heavier, and for a moment she wondered if she'd misheard and the huge fat drops had simply blurred his words into something she wanted to hear.

'*Are* you up for it?' Ade said again.

'Wow. Oh my God. Yup. I mean, yes,' she said, with at least four unnecessary words. 'Yes, I totally am. That's amazing news, Ade, thank you.'

She listened to him talk gently about starting days and probation periods, and it slowly dawned on her that he was really, truly offering her the job.

'Hello? Are you there? Charlie?'

She blinked and straightened. 'Yes, Ade,' she said. 'That's fantastic. I'll see you in two weeks.'

Celebratory coffee. Celebratory look in the expensive ethical womenswear shop. She still had a credit card, after all. And credit was on its way, imminently. Charlie sauntered down the road, umbrella restored to its rightful place, feeling more fabulous than she had five minutes previously. South London in the rain was glorious.

Passing the grocer's made her remember where she had last seen apples, hanging limply from the tree outside that cottage. With a few days' distance, Lydia didn't seem quite so exhausting. Just... effusive. It would be cute, living in a cottage and helping run a farm.

'What the hell,' she said. When she got back home, she would phone Lydia to tell her she'd take the room if it was still going, and she'd use any money she saved wisely, for once. This was the start of a whole new Charlie.

'Hey,' called a man's voice, somewhere to her right.

'Hey,' said Charlie, automatically, looking up to see a cyclist passing her with a half-wave, the hood of his jacket up, and realising that it was the Hungarian guy. The man who'd been reading *Animal Farm* and had therefore basically led her to this exact lovely moment.

She opened her mouth to call after him, and at exactly the same time, he turned his head back to her and began to say something else; as they locked eyes, the door of a gold car parked just ahead of him began to open, and his bike glanced violently off the edge.

It was a moment that seemed both sudden and suspended.

The bike spun sideways and toppled before skidding – with the guy caught underneath it – into the middle of the wet road.

A split-second of silence as the traffic stopped.

'Oh, my God,' said Charlie, her heart rocketing to her throat, and she began to dash towards him. Several others did, too.

The bike's wheels were still turning. The guy was lying awkwardly, his foot caught under the frame, and two bystanders were carefully lifting the bike off him.

Charlie crouched down by his head. 'Oh, my God,' she said again. 'Are you OK?'

He blinked slowly at her. Green-ish brown-ish eyes. 'I'm all right,' he said, in an odd, unemotional voice. He swallowed, looking upwards, the rain hitting his face.

He didn't really look all right. It had been a horrible, juddering movement. He hadn't been wearing a helmet.

'Do you think you can move?' she said.

'Shall we get you up?' said another lady, next to her. Cars were waiting on both sides of the road, a bus sighing to a stop.

Another slow blink. 'Yes.' A hiss as he lifted his arm, a dark gash at his wrist. One trouser leg had torn, the skin full of gravel. He quietly muttered an *ow*, the vowel soft.

Someone was remonstrating with the driver, a woman with a child's car seat in the back. A teenager in school uniform was calling 999.

'Come and sit down over here,' said Charlie, gesturing to the kerb.

He sat up, slowly. 'My bike.'

The man and woman had already moved the bike, which was looking the worse for wear. 'It's over here, too.'

She helped him up, taking his elbow, and he limped over

and sat on the edge of the kerb. The traffic began to inch past again.

Charlie sat down next to him, and held her umbrella over his head. 'She totally wasn't looking. Wing mirrors are there for a reason.'

He gave a gentle, pained hum, looking at his wrist and leg, before putting a hand to the back of his skull. 'I think I hit my head.' As he said *ow* again, he slowly leaned over until his head was resting on Charlie's lap.

'Oh, *God*,' she said. 'It's my fault.'

'I think it was mine,' he said from her lap, and it really didn't seem awkward or wrong that he was lying there. A couple of people were standing with the owner of the gold car, who looked very distressed, and several others hovered around her and Charlie.

'Don't go to sleep or anything,' she said, making sure that her umbrella was still sheltering him. 'That's definitely not allowed.'

'OK,' he said.

His head was very heavy. He was gazing up at her in a foggy, undetermined way that probably meant he was utterly concussed. There was a small gash at the edge of his eyebrow, beginning to weep a little. She pulled her jumper cuff down, dabbed at the blood, and saw that her hand was trembling. *Jools*, she thought, fleetingly, before forcing herself into the present.

The driver of the gold car had come over. She seemed aghast, tearful. 'I'm so sorry. I just didn't see you, I was—'

'It's OK,' he said, rather courteously for someone lying injured in a stranger's lap. 'I'll be fine.'

The woman wrote down her number on a scrap of a magazine. 'If there's anything I can do.' Her child was screaming in the back seat of the car over the road. 'Pay for your bike, if it needs fixing, or—'

'It's fine,' he said.

'He'll take it,' Charlie said, more firmly, and put out her hand.

After the woman had gone, the other pedestrians who'd helped out drifted away, and it was just the two of them left on the kerb.

'I like your coat,' he said. '*Vörös*.'

'Thank you,' she said. He was definitely concussed. 'Don't worry, it'll all be cool. The ambulance is coming. The hospital's only up the road. Luckily for you.' She resisted the urge to stroke his damp hair. Though the danger was over, part of her body seemed to be ringing an alarm bell, a deep, distant fear that she understood but didn't dare get close to right now.

'I don't know your name,' he said.

'I don't know yours.' She clenched her fist to stop it trembling.

'Gábriel,' he said, the first syllable as an *ah* sound.

'Hi, Gábriel,' she said. 'I'm Charlie. You're my lucky charm, you know.'

He gave a mild, rather beatific frown.

'Down to you I've got a new job, and a place to live, hopefully.'

'OK,' he said, sounding a little confused.

There was the angry squall of a siren, and an ambulance came burrowing through the traffic.

'Your lift's here,' she said. He looked rather pale, and was beginning to shake, the shock finally hitting him. She felt a pang of sympathy. 'Do you want me to come with you?'

He took her hand, and she let him hold it, purely because he was half-conscious. 'Yes, please,' he said.

. . .

Gábriel didn't die, or slip into unconsciousness. He didn't even have concussion. Charlie rode with him in the ambulance, a novel excitement in itself, and waited in a miraculously quiet A&E while he was checked out. After messaging Lydia – who had texted back with the word *HOUSEMATESSSS!* – she finally allowed herself to take in what had happened: the brief horror of Gábriel's body sprawled on the road, cars stopping and people remonstrating. How it took her straight back to being aged six, the memory scratched into her bones.

Jools had been allowed to go round to her friend Josie's house on her own, because Shakespeare Road was parallel to theirs. She'd returned from school with news of Josie's new rabbit, and Nellie had said she could pop over for half an hour before tea. Charlie had spent the day in bed with an ear infection and while she sulked into her warm orange squash, Jools changed into her favourite purple tracksuit trousers and hi-top trainers, and dashed out. And never returned for tea.

There was a court case, but another witness, a pedestrian, backed up the driver's story. It was so simple, and so futile. Jools had been excited, forgotten to look, and had been hit by a car not even going that fast, and gone under the front wheel.

Charlie could still hear the sound Nellie had made after answering the front door, wild and strange, before she ran out in her bare feet, the door left open. *Stay here, love,* Josie's mum had said, her face bleached with shock. Charlie had stood in the hallway, ear and heart throbbing like a bass drum.

Nellie had to go through the last three months of pregnancy with Casey in a deep, all-consuming grief that seemed to continue through Casey's first year. Charlie had found herself alone, and then the big sister to a baby that seemed alien.

In the waiting room, she felt herself doing what she used to: imagining Jools's body, how and where it might have been broken, crushed. Limbs facing the wrong way, blood on the road. She took a deep breath and made herself rise and fetch herself a cup of sugary tea from the café.

She was just finishing it when Gábriel emerged with a few bandages, limping awkwardly and texting the friend who had gone to pick up his bike.

'How are you feeling?' Charlie said.

He looked tired. There were three tiny strips of bandage over the end of his eyebrow. 'A little stupid. It's really nice of you to wait. You didn't need to.'

She gathered her bag to her side. 'No biggie. I wanted to make sure you didn't snuff it.' She managed a grin she didn't entirely feel.

His smile was perplexed and a little adorable. 'I don't know what that means exactly, but I don't think I did snuff it.' He had a sweet, slightly formal way of speaking, like someone who had learned English rather than grown up with it.

'Definitely not.'

'Are *you* OK?' He was gently frowning at her.

She tried to lower her shoulders from their position near her ears. 'Oh, yeah. I'm… I'm all good.' She forced another breezy smile as she stood. 'Are you OK getting home?'

'My friend is coming to pick me up in a minute. He has my bike already.'

'Cool.' She looked at him. 'I'm really sorry. I swear it was my fault.' If she hadn't been there, he wouldn't have been looking round when the car's door had opened. If she'd have gone with Jools, she might have stopped her running.

'No way,' Gábriel said. 'Don't think like that. The driver should have been looking. And it might have helped if I'd been facing in the right direction.' A sheepish smile, before he looked down at his feet and back up again. 'Do you go to the Tailor's café a lot?'

She shrugged. 'Some. I keep trying to avoid Mumageddon but they're always in there.'

He looked puzzled.

'Mums,' she said, though she meant a certain type of mum – massive car, member of an expensive gym, buys face serums from Goop. 'Five o'clock's my new slot. Kids are home for their dinner.'

'Maybe I'll see you in there,' he said.

'Sure, maybe,' she said.

'Tuesday?' he said.

'Oh.' Well, it was the least she could do. They could both spend it telling each other repeatedly that it hadn't been the other's fault. 'OK, sure. Tuesday.' She put her bag over her shoulder. 'Later.' She pointed a finger. 'No cycling without a helmet.'

'No cycling without a helmet,' he said, and held up his hand.

On Tuesday, she was back in the Old Tailor's, reading about rare breed sheep on her phone and Insta-stalking Alex. It was obvious enough now that he and the French *fille* were together. They left copious heart emojis on each other's posts and each one drilled a hole into Charlie's own less fulsome heart.

'Bastard,' she said.

'Hi,' said a warm, recognisable voice from behind her.

She hastily put her phone down. 'Hello,' she said, turning around.

'I don't mean to disturb you,' said Gábriel, glancing at her phone. He was clutching a small plastic bag and looked less scruffy than previously. A mottled grey polo shirt and a dark-green bomber jacket. There was a thin scar at the edge of his eyebrow and some purple bruising.

'I'm not disturbed,' she said, before turning her phone over and shutting one eye. 'Most of the time.'

They grinned at each other. He passed over the bag as he sat down. 'It's to say thank you for looking after me. It's just a little thing.'

Charlie unwrapped the bag and took out a tray of meat cutlets as the waitress came to take their order.

'From the shop,' he said, once they had ordered. 'Lamb. The best.' He looked slightly embarrassed. 'You're not a vegetarian, are you? My friend said I was mad to bring you meat. So I brought you some chocolate as well.' He leant down into his bag and put a large bar, with cherries and almonds, on the table.

'Oh, um, no,' she said, still gazing at the chilled package in her hands. She'd never been given lamb before. That was... unusual. 'Thanks. That's very nice of you. I'll use them tonight. My dad loves lamb.'

'You live with your parents?' He seemed surprised.

'Very temporarily,' said Charlie. 'I've moving in to a new place next week.'

'Oh, OK.' Definitely some faint relief there. He hunched his shoulders, hands in his pockets. He seemed shyer today.

'So, how's your bike?' she said, once they'd had their coffees served to them.

'Getting repaired. I messaged the driver to say I was OK and she said she would pay for it, so…' he shrugged.

'You should get a full service, then,' said Charlie. 'New seat, fresh tyres, go-faster stripes.'

'No.' His smile was abashed. Obviously far too honest for that sort of thing. 'But I'll be happy to get it back,' he said. 'I like my bike.'

'I should get one. My new job's the perfect distance for it.'

'Yeah? What's your job?'

She told him, and his eyes lit up. 'That's cool. I didn't know there were farms around here.'

'Well, stay away,' she said. 'You're not killing my sheep.'

'I don't kill them myself,' he said, grinning at her. 'I like sheep. I grew up on a farm.'

'No way.'

She listened as he told her about his family's small farm in the central plains of Hungary, an area called the *Alföld*. He showed her a photo of the native woolly pigs they'd had alongside the black-headed sheep bred mostly for their milk, as well as a hilarious photo of their breed of sheepdog, with a long corded coat that made it look like a kitchen mop.

'You'll have to give me some tips, then,' she said.

'Maybe I will come and visit you,' he said. 'See how your English sheep are doing.' He held up his hands. 'I promise not to butcher them.'

'Hmm,' she said with a smile, as she picked up her mocha. 'Maybe.'

There was a silence as they both drank from their mugs, Charlie trying to picture herself making her first cup of tea in the morning and fielding phone calls about allotment waiting lists or half-term activities or—

Oh God, she really didn't know what she was letting herself in for.

'Um, I was wondering...' Gábriel put down his cup and looked at Charlie with a rather earnest, soulful expression. 'I was wondering,' he said again. 'Would you like to go out with me sometime?'

'Oh,' said Charlie, and wondered why she hadn't realised that this was coming. She looked at him. He seemed nervous, those big hazel eyes fixed on her unwaveringly. 'Wow. That's nice of you.'

He gave an uncertain smile, and when Charlie didn't say anything, he sat up. 'I mean, it was really nice that you came to the hospital with me.' He looked down at the table, shaking his head at himself, before making eye contact again. 'Not just that. You seem really cool. And funny.'

'Oh,' said Charlie. 'Thanks. It's so sweet of you to ask.'

A more assured smile. 'I didn't know if you'd say yes.'

'Oh, I'm not saying yes,' Charlie said, and his face fell. 'I can't.'

'You have a boyfriend.'

'No.' She shook her head decisively and clasped her mug. 'No, I absolutely do not.'

'Girlfriend...?' he asked.

'No, no. That's not what I meant. I'm not doing guys right now.' Classic. She put her hand to her forehead. 'I mean, I'm just not looking for anything at the moment. I've just come out of a relationship and I'm going to focus on work.' She was not going to segue her romantic partners, even if Alex had.

'You can do both.' His smile had a very simple sense of conviction.

'No, I can't,' Charlie said, and even though she didn't entirely know what her job was going to entail, she knew she had to throw herself into it and not be distracted. Just like fickle, French and new-media-loving Alex had said. 'I'm going to be independent for a while.' She nodded assertively, self-convincingly.

'It doesn't have to be a big thing,' he said. 'We could just go out. For a drink or film or something.'

'I have zero money right now.'

'I can pay,' he said, with an easy shrug, somehow managing not to be patronising.

'I just want to keep my head down and work,' she said.

Gábriel was watching her, as if hoping she might still change her mind.

'It's really sweet of you,' she said for the second time, and gave her kindest, gentlest smile.

He looked at his coffee. 'OK.' He shrugged and gave a gracefully discomfited sigh. 'Well, come and buy some meat sometime if you want.'

In the following weeks, Charlie didn't go to the butcher's in Peckham. It felt too awkward.

The lamb cutlets, however, as Aidan attested, were exquisite.

FIVE

The Farm – A Baptism – A Mistake

'Rihanna. Or RiRi.'

Charlie was walking along the narrow woodchip path between the pens. On one side was a large area with three alpacas, all with alarmingly long necks and deranged expressions.

'Beyoncé. Bey-Bey for short.'

On the other side was a pen with several variously-coloured sheep.

'Gaga. Lady Gaga, to give her full name. Missy. AKA Missy Elliott.'

Lydia, AKA Charlie's new landlady, was showing her round. So far, they'd covered the community allotments, the herb garden and raised beds, the equipment store, the compost corner, the hens and chickens, and the pigs, all introduced with extreme enthusiasm. Lydia really did everything with extreme enthusiasm, from her greeting hug (long, crushing) to her walking (breathless, erratically stopping and starting) and now with her introductions to some of Charlie's new and more woolly officemates (accompanied by capacious arm movements).

'Give her a pat,' said Lydia, nodding down to Missy.

'Um,' said Charlie, rather more hesitatingly.

Lydia dashed her a curious look. 'She won't bite. She's a right bloody softie, this one.'

Charlie, though she had very much pretended otherwise in her interview, was not the most outdoorsy of people. Concrete and corner shops, high-rises and sirens were more familiar than flora and fauna, farm-based or otherwise. If she had a choice, she'd go to a gallery or some indie shops rather than march up a mountain or dip *al fresco* in a river. She knew her local parks well, but tended to sit on picnic blankets with her now-departed best mate, drinking sparkling wine until the sun had gone down. The one time she and Alex had stayed in a cottage in the Brecon Beacons, she'd been completely freaked out by the blanket of darkness and silence at night; she had been convinced, as they walked back from the pub using their phone torches to light the way, that a slavering wild beast was going to jump out of the hedge.

Now, she reached over and gingerly touched Missy's deep-brown brow with her forefinger, and then her palm. The lighter brown wool on her skull was very dense, almost oily. Missy was definitely giving Charlie side-eye, as if she could see straight through her.

'And this little mucker's Britney,' said Lydia, pointing a final finger down at the smallest, palest sheep who was gently butting the fence. They were Shetlands, a breed, as Lydia explained, that came in a wide variety of colours. 'She's got the crappest *baa*. Bless.'

'How do all the animals get named?' asked Charlie.

'Depends. A school class named most of these girls, and

otherwise it's down to whichever staffer's turn it is.' She nodded downwards. 'I had to fight tooth and nail to name Britters.'

Lydia's hair was tucked into a cap with the words COUNTRY GIRL stitched into it. She was in mud-caked wellies and seemed utterly in her element. Charlie, aiming to dress down, was in high-waisted cigarette trousers, a T-shirt and blazer, and was still obviously wearing completely the wrong thing. At least she'd got trainers on, though they were her best gold ones.

'And what about those guys?'

Lydia glanced round at the alpacas. 'Oh,' she said, sniffing dismissively. Two were chocolate brown and one was a dirty shade of cream, and they were all looking at Charlie with an unnervingly evil glint in their eyes. 'I didn't name them. They're Barry, Maurice and Robin.' She pointed to the chalkboard sign on the gate. 'The last person in charge named them. Benji.' Her tone suggested she hadn't thought much of him.

'Are they the ones that spit?'

'They can do. If you really piss them off. Basically, don't sing anything from the 1980s and you'll be all right.' She squinted at Charlie with the same curiosity as before. 'You do know about animals, don't you?'

'Um,' said Charlie, sneaking a look back at her. 'I know about *some* animals. But I'm betting you can tell me absolutely everything I need to know.'

'I'm your wingman,' said Lydia, doing a fist-bump. 'You are going to be recognising whose shit is whose by the end of the day.'

'All right, newbie?' Jan was ambling over, hands in the pockets of her long cargo shorts.

Charlie still felt slightly terrified of Jan. She gave the air of it being a very bad idea to get on the wrong side of her. 'Good morning.'

Jan leant on the fence. 'This one giving you the tour?' A slightly amused look at Charlie's outfit.

Charlie nodded.

'First vegan I ever heard of working on a bloody farm.'

Charlie looked at Lydia. 'You're a vegan?'

'Oh, yeah,' said Lydia, unfussily. 'I didn't tell you when you came round. I've been one since I was sixteen. I did a project on McDonald's for my GCSEs and it turned me right off. I'm proper into animal welfare.' She glanced over at Charlie. 'That's not a problem for the cottage, is it? I don't care what you eat. Just got to wash the pans and that.'

'No, it's fine. If you're definitely OK with it.'

'Sorted. Right,' said Lydia, clapping her hands. 'Got to do the donkeys. See you in a bit.'

Jan finished off the tour rather more succinctly – 'Goats,' she said, nodding to them – before walking her back towards the café. 'Gonna live with Lydia, are ya?'

'Yeah, I moved most of my stuff in yesterday. In properly on Saturday.' Aidan had driven Charlie round with two suitcases of clothes and several boxes. He had been just as charmed as his daughter by the cottage, though he had giggled and said *well, la di bloody da. Someone's fallen on their feet.* Lydia had, of course, thought him awesome.

'Bloody hell,' said Jan. 'Good luck with that. The kid never shuts up.' She grinned, before nodding at the classroom. 'Little blighters in there most days of the week, mid-morning and mid-afternoon. Ade will talk you through the weekly schedule when he's in. Can you do first aid?'

Charlie shook her head. Best not to lie about that.

54

'Ade'll probably send you on a course,' Jan said as they entered the café. 'Me and Lyds are the main first aiders but every little helps. 'Now here's the one you want to be your friend.'

Jan introduced Charlie to Moonie, a very pale, gothy-looking teenager with turquoise-streaked hair and a little white pin saying THEY/THEM, who stood behind the counter. 'This diamond makes the best coffee this side of the river, don't you, mate?'

'I do what I can,' said Moonie, in a quiet, wry voice.

Jan leaned her elbow on the counter as the coffee machine erupted into noisy life. 'The animals you can mostly leave to me. Though it'll help if you can muck in a few times, just to know what you're asking volunteers to do.' She scratched her head. 'I could do with about seven extra pairs of hands.'

'No probs,' said Charlie, a little too over-confidently, seeing as just touching one docile sheep had proved a challenge.

Jan told her that all the city farms were understaffed and how Mudchute Farm on the Isle of Dogs had been trying to poach her since she started. 'Told you,' she said, as Moonie set down two coffees in front of them. 'This one's an artist.'

Charlie looked down to see the outline of a sheep drawn perfectly in the foam of their lattes.

It was once the sheep-foam had been slurped away that Charlie learned how she'd been Ade and Jan's third choice, the first two declining for jobs with higher salaries. She tried not to let her self-esteem completely deflate at that. She had a job, and that was the main thing.

'Says it all, really,' Jan said. 'This sort of job isn't for someone wanting to make their millions.' She sat back with a sigh. 'To be honest, you came across as a bit... eccentric in the interview. But I liked you, and you've got to be better than your predecessor.'

'Do you mind me asking why he left?'

'He didn't leave. He was fired, good and proper.' She sighed. 'It's been a bloody nightmare.'

'Really?' Charlie suddenly felt apprehensive. Perhaps her next dismissal was just around the corner.

Jan shook her head, leaning back and folding her elbows. 'The arsehole swindled us.'

'Seriously?'

'Yep. Callous fucker. 'Scuse my French. He turned out to be a total fraudster, siphoning off money every month. As if this place makes any bleedin' money in the first place.'

'That's awful.'

'Yep. It's been going through the courts. He's put up a right fight, though fuck knows how he can afford the legal aid. I would say pig-headed bastard, but that's too harsh on the pigs.'

'Wow. I'm so sorry.'

Jan gave a half-smile. 'Anyways. He'd had more farm experience but we decided we just needed someone who could boss all the admin and not steal what little dough we make.' She cast over an astute look. 'You're not going to be shit now, are you, Charlie?'

Charlie shook her head, though she suddenly felt the weight of responsibility on her shoulders. There was something about this place. It was sweet, a little dishevelled, had been through the wars. 'No,' she said. 'Hand on heart. I'm going to—'

'Amaze us all,' Jan cut in. 'Your exact words.' She clasped her hands behind her head. 'Don't know how you're going to do that exactly, but you could try and get us out of the red for starters. The trustees have been pulling their weight, but we're skint.'

Charlie's first day continued in very unprecedented style. Ade and Jan had, perhaps, on the day of her interview, been very deliberate in not showing her where she'd be actually working. This time she wasn't walking into a bland new-build, with desks separated by dividers, a long meeting room, flat screen TVs displaying the company's trite philosophies. Her office consisted of a tiny box room with a wonky desk shoved into a corner next to a filing cabinet, and teetering piles of papers all over the place. They definitely didn't have a cleaner in every morning. It was also on the chilly side; there was an electric heater that looked like it had seen better days. The desktop computer was ancient, perhaps donated by someone. When it did finally rumble into life, she spent an hour trying to understand the hot mess of the folders system, before deciding she needed a cuppa and some air.

This was better. It was lovely to see toddlers around, their parents following slowly behind with pushchairs, or kneeling down to help them with the bags of feed. One little girl in a tutu was shouting 'Go. A. Way!' in a very committed fashion at the pygmy goats, who stood atop their haphazard log and box construction as if they had summited Everest.

The smell wasn't so bad, really. Though she definitely needed a harder wardrobe, one that combined sassy, managerial vibes with wipe-clean materials. With slight self-consciousness, she greeted the RPF Farm Club, a small group of teenagers and young adults with learning disabilities, and watched them work on the allotments with a regular adult volunteer, Marianne.

Ade popped by in the afternoon – his permanently harried air explained by him having three part-time jobs and, despite being in his early fifties, a new baby – to talk Charlie through everything, including the accounts. As well as the council and trusts, the funders included many small grants and a national bank.

Charlie nodded confidently, whilst making a mental note to order several dummy guidebooks on accounting as soon as he had left the office. She felt completely out of her depth, but she absolutely wasn't going to tell him that.

The next morning, Charlie was woken by Casey's foot, digging into her thigh.

'Aren't you supposed to be up by now?'

Charlie's stomach hurt. The heaviest part of her period always made her foggy-headed and lethargic. She pulled over her phone and gazed obliquely at the time, which seemed to be telling her an hour later than it should. She sat up with a jolt. '*Shit.*' In the space of three seconds, she was up and pulling on yesterday's clothes. 'What is wrong with my phone? I set an alarm.'

'Oh. I might've turned it off,' said Casey, who was still in her own bed.

'What? Why?' Charlie shrugged off the trousers and rummaged furiously in her suitcase for a pair of jeans. 'Casey. For fuck's sake. Are you *trying* to ruin my life?'

Casey shrugged. 'I was half-asleep. It was really early.'

'Early because this is my new job and I'm trying to make a good impression,' said Charlie, feeling the urgent need to get to the loo before she leaked everywhere. 'You're a nightmare.'

Casey brought her duvet back up to her chin. 'Move out, then.'

'I am. I will.' She'd been planning to move properly into Lydia's cottage at the weekend, but the idea of spending one more night next to Casey was more than she could bear. 'Believe me. I'm gone.'

'Was beginning to think you'd had second thoughts,' said Jan, leaning on a shovel as Charlie came dashing in at 9.45am.

'No. Definitely not. I'm so sorry.' She thought about just blaming Casey, or lying about the buses, but decided to take responsibility. 'My period can knock me out. I slept through my alarm. I will totally not do that again. I'll stay late. Sorry.'

'Mate,' said Jan. 'I hear ya. Try not to do it again though, eh? The volunteers need people to look up to. Easy for them to stray.'

Today, there was a group of youth volunteers who came together on Tuesdays after school; some came more regularly, and all made Charlie feel welcome. She was surprised at how diverse the volunteers were – certainly not just the scrubbed-rosy cheeks of white middle-class folks on a jolly. Joe, a cheery, white fifteen-year-old from one of the big blocks of flats in Loughborough Junction, had breezily told Charlie that he'd come originally on some community service for dealing weed. 'Stayed, though, din't I?' he said, his grin displaying a gold tooth behind his braces. Tallboy, a couple of years older, was a handsome young man with a dyed blond, high-faded haircut and neon-blue eyeliner that contrasted with his bronze-brown skin; he did contemporary and street dance at the weekends and moved through the farm with an ethereal grace. Marianne, whom she'd already met, was their supervisor, a black retired professor of education with long grey dreadlocks and an alternative vibe, who had named the nanny goats after a range of feminist thinkers.

'Hello, newbie.' Two days later, towards the end of the day, Jan was at the door.

Charlie hastily shut her accounting book. 'Hey. How's it going?'

'Mint.' She jerked her head back behind her. 'Right, look lively.'

'What do you need?'

'The question is what do *you* need,' said Jan. 'I reckon you've been spending too much time in this little hidey-hole.'

It was true that Charlie's first week had largely focused on trying to make sense of the admin apocalypse; the box files of documents lacked any chronology and there was a bag of shop receipts that had clearly just been flung in. She was still surrounded by piles of paper like a mini cityscape. 'OK, so—'

'Time for your farmhand induction.'

'Oh. I didn't know I was having one of—'

'I've just decided.' Jan winked. 'My farm, my rules. Chop chop.'

'Is that mud or, um, poo?'

It was very hard to say no to Jan, who was three parts genial to two parts menacing. Charlie really did want to prove that she *was* worth employing, even as a third choice, and that the late morning had been a one-off. Hence she was now sporting a pair of wellies, a farm jumper over her own, and standing with some trepidation outside the pig pen.

She had already weeded one large vegetable bed, sieved some rotten woodchip to add to the compost pile, and fed two goats as they were getting settled in their stable for the night. She'd been initially hesitant until a forthright toddler had shamed her by shoving their hand right between the fence posts; the light nibbling of the goat's lips and teeth had not been as disgusting as she'd anticipated.

'Mostly the latter,' said Jan, opening the gate of the pig pen and holding it for her to enter. 'Come on, missus, what are you waiting for?'

Courage, Charlie thought. A plastic boiler suit and gas mask. 'Um,' she said. 'I was once chased by cows.'

'Cows can be right crazy fucks,' said Jan. 'But this lot are soft bastards. Trust me, you're not going to be trampled by pigs. They'd sooner slobber you to death.'

The two sows, Annie and Ethel, were Oxford Sandy and Blacks – big-bellied, big-butted beasts, ginger with black spots, who'd each given birth to a litter a month ago. Most of the piglets – not the teeny, cute things one might expect; these came up to her knee – were asleep in the shelter. Annie – who had fewer black patches – gave a guttural grunt and shuffled up as Charlie reluctantly entered the pen. Her snout was wiry, dribblingly moist, and there was straw stuck all around her mouth. She didn't *look* particularly soft.

Jan handed Charlie half an apple. 'Down the hatch.'

'Oh, my gosh,' said Charlie.

The sow gazed up and began to put her head against Charlie's thigh.

'Just hold it up and she'll stop,' said Jan. 'Drop it in. You don't have to touch her if you don't want to.'

The sow caught sight of the apple and opened her mouth, displaying a horror film's worth of pink gullet, ridged tongue and teeth. Charlie dropped the apple hastily and it disappeared in a moment, accompanied by noisy, open-mouthed chomping.

'That is an extra level of gross,' said Charlie.

Jan snorted as she put down a metal bowl of vegetables. 'Pigs are clean, mate. They shit outside their pens, unlike most animals.'

'Yay,' said Charlie, weakly, looking down at her feet.

'Normally we muck 'em out in the morning, but seeing as you're here…' There was a devilish glint in Jan's eye as she handed her a rake.

Under Jan's casual instruction, Charlie forked up the clean-looking hay in the pen into one corner, before gathering up the filthy straw to go into a wheelbarrow. There was sweeping, and rinsing down with a bucket of water, and sweeping again. She made an extremely conscious effort to think about salted caramel chocolate, wine and bubble baths, whilst breathing through her mouth and trying to avoid the animals.

'Done, I think?' she said, after ten minutes.

'Missed a bit there,' said Jan, waving to a corner where Ethel doughtily stood next to the wheelbarrow, her head in the metal bowl as she polished off the vegetables.

'She's in the way.'

'Just shove her; she'll do as she's told.'

Charlie eyed Ethel, and Ethel eyed Charlie. 'Um,' Charlie said. 'Hello. Please move.' Ethel gave a chortling sort of grunt, and stayed put.

'Go on,' said Jan, amused. 'Show her who's boss.'

Charlie hesitantly shuffled beside Ethel, and nudged her flank with her own thigh. It was like asking a wholesale sack of flour to move. Ethel continued munching, oblivious. Charlie nudged again. Nothing. Finally, she pushed her with more might, and Ethel looked up with a mouth full of carrot, brutishly shoving her thick neck at Charlie, before turning and butting her full weight against her.

Charlie yelped and backed off at speed, and as she did her ankle twisted, causing her to stumble against the wheelbarrow. In one swift moment, she had slipped, grabbed on to the wheelbarrow and dumped half of the shit-covered and urine-dank straw onto her lap as she landed on the concrete.

'Jokes,' said Joe, who'd come over to watch and was leaning on the fence. 'You got *got*, fam.'

The water Charlie had washed over the pen was now soaking, coldly, into her bottom.

'Bad luck, mate. Up you get,' said Jan, not unkindly. 'Ethel was only being friendly, but you weren't to know. Baptism of fire, eh?'

'Baptism of shit,' said Joe, laughing.

Charlie allowed Jan to haul her up, hot with embarrassment and fury, mostly at herself for being so cowed – or *pigged*. She brushed herself down with the backs of her hands, knowing full well she was only getting more traces of animal effluent on her.

'Reward time,' said Jan. 'I reckon you've done enough for one sesh.'

'Reward?' said Charlie, who wanted nothing more than to crawl into a non-shit-smelling hole.

'Yep,' said Jan. 'We'll go by the sinks first. Then to the hutches. Time to cuddle a bunny.'

• • •

'Come and celebrate your new crib! I've got two-for-one cocktail vouchers for this gay bar in Clapham.' Lydia had returned from her late afternoon lecture, stuffed her face full of corn chips and salsa, and come back downstairs sporting a tiny silver skirt and an impressive amount of eyeliner.

Charlie was curled up on the sofa in the cottage with a bowl of spinach tortellini and very achy muscles. Her calves hurt, her lower back hurt, her biceps hurt. Shovelling, sweeping and weeding was a surprisingly rigorous workout. 'I'm wiped,' she said. And, however much cuddling one of the floppy-eared big rabbits had soothed her, she still felt ashamed over the wheelbarrow calamity.

Lydia made a cheerfully dismissive sound. 'Bet you've still got it in you. Come on, you've lived here two days. We've got to toast it.'

Charlie hummed a fairly definite no.

Lydia watched her for a moment. 'You'll have won Jan over, you know. She doesn't really like anyone until they've got animal shit on their clothes.' She waved the vouchers again and sang a fairly tuneless version of 'Voulez-Vous Choucher Avec Moi?' 'We don't have to go to the gay bar. We can go boy-hunting if you want. Always up for that.'

'Not up for that at the moment, as you well know,' Charlie said. Lydia had already got the entire lowdown on her love life from the age of thirteen to the present day out of her. Charlie had omitted to mention Gábriel asking her out the other week, because that didn't count. 'I will come out with you,' she said. 'At the weekend. Promise. I've still got stuff to unpack, anyway.'

Lydia pointed a dramatic finger. 'Never make a promise you can't keep.'

'Hand on heart,' said Charlie. Lydia was at least more fun

than Casey, who would sooner bash her head repeatedly against a wall than go clubbing, ever.

The beams of the cottage shuddered as Lydia slammed the door. Charlie tucked her feet up underneath her and wrinkled her nose. Though she had changed and showered, she was sure that, underneath the smell of pasta sauce, she could still smell pig shit.

Autumn begins to find itself. There is little rain and the leaves begin to crisp. In the park, there are long-tailed tits among the crab apple and silver birch trees, and the rattle of crows' throats accompanies the brass funk sextet that practise on the bandstand. On the farm, some of the teenage volunteers are discussing their newest administrator.

'I dunno, man. She don't like the animals much. Seems a bit scared of everything if you ask me.'

'Nah, she helped me muck out the goats the other morning. She's bless.'

'For real? I thought she'd never go in the pens after her face-off with Ethel.'

'She did. Came in early. Said she was getting on Jan's good side.'

'Did you see her wellies? One pair's red, the other silver.'

'At least she's *got* wellies now. And nothing wrong with keeping yourself looking good, fam.'

'And she looks *good*, trust.'

'Oh my gosh.'

'What? I'm not allowed to say that?'

'No, because there are girls present, i.e. me.'

'Someone's getting jealous.'

'*Someone's* asserting a lazy right to patriarchy.'

'You love it. Bruv, look at those alpacas. Maurice is totally smacking Barry-boy down.'

For the next couple of weeks, Charlie tried to adjust to her new job. She bought a proper alarm clock, putting it a few inches from her pillow. She began to familiarise herself with the nooks and crannies of the farm, making sure she knew where everything was, from the wheelbarrows to the wellies store to the school visit clipboards. It was obvious, even to her, what a mess Benji had left, not just clerically but in the disassembled look of the whole place – the storage area of the barn was a jumble and some fences looked like they needed repairing.

She met more of the volunteers, discreetly ticking them off on a list on her phone next to a description so she'd remember them. In her most recent jobs, her colleagues had been variations on a theme: suits and pencil skirts, eating at their desk and juggling three mobile phones, overusing jargon like *ducks in a row* and *moving forward* and *blue-sky thinking*. Now she was working out how on earth to talk to a range of people from teenagers to retirees with varied backgrounds. Walt, their oldest volunteer at seventy-five, came in once a week from his serviced flat in Tulse Hill and delighted in telling her, in very detailed fashion, what farming had been like in 1950s Lincolnshire. She ate in the café with Leila, the Scottish-Iranian chef, who enjoyed feeding her up on massive portions of stuffed aubergines or chicken and walnut stew, telling her about her five grandchildren, and lamenting Lydia's veganism.

And she got to know the animals – the breeds, as well as the names. There were the Anglo-Nubian goats, with their distinctive curved noses and long, floppy ears. The stocky fringe-haired Oxford Down sheep, as well as the Shetlands. Elton, the white-crested Polish cockerel, and his comedy-wig feathering. She rubbed behind ears, collected eggs, and held her hand out with feed, managing not to run away at the sensation of Barry the alpaca's lips on her palm.

Soon enough, Charlie had begun to divine that they had as much personality as the staff. Audre was the friendliest of the pygmy goats, always first up with her front hooves on the fence when visitors were around. Bette, one of the two donkeys, was much more likely to allow her ears to be scratched than Joan, though both of them retained their countenance of exquisite, long-lashed melancholy. The dark-brown chinchilla, Caramel, chattered in a sweet, burbly fashion all day long, no matter whether her companions were awake or not.

'That's RiRi,' Charlie said, pointing out the steadily-chewing Shetland to her dad, who had accompanied his Year 4s and their teacher on a visit. 'She's not really a morning sort of sheep. Never likes taking food from the kids until after 1pm.'

Aidan was leaning his big forearms on the fence of the sheep pen. 'I never would have thought it,' he said. 'My girl-about-town running a farm. My ancestors will be having a drink to your health around about now.'

'Not running, Dad,' she said. 'I'm just the admin person.'

'Looks like it to me,' he said proudly, before bellowing to a pair of pupils who were bickering over their bag of feed. 'Ava! Keisha! Stop with that rowdiness right now, you two.'

In the classroom, Charlie watched as Marianne introduced the Year 4s to the smaller creatures. Some of the kids had never seen farm animals before – several didn't know where milk came from. Kaa, the red and white snake, came out to gentle gasps of delight and wide-eyed fear, and the bolshy boy who stood up first to hold it chickened out and ran to the back of the room. Aidan loudly nominated Charlie as the first person to touch it and, because she could never be a wimp in front of her dad, she held the cool laminated body in her hand, her heart not beating as rapidly as she'd thought it would.

'Snake charmer right there,' Aidan said, boomingly. 'Now come on, you lot. Who's next?'

Half the class raised their hands, and Charlie passed Kaa back to Marianne, watching as a girl in a hijab and bright-pink glasses came up.

This is what it's about, thought Charlie, with a small bloom of understanding in her chest. This was why this place existed: to create thirty pairs of wide eyes, and thirty beaming smiles.

At 11am on the Saturday morning after her third week, Charlie was still lying facedown on her pillow, increasingly aware of her phone vibrating on the bedside table by her head. When she dragged it over to her face, there were four missed calls from Lydia, two from Jan and one from Ade.

Charlie sat up in alarm, her heart suddenly inflated, and decided to call back the person who might shout at her the least.

'Mate, where've you been at?' shouted Lydia.

'I'm sorry, I was asleep.' At least this time she was allowed to be asleep. It *was* the weekend. 'What's up?'

'Red alert. There's no chef in the café.'

'What?' Charlie's brain shifted up a gear. 'But isn't Leila—'

'Nope, Leila's off til Wednesday. I remember, she's gone to

see her mum in Glasgow. She'll have marked it on the staff forms.'

Staff holiday forms. That rang a bell, she thought, with an increasing sense of trepidation. That was supposed to be her thing. The café was a serious source of income for the farm, and if there wasn't any food on their busiest day, they'd lose out.

'Yeah, anyway, I've been holding off the parents for a bit,' said Lydia. 'But people want their fry-ups. Might get ugly.'

Brilliant, thought Charlie, with both panic and a sense of impending doom. She'd been here precisely three weeks and she was going to be fired already.

SIX

A Fresh Start – A Fire – A Hiring

'Well,' said Ade. 'It was certainly unfortunate.'

Monday morning. Charlie hadn't even made it to her first probationary meeting before Ade had to call an emergency one-to-one, and they were crammed in the office, their knees almost touching.

Definitely no way out of this. Charlie took a deep breath. 'I take full responsibility,' she said. 'I'm so sorry. I missed it.' She wanted to blame Benji and the calamitous disorganisation of just about everything, but she knew that wasn't going to cut it. 'It's OK.' Another brave breath, and the acceptance that she would be back on the camp bed listening to Casey snore for England. 'I'm ready. Do what you need to do.'

Ade gazed at her with mild curiosity. 'Charlie, it's just a mistake. I know Benji Pennyways left you without a handover. I take just as much responsibility for having hired such a…' He looked about the office – which Charlie had made into a worse mess in order to try and sort everything out – and shook his head, as if swallowing a swearword or two. 'It'll take time. So you mislaid the forms. Teething problems are perfectly natural.' He smiled. 'Anyway, I was grateful for your resourcefulness. You've got a very obliging father.'

After going into a brief meltdown and googling too-expensive, all-unavailable caterers for ten minutes on Saturday morning, Charlie had phoned the one person she could think of who would drop everything and rustle up some tasty meals. Aidan had come in just after she'd dashed down to the farm herself; he cheerfully donned Leila's apron and managed two vats of lamb stew, as well as maintaining a high turnover of jacket potatoes and sandwiches. Charlie had helped, and Casey, under extreme duress ('I rest my brain on Saturdays') had come in the afternoon to keep the salads and sandwiches going when everything else had run out. She'd managed to find a freelance caterer in West Norwood who would cover them for the remaining days. She really owed them all.

'So...' she looked at him tentatively. Having a sister killed the way Jools had been had always given her the tendency to catastrophise. 'You're not going to give me a warning?'

'No, no,' said Ade, before clapping his hands on his knees and looking around him. 'Now. What can I do to help you sort all this out?'

'My great-gran says always leave work at the door,' said Lydia merrily, a few weeks later. She was finishing off a bowl of oven chips with her fingers and wearing her star-print onesie with the hood up.

'She wasn't tasked with making a farm earn money,' said Charlie, who for the first time in her working life had her laptop open at home, glasses on, and two notepads by her feet, as well as the remains of a takeaway Thai red curry (extra chilli). 'With zero offence to your badass great-gran.'

After Ade had generously sifted through papers with her that afternoon in the office, as well as talking her through contracts and rotas, a fire had been lit in Charlie's belly. She would address things that felt achievable: first, she bought two armfuls of stationary, and slowly the piles of paper shrank from mountains to hills to knolls to nothing as they were divided into ring-binders and filed in the cabinet. She tackled the farm website – which was pretty dreadful, and done on a budget – persuading Casey to advertise at King's for a student web designer who might want a project for their degree. The volunteer system was started from scratch, with lists and new timetables that could be put online. Ade was giving her a chance, and she was going to take it.

Currently, she was working her way through an audiobook on running a small business, and making a long list of things to be improved, with *fake it 'til you make it* as a mantra on repeat in her head. Though her job was termed as Administrator, really it seemed that they needed more from her. She hadn't worked this hard since… well, ever.

'But you've got to have a break sometime,' said Lydia, chomping on a chip as she sat down next to Charlie. 'You literally made notes and said, "analyse and capitalise" whilst eating your dinner.' She clicked her fingers. 'Oh, my days. I've got it.'

'Huh?' said Charlie, heading three columns with the words *short*, *medium* and *long-term goals*.

'*Makeoverrr*,' said Lydia, in the same gleefully daring tone with which you might suggest bank robbery, or doing crack cocaine.

'Mmm,' said Charlie.

Lydia put her bowl on the floor and knelt up on the sofa. 'I've got three younger sisters, so I always had lots of models to practise on. I always wanted to either be a vet or a hairdresser. But my mum said I had to do a proper degree, give myself some options.' She screwed her nose up in the general direction of Charlie's head. 'I'm not, like, an expert in curls but I could give it a good go. Or maybe make-up?'

'I'll let you do my face if you help me with something.'

'With what?'

'I need ideas. For the farm.' Charlie realised that, unlike old jobs where there were always meetings and directives, *she* had to make the work. A new part of her brain was kickstarting into life, giving her an energy she didn't know she had. 'I think we can bring in more money, and if we do, we can probably get more funders in.'

'*Yasss.*' Lydia bounded up from the sofa, slid over the floorboards to the kitchen, and came back with a bottle of budget rosé and two mugs. 'This is going to be awesome.'

There was other research to be done, too. The next day, her face scrubbed back to normal after Lydia had attacked her, Charlie took most of the day to visit the farms at Mudchute and Vauxhall. They were much more established and she took photos and made notes on her phone, feeling covert and envious of their set-ups, before deciding to knock on the farm manager's door at Vauxhall and introduce herself. The manager was lovely, open and helpful, and they made a date to meet up properly another time.

Returning, she'd got off the bus by the hospital and was

scrolling back through her photos as a fire engine roared past. And another. She looked up the hill and saw it turn into the hospital driveway just by the corner of the park.

'Oh God,' she said, and ran towards it.

Don't let it be the farm, she repeated in her head. *Don't let it be the farm*. But there were the firefighters in their dark, bulky uniforms, coming from the truck and heading through the gate nearest the farm, the hoses snaking out. Smoke trailed up above the trees, and people were hovering on the pavement outside. What if it had been her? Maybe she'd left the rickety old heater on, and it had sparked, gone up, and she had burnt down the farm, and the *animals*—

She pushed past a small crowd towards the barn.

'It's OK,' said Jan, seeing her race in. 'Don't freak out.' Her hands were grimy, cheeks unnaturally red. 'It's under control now.'

Charlie stopped dead. There were several firefighters with a hose, but most were standing around, making sure everyone was far back from the entrance to the barn. Just the barn, not the office. There was a bright flicker of flames in one corner.

'Is everyone OK? Are the animals OK?'

'Everyone's fine, mate. All good.'

Her breath was beginning to level. She looked around. Joe was videoing the entire thing on his phone, occasionally putting himself into shot to commentate.

'What happened?'

'Not too sure yet,' said Jan. 'The hay started to go up. Just as well we had a visitor spot it, otherwise it might have taken more quickly. He came straight in to help, too. Sorted all the volunteers into a line, got the buckets going before the big guns showed up.'

Charlie followed the direction of Jan's nod to see a familiar figure watching the firefighters extinguish the remaining flames. Tall, bomber-jacketed. She watched him for a moment longer, before walking over.

'Gábriel?'

'You deserve all the cake,' said Charlie, sitting down with him in the café and placing a cup of tea next to his plate. She'd made herself one, too. They had closed the farm while the firefighters investigated the origin of the fire. She felt shaky, though in truth there'd been no great harm done. If it had been a hot summer's day, it could have been catastrophic.

Gábriel looked a little shaken, too. His face was as red as Jan's, and there were flakes of black ash in his hair. He was carefully slicing the red velvet cake Charlie had got him from the cafe's industrial fridge, having said he would clean himself up when he got home.

'What were you doing here?' Charlie asked, gently. 'If you don't mind me asking.'

'I thought I would come and look at the farm,' he said, glancing up, and she knew, with awkwardness, that he must have come to see her, just as he'd said he might. He stretched. 'I was just leaving when I saw the flames in the barn.'

'Thank you so, so much. If you hadn't…' She looked up at the ceiling and shivered. 'It could have been a lot worse. And thank you for helping.'

He shrugged. 'It was no problem.' He put another forkful of cake into his mouth.

'How are you, anyway?' She knew, even as she asked the question, that he wasn't good, and that it wasn't just the shock of the fire. He didn't have the same air of easy confidence as during those few times they'd met at the café. There were dark shadows under his eyes and he had long stubble, though not quite enough to be a decent beard. His free hand was shoved deep into his pockets.

'I'm all right,' he said, in the same way he'd replied after slamming into that car door with his bike. He looked up at her. 'This place is really nice.'

'Yeah. It's definitely different.' She wanted to tell him how overwhelmed she was by the responsibility, and how she didn't entirely know what she was doing. 'How's the butcher's shop?' She tried not to feel embarrassed about the last time they'd met, him giving her lamb cutlets and asking her out, her saying no.

He drew in a long breath, and sighed. 'Not happening.' The words were lightly delivered.

'Not happening? How come?'

He spoke to his plate. 'There was a problem with some lamb. A lot of customers got food poisoning. We had inspectors come in.'

'Oh, shit.'

'Yeah. And then there was a pipe that burst on the road. The whole row of shops was flooded. Did you hear about it?'

Charlie remembered the local news reports. She hadn't realised that his shop was right there. 'That's awful. Did it get damaged?'

He nodded. 'We didn't have proper insurance. I thought we did but—' He scratched his head. 'Geórgi was supposed to be in charge of that. So we lost most of our money.' He looked over and gave a subdued smile. 'We had to sell it, and that money all went back to the bank.'

'I'm really sorry.' She put her cup down. 'That totally sucks.'

'Yeah, it sucks,' he said, through another big sigh. 'It all happened very fast. My contract finished on the flat I shared with Geórgi, and he is going back to Hungary now.'

'You haven't got anywhere to live?'

'I'm sleeping on a friend's sofa. I need to find some more work so I can get somewhere better.' A brief, wry glance over. 'Do you have any jobs here?'

Charlie looked at him. Maybe he had appeared at exactly the right time. 'I might do, actually.'

He blinked, surprised. 'For real?'

'Yeah. How are you with power tools?'

'I'm OK, I think.' He looked puzzled.

She got her phone out of her pocket. 'Give me your number.'

Charlie had given a few presentations in her previous jobs. Usually, they had featured projectors and graphs, and people had snuck quiet looks at their phones or watches. This time – for the second half of her probation meeting – she was perched on the edge of a classroom table, holding the first of two single A4 pieces of paper up in front of Ade and Jan.

A deep breath. *Fake it 'til you make it.* 'So I've been here six weeks now,' she said. 'And I've got more of a handle on how everything works. I've seen what the other farms do and I think we can start to up our game. We can make more money hiring the farm out for children's birthday parties and other events.'

'It's a community farm. We don't shut it for private events unless we can help it,' said Jan, her arms folded.

'I thought it could still stay open to the public, actually. We'll just use the classroom and make sure we have volunteers. There'll be loads of parents queuing up for it. If we open seven days a week, that'll be a whole extra day's income. And I've been thinking about a few other things for further down the line.'

Charlie went through her list, which included yoga and art classes, broadening the adopt-a-donkey project to all other livestock, and a membership scheme for adults. Most of this had been brainstormed with Lydia over the bottle of rosé, though Lydia had also been shouting about animal disco and how the pair of them would be running the world soon enough.

'Blimey. You're ambitious, aren't you?' Jan glanced over at Ade. 'We're only a small site, you know. And you'd have to pay the teachers.'

Charlie shook her head. 'My mum's friend will do the yoga class for nothing,' she said, grateful for Nellie's close circle of gently alternative friends. And Aidan had agreed to loan out his school's specialist art teacher in return for an occasional small animal visit to the nursery and reception kids. 'I want the farm to be the best in South London. The best in *London*.'

Ade looked mildly impressed.

She was on a roll. 'Also, I was looking into doing a mobile farm thing – so that some of the bigger animals could be taken offsite to visit schools and community centres, and some could be here, so we could potentially double our income. Prices start quite high for mobile visits on the other farms. And we've got the van already.'

Jan shook her head. 'Bloody Nora. You're talking as if there's two of me, mate. Especially if you're wanting to open seven days. I'm up to my ears as it is.'

'No, I know,' said Charlie, and looked at them both. 'I had an idea about that.'

Three days later, Charlie was by the fence watching Barry and Maurice glare at some five-year-olds from their alpaca pen, when Gábriel came out of his interview. He'd brushed up, was clean-shaven, and looked sweetly formal in a plaid shirt and tie.

She turned to him. 'How did it go?'

He joined her. 'Good, I think. They said they would call me tomorrow.' He looked over. 'This was a really nice thing for you to do.'

'You basically saved the farm from burning down,' she said, grinning. 'And I'm still feeling guilty about causing you to fly off your bike.'

'I got a helmet now, you know.'

'I should think so. Come on, I'll shout you a cuppa.'

A little while after he'd left, Jan came and found her, a smear of mud on her forearm. 'You're good at spotting them, aren't you?'

'Am I?'

'Seems like a good lad, that Gábriel. Though he was doing his best to pretend he wasn't desperate for a job.' A quick, amused look over. 'Bit like someone else we know around here.'

'I have no idea what you mean,' said Charlie airily.

Jan gave a deft grin. 'Anyway. The boy knows his pigs and sheep at least. I reckon he can do quite a bit actually – said he was up for supervising all the maintenance stuff as well as the beasts. Might give me a chance to do a bit of moonlighting over at Mudchute.'

'You're employing him, then?'

'Ade's giving him a call. Starts on Monday.'

Charlie couldn't help the gentle buzz of pride as she cleared up the mugs.

SEVEN

Gábriel on the Farm - Gossip

At the beginning of the next week, Charlie got up especially early and walked to the farm, wrapped up in a voluminous winter scarf and woolly hat. She needed to clear the remaining fog from her head after Saturday's night out at Lydia's favourite terrible club in Clapham – there'd been the slight dread of seeing Alex there, possibly sucking on the neck of that French girl, as he and Charlie had often gone out together on the high street. Although in truth he wouldn't have been seen dead in a place that served Bailey's-heavy cocktails called Boys Are Stupid and played the Sugababes. She really did have to school Lydia in some better places to go – perhaps she'd take her up to Elephant and Castle, introduce her to the sort of rib-destroying bass she currently had playing through her headphones.

She powered through Brockwell Park and up the hill, the scarf too hot now, her chest heaving and armpits damp, but feeling much better for it. She was beginning to rather enjoy her morning walks; they beat tube commutes hands-down.

Gábriel was waiting by the gate to the farm, wearing a long

winter coat and holding a cup of coffee, his breath coming out in clouds.

'Oh. Morning,' said Charlie, taking her headphones off, suddenly wishing she didn't look sweaty and disgusting. 'You're here bright and early.'

He smiled. 'I wanted to make a good first impression for the boss.'

She glanced at him as she unlocked the gate, wondering if there was a hint of mockery there, but he seemed genuine enough. 'Welcome to the farm,' she said, and beamed.

She sat down in the office with him and made them both a cup of tea, conscious of how tall he was and yet how he didn't seem to need to take up every inch of space. His shoulders were curved inwards, head slightly dipped as he looked at the job description she'd drawn up for him, with Ade and Jan's help.

She talked him through it, feeling strange that she'd only been here two months and yet was his co-line-manager, along with Jan. 'Aside from the animals, there's loads to do. I'm not exactly a DIY expert, but even I can see that some areas could do with a bit of love. There are usually volunteers around to help, too. I've realised it's about working out how to get the most out of them. How are you with kids?'

'I don't know. I said I was great with them to Ade and to Jan.' He smiled at the sheet of paper.

It was rather comforting to know that she might not be the only one chancing it. She cast him a more tentative look. 'To be honest, I'm still finding my feet.'

'You seem like you're doing great.'

She felt a faint flush of pleasure creep up her neck. 'We'll see.' She wasn't sure that she completely trusted herself not to make a calamitous mistake yet. She looked out of the little window and gathered herself. 'Anyway, don't feel like you have to do much today. Just get yourself acclimatised, and Jan'll be in soon. Um, shall we get you kitted out?'

'He says he was a butcher,' said Lydia later, having been in lectures all morning. She and Charlie were watching Gábriel shift wire mesh fencing from the equipment store to the sheep pen, now clad in his green RPF jumper and some spare wellies.

'He was.' It seemed wrong to put it in past tense. There was every chance he would be again. She hoped he didn't feel totally crap for doing such menial work, compared to running his own business.

'Not sure I want to be associating with someone who chops up animals for a living.'

Charlie could still not entirely get over the fact that Lydia was a vegan and working here. 'It was very ethical, from what he told me. Not exactly fast-food levels of production.'

'Yeah, well,' said Lydia. 'We'll see. I've got my eye on him.' She forked her index and forefinger to her eyes and then pointed them, somewhat menacingly, in his general direction.

———

Late November. The days tighten. Leaves and crisp packets clog up the drains. On one side of the park, the trains shuffle past, beginning to pick up speed after leaving Denmark Hill station. There's an occasional flurry of ambulance sirens as they converge on A&E at the hospital, mixed with the abrupt, alarm-style calls of the parakeets, neon green in the trees. On the farm, some of the younger volunteers gather on their break, consuming energy drinks and crisps, stamping their feet to keep their toes warm, and chatting amongst themselves.

'Yo, did you hear about Benji P? Court case is a done deal.'

'No way. Really?'

'Trust. Man is going down.'

'Is he getting banged up?'

'Nah, civil lawsuit. He just gives the money back. Maybe he has to pay for their lawyers' fees. I dunno.'

'I think we got our laywers for free. Pro bono.'

'He got off *easy*, fam. You know they think a cigarette butt started the fire?'

'No way. You can't smoke in here.'

'Sabotage, innit.'

'What, you think Benji did it? Someone would've seen him.'

'Or he put someone up to it.'

'Fuck.'

'Charlie's gotta be better than that crim. Where's she at today?'

'Training day. Social Farms and Gardens.'

'Think she's finding her feet now?'

'Yeah, she doesn't look so frightened. You know the farm's on Insta and Twitter and all that shit? She's asking us all to post farm stuff. #RPHforlife.'

'I heard her talking about merch for the shop. T-Shirts, caps, beanies, stickers. I said they should do keyrings and bookmarks too.'

'Bookmarks. When did you last read a book?'

'This morning. Halfway through *Brave New World*. Suck it.'

'Ah, you got me, G.'

. . .

Gábriel had already impressed everyone by quietly getting on with things at the farm. He cleared shrubbery from the back of the sheep pen and swept the puddles. He hefted big bales of hay onto his shoulder, and wiped his hands on his jeans before greeting every new volunteer he met. He took apart and reconstructed some shoddily made fencing at the end of the pigpen. Jan took him in the van to go and pick up the Anglo-Nubian billy from Mudchute for breeding.

'How are you finding it?' Charlie had said, after the first couple of days, watching him squat down next to one of the hutches with a screwdriver. Suarez and Messi, the Continental Giant rabbits, had lolloped to the corner away from him.

'It's nice,' Gábriel said. He had on faded jeans and a dark-green woolly hat, and there were shreds of straw on his jumper. 'Cute.' A gently amused glance up. 'Not like a real farm.'

'Hey, don't you be beating up on the farm,' said Charlie, feeling a sudden unfamiliar defensiveness. 'It's *better* than a normal farm.' There were no cows, for a start.

'Yeah, maybe,' he said, smiling.

He still seemed a little subdued, and she was aware of the new dynamic between them now; having got him the job and being his line manager there was the slightest hint of subservience from him, but she never felt uncomfortable about it. She had told him he could get a free lunch every day from the café so he might as well pile his plate up, and she swore he looked grateful.

'He's fit, though, isn't he?' said Lydia later that day at the office door, craning round to where Gábriel was working outside.

'Um,' Charlie said, noncommittally, though there was a small flare of an indefinable feeling in her stomach. 'I suppose.'

Lydia was still watching him. 'I mean, he totally is. Look at those shoulders. D'you reckon he's single? Probably totally got a girlfriend. They always do, the really nice ones. That's why I always settle for second best. Or third best. Whichevs.'

'You'll never know unless you ask,' Charlie said to her computer, wondering if the feeling in her stomach was jealousy.

'What, ask him out? Don't know. Don't fancy my chances much. You don't want a go?'

'I'm kind of his boss,' said Charlie, stretching and putting her glasses back on. 'That would be very unprofessional.' Did she think of him like that? She wasn't allowed. She was a career woman now, and no man was going to get in the way of it.

''Spose,' said Lydia, checking out Gábriel again. 'Yeah, you know what? Sod it! Maybe I bloody well will. I'll get a few pints in him tonight at The Sun and his defences will be down. He'll have no chance!'

'Sounds perfect.'

'You coming?'

'Not tonight. I've got my sister coming round,' Charlie lied, finding herself not wanting to be witness to such an onslaught, and realising that in fact she did feel delicately, but undeniably, jealous.

She decided to go over and see the family, to make that fiction nearer reality. Incredibly, Casey was out with friends, though it was to see a sci-fi film that she would only dissect afterwards in order to point out all the astronomical mistakes. Aidan cooked moussaka, heavy on the aubergine, turned down the pirate radio station and sat with Nellie as Charlie filled them in on the farm news, all the while trying not to think about the staff and volunteers round the fireplace at the pub, and Lydia making eyes at their most recent employee.

'So I asked him,' said Lydia in the morning, looking a little worse for wear as she waited for the kettle to boil. 'Jesus, I feel rough as fuck.'

'Asked who?' Charlie said with careful blitheness, as she chopped root ginger for her breakfast smoothie.

'Gábriel.'

'Oh. Great.' She put the ginger into the blender. 'Want one?'

Lydia took a rather puce look at Charlie's ingredients. 'Ugh, shit, no thanks. I need six pieces of toast, heavy on the Marmite.'

'So how did it go?'

'Huh?'

'With Gábriel.'

'Oh. Yeah. Not a sausage. Not even after four pints. He said he wasn't really looking at the moment. I said it could be no-strings, that I wouldn't be all, you know, *girlfriendy* with him, but he said no, thanks. He was pretty nice about it, really. I've had men run,' she said, before clarifying. 'Sprint.'

'Bad luck,' said Charlie, not meaning it one bit, before pressing the button on the blender, the sound making Lydia run out of the room.

Charlie came onto the farm one Saturday, having been away in Nottingham for the christening of her cousin's baby the day before. The farm was often busier at the weekends, older children in as well as toddlers, a few teenagers and arty twenty-something couples taking photos of the pigs, phones stuck right up to the fence wire. Gábriel was in, too – it had been arranged that he would do some duty manager-ing on the weekends – smiling at the kids and crouching down to help a few of them with the feed dispenser.

He was in the café at lunchtime, and nodded when Charlie sat down opposite him, she for once having managed enough willpower to order a big salad and not the most fattening thing on the menu.

'It's not too much for you, is it?' she said. 'Doing the weekends as well?'

He swallowed his mouthful. 'No, it's fine. Overtime is good right now.' A faintly uncomfortable, abashed look.

It was the first time they'd really sat down to talk since he'd started. She had been to the pub after work a couple of times with the volunteers and staff, soaked up the highly-charged banter ranging from football to dance crazes, cat videos to sheep breeding, but she felt the need to be slightly removed, professional. Gábriel on his own, however, was a much calmer proposition. He had a way of making her feel extremely level, just by sitting there and listening, and Charlie found herself telling him about her family: Nellie's five loud sisters up north, and Aidan's mother in County Cork, who owned a tea shop on the south coast that also sold crystals and jewellery. She exaggerated Casey's impossible stoicism and how she was likely at the very least to name a new star. But she didn't tell him about Jools. It hurt too much.

Gábriel said he had an older sister who had lived in

Hamburg for a while, but had moved back to Hungary with her son and daughter, of whom he seemed fond. He spoke of going to university in Budapest and coming over a few years ago with his friend. Geórgi, Charlie remembered, though Gábriel didn't utter his name. He talked of how he'd thought this country might offer something he couldn't get back home. How he'd nodded and smiled a lot in the early days, because it had been hard, even with his extra English classes, to understand anyone in the city. How polite everyone was here, and that he sometimes missed the typically straight-talking Hungarian manner.

'So,' he said finally, sitting back in his chair, and giving Charlie a frank, gentle look. 'You found a job you like. I remember you said that's what you wanted.'

'Yeah. Maybe.' She found that she was liking it, more than she'd anticipated. There was something grounding about being here; a new sense of sureness in her bones. She took her elbows off the table. 'I hope it's OK for you. I know it's not exactly your ideal.'

'It's great,' he said. 'I'm grateful.'

'You scratch my back, I'll scratch yours,' she said.

He looked faintly perplexed.

'Oh. Just a saying,' she said, and his face cleared. 'Back to it?'

He nodded. 'Back to it.'

It was silly, she thought as she followed him out of the café, to have been jealous of Lydia. It felt comfortably amicable between them, and that was all she needed right now.

Gábriel seemed particularly attached to a new volunteer, a teenage boy with Down's Syndrome, very small for his age, with deep-brown skin and short zigzagging corn rows. Kaden was obsessed with the sheep, and Gábriel would invent jobs for him so that he could go into the pen and put his hands on the wiry, greasy wool. Lydia taught him a relevant song for each of the Shetlands, and he was currently crooning 'Crazy in Love' at Bey-Bey, who continued munching her hay impassively as Gábriel heaped more into the grate above her head with a garden spade.

'You don't get that in some city office, now, do you?' said Jan, passing Charlie as she stood in the doorway with a cuppa.

'You really don't,' said Charlie. The only things she found herself missing from her last place were the non-wonky office chair and the heating.

'Did he tell you I'm about to be his landlady?'

'Who?'

'Gábriel,' Jan said, as if it were obvious. 'Me and the wife have got a spare room going to waste. Might as well give it to the strapping Hungarian. Speaking of,' she said, nodding towards the sheep pen, where Gábriel was taking off his jumper. In doing so, his T-shirt rose with it, revealing quite a lot of lightly-tanned back and a glimpse of a large tattoo between his shoulder blades. From here, it looked like a very detailed tree trunk.

Charlie averted her eyes just as Kaden finished his brass riff and Gábriel pulled his T-shirt down, turning towards them as he did so, almost definitely seeing her looking.

Jan waved at him. 'Just telling missus about your new digs,' she shouted.

He held up his thumb.

'So you'll never guess what I heard,' said Lydia.

Charlie was sitting on her bed, attempting some cross-stitch on Nellie's suggestion – her mum was obsessed with knitting and said that crafting was very mindful. Charlie had countered the fear of becoming an old lady by being halfway through a circular pattern that said BITCHES GET SHIT DONE, whilst catching up on some TV, until Lydia knocked on her door.

'Hey.' Charlie rested her needle on the fabric and pressed pause. 'What?' The wind was picking up, the apple tree tapping on her windowpane.

'Some of the teenagers were talking. One of the newish volunteers, the kid who comes on Thursdays – what's his name, Marcus or Marco? – and some of the others. I was round the back and they didn't see me. They were saying—' She glanced at Charlie. 'They're just kids, I mean, I hope it's all right to say.'

'It's fine, Lydia, just tell me.'

'Well, they were just talking about you. In a nice way, really, but they're teenagers trying to impress each other, so, you know. They were talking about you mostly being in the office, not being able to tell a billy goat from a nanny, and how you're not really serious about it. Which is obviously bullshit. It was mostly the new kid, not the others. I was round the back and just starting to think I'd go round and give him what for, but I didn't need to.'

'Why not?'

'Because your man Gábriel hadn't been too far away in the barn and he walked over there and said that if he ever heard him talking about you like that again, he'd have him to deal with. I think it took him a second to get what he meant because he said it so nicely.'

'And what did he say?'

'Didn't say much after that. Bit embarrassed, I reckon. They all like him – I think they look up to him, really. I'm making fajitas – want some?'

'I'm good, ta,' said Charlie, remembering the last time she'd agreed to eat something made by Lydia, and subsequently spending the next few hours feeling very ill. She went back to her cross-stitch and her box set, the branch of the apple tree knocking doggedly on her window.

EIGHT

A Christmas Party – A Board Meeting – A Discovery

'Higher?' said Tallboy, whose willowy height Charlie was putting to good use.

'A bit higher, I reckon,' she said.

'Here?'

'Perfect.'

Charlie had helped organise one office Christmas party before, but that had mostly involved ordering wholesale amounts of booze and drinking a great deal of it whilst trying to avoid the sleazy account manager and his red onion breath. It had rather less involved sending volunteers out to nick holly from the other side of the park, taste-testing Leila's insanely alcoholic Christmas cake, and overseeing the brief modelling of tinsel around the ears of the more acquiescing animals for social media – Charlie had wanted mistletoe until Jan had sanguinely pointed out that it might poison them.

Other farms had public Christmas fairs, but Ade had suggested that Charlie save herself for the Spring Fair next year. Part of her wondered if he didn't yet trust her with something bigger, but he said it so kindly, as if it was really a favour to her. So this was a private party for funders, from the corporate sponsorship manager at the bank – who probably wouldn't turn up – to the individual donors and trustees. She'd made a fabulous playlist of crowd-pleasing and slightly quirkier Christmas tunes and was now supervising Tallboy and Lydia in decorating the café.

'This party is going to blow everyone's minds,' said Lydia ambitiously, as she jumped down from the chair she was standing on.

'This party is going to be extremely civilised and create no mess,' said Charlie, who was feeling nervous enough to be representing the farm to the bigwigs. Last time she tried hard to entertain in a professional capacity she almost burnt a restaurant to its foundations. 'No mess at all.'

It was somewhere in between the two, in the end. The volunteers had all been invited, and came in a mixture of sparkly dresses and their best bad Christmas jumpers. Charlie was sporting a deep-red velvet miniskirt and a gold sequinned jacket – a little over-glam for the farm, but she had to have *some* outlets – while Lydia was wearing reindeer antlers, stripey elf leggings and a snow-scene jumper with flashing LED lights. Joe had on a jumper saying F*** XMAS and Tallboy had made himself a mistletoe headband, though you'd have to stand on a chair to have a chance.

'That's far too tasteful,' Charlie said to Gábriel, who was in a knitted jumper with a Scandinavian pattern, standing by the entrance to the café. There was a blast of cold air from outside.

He smiled. 'Kaden is doing all the work for me,' he said, as his protégé bopped over to them.

'Check it out, Charlie,' Kaden said, pointing to his chest. He was wearing a T-shirt saying GÁBRIEL'S LITTLE HELPER along with his Santa hat.

'Oh, nice one, Kaden,' Charlie said. 'Did you make that?'

'Yeah,' said Kaden. 'Kind of. OK, my mum made it. But I helped.' Gábriel put his hand on Kaden's shoulder. 'Can I go dance now?' He bopped off again.

They stood together for a moment, and Charlie waited for Gábriel to say something about her own outfit.

'You made the farm look really nice,' he said, nodding vaguely around him.

Maybe not, then, she thought. That put paid to any question of him still liking her. He'd obviously just been professional in defending her to the volunteers. 'Thank you.'

It was true, though, she realised as she drifted to the kitchen door, where Lydia was topping up glasses of mulled wine and taking surreptitious slurps from the ladle. Charlie hadn't panicked and put her hand in the (non-existent) kitty jar, but instead asked volunteers for ideas, and everyone had pitched in to help. The fence-posts were wrapped in fairy lights. The donkeys, Bette and Joan, stood wearing their animal-friendly wreaths and their best French noir faces while funders stroked their ears. Marianne knew a wine stockist and had coaxed them into donating free boxes of Merlot. For once, Charlie had managed to arrange something significant at work without disaster. Maybe she really *could* do this.

She turned to watch the room again, to make sure she had greeted everyone.

A broad, relatively tall black man had just arrived, looking a little out of place in a suit and smart overcoat as he exchanged words with Gábriel by the door. He was probably in his forties, with prominent cheekbones and an artful goatee.

'Who's that, Lydia?'

Lydia came and joined her, holding a fresh tray of drinks. 'Oh, that's Mr B.'

'Mr B?'

'Boadu. He's one of the trustees, or maybe on the board, or both. Can't remember.'

'Boadu,' Charlie said, remembering the name from the short list of apologies for absence in the board meeting she'd sat in on last month. She watched as he moved past some of the guests.

'He's well posh,' said Lydia. 'He's got a CBE and everything. Or is it an OBE? One of them. He's not a lord, but he probably will be. And he's an MEP.' She began to move off, saying 'MEP, JCB, TCP, you know, the full works,' a little too loudly, heading straight for the man called Will Boadu.

Charlie thought it best to follow.

'Hi, Mr B,' said Lydia, holding the tray up to him. 'How's it hanging?'

'Hello, er…' the man looked stiffly bemused.

'This is Lydia,' said Charlie hastily, joining them properly. 'She's our intern at the farm. She basically runs it.'

'That's not true,' said Lydia. 'Charlie's mistress of everything, since September. She's totally bossing it.'

'Is that so?' said Mr Boadu with a brittle expression, and the briefest of glances at Charlie's outfit. 'Very good. I'm glad to hear it.' He gave an oddly formal bow, and took another mildly puzzled glance at Charlie before moving off.

'He's very serious.'

'Who, Mr B?' Lydia watched his retreating back as he moved into the crowd. 'Nah, he's just a bit shy, that's all. He loves the farm. He's proper generous. Comes every so often to see how everything's going. He set up a stables, too, not far away.'

'A stables?' There she was, thinking that London was an urban metropolis when in fact there was a horse or a hen stuffed into every available corner.

'Yeah. For, like, gang kids and that. They ride the horses and it distracts them from the shit they've got going on. He's a diamond.'

Charlie looked him up at home later, feeling very tipsy after several glasses of mulled wine and a probably ill-advised eggnog, made with the farm's own eggs. There was a biography on his own website, Black Sheep Foods. Will Boadu had grown up in Leeds to Ghanaian-born parents and established an organic farm in the Yorkshire Dales fifteen years ago – a documentary had been made about him, it still being rather unusual to be black and a farmer. There was a picture of him on the home page wearing some stout country tweeds and holding a shepherd's crook. He was an MEP for the Liberal Democrats and the patron of several charities, including being the chief funder of the farm, and had founded a community stables in Loughborough Junction. And all at the age of – verified with his Wikipedia page – forty-three.

He's rather striking too, said one half of her brain.

Shut up, replied the other half.

The New Year brings cool, hard days. People keep their heads down as they go to work in the dark mornings, battling with resolutions to read more, spend less, resign from their jobs and join gyms. In the centre of London, a young man and a younger woman are arguing, he holding her hand, she looking away – but perhaps we shall come back to them later. Frost finds the edges of everything, from the stems of the wildflowers in the park's labyrinth garden to the limp bunting on the gable of the farm café. The tennis courts are empty. The kids visiting the farm are wrapped up tight and warm, their cheeks bright with the cold, dropping feed with their padded gloves, though the animals mostly linger in the gloom of their shelters.

Charlie had gone round to her folks' for Christmas Day, where Aidan had put on a massive spread including Guinness-soaked roast beef for the family and his two London-based cousins. As usual, they'd made the traditional toast that filled Aidan, Nellie and Charlie with their own private melancholy, finishing off with so much Christmas pudding and cheese that none of them could move for hours. The next day, they'd driven up to Nottingham to see the 'Robin Hood fam', as Aidan liked to call them. Lydia sent photos of her massive extended family in Dorset, all toasting the camera with glasses of Bailey's. Charlie made sure she texted Gábriel, who had volunteered to do the rounds at the farm before heading to Hungary on Boxing Day. He sent her a picture of Gaga and RiRi:

The sheep say Boldog Karácsonyt,

he'd messaged, simply.

In January, the farm closed to visitors at four in the afternoon, the winter's darkness still shrouding everything, though staff and volunteers stayed longer. One day at the end of the week, Charlie did a final sweep and saw a figure by the sheep, scratching a head or two. 'Hey Joe, time to bounce,' she said.

'Safe, yeah, in a sec.'

She jingled her keys. 'I'm locking up.'

He shuffled over to her, obviously reluctant.

'I'm sure you've got some dinner waiting for you at home.'

He gave a small, rasping laugh that turned into a cough. 'No way, man. Morley's for me. Spicy wings and chips.'

'Oh. OK.'

'Home ain't all that. I try and stay away. Christmas was, like, black hole ting.'

She didn't entirely know what that meant, but it obviously wasn't good. She'd heard him say once before that he had an older brother in prison. 'I'm sorry, Joe. Is there anything I can help with?' She was feeling more comfortable talking to the volunteers these days, striking a balance between friendly and efficient.

'Nah, man, nah.' A brave smile. 'This is what helps. It's sick.' He put his coat on properly. 'Roll safe, yeah?' A wave, and he disappeared.

'Blue Monday, ugh,' said Lydia by the hutches, on apparently the most depressing day of the year, three weeks into the month. 'I feel like total crapsticks. I miss the holidays.'

'That's sobriety for you,' said Charlie.

Lydia had vowed to do a dry January and spent most of the time at home staring wistfully at the one bottle of Lambrusco on the top of the kitchen cabinet and eating a great deal of pickled onion flavoured crisps. Charlie was more realistic, substituting most, but not all, of her rum and wine cravings with very posh lemonade. She'd also started bringing back the odd surplus vegetable from the farm shop to replace her tendency for takeaway Thai curry.

'Bring on February,' Lydia said, hefting a big plastic bucket of sawdust and pellets onto her hip. 'Good luck tonight, mate. You're going to rock that bitch.'

The evening brought her first official board meeting, and she felt jittery. Ade was going to set out the next twelve months, which included some of her proposed plans; she had, on his advice, reined herself in a little. 'You mean animal disco has to wait?' Lydia had said, outraged and crestfallen in equal measures.

Everyone was there, including Will Boadu, who'd greeted her just as formally as at the December party. As Ade summarised their opening year, and filled them in on the successful court proceedings with Benji Pennyways, she was aware of Boadu's presence in the room, and though she wasn't looking at him, was sure that his eyes kept falling on her. She felt a faint burning sensation on her neck. He had on a dark-pink shirt with his suit, everything looking well-pressed and expensive. She wondered how much he'd ever really got his hands in the mud or up a cow, or whether he just managed everything from the comfort of his Battersea flat.

'So, Charlie.'

She blinked and looked at Ade, who seemed to be waiting for something.

'Oh,' she said, sitting up and gathering her papers. 'Yes.' She looked around at everyone, their faces largely open and interested, apart from Will Boadu's, which was flinty and unreadable. She faintly wondered if he had a problem with women, and how boring and disappointing that would be. Charlie took a deep breath, and talked them through her ideas for the coming year.

It went well. Mostly. Various board members asked questions, which she largely managed to find answers for; there was an extended discussion about the potential challenges of inviting homeless people to work on the allotments, and the best area and time for yoga classes. Then, a question from Will Boadu.

'I have to ask, Miss Hughes,' he said. His voice was rich, resonant, and commanded respect from the room. 'These are commendable plans, and very ambitious, but do you really think you can implement them all this year?'

'Hell, yeah,' she said, feeling prickly, before catching Ade's eye. *Down, tiger-pride*, she thought. 'I mean, I believe so. Yes.'

He remained in the same position, his legs crossed, hands folded on his thighs. 'All the on-site classes seem practical, but exporting the animals to this number of care homes and more schools will require extra volunteers, and you'll always need a driver.'

As everyone looked at Charlie, she had a brief memory of Andreas and a roomful of people staring at her PowerPoint while she tried to laugh off the accidentally visible folder titled *SUCKY WORK SUCKS*. She swallowed, straightened. 'I've thoroughly researched how the other farms have done these sorts of things, and I got advice from the Social Farms and Gardens network,' she said. 'Nothing's been suggested tonight that I don't know the cost implications for. We've got a new member of staff, as Ade said, and he's got a provisional license to drive the van. And I can secure more volunteers.' She held his gaze, hoping she conveyed serious power-woman vibes, and it was he who looked away first, his lips set firmly together.

'I have every confidence,' said Ade cheerfully, and there were murmurs of assent, before the conversation developed into a brainstorming session on potential new funders. Charlie furiously made notes on her laptop, trying not to glare at the moody, contrary MEP in the corner.

'Miss Hughes,' Will Boadu said afterwards, from behind her.

She felt a rash of impetuousness as she turned. His formality was ridiculous. 'Charlie is fine, Will,' she said, holding out her hand.

He looked at her outstretched hand for a moment before taking it in a warm, startlingly firm grip. 'You seem to be doing well here. Thank you.'

'Oh. No probs,' she said, wondering why he hadn't said that in the meeting, rather than trying to pick holes in her proposals, and why his solemnity made her feel rather petulant. 'Going to come and do the yoga class?'

'The...' His eyebrows rose, as if he was trying to work out whether she was joking or not. 'I don't imagine so. I'm sure it will go well.'

'Awesome,' said Charlie, and flashed him a massive defiant smile.

———

More wintry days. There is rain that almost becomes sleet, and condensed windows in the dry cleaner's and the barber's shop. The January sale signs are taken down. Outside King's

A&E, patients in hospital gowns smoke furiously, the veins blue and prominent on their pale legs, and a very overweight man sings Michael Jackson songs as he pushes a great trolley of green, yellow and red paraphernalia down the hill, including a banner saying THE END IS NIGH. On the farm, the ewes are bulging, their movements sluggish as they near the end of their pregnancies, and Jan monitors them daily.

It's dark in the morning when Charlie arrives, but she still likes to get there in good time, to fire up the computer and make her first cup of tea. She likes the quiet moments before the volunteers start coming, when she can gather herself, check her emails and make a to-do list for the day. She has worked out how many layers to wear in the freezing office, with the addition of fingerless gloves, scarf and hat, and now has a comfy cushion to sit on, and a cheery pot plant.

As if by magic, things started to happen. Except it wasn't really by magic, but by Charlie methodically crossing items off her list – and no matter how simple they were, she always felt a novel fizz of satisfaction. For the first time in her life, her work days seemed a little brighter, easier.

It helped that Jan and Gábriel were supportive of everything; and wherever Jan cast doubts on the availability of staff, Gábriel always said he could do it. Charlie updated the website to include the new classes, the corporate farm gym event and the expanded adopt-an-animal. She got in touch with several homeless charities to set up meetings, talked to the council about part-funding her care home scheme, and borrowed Aidan's school camera to take new photos of all the animals. She advertised for new dedicated volunteers and inducted twins Jami and Badiha, seventeen-year-olds dropped off by their mother. Badiha had her hijab tucked into a big woolly roll-neck jumper and proclaimed each animal cuter than the last one, whilst Jami rolled his eyes. Casey finally visited, though she plodded round like a dead woman walking, scowling at the alpacas, who scowled right back.

Late one afternoon, Charlie was just leaving when her phone buzzed. Lydia.

> *Lydia: U WILL LITERALLY NEVER GUESS WHAT [open-mouthed emoji]*

> *Charlie: What?*

> *Lydia: u will never guess omg haha [four crying/laughing emojis]*

> *Charlie: ????*

> *Lydia: its too good [upside down face emoji]*

> *Charlie: Tell me later x*

She put her phone back in her pocket. Lydia loved gossip that was completely irrelevant to Charlie. If it wasn't something about a pregnant pop starlet going out with an actor who'd been going out with a much older actress but now wasn't, it would be something about her lecturer, the woman with the booming voice, or her student friends and their latest drunken escapades involving street cones and animal costumes.

• • •

'Oh, wow.'

'I know. *Told* you.'

As it happened, Lydia's gossip did turn out to be a little more relevant. She had thrust her phone screen in front of Charlie's face as soon as she'd shut the front door, and on the phone screen was a photo of Will Boadu. On a dating app.

'So my mate's friends with a real posho, yeah, she's like a sort of *Made in Chelsea* Sloane Ranger Minor Royal sort of thing, and she's on this app that's only for other poshos – you have to get like, vetted – and I was looking over her shoulder while she was swiping through a whole load of posho men, and then Mr B's face came up and I literally fell off my chair in the library canteen. It was properly hilarious. My hip hurts like fuck.'

Charlie was still holding Lydia's phone. The photo was a close-up, probably a professional job; Will Boadu was looking directly at the camera, wearing a dark-green shirt and a black tie. 'But how are you looking at it now if you're not a member?'

'Suzie gave me her login so I could show you. I had to promise not to mess up her account. Look at him. So adorbs. There are more photos than that.' Lydia leant over to touch her screen.

'Oh God, Lydia, don't.'

'Why not?'

'Because it's intruding. This is personal stuff. He wouldn't expect us to be looking at this.'

'Yeah, because we're not raging poshos. But exactly – he won't ever know we've seen it, will he?' Lydia put her finger on the screen again.

'Oh, man,' said Charlie, pulling Lydia over to the sofa.

The second photo showed Will in a sports car in the countryside, wearing a flat cap and driving gloves, and in the third he was in a white linen suit with pyramids looming behind him. His avatar name was Black & Proud Country Man.

Lydia read out his blurb which, unlike most dating apps, was in the third person, as if they were being introduced to you at a ball. '*This handsome gentleman can be found in the city and the country. Deeply engaged with European political affairs, he works in government, and feels strongly about his role in the community. But he is equally at home in the countryside, where he runs a farming business, enjoys long walks and even longer drives in his 1969 MG.*' She snickered.

'Don't be mean,' said Charlie softly, nudging her and taking the phone. '*He is looking for a serious, long-term relationship with a strong, independent woman who can happily adapt to urban and rural living.*'

'Sounds like someone I know.' Lydia raised a suggestive eyebrow.

'Shut it.' Charlie continued reading aloud. '*A shared love of cinema, theatre, concerts, jazz, horse-riding, and in-depth conversation are desired.*' There were symbols on the right of the blurb, and several highlighted: long-term relationship, marriage, children. 'Well, I can't ride a horse,' she said. 'Phew. Let off the hook.'

A choked snigger from Lydia. 'He is pretty hot, for an older guy. A proper catch for the right posho.'

'Mmm,' said Charlie. He was handsome, in a stern sort of way, and it made her think of him a little differently, seeing him put himself out there like this. It was actually rather sweet. Good on him.

'I'm just saying what I see. And he's very proper. A gentleman. Old-fashioned. But nice. He's totally not going to be the sort to send you a dick pic. I mean, not that I mind that sort of thing. Bring them on, I say.'

'Of course you do,' said Charlie.

Maybe *she* should go on a dating app, Charlie thought later, from under her duvet. It had been five months since Alex dumped her over the phone. But the thought of dating made her shudder – even looking at this site, and how polite everything seemed, simply did not appeal to her right now. '*All the single ladies,*' she quietly sang to the ceiling, slightly mournfully. Beyoncé – and Bey-Bey, the pop princess's avatar on the farm – would keep her strong.

NINE

A Valentine - A Proposal

The lambs came. Visitors and staff went crazy over the new arrivals as they tottered over the grass and tugged at their mothers' udders, and Charlie documented each one for social media posts festooned with sheep and heart emojis.

She stayed late one Sunday evening, watching Jan and Gábriel crouched over RiRi in the shed, having topped up their flasks of coffee for them. The ewe was on her side, head raised, making no noise. After an hour, Jan washed her forearms in the bucket of soapy water and inserted her hand. It was a quiet, church-like moment – only the sound of rustling straw and the faint hum of traffic, the ewe bathed in the unnatural orange glow of the electric light.

'Do we need the vet?' asked Charlie softly.

Jan shook her head. 'Legs back,' she said to Gábriel, who nodded, left the shed, and came back a minute later with a short corded rope.

Charlie didn't really breathe as Jan inserted the rope into the ewe's uterus, her face full of concentration, and there were a few small, fierce exhalations from both of them. Jan shifted her kneeling position, and finally began to withdraw her arm; a glimpse of two hooves, then legs with the rope around them and suddenly the whole body slipped out, glistening and coated in mucus. A tiny, brown lamb. Gábriel cleaned its nostrils, rubbed his hand on its little flank, and brought it over to RiRi to lick.

'Wow,' said Charlie.

He looked over at her. 'Do you want to name her?'

'Is she going to be kept?'

'Not sure yet,' said Jan. 'Could do.'

Charlie looked at the valiant, trembling body. 'Whitney,' she said.

'Lovely,' said Jan.

Charlie arrived home knackered but glowing, feeling like she'd witnessed something from another realm. The most exciting thing to happen in her last workplace had been the arrival of a barista-style coffee machine, not actual new life. Lydia was on the floor with glittery paper and pens scattered around her legs as if she were an eight-year-old, although the bottle of wine suggested otherwise. She had happily gone from dry January to sodden February with full determination.

'What are you up to?' Charlie said.

Lydia didn't look up from cutting her card. 'Doing a Valentine.'

'For who?'

'A guy in my Tuesday seminar. He doesn't like me, but I don't care. Got to spread the love. You should totes do one.'

Charlie thought back to last Valentine's Day, when she and Alex had gone out to the Institute of Contemporary Arts to watch a film with an entirely blue screen for seventy-nine minutes, during which she had fallen asleep and he had got annoyed. She poured herself a glass of wine. 'Mmm. No.'

'Go on. It's *tradition*. I make one every year, no matter what. Bespoke. My mum says you have to do one otherwise it's fourteen years' of bad luck. She would know. She's been divorced fourteen years. Not even lying.'

Charlie sat down on the sofa. There were flecks of gold glitter on the cushions. 'I haven't got anyone in mind.' Earlier today, she'd looked at Alex's Instagram feed, which she hadn't done in a while. He and the French girl, Elodie, had gone to the ICA, and she looked happy about it. *Never had a love like this before*, he'd written, and she was surprised at what little hurt she felt. She'd been blithe, too hopeful, simultaneously wanting Alex to be everything and trying to be the person he wanted her to be.

'Not on the farm or anything?' said Lydia. 'What about Gábriel?'

'No.'

'But he's so rockin'. And he doesn't have a girlfriend. I bet he'd well like a Vally card. He'd sit in the barn on a hay bale gazing at it all afternoon. You can do it anonymously.'

'No.'

'Maybe he's gay. Just imagine him with a sexy boyfriend.' She rolled her tongue, making a noise like a horny dove.

'He's not gay,' said Charlie, offhandedly.

'How do you know?'

'He's just not.'

'But how do you *know*?'

Charlie felt a rash of impatience. 'Because he asked me out once.'

Lydia stopped her work then, and looked delightfully scandalised. 'When?'

Now, of course, she wished she'd kept that to herself. 'Before the farm.' She took a glug of wine.

'You knew each other before the farm? Have you got a history with him?'

'No. Not really.' She did sometimes wonder if he still liked her, and whether indeed she liked him; but somehow, it just didn't feel right when she was working so hard to do well on the farm. They shared an amiable rapport, and she didn't want to ruin it. 'Don't say anything.'

Lydia popped open the lid of a new pen. 'Can't believe I didn't know.'

'You didn't know because nothing is ever a secret with you.'

'I can keep a secret,' Lydia said, her pen lid now in her mouth as she filled in another cartoon heart.

'Anyway, not him.' Charlie turned on the TV. *Countryfile* had something on superfood crop cultivation, and she didn't change the channel as she would have done six months ago.

Half an hour later, Lydia – having poured Charlie her second glass of wine – sat up very straight, or as straight as she could after four (and a third) glasses. 'You know who you could send one to.'

'Not a volunteer. That would be weird.'

Lydia shook her head, and her next words were spoken wide-eyed, as if telling a ghost story around a campfire. '*Mister. Boa-Du.*'

'Oh my God, Lydia,' said Charlie, letting out a laugh. 'You are so bad.'

'Bad meaning good, you mean.'

'Bad meaning *bad*. The poor guy. He's just looking for love.'

Countryfile was just finishing, the presenter on the TV shoving a drench gun into the mouth of an unhappy sheep.

'Exactly,' said Lydia, enthusiastically. 'Just imagine how warm his heart will be when he gets a *Valentine*.'

'It's cruel. And disrespectful. I don't want take the piss out of him.'

'I'm not, honest. Getting a Valentine is the ultimate best.' Lydia threw her hands outwards, and glitter powder drifted from her fingers as if she were a fairy godmother. 'It'll be anonymous. Didn't you feel good when you were younger and you got a card and you didn't know who it was from so you could imagine it was from the fittest guy in the school and that he was hopelessly, madly, wildly in love with you?'

Charlie thought back to the occasional card slipped into her bag at secondary school. The clandestine tingle in her belly. 'Yeah,' she said, a little less doubtfully. 'I guess it could be nice. Even if *she* didn't want that, maybe he would.

'Shall I do one, then?'

'It's too late to send anything now.'

'E-card,' said Lydia.

'No one sends e-cards. E-cards are very 2007.'

Lydia was already pulling over Charlie's laptop.

'Oh, God.' There was a part of Charlie that always wanted to go the extra mile to cheer people up. She knew where it came from, deep down – the primal desire to preserve her parents' happiness when an immoveable cloud of gloom had settled upon their house. She tried to imagine Will Boadu's granite countenance yielding a little. Maybe it wouldn't be so bad to give him a diverting moment of joy. Everyone deserved a Valentine, really. 'Anonymous, though.'

'Deffo,' said Lydia, before letting out a gooey sort of gasp. 'It's perfect.' She swivelled round the screen, on which there was a rectangular image of two cartoon pig silhouettes facing each other, one white and one dark pink, with a tiny heart between their two heads and the words THIS LITTLE PIGGY FELL IN LOVE. 'You have to,' she said deliriously. 'It's literally meant to be. I'm going to look up his MEP email address.'

'"Fell in love" though?' said Charlie. 'Isn't that a bit much?'

'Nah,' said Lydia. 'Valentines are supposed to be over the top.'

Charlie downed the last of her wine. 'Fine,' she said. 'Just because we are generous people trying to cheer up a stern-hearted man.'

'We are literally the nicest people in the whole universe.'

'Anonymously, Lydia.'

'Yeah, yeah,' said Lydia, already absorbed in writing the card.

Halfway through the next morning, Charlie opened her junk mail folder in the office to find an email headed THANK YOU FOR YOUR VALENTINE E-CARD PURCHASE and felt her heart plunge to the floor.

On opening it, she realised that the very worst thing that could possibly happen had indeed happened: that Lydia, doubtless through a fog of cheap Chenin Blanc, had not opened her own email account as assumed, but sent it from Charlie's work email, and though the card had been signed 'an admirer from afar', the recipient would still see that it had come from *cbhughes@ruskinparkfarm.co.uk*.

'Fuck,' said Charlie. 'Fuck, fuck, fuck.'

A knock and Gábriel was suddenly in the doorway. Charlie went to close her laptop screen, except that this was a desktop computer and he'd still have seen something of the email header before she remembered that she could close the window.

His eyes flicked very quickly from the screen to her. 'Just wanted to remind you that I'm out before lunch to go to the dentist.'

'Yep, yep, totally, absolutely awesome, sick,' said Charlie, beaming, before deciding that the beam was wrong and making her face extremely serious instead.

Gábriel looked faintly perplexed, in that very subtle way of his. 'OK,' he said, and lingered for a moment longer, as if about to say something.

'Any more lambs?' she said.

'Not yet.' He glanced at the computer again before he disappeared.

Charlie hit her forehead with the heel of her hand three times, very deliberately.

Thankfully, nothing happened at all. Charlie waited for some sort of retribution: to be called in by Ade for a dressing-down; to get some sort of ticking-off from a *europarl.europa.eu* email; she scanned the farm every so often to check that a well-dressed man wasn't striding towards her with a summons about harassment. She also stalked him on Twitter, where he put occasional updates from European cities – fact-finding trips to observe community-based business schemes. Occasionally, she woke up in the middle of the night and remembered what she'd done, curling up with embarrassment. She cursed herself for the over-enthusiasm and impetuosity she was supposed to be training herself out of. Getting Alex to live with her after three months, not double-checking those flights to Maine in her previous job, the Sambuca fireball, an anonymous-actually-extremely-*non*-anonymous Valentine. She should have supervised Lydia, not left her to it. She shouldn't have done it at all. Her housemate and landlady was contrite, but flippantly so. 'He probably gets loads. I mean, how many fit MEPs are there?' she said, shrugging. 'He probably doesn't even look at that email address.'

Two weeks after Valentine's Day, when she had all but forgotten it, she answered the office phone one afternoon to hear a richly formal voice on the other end.

'Miss... Hughes? Charlie?'

She froze. 'Yes. Speaking.' She already knew it was him, and waited for all of the worst things to transpire.

There was a slight pause, and for a moment she thought he must be on a mobile and had lost signal. 'It's, er, Will Boadu here.'

'Hi. Yes. Hello.'

Another short pause, in which people in any normal sort of conversation would have been asking how the other was.

'My apologies,' he said. 'I've been away.'

She didn't dare respond.

'I have a proposal for you.' He coughed lightly. 'Of sorts.'

She felt utterly rigid. Outside, as if to perfectly highlight her idiocy, a child made a very snorty *oinking* sound.

He took a long breath. Another pause. 'My stables. I don't know if you've heard much about them. They're very near to you. Coldharbour Lane. I wondered if you'd like to visit them. I know you don't have horses, but...' For a moment, it sounded like he might be chiding himself. 'Yes. Would you like to come and see it?'

Charlie stared at the small cobweb in the corner of the window, the tiny spider's legs working methodically. 'Yes, of course,' she heard herself saying. 'That would be lovely.'

SW9 Stables was on an overlooked patch of land between Loughborough Junction and Brixton, with the elevated train line on one side and great blocks of council flats on the other. There was a mixture of stubbly grass and two large fenced enclosures, one with some jumps, the blue and white poles low and parallel to each other. Other brightly coloured apparatus lay dismantled in the corner. A low row of brick-built stables ran along the end of the site.

Will Boadu had picked Charlie up from the farm, arriving in a gleaming black Audi and using the entrance meant only for the two vans. At least three of the volunteers saw her greet him and get into the passenger side, as much as she'd tried to be subtle. Though not in a suit this time, he still exuded propriety in dark trousers, a grey cable-knit jumper and an overcoat that probably cost five hundred quid. She'd held her breath for the first minute of their journey, waiting for the worst to be said, but when he spoke, it was of the weather, the traffic. Safe, non-Valentine-y things. Maybe he was OK about it after all; had understood the lightness of the gesture, and didn't plan to bring it up. She wouldn't need to pour out her apology, honed and rehearsed countless times in her head.

At the stables he introduced her to a spotty teenage boy with an abrasive, croaky voice, and a cheerful young girl in yellow wellies, the latter holding the reins of a very squat, fat pony as she told him about her dance show at school. Charlie watched how Will listened to her as seriously as someone telling him their political grievances, but with warmth in his answers.

'You're very good with kids,' she said, as the little girl dragged her pony away.

He looked faintly disarmed. 'I— Thank you. Well. I like to see them excelling.' They continued walking, and he explained that the boy they'd met had ADHD and a disruptive home life, and had been getting into less trouble since being here, and how the girl had previously been bullied at school. He talked of how he'd been introduced to horses as part of an adventure week with his school up north, and how that had eventually led him to farming, following in the footsteps of his great-grandfather in Ghana, although that had been sweet potato and maize rather than grass-reared beef and lamb.

A group of teenagers, all sporting black hard hats and bright-blue fleeces bearing the club's logo, were leading out their saddled bridled horses.

'We should really link up,' said Charlie, gazing at the red-brown mud of the enclosure. Her friend at Vauxhall Farm had encouraged her to make alliances with like-minded organisations, and she was starting to feel more confident about the idea.

There was a rustle of Will's coat as he turned to look at her. 'Do you think so?' he said, in quite a different voice to the first time she'd met him.

'Definitely,' said Charlie, before realising what she'd just said, and speaking more quickly. 'I mean, there's so much opportunity. Not just to mutually advertise but actually run joint clubs.'

A train rattled past. 'Yes,' said Will, and didn't say anything else until the train had disappeared. 'Indeed.' He drew in a demonstrative breath. 'Now then. Shall we?'

Charlie looked at him. 'Shall we what?'

He attempted something approaching a smile. 'Get you saddled up?'

· · ·

As much as she'd tried to protest, Will insisted upon her riding. Seeing as at the board meeting she'd been trying to demonstrate how capable she was, there was only so long before she gave in. A sweet teenage girl with braces helped her find the right size of helmet, and Will led her to the end of the stables to a speckled white horse with a large black patch over one eye.

'He's very big.' She looked up at the strong neck and beautifully brushed mane. One ear turned slowly, like the Queen waving.

'She,' Will said, taking the reins and holding his other hand out towards her.

Charlie took it. 'Oh, my gosh,' she said. 'Here goes.'

It wasn't so bad. Probably due to the fact that Will was still leading the horse around the enclosure, rather than her having to actually *do* anything. She felt very high up, but anchored by the warmth of the horse and the firm movement of the muscles underneath her.

'What's she called?'

'Elle.'

'After the magazine?'

He looked up, amused. 'After a film character with an eye patch, I believe.'

'Hello, Elle,' Charlie said, realising that Will had let go and that she was on her own. 'Agh.' She gripped the reins more tightly. 'I can't even drive.' She'd decided a long time ago that driving in London was pointless, specifically after failing her first, second and third tests aged seventeen.

'This should be easier,' Will said as he backed off. 'There are no gears, or indicators, or handbrakes.'

She concentrated, trying to turn Elle slightly to the right, feeling the gentle sway and bump as the horse shifted. The sound of the traffic faded away and she worked on tugging the reins just the right amount.

'You look good up there,' he said.

'Oh.' Did he mean as a competent horse rider, or as something more romantic? 'Um. Thanks. I still feel very weird.'

'You look perfect,' he said, in such a serious, heartfelt way that she glanced over at him again, realising what she was walking – or rather trotting – into.

'Well done,' he said in a faintly avuncular fashion, as she passed the reins to a staff member ten minutes later.

'Thank you.' She removed her helmet and tried to sort her hair out.

'Thank *you*,' said Will, rather quietly. 'For coming over, and for...' He looked at her. 'I wondered, if it's not an imposition, if you might like to come out for dinner? There's a charming place I know near me in Battersea. It's very good.'

Here it was. He had received the Valentine, and he had believed it.

'Um,' said Charlie, flooded with panicked guilt. 'I can't tonight. I've got a... thing.'

'Right,' he said. 'Perhaps later in the week?' He lifted a hand to brush a horse hair from her arm.

'Um.' She took a deep breath. 'I'm so sorry, I... I think you've got the wrong impression.'

'Oh.' Will dropped his hand immediately and gazed at her, his lips beginning to inch into an uncertain smile that disappeared just as swiftly.

Charlie moved fractionally away. 'Oh, man,' she said. 'This is so hard. I feel terrible.'

'But…' He looked perplexed, in that perfectly polished way of his. 'Sorry. Maybe I got mixed up. I'm not very good at… reading signals. Not too much time for it, really. But I thought… that is to say… I'm rather certain that you sent me this.' He reached into the inside pocket of his coat and produced a piece of paper. He'd printed it out, and now was unfolding it from a small square to an A4 sheet, the lines worn and tufted. The two pigs facing each other. The word *love*. 'It's… yours, isn't it?'

She had to own up. It was from her email address. 'It is. Yes. But, um…'

He watched her floundering. 'It's OK. I'm quite shy, too. Not that the wider public know that.' A gentle, hesitant smile, so unlike when she first·met him.

'No. Not shy. Just…' She looked up at him properly. 'I'm really sorry, Will. It wasn't meant in the way you might have taken it.' He was obviously a good man, something deeper there underneath the courtesy, and he was handsome, but… no. She didn't feel that way about him.

He stared at the paper for a few seconds, before looking at her. 'It's a Valentine's card,' he said gently, but as if that was the final word on it. 'I admit, I haven't had one of those since I was rather younger, so maybe things have changed. And I was surprised to receive it, being a fair bit older than you…' He looked subtly, elegantly pained. 'But I suppose I thought—'

'I know,' she said. She was working very hard to think of the right words, to say them carefully, one after the other, little pebbles dropped into a pond. 'I know you did. And that makes me realise how'—*stupid, reckless, wankerish, wasteman*—'thoughtless I was.' She swallowed. 'It was meant very lightly.'

A horse harrumphed behind them. His gaze fell to the piece of paper he was holding in both hands, and then to the mud at his feet. 'You mean as a joke?' He spoke quietly, and she knew he was hurt, but there was something of the MEP there, the person trying to call his opposite number out.

'Not a joke,' she said, not wishing to wound him further. But there was the slightest hint of hope in his eyes, and she went on more hastily. 'But not serious.'

He was standing very still.

'It was supposed to be anonymous,' she said in a small voice.

'So you…'—he frowned again—'you did *want* to send it, but you simply wanted it to be anonymous?'

'Um,' said Charlie, wondering how she would ever get out of this.

He misread her hesitancy. 'I'm sure you can imagine, having something of a profile often makes one desire anonymity. To disappear behind a mask. However, in this case…' A quizzical near-smile, intended to be encouraging. 'You must have known that I would see the email address it was sent from.'

'That's just the thing,' said Charlie, her stomach now in a tiny ball. 'I didn't. I made a mistake.'

'With the Valentine or with the anonymising of it?'

It was Lydia! she wanted to shout, before running away. But that would only make this worse than it already was. She had to take responsibility. He was earnest and far sweeter than she'd realised, and she'd accidentally totally played him. 'Both,' said Charlie, and though she said the word as delicately and inconsequently as possible, there was no mistaking its effect on Will.

His face, which had become sincere and more inviting,

began to form a cool glaze. 'Right,' he said. 'I see. That's —' He swallowed, and seemed to nod to himself in a faintly self-deprecating way. 'Right.'

Charlie walked out with him and watched him get into his car, both of them incredibly polite as they said their farewells. She stood on the pavement as he drove off, as the car reached the far end of the road, signalled and turned the corner, and watched as a man pushed a small supermarket shopping trolley on the other side, whistling.

'I am such a fucking idiot,' she said very simply.

TEN

An Argument – An Emergency

'Blud. Blud.'

'What? I'm busy.'

'You ain't busy. Did you see Charlie and the big man yesterday?'

'Who?'

'The big man. I dunno, he's like a money man, politician, gives to the farm.'

'What about them?'

'They went off together, didn't they.'

'So?'

'So? What d'you think they're doing? Gonna park up somewhere, steam up the windows. Proper sugardaddy situation.'

'He's gonna get a slap.'

'Nah, but didn't you hear? She sent a Valentine to him.'

'You're lying.'

'No lie. Told him she wanted to get down with him, give him a *good* time, you get me?'

'Shut up, fam.'

'He's making his moves on her. Crossing his fingers she don't bounce on him. Best behaviour.'

'Why's that?'

'Man was engaged, yeah, few years ago, and she blew him off before the wedding. Like, the *day* before. He was proper shamed.'

'No way.'

'Swear down. I got my sources. Word on the street.'

'Word from your nan, more like. Nah, Charlie wouldn't go for him.'

'What, you think she's gonna give it up for *you*?'

'Liberty, man. Come on. Donkeys need mucking out.'

The weekend brought uncommonly cold spring weather. Charlie came in at Saturday's close to watch the end of a bench-making workshop being wound up by a woman from an East London guild. She was meeting the teacher afterwards to discuss the other classes offered, from blade-smithing to bowl-carving, with the possibility of inviting them back for the Spring Fair in May – instead of blindly booking it, as she might have done in the past. To her surprise, Gábriel was in, too, seated on the floor of the barn in the corner holding a slim wooden bench leg – he nodded to her, though there was something a little closed in his face. The small group of adults was quietly working with medieval-style hand tools, and all of the materials were recycled. Charlie hovered, listened to the workshop leader talk about drawbore joints and tenon cutters, feeling not for the first time as if she were in a completely different era and place, before slipping away to answer a few emails.

Later, after closing time, Charlie was on her way out when she heard a scraping sound in the barn and went to investigate.

Everything was being left overnight ready for tomorrow's workshop. The floor was scattered with squat logs and slim bark peelings, with spirit levels and hand tools stacked in a corner. Gábriel was still there, leaning over his bench, the long seat dark and glossy, the three attached legs angled slightly outwards. It was rustic, the grooves made by the tools clearly visible, but definitely resembled an actual bench. He looked up briefly before going on with his work.

'You know you're supposed to go home at some point,' she said.

'I wanted to finish this,' he said. 'I'm making it for Jan and Beth. A surprise for when they come back. Everyone else finishes theirs tomorrow.'

Jan and her wife had gone to Costa Rica for ten days to celebrate their first wedding anniversary. She'd shown Charlie photos of their wedding before she left, bride one resplendent in an elegant satin gown, and bride two equally resplendent in a burgundy tux.

'That's nice of you.'

He gave a shrug.

She sat down on a log-stump and rested her head against the wall, bringing her scarf higher around her neck. There was something easy and companionable about the two of them there together. They didn't have to talk. She breathed in the rich, peppery scent of the wood and watched him work.

The bench was on its side, and Gábriel was shaving the top of the fourth leg, testing it in the socket, shaving a little more. He was crouched over, a patch of lighter skin exposed at his neckline, the barn's lamplight finding gold in the strands of his hair.

'Can I have a go?' she said.

'Sure.' He moved aside.

'I don't want to mess up your bench.'

'You won't.' He seemed sullen, and she suspected that she knew why. She thought she'd overheard a couple of the volunteers talking. Gossip spread easily amongst the sheep and pigpens, it seemed.

She knelt next to him on the cold concrete floor. He passed her the bench leg, mostly smoothed, and a small metal contraption that fit over the end.

'Turn it around,' he said, and moved closer, putting his hand over Charlie's to show her. He smelt woody, too.

With his hand over hers, he turned the plane and small shavings peeled away. 'Just a little bit. Not much.'

She put her elbow back, a gentle shove into his upper arm. 'I can do it.' A flare of pride she regretted as soon as she'd spoken.

He removed his hand and sat watching her.

She turned the plane around on her own, watching the blonde wood curl and lift clean. 'You get on so well with everyone. All the volunteers, I mean.' A glance over at him. 'They do talk shit sometimes, though.'

'They talk a lot,' he said impassively. 'I try and ignore it most of the time. That's fine now.' He put out his hand for the wooden leg.

'What did they talk about today? Or yesterday?'

He brushed the shavings from the tapered end of the leg and examined it. 'Do you really want to know?'

Perhaps not in so many words. 'Yes.'

'About you and Will Boadu.'

'What about us?'

'Just dirty things.' He blew away a few final flakes of wood and leant down to his bench.

Charlie didn't really need the details. She stood up again, swiping the shavings off her jeans. 'Can you tell them to stop talking about that? Or about anything.'

'Why?'

She folded her arms. 'Because… because it's not true. I know they have loads of banter, but it's not cool. They're volunteers, and they should, you know, act appropriately.'

'It's not my job.' He began to work the leg into the borehole, with tiny, tight exhalations of breath as he twisted it. 'You can tell them if you want to.'

It really wasn't his job, but she was annoyed that he wouldn't try and help her out. He had more of a connection with them, being a staffer working across all the areas. Lydia had told her how he'd defended her previously, so why wouldn't he now? 'What, so you won't? Just to help me out?' She shut one eye, an attempt at being cutely beseeching.

He stopped and looked at her, his gaze surprisingly austere. 'I can if you want. Or I can tell you what I think about it.'

He'd never talked to her like that – as if, underneath it all, he was spoiling for a fight. Well, she could give as good as she got. She dropped her cute face and stared right back. 'No, I'm good, thanks.'

'Fine.' He leant behind him, picking up a small wooden block-hammer, and bashed at the end of the leg.

Charlie loitered, watching him, and leant her shoulder against the wall. She couldn't leave it like that, without knowing what he meant. He'd spoken once of Hungarian people often telling it like is, straight to your face. 'OK, tell me, then,' she said, as breezily as she could.

He ceased his hammering and looked at her simply, but in a way that made her itch. 'You shouldn't have done that.'

'Done what?' She assumed her most polished face.

There was the slightest admonishing breath through his nose. 'You think anything Lydia has anything to do with stays a secret?'

No. Of course not. Another reason that her action was extremely thoughtless. Charlie folded her arms and looked past him. 'We meant well. It was just a light-hearted thing.'

'Not for him.'

'How do you know?' She knew he was right, and she resented him for it.

'Because I've talked to him. Because he seems like a serious guy. A good guy. Not one to make fun with.'

'Fun *of*.'

His look was blunt, but she knew he was hurt at being corrected. 'You said it.'

'Maybe someone's sad that they didn't get one.' She was passing it off as a joke, eyebrow raised, but she knew the peevishness underneath it wasn't completely concealed.

He gave a quiet, incredulous laugh that didn't really have any mirth in it, as if he couldn't believe she'd stoop so low. 'What, from you? I didn't think of it. I've forgotten that and I wouldn't want it anyway.' He turned back to the bench. 'I'm just saying it was a mean thing to do to a man like him. Not cool. I thought you were better than that.'

His words hit as keenly as a wasp-sting. 'Wow.' She put her hands on her hips then removed them. 'You know, it's pretty fucking rude to talk to me like that.'

Gábriel gave a small shrug and another not-real laugh, and gripped the leg, testing its security.

'I'd never have been able to talk to my'—she almost said *boss*—'colleague that way.'

'What do you mean?'

'In my previous job. I'd have got a warning.'

He stopped and looked at her, hard, and she wished those words right back. 'You want to give me a warning?' he said.

'No!'

'For telling you what I think?'

'Of course not, I'm just saying—'

He didn't let her finish. 'Forget it.' He stood up.

She felt everything spiralling out of control. 'Excuse me?'

'Forget about your warning.'

'I'm not *giving* you a warning. Of course not. I don't think I can, anyway, even if I wanted to. Which I don't. I was just saying that in—'

He turned the bench over, put his palms flat on the seat, and pressed on it. It didn't wobble. Then he straightened and his expression was strange, challenging. 'Forget it. I quit.'

Her mind suddenly blotted, before beginning to feather. 'What?'

'I quit.'

'Gábriel, that's ridiculous.'

'I'm ridiculous?'

'No. You don't have to be so dramatic.'

He shook his head. 'You asked me what I thought. I told you. Now, you say—' He stood up, and shook his head again.

Stalemate. She was suddenly aware of the barn's wooden walls, clicking, and the sound of a goose further off. He seemed to be waiting for her to say something.

'Fine,' she said. 'Do what you feel.'

'Fine.' He picked up the bench, hefted it over his shoulder, and left.

• • •

It was too cold to walk. Charlie rode the buses home, sitting amongst people on their way out to house parties, plastic bags full of clinking bottles by their feet. She found herself rubbing the thumb of one hand into the palm of the other. She felt furious, and horribly guilty, and furious again. When did he get so sanctimonious? Just because he plodded around, always so bloody reliable, so much better than everyone else. There was a sudden, vivid childhood memory: her dad advising a better way to set off on her new bike in the park, and her careening into a fence. She'd pushed the bike over and shouted to her dad that he'd been wrong and she hated him more than anyone else in the whole world, before storming off and hiding under a tree by the tennis courts. She'd stayed crouched under there for hours, looking at her grazed knee, knowing there was only one person whose advice she'd never doubt, would follow to the letter, and that person wasn't there anymore. She had headed home at teatime to find her dad at the end of the road, his brow slick with sweat, and her mum, sobbing with angry relief as she told her off.

Every time the second bus sighed to a halt, a little more of Charlie's fury began to fizzle out. This was the adult version of that memory; subtler, but only just. What had she just done? She'd felt stung by him essentially saying he wasn't attracted to her anymore, which was ludicrous, because she didn't want him to be. *He* was proud, too, she thought – but that couldn't be an excuse. He'd left a gap for her to tell him that she very much didn't want him to quit, and the tiger-pride had reared its head, snarled out the words before he'd had time to take a breath. *Do what you feel*. Why had she said that? Oh God, what would Ade say?

It was only when she got home that she remembered Jan was away and Gábriel was the duty manager and on call for any emergencies. Dammit. She phoned Lydia, heard her pick up and was about to speak when she got a blast of distorted bass, as if there was a hurricane on the end of the line.

'Lydia?' A garbled response through the white noise. 'Lydia, can you hear me?' More of the same, and unintelligible. She hung up and messaged instead.

Lydia ru OK?

The response came quickly.

yasss [four thumbs-up emojis]
am in camden
sick party [explosions emojis]
am wasteeeeeed

There followed a video that to the untrained eye might have seemed like the apocalypse, all flashing lights and screaming and thudding sounds, finishing with a close-up of Lydia's open mouth and tongue.

'Great,' said Charlie.

She got up early the next morning to get to the office and come up with a contingency plan. She'd slept dreadfully, waking up every hour and remembering the argument with Gábriel, how disbelieving he'd looked, the sudden flash of not-quite-arrogance. It had been so windy in the night, the apple tree branch banging against the window until she'd yelled at it to shut up.

On the farm, everything seemed eerily quiet. Wrapped up in her coat and scarf, she had a quick wander along the main paths, slightly slippery with frost, and went into see the ewes and their lambs in their separate makeshift pens. Whitney was now Whitney Eweston, christened in full by Lydia, who had consequently laughed so hard that she had run to the loo for fear of wetting herself. There she was, the little brown lamb, curled up against her mother's back, fast asleep.

'Hello, Whitney,' said Charlie, leaning on the fence. 'Hello, Whitney's mum.'

Whitney's mum, RiRi, lifted her head to look impenetrably at Charlie.

'So you hate me, too,' she said, watching a moment longer before moving to the next pen.

Missy's two lambs had been the last to come. One of them was nestled, fast asleep, in the hay. The other...

Charlie paused, bent down, and looked properly. The other didn't look right. The second lamb – mid-brown, with black legs and a streak of white on its nose – was lying on her side, twitching. Shaking, really.

'Shit,' she said.

'I dunno,' said Tallboy, the first one in, looking beatifically sleepy as he crouched over the lamb, his hood up. 'I think she's ill.'

'She's definitely ill,' said Charlie.

'And the vet's not there?'

'They can come this afternoon,' she said. The main veterinary practice used by the farm was in Hertfordshire, and their visits were usually booked far in advance.

Tallboy put both hands underneath the lamb and shifted

her over to Missy's udder. The head was limp, cradled by his hand. He looked up. 'Feels cold.'

Charlie had tried calling Lydia, but had only received a message back.

sorry i missed u sooooo literally dead rn

She hadn't come home last night and was doubtless lying semi-comatose on a fellow student's floor in North London. Jan was probably drinking cocktails in Costa Rica at this exact moment.

'Gábriel will know,' said Tallboy.

Charlie avoided his gaze, biting on her thumbnail. 'I'll try another vet.'

The other vet, based in Surrey, said they could come out in five hours, and seemed confused as to why there wasn't a staff member who could help. Charlie sat watching the lamb, Tallboy squatting down and gently rubbing her. The lamb was still trembling, tiny tremors across her side, but less frequently. A dark-pink tongue peeked out from one side of her mouth. Charlie tried not to think of Jools's limp body being lifted into an ambulance.

'Is Gábriel not answering?' said Tallboy.

Charlie took a breath, went to affirm. Couldn't pretend. Now was not the time to be imperious. She brought up his name, a tiny picture of a goat. *Gábriel is online*, it said on WhatsApp.

Gabriel, are you there?
It's not about me. It's the farm

133

Two blue ticks. He was there, and watching the messages come in, and not answering them. Probably lying broodily in the dark of his bedroom, the screen lighting up his face.

One of Missy's lambs is really sick
Looks really ill, shaking, not feeding
No vet free for hours
Please answer me
I know you're there

With relief, she finally saw that he was typing back, and clenched her mobile harder. Waited.

Phone me and ask me properly.

'You have got to be kidding me,' she said aloud, and Tallboy looked up. She stared at the wall for several moments before finally pressing the call button.

He picked up after four rings, and didn't say anything.

'Please come and help me,' she said. 'No one else can.'

There was a long silence on the end of the line. She listened to her own breathing.

'All right,' he said.

When Gábriel arrived, he took one look at the lamb and lifted her out of the pen in one hand. He worked his index finger into her mouth and remained there for a moment, before handing the lamb to Tallboy.

'What is it?' Charlie said. 'What's wrong with her?'

'Too cold,' he said. 'And she has not been feeding.'

He had picked up the thermometer from the supply store

on his way through the farm, and got Tallboy to turn the lamb around. He inserted the thermometer into the lamb's bottom. The animal barely moved.

'We have to know how cold,' Gábriel said, mostly to himself, before withdrawing the instrument and looking at it. 'OK.' He looked at Charlie. 'I think we do not need the injection. Which is good 'cause I haven't done it before.' He took the lamb back from Tallboy. 'Milk?'

'Yeah.' Tallboy had been instructed by Gábriel on Charlie's phone to draw some milk from the ewe, and now he leant down and picked up the small beaker.

Gábriel looked over at Charlie. 'Go and warm it.'

She took it from Tallboy. 'How hot?'

'Like... how do you call it? The same as for babies.'

'Body temperature,' she said.

He nodded. 'We will be in the barn.'

When she brought it back, Gábriel was sitting on a hay bale with the lamb between his knees, facing forwards, the gangly front legs hanging down. He was holding a length of red tubing, and glanced up when she entered.

'OK,' he said. He put the thinner end of the tubing into the side of the lamb's mouth and began to feed it down, stopping and bringing it back, and doing the same again.

'Have you done this before?' she asked, her voice very small, trying not to imagine the tube jabbing the back of the lamb's throat.

'A long time ago,' he said, finally pushing it down until there were only a couple of inches visible. The lamb seemed a little more awake, her mouth moving as if trying to chew on the tube. 'My dad showed me.' He put out his other hand to

Charlie for the beaker, then gave it to Tallboy, who was kneeling next to him. 'Fill that up.'

Tallboy was holding a big plastic syringe with measurements along the side. 'All the way?'

'Yeah.'

Tallboy did as instructed and passed it over. Gábriel worked the milk-filled syringe into the end of the tube and slowly injected the liquid into it, his other hand cupped over the lamb's mouth. A little milk dribbled out. The process was repeated, the syringe filled and drained into the lamb's stomach. Charlie watched her small hooves, resting on Gábriel's knees.

He pulled out the syringe and tube very quickly, holding the lamb under her chin, before craning over to have a look.

'Epic,' said Tallboy.

'Will she be OK now?' asked Charlie.

'Not yet. Now we need to get her warm.'

The lamb was put into a small crate-like box in the barn, one with a metal grate at the bottom, and the purr of an electric heater under it. As volunteers arrived and the first visitors began to amble in, Gábriel monitored her temperature, bringing her out every half hour and taking her back to the mother to attempt suckling. Eventually, she began to blurt out tiny stuttering calls, and was placed back in her own pen, with a red heat lamp overhead. Tallboy was put on lamb-watch.

Gábriel's ears and knuckles had gone red with the cold. Charlie fetched them both a bowl of maple syrup porridge from the kitchen and they sat in the office, the windows steaming up.

'What happened?' she asked quietly. 'I mean, I know it was cold last night, but all the other lambs are OK.'

'Could be a few things. The mother could not be interested enough. Or the lamb could not be feeding properly. I'll stay until the vet comes.'

Until the vet comes. Then never again. Charlie put her bowl on the side of her computer desk. 'Gábriel,' she said. 'I'm really sorry. Hand on heart. About before.'

He glanced over but didn't say anything.

She drew her gaze up to the fogged glass of the window, and the little gauzy mass of spiders' webs in the corner, before turning to face him properly. 'Can I erase the last eighteen hours from your brain, please?' After a moment, she held up an imaginary futuristic contraption and made a buzzing sound, *Men In Black*-style.

He almost smiled, but not quite.

'Can you forgive me, at least? And…' She had to be better. Humble, less rash. Less tiger. It was for the farm. She bit her lip a little and straightened. 'Please can you come back?'

He blinked once, twice. Stared down at his bowl, and looked up again with the faintest, most muted shine in his eyes. 'OK,' he said.

ELEVEN

The May Spring Fair - Festivities

Spring finally arrives, bringing rain followed by blue, breezy skies. The parks erupt into colour and the owners of flats compete for the most ostentatious hanging basket. As the city wakes, the calls of great tits, blackbirds, blue tits and chaffinches tangle together. On the scaffolding of the hospital, peregrine chicks have hatched, and the male adult endlessly forays out over the skyline for pigeons and parakeets. Once, he flies as far as Battersea Park, arcing over great oak trees and a hornbeam, next to which a certain politician and farm trustee you might recognise is sitting on a bench, gazing at his phone. If the peregrine were to descend further, he would see this man swipe gently over photos on the Instagram account of a certain farm. He pauses so very briefly on the photo of a certain farm administrator with a flicker of regret, before turning his screen to black and putting it in his pocket.

Back at Ruskin Park, the gates are unlocked every dawn, one or two joggers already waiting. Nuthatches hop up the tree trunks, streaks of dusky blue and orange, and the traffic begins to collect into a long, blurred hum. On the farm, the beds are full of the open scents of basil, mint, rosemary, tansy and sage. Goat kids are born. The lambs are almost half the size of their mothers now, and almost none have been named, so that no one gets attached to them. Lydia maintains a tragically noble countenance when they are taken away.

'So,' said Ade. 'You can be honest now. How have you found it?'

Charlie's second probation meeting had been nothing more than a genial chat. They'd gone over what she'd accomplished so far, the key dates in the diary for the rest of the year, and more training days she might be able to go on.

'It's good,' she said. 'I think I wasn't really sure what to expect, but...'

'But you're getting into the swing of it,' Ade said, nodding at her fingerless gloves and muddy trainers.

'Yeah. I guess I am.'

He nodded. 'The word on the street – and by street I mean woodchip path – is that everyone's happy.' He spoke more thoughtfully. 'I'm going to see if we can up your salary a bit.'

She looked at him. The farm didn't work in the same way as most businesses, with payment structures and salary review dates. She thought she'd need to ask, at some point, but wasn't really sure she'd yet earned the right. 'Don't you want to see how the Spring Fair goes?'

'I think you've proved yourself enough,' he said, and the lines in his cheeks multiplied.

Charlie blushed. No one had ever said that to her in the workplace. 'Wow. Thank you.'

Ade tapped the tabletop and stood with a gusty sigh. He

looked exhausted. Benji Pennyways was appealing his conviction, causing more frustration and financial concerns.

'How's the baby?' she asked.

'Glorious,' he said. 'And gloriously awake, almost all of the time.' A trace of a wink before he put on his coat. 'It's good to know that the farm is in safe hands, Charlie. Keep it up.'

It was May half-term, and their first Spring Fair. Most of the city farms did something similar, but it had been too early in Ruskin Park Farm's first months last year. Charlie had spent weeks preparing for it, gleaning some tips from the farm managers at Vauxhall and Surrey Docks. Today, she'd got here extra early to supervise the set-up, finding herself biting her thumbnails far too often. But it turned out that she *did* know where each stall needed to go, and what time everything was happening. Now, the whole site was abuzz, and they'd been blessed with sunshine and fast-moving clouds. There were stalls from local craftspeople in the yard, some of whom were regular traders at the Herne Hill Sunday market. The woodcraft workshop had been set up in the barn, and a semi-circle of dads was solemnly whittling at squares of native green hardwood. At several points in the day, a South West London Morris side – which comprised, hearteningly, not just of portly white men with beards, though there were several – performed some routines, clad in their green velvet trousers and calf-garters, sashes and rosettes. Until talking to her Surrey Docks contact, she'd had no idea that anyone still did this kind of thing. Joe stood tittering at them and half-heartedly throwing in some occasional beatboxing, while Tallboy stood close by, watching the dances intently.

Moonie had become increasingly interested in baking and

was selling an impressive tray of wares at one of the trestle tables, next to Badiha, who was serving fresh lemonade and trying to get extra donations out of everyone by blinking her false lashes at them. Aidan had generously come along to do a shift at the BBQ, and was currently standing with Jan's wife, the pair of them dishing up burgers, some made with farm pork, to be slathered in mustard, ketchup and brown sauce. Lydia steered well clear.

The main focus, however, was the sheep shearing. People crowded round the sheep pen with pints of cider or ale, watching the work. Jan and Gábriel alternated, grabbing one of the ewes and turning them over, belly outwards, forelegs hanging down. The wool was snipped away with hand shears under the neck, the sheep's legs flailing in protest as the softer, smoother underside of the fleece became visible. It was removed from around one front and back leg before the sheep was turned, and the fleece became a wing, a cloak, and was finally cut free to a gentle cheer. Gábriel just smiled and turned his sheep back over for a final belly-trim, but Jan stood with shears aloft, still holding the sheep, like the champion of a boxing match.

The alpacas got a haircut, too, their long legs and necks cropped short, their heads left alone, teeth jutting alarmingly for the many photos that were taken. If you didn't know any better, you'd think they looked vengeful.

'This is so lovely,' said Nellie, her hair framed in a new jaw-skimming bob, her face festooned with painted flowers. 'Well done, darling. What a May Queen my daughter is.'

'Thanks, Mum. Nice face.'

Nellie smiled. 'There's a part of me that will always remain a five-year-old girl, no matter how many wrinkles I get.'

It was mid-afternoon. Charlie and her mum were watching an elderly black woman methodically feed grey wool through her fingers, her foot working the spinning pedal, all the while carrying on a conversation about politicians and lies being printed on buses.

Nellie put her arm through Charlie's. 'You really seem to have settled in to this. Maybe you've found your calling.'

'Maybe,' said Charlie, though she was feeling pretty good right now with how it was all going, as well as happily full of barbecued pig. There was a less familiar sense of pride – not the up-in-your-face tiger kind, but something warm and melting in her chest. *She* had put this together, and all these people were enjoying themselves.

'Dad's very proud,' said Nellie. 'Telling everyone within earshot how you're his offspring.'

Charlie looked over at the barbecue stall to see Aidan serving Will Boadu. 'Oh, God,' she said, unlinking arms with Nellie and feeling a prickle of shame spread across her chest.

'Charlie? Are you all right?'

'Yep. Just got to—'

She made every effort to saunter, rather than run, over to the stall. Obviously Will wasn't going to tell her dad about what an arse she'd been, but what if he *did*, and Aidan dressed her down in front of all the employees, including Ade, who was just over there, and her job was—

She reached them just in time to hear Aidan saying, '…that's what I mean. Those eejits don't have the first bleedin' clue how to educate our children. Charlie!' He gave a huge beam. 'Hello to you.'

'Hey, Dad. Hello, Will.'

Will Boadu was the most casual she had seen him, in a blue crew-neck jumper, shirt collar and light-grey trousers. 'Charlie.' He nodded at her, and his smile was small and uncomfortable.

She looked between them both. Having charged up here, she wasn't entirely sure what to say next. 'So, um… what were you two talking about?'

'We're putting the world to rights,' said Aidan, flipping a burger. 'Someone has to. And, just before that, talking a little bit about you.' He pointed his slice at her.

Well, she deserved this. She waited for Will to elaborate.

'It all seems to be going well,' said Will.

'Oh,' said Charlie, crossing her arms and uncrossing them again. 'Yeah. So far. Thank you.'

'Once she puts her mind to something, there's no stopping this girl, my friend. Nothing will stand in her way.'

'Is that so?' said Will, but he spoke with detachment.

She gave an awkward smile and quickly looked behind her towards the alpaca pen and beyond, as if needing to check on something very important.

'And you're going to the big shindig this evening, sir?' said Aidan.

'The big…?' Will looked enquiringly at him, and back at Charlie.

'Oh,' said Charlie, hoping she sounded flippant. 'We're just going out after it's all finished. I promised karaoke if everyone could leave the farm the way they found it. It's not really a *big* thing, you know, as such. Low-key, really. And trashy. Really trashy.'

'Do you sing yourself now, Will?' said Aidan, turning over another sausage so that it steamed and sizzled.

Will put his hands behind his back. 'Actually, I do,' he said.

'Or rather, it's been known. Once I've had a sharpener. To be honest, I'm more of a trumpet player.'

'Is that right? I imagine that's quite a hard instrument to make sound good.'

Will smiled. 'Not if you've had a sharpener.'

'It's a no-brainer, then!' said Aidan. 'You know, my girl has the most beautiful voice.'

Will's eyes fell on her. 'Does she?' He still sounded frosty, and who could blame him.

'Like an angel.'

'Really not like an angel, Dad,' she said, wishing she could go and hide in a giant bale of hay.

'Well, I'd be happy to hear her,' Will said, with utter courtesy.

'Come down, man,' said Joe, who was queuing with Jami for a burger, and blatantly listening in. 'Farmdem let loose on the mic. It'll be peak.'

Will gave another warm smile. He did seem to respond especially graciously to young people. 'Well. Perhaps I'll let you twist my arm.' He glanced impenetrably at Charlie. 'But of course only if it's acceptable to Charlie.'

What could she say? 'Um.' She looked around, at the long queue of people waiting for burgers, the mother slathering her small child in sun cream and putting some on her own nose. Aidan was beginning to frown at her. 'Yes, of course it is,' she said. 'You're so welcome.'

Charlie had always held a profound love for karaoke. She and her uni mates had quite often ended up in some appallingly tacky Soho bar, crowded around a screen and squalling theatrically into their microphones (Charlie on harmonies).

Now, though, she had a great desire to be somewhere else entirely, such as under her duvet, with earplugs in.

Her promise of karaoke had been spontaneous, one of those throw-away comments that she was supposed to be curbing in favour of careful thought and patience. But it had been talked up so much by the volunteers – Lydia stoking the flames – that she had followed through. On Marianne's suggestion, she'd put out a collection box for the volunteers at the Fair to cover their table bookings and a round of drinks, and she privately determined that there would be no shots and no fire hazards.

Despite her protests to Will about the night being trashy, it really was the best it could be, as far as karaoke entailed. Unlike most set-ups, plucky singers fronted a live five-piece band in the back room of a much-loved establishment in Nunhead. The Ivy House was proud of its status as London's first co-operative pub; locals had banded together and raised a million pounds to defy a property developer. It had a Grade II listed 1930s interior featuring oak panelling (a definite fire hazard, but only if flaming sambuca was served, which it would not be) and original gig posters from the likes of Joe Strummer and Doctor Feelgood. It sold locally brewed real ale and craft beer, and hosted events from jazz nights to a knitting circle. The tiny music stage had splendidly gaudy red velvet and gold lamé curtains.

Whilst there were other locals present, most of the room was taken up with the farm's staff and volunteers. A few of the younger ones had been let in on the proviso that a strict eye was kept on them, and Charlie had bought a round of Cokes for them all. Will hadn't yet arrived, and she lived in hope that he had merely been civil in accepting, and in fact loathed any such nonsense and was in bed with a cup of hot cocoa and a later season of *Mad Men*.

Currently, Lydia was onstage in front of the quintet, bawling out 'Bad Romance' to general sniggers from the crowd, whilst wearing a T-shirt that said FARM GIRLS AREN'T AFRAID TO GET DIRTY. Tallboy had already sung a David Bowie number, and Marianne had done an impressively zany Kate Bush impression. Walt had brought tears to several eyes with a surprisingly affecting rendition of John Lennon's 'Imagine,' although he found the band too loud. Joe, who had already tried to persuade the band to diverge from their offered list and do one of his suggested tunes, gave up and instead changed Will Smith's track to 'Gettin' Piggy With It,' not needing to look at the words once.

Lydia bounced off the stage. 'You not singing yet?'

'Soon,' said Charlie. 'More drinks first.'

When she returned from the bar, Gábriel was part of the way through 'Should I Stay or Should I Go'. She hovered at the back and watched him as he stood with a beer in one hand and the mic in the other. He was a little understated in his performance but almost perfectly in tune, and sang with his eyes fixed on the screen, apart from looking up to grin when Lydia gave a piercing whistle through her fingers.

The atmosphere between Gábriel and Charlie had settled since that night over two months ago. If anything, it seemed better than before. Charlie was more respectful and collaborative: she let him sort out his own volunteers for all the maintenance and some farm jobs; agreed that they could make the half-term holiday Junior Farmers Club into a regular Sunday morning event. They sat down to discuss his idea of converting the hens and geese section into a little orchard with beehives. He had seemed pleased when she'd brought him in a

New York baked cheesecake for his birthday last week, and saved her an extra slice once he'd divvied it up around the volunteers. He had the same easy manner as ever, and she was very grateful that he was not the type to hold a grudge.

'You're pretty good,' Charlie said, giving him a gentle shoulder-shove when he came offstage and sat down next to her. Jan was just starting Katy Perry's 'I Kissed a Girl.'

He smiled and swigged his beer. 'You don't have to pretend.'

'I'm not.' She held up her rum and Coke.

He narrowed his eyes at her, feigning suspicion, before gently clinking his bottle against her glass. Squeezed in between others, they were sitting rather close, arms touching, and he felt very warm. Onstage, Jan was performing with the élan of a cabaret singer.

'Hey,' she said. She'd begun to relax a little more now, the rum loosening her. 'We're good together, aren't we?'

He hummed a slightly impervious, questioning sound.

'You and me. Farm shenanigans.'

A slight pause. 'Yeah. We are.'

'You're the bees' knees.'

'The… what?'

'Bees' knees.' She raised her eyebrows.

He looked bemused and a little abashed. 'I don't know what you're talking about.'

She leaned a little closer to shout in his ear over Jan's expansive belting. 'It's an expression. It means you're great. Awesome. I don't really know where it comes from, or indeed if bees even *have* knees. If we get funding for the hives, we'll have to check.' A wink and a self-affirming nod.

'OK.' He laughed, the slightest exhalation through his nose.

'Yes,' she said, getting into her stride. 'You're top banana.

Eggy bread.'

'You're just putting weird words together.'

'I'm not! They're real ones, I'm telling you. Hand on heart.'

He watched as she placed her palm on her chest, and he said something, rather quietly, in Hungarian.

'Say what?'

He shook his head. 'No. That's just for me. If you're going to say funny English words that don't make sense then I'm going to speak my own language.'

'But what did you say?' She nudged her knee against his.

He shook his head, retaining the smallest daydreamy look that suggested he was weighing up whether to tell her or not.

'Tell me,' she said, in a breathily commanding voice.

'Right, woman,' said Lydia, bounding up. 'You're on next. I'm not taking no for an answer. They've got Whitney, for crying out loud. Whitney *Eweston*.'

'OK. You win.' She turned to Gábriel. 'Look after my drink for me?'

He nodded, still seemingly caught in his daydream, and took it.

It was as she simultaneously opened her mouth to sing her third favourite Whitney Houston song and looked up at her colleagues, that she saw Will Boadu at the entrance to the room, holding a tumbler of something golden. She clutched the microphone tighter and missed her entrance. The drummer played a fizzling little fill and the band came back round again.

'Go on, Charls!' yelled Lydia.

'OK, love?' said the keyboard player to the side of her as he repeated the introduction. 'You can do it. Do you want me to count you in?'

No, she thought, smarting, because she knew 'I Wanna Dance with Somebody' inside out, and began.

The lights felt very hot. She spent most of the song holding her microphone in both hands, singing much more demurely than if she'd been with her old friends and trying very much to seem like she didn't really mean it. Gábriel had given Will a nod and moved over to allow him room to sit down, before eyeing the two drinks in his hand and putting Charlie's on the table.

She sang to the ceiling, only twice daring to look in their general direction. Helpfully, just as she was singing '*a love that burns hot enough to last*' Will looked up at the ceiling and Gábriel looked down at his drink. She sang the last choruses rather poorly and tailed off before the end with a quiver. Nonetheless, there were rapturous whoops and cheers as she took the little stairs off the stage, walking straight into the ladies' where she hid for ten full minutes, wishing back the last few weeks.

'Right, you lot,' said Lydia – who seemed to have ended up being MC for the evening – as Charlie finally returned. 'We've got a treat for you now. The one. The only. Mister Will.I.Am Boadu!'

To semi-enthusiastic applause, Will got up and nodded at the room, and she saw again the politician in him, someone who was used to standing up in front of people.

The band started. Please don't let that be 'When a Man Loves a Woman', she thought, because it really sounded like 'When a Man Loves a Woman'.

'He's only doing 'When a Man Loves a Woman',' said Jan, loudly, to her wife. 'Yes, my son!'

He did, rather beautifully, an octave lower than the original, in a smooth baritone voice. Joe stage-whispered something to Tallboy, who nudged him unsubtly. Charlie stared very fixedly at her drink.

When he finished, Lydia did another of her shepherdess-whistles over the applause from her position next to Charlie. 'You are the *man*, Mr B! Seriously,' she said to Charlie. 'He is a ledge.'

Charlie managed to float about the room for a while, always aware of Will in her peripheral vision as he chatted to various farm workers. She felt terrible. He'd had the dignity to come out tonight, despite what she had done, and was a good sport. Whilst Badiha and one of the newer girls, Charity, had a go at Taylor Swift in a performance that was more composed of giggles than singing, she managed to get into a very in-depth conversation with Marianne about meditation, nodding in an overly impassioned way, wondering what Will really thought of her now.

'Duet time!' said Lydia too loudly into the mic, on stage, as Moonie finished Radiohead's 'Karma Police'. 'This is a special request from I'm not telling who. Charlie'—she pointed one definite forefinger—'Mr. Boadu'—and another at him—'it's time.'

Charlie's heart dropped to her feet.

'Oh, how exciting,' said Marianne, putting a hand on Charlie's back.

Will was looking at her from two tables away.

Charlie glared furiously at Lydia, who frowned at her, mouthed '*what?*', and frowned again. Maybe it had been Joe, then. 'I think I've done enough singing for one night,' she called.

'*Char-lie!*' Lydia started the chant. '*Char-lie!*' The room started to join in, stamping and banging on the table. Gábriel was looking at her with an uninterpretable half-smile, no help at all.

'Islands in the Stream.' 'Nothing's Gonna Stop Us Now.' 'You're The One That I Want.' Charlie tried hard, as the introduction started, to think of a duet that *wouldn't* have made her want the rickety wooden staging to collapse beneath her, but somehow, this one was the worst.

'I'm sorry,' said Charlie, very quietly, as they got up on stage. 'I promise it wasn't me.'

'Let's just get it done, then,' Will said dispassionately.

So, standing very stiffly next to Will, she did her very best to imagine that she was somewhere else entirely, and together they sang '(I've Had) The Time of My Life', whilst Lydia attempted to entice anyone in the room into doing some dirty dancing with her, and Joe worked on his wolf-whistle.

'Bloody hell,' said Jan as they came offstage. 'That was bleedin' beautiful. You nailed those harmonies and everything.'

'Thank you,' said Charlie, feeling rather faint. Will was moving away. She touched his arm, very briefly. 'Will.'

He stopped and looked at her.

'Can I buy you a drink? Just... just a drink.' Fifty drinks wouldn't make up for it, but she had to start somewhere.

'Sure,' he said.

When she returned, a really quite tipsy Lydia was belting out 'Teenage Dirtbag' whilst playing air guitar. Gábriel was now talking to Marianne, probably about meditation and probably more genuinely than she had.

'You *are* a good singer,' she said, sitting down opposite Will. 'Sharpener or no.'

Will, who had been looking a little wary of her, smiled. 'I'm still glad there was no press around to hear it.'

'Do they follow you around a lot?'

'Not often,' he said. 'The black farmer thing pops up occasionally, far more than all the work I'm doing as a politician.'

He told her about growing up in Leeds, the only black child in his class at primary school in the early 80s, and how he was bullied. 'But I realised that talking at them – not *to* them, but actually at them, until they got bored – worked in the end.' He went on to say how he'd gone to a prep school in North Yorkshire on a scholarship. 'There it was more of a problem having a broad West Yorkshire accent, so I had to lose it rather quickly. And now of course, for some, I am too posh. Not representing my people.'

She admired him for being so open about race – she'd noticed that, reading his biography and seeing him in the news – how important his black identity was in all the work he did. 'That sounds challenging,' she said, knowing that she could never really understand, hoping that her empathy would be enough.

'Ah. There are worse things,' he said. 'I just try and stay true to myself.'

'Do you really play trumpet?'

'Oh, hardly at all these days. No matter what I'm doing, though, there's always a part of me in a little smoky basement club, belting out something mournful.'

They exchanged an awkward smile and sat in silence for a moment, watching several of the volunteers pile on stage to sing the Spice Girls.

'Right. Time for me to head off, I think,' said Will. 'Do say goodbye to everyone for me.'

She hadn't apologised yet. 'Wait. I'll come out with you.'

They stood outside the pub, a little way off from the smokers. It was a suburban street, a motley collection of semi-detached houses, cars parked nose to end on both sides.

'Will, I just wanted to say…'

He turned to her, his phone in his hand.

'I really messed up, and I shouldn't have. You're obviously a lovely guy, and it wasn't right for me to do what I did.'

Will gazed at her for a moment, before nodding. 'Well. It's done now. Perhaps I give the impression of not giving a damn, but… I do actually have a heart.'

She wanted to melt into the paving stones beneath her. 'I know. I see that. I really don't want it to affect your opinion of the farm.'

He looked perplexed and faintly admonishing. 'Is that what you're worried about?

'No,' she said. Of course it wouldn't. Because he was solid and principled, and she was a needy idiot. 'I don't want it to affect your opinion of me,' she said, more sheepishly. She suddenly found that she wanted to be friends with him.

Will gave a strange, quizzical smile over to the houses opposite. 'Look, Charlie.' He cleared his throat. 'I'm going to be busy with work for a bit. I'll see you when I see you.' He nodded at an approaching car. 'My taxi's here. Take good care.'

Charlie watched him leave, then walked to the end of the street, and over the road and past the first bus stop, and the second and the third, and she kept walking until she found herself at her own front door.

TWELVE

Two Encounters

The summer moves on. Rain comes and disappears just as swiftly, leaving pearls on the leaves of the dawn redwood and the maple trees. Volunteer litter-pickers meander along the paths, and pigeons dawdle around them. A man wearing a safari hat moves slowly with a walking stick, playing 1950s rock 'n' roll from a portable speaker strapped to his chest. High up on the hospital scaffolding, the peregrine chicks are now scraggy, brownish things, endlessly screeching for food. In the second week of June, there is a strange shift, in which the country seems to tilt. In London, the mood is largely of despair and uncertainty, though of course not for everyone. Some of the staff and volunteers move sluggishly, reading the news on their phones at every available opportunity. Two are insulted by members of the public, one on the street and another in a taxi, and wonder if this is the state of things to come.

The animals and their daily routines provide constancy for everyone: the feeds, the mucking out, walks and petting excursions. The two sows, Ethel and Annie, suddenly show their pregnancies, though it has been almost three months. Their abdomens appear swollen and their udders swing. They have a new brick pen, built by Gábriel and some volunteers, and spend more time than usual in the straw. In July, a homeless charity brings volunteers for the first time, and three return the week after to work on the allotments. The two men – one from Essex, the other from Syria, are gaunt and full of nervous energy. The young woman from Somalia barely speaks, just looks at the soil that gathers in the creases of her palms. Leila provides stew and rice, and gives them rolls to take away.

'Oi, oi, missus,' said Jan, popping her head round the door. 'Percy Sledge is here. You're meeting him to talk horses, apparently.'

Charlie, composing an email to a prospective company about a corporate farm away day, gave no indication of her genuine feelings, and nodded. 'OK. Thanks.' She remained firmly in her seat.

Jan cast her a shrewd, amused look. 'I'll tell him you're on your way?'

'Yep. In a sec.'

'He's by the alpacas. Probably telling them off for voting Leave.' She tapped a short rhythm on the side of the door before disappearing.

Will had been largely absent for the last six weeks – he was in Brussels a lot, and Charlie had seen news reports praising a speech he'd given about renewable energy. He'd replied to her email about a joint enterprise with the community stables –

she'd decided the farm should come before her shame – in a businesslike manner. He had been present at the summer board meeting, and Charlie had been ill, with a streaming red nose, sore throat, and strong need to get home to bed. He was briskly sympathetic, talked about a spiced ginger tea that his secretary always gave him when he was under the weather. When she returned to the office after two days off, she found that he'd sent her some.

Now she wandered over to the animal pens to find Will talking to Gábriel, who was on a brief break from supervising Kaden in feeding the alpacas. Will seemed to sense her before she reached them and turned. 'Charlie,' he said. 'Good to see you.' He'd definitely retreated to his detached manner again, if not as stern as their first meetings.

'Hello,' she said.

'I've been learning about Hungarian pigs,' he said. 'Fascinating.'

Gábriel glanced between them and gave an oddly deferential nod, before taking a few steps back with his bag of feed.

Will put his hands behind his back. 'He seems like an excellent man to have on the farm.'

'He is,' said Charlie. 'The best. We're very lucky.'

'And how are you? No more colds, I trust?'

'No. I'm all good. Healed up.'

'And the tea? Did that help? I hope you didn't think it… an imposition.'

Gábriel was still within earshot. She was aware of him moving the alpacas away from the entrance to their shed with a quiet *tsssk-tsssk* noise.

'Oh, no. Of course not.' In truth, she had thought it touching. 'I'm sure it helped. It was very kind. Thanks again.

Shall we go out?' In truth, she didn't want any more gossip forming if they had their meeting on site.

'Sure,' he said.

Love Walk Café, at the end of a tiny cobbled street of the same name, was a favourite of nurses, doctors and art students, and purported to celebrate the relationship of Victorian poets Robert Browning (born in Camberwell) and Elizabeth Barrett. It was a regular haunt of Charlie's, but she'd never really been as aware of its unfortunate name until now, a perfect reminder of her slight to him. She mentally bashed herself about the head whilst hoping Will had not noticed the illustrated hearts all over the menu.

Still, she had to hand it to him: Will was gracious, convivial, and she relaxed. Over eggs benedict and coffee (Will) and an Immune Swoon smoothie (Charlie), they talked in a perfectly professional manner and with no mention of karaoke duets or Valentines. There was the inevitable subject of Europe and his job, the mutual shaking of heads at how it seemed to have unleashed a new level of open bigotry. Will spoke a little about his family up north, and his worries over his dad, who kept falling ill, before conversation turned to the stables. Charlie asked him to tell her more about the horse, Elle, remembering how much she'd enjoyed riding her. The calm and poise, the way of seeing the world at a slight elevation.

Will was mopping up his egg yolk with a last forkful of English muffin in a dignified fashion. 'You know you're welcome to come and ride there any time you like.'

Charlie, on the other hand, slurped the dregs of her smoothie. 'Thank you. But it's for young people in need. I'm not in need.' Apart from needing a time machine to make sure that she never let Lydia send that Valentine's card.

'I'll arrange it,' he said unfussily. 'It's fine. As long as it's in the later part of the day, you'd be most welcome.'

'That's very kind,' said Charlie, imagining feeding Elle some polo mints and brushing her mane. 'Thank you.'

Back at the farm, Charlie leant on the fence post, watching a child feed Bette, thinking over her afternoon with Will. She'd initially read him as haughty and stiff, whereas in reality he was considerate, magnanimous, a little shy. If she'd only spent time getting to know him first, she'd have never sent the card. She liked him. She actually—

'You the new one, then?'

She looked over to see a white man in his forties, with thick sideburns and a shiny forehead, wearing a navy polo shirt embossed with the words WEST KENT OFF-ROAD CAR CLUB.

'Sorry?' she said.

'You the new one, then?' he said again, more loudly, as if she were deaf. A sharp-edged South London accent.

'I'm… not sure what you mean.'

'Manager.' He nodded around him.

'Oh.' She straightened. 'Administrator. Yes. Is there anything I can help you with?'

He gave a vague, greasy grin and looked about him in a manner that suggested familiarity. 'How you finding it?' He spoke in a familiar way too, as if they knew each other.

'Um, fine, thanks.'

He seemed to be out of breath, and there was a coarse quality to his exhalations. 'Getting your feet dirty?' He flashed her an up-down look that told her exactly what sort of man he was.

She felt herself tense. 'Sometimes.'

Marianne came past with a garden hoe and cast him an inquisitive look that clouded over swiftly. 'Oh, Benji. Hello,' she said, and looked keenly at him, and then pertinently at Charlie.

'Marianne,' he said, a little more stiffly.

Benji. That was the name of the previous manager, the one who'd swindled the farm and left it in a mess. Suddenly it made sense.

'Just passing through, are you?' Marianne said with a hint of challenge in her voice, and didn't wait for an answer. 'I'll just get these put away, Charlie, and I'll be right back. Give me two ticks.'

Benji watched her disappear. He remained leaning on the fence, the same guttural breathing, for far too long. 'Thought I'd come and see if everything was still standing.'

Charlie was trying to work out what to do. Should she be calling the police right now? 'I don't think you should be here,' she said, as measuredly as she could.

'Says who?' he said, looking amused and folding his arms. His presence was sizable, meaty.

'Me, actually.'

'It's like that, is it?' he said in a righteous, musical tone.

'You stole from the farm,' she said. 'From the community.'

'That's down to the courts to decide.'

'They have decided.'

'Not by my reckoning,' he said.

'Well, I heard plenty about it.' She made herself face him. 'It's time for you to go now. You're really not welcome.'

His eyes had a flat crocodile gleam to them. 'Blimey,

madam. All right.' His tone was defensive and suggested she was overreacting. Jan was approaching, and he held up his hands when he saw her. 'I know where I'm not wanted.'

As he turned, he uttered the words she feared he'd been thinking all along. 'You're not up to it, are you?' He muttered something else she didn't quite catch, and at the same time Jan had reached him.

'Out,' Jan said.

'I hope you all rot. You and the animals.'

'Right now,' Jan said grimly.

'It's a free country,' he said, though he was beginning to walk away. 'Gonna be freer than ever, soon.'

'You're embarrassing yourself,' Jan said, walking right behind him. 'Sling your hook, mate, and don't darken this door again. You're fucking barred. I'm reporting this.'

He held a hand up with the middle finger raised, and carried on walking towards the exit.

There was a quiet knock on the open door of the office, and Charlie blinked, suddenly registering that there had been another knock a few seconds ago.

Gábriel was by the door. 'Are you OK? Marianne just told me about what happened.'

'Yeah.' She shrugged. 'I mean, no, not really.' She let out a light, forlorn laugh, and shivered. 'Um. He was just a dick.' She put the heel of her hand to her forehead, brought it down again. It had been nothing, really. Yet she felt so rattled – she'd been slowly building up her confidence and it took a couple of throwaway words to make it all tumble down again.

He leant against the door, watching her. 'Can I do anything for you?'

Charlie let out a short sigh. 'I could do with a hug,' she said, rather plaintively.

Gábriel gazed at her somewhat obliquely for a moment, and she almost told him to forget it. But then he stepped forward, and so she stood up from her chair so that he could put his arms around her.

She placed her hands lightly around his back and rested her forehead on his chest, and though they'd never hugged, it didn't feel awkward. His T-shirt was warm, smelt faintly of deodorant, and faintly of sweat. She wondered how long she could stay here like this. She heard the slightest pressure of an exhalation in his throat.

'You're good at this,' he said, from above her head. 'The farm.'

'Yeah?'

'Yeah.'

As they began to pull away from each other, he held on to her forearms for a moment longer before letting go. 'He's just some stupid guy.'

'Yeah. I know.'

Gábriel gave the slightest smile before stepping away from her and stretching, self-consciously. He wore his height so unobtrusively sometimes, as if he were embarrassed by it. His second smile was more assured, comforting, and for a strange, suspended moment, she wondered if he was going to tell her that he still thought about her, cared about her.

'Shall I go and get you some chocolate?' he said. 'From the shop?'

Of course not. He'd told her already he wouldn't have wanted a Valentine's card from her. But he did know that salted caramel chocolate was her favourite, and where they sold it.

'Yeah,' she said. 'Yes, please.'

'How much further?'

'Two streets.'

'That is literally miles.'

'It is literally one hundred metres. We can make it because we are fierce ladies.'

Last night, she'd lain next to Lydia on the sofa and watched a very mediocre romcom about a woman wanting a baby and trying to choose between several potential fathers. Lydia's first attempt at cheering her up was followed by her second: insisting they went out on the lash at the weekend to dance their arses off. Part of Charlie wanted to remain welded to the sofa, doing cross-stitch (current pattern: RIOTS NOT DIETS) to 90s RnB playlists all weekend, but another part needed distraction.

The Fir Tree was a large, community-run music venue in Clapton, a comfortable walk from the train station – comfortable, that was, if you weren't walking in heels. The two of them limped along the road, Charlie having decided to show Lydia how a good night was *really* done. Tonight, Charlie was wearing a holographic purple ruffled mini-skirt and a sheer silver top over a black sports bra. Fabulousness might override hurt, if she really went for it.

Contrary to its rather bucolic name, The Fir Tree was a ramshackle building and part of an old printworks. It had slanting floorboards, a great deal of multi-coloured bunting, and some unsavoury toilets (only one with a functioning lock). There were workshops, grassroots political meetings and film screenings during the day before it transformed into a bacchanalian club most evenings. It had always had an anarchic, all-welcoming feel.

Tonight, a seven-piece Afrobeat band were crammed onstage, two saxes and a trumpet next to a beautiful singer in metallic gold trousers. The packed crowd in front of them was sweaty and blissfully happy, a mixture of students and locals of all ages, even a couple of grizzled guys in their sixties, benignly nodding to the music in the corner from under a rasta hat and a lopsided Stetson respectively. There were fairy lights and disco balls, and silkscreen-printed material that billowed down from the ceiling.

'This place is majorly awesome!' shouted Lydia in Charlie's ear. She was sporting a glittery pink boob tube and extremely tight jeans.

Charlie nodded serenely, before leaning over. 'Drinks,' she said.

'Look at the arse on that,' shouted Lydia, suddenly bumping up to Charlie's ear at the bar, where she had finally got in an order after fifteen minutes. 'That is like a work of art, that is. Put that boy in a museum! I'd buy postcards of that arse.'

Charlie craned round. Lydia was pointing out a guy, slight, wearing a jacket with lots of zips, and who frankly looked like a model. He was currently having his face painted in neon stripes, chin upturned to the very tall girl in platform heels, grinning at her as he talked and occasionally scrunching his eyes up.

'Hot,' said Charlie, half-heartedly, waving at the barman to remind him where she was.

'Tell me you're going after that,' Lydia said. 'He keeps looking at you.'

Charlie turned around again as she collected the two bottles. Sure enough, the guy was looking over at her as a final streak of luminous lime-yellow was added to his cheek. He gave her a slender, knowingly louche smile.

'Not interested,' she said.

'What are you like? You've literally been single the whole time I've known you.' Lydia, on the other hand, had experienced a range of mostly unsuccessful dates, recounted in luridly extreme detail each time. The last one had involved paintballing and an accusation of nearly blinding him.

'I'm here to dance.' Charlie pulled Lydia back towards the main room. 'And that's what we're going to do.'

An hour later, Charlie was coming out of the ladies' and down the murky packed corridor towards the stairs, occasionally putting a hand lightly on a shoulder or waist as she slinked back towards the sound of the jangling guitars.

As she brushed very close to someone, there was the sensation of being tugged backwards. She stopped, and tried to move on again, but something was gently pulling her.

'Hello, goddess,' said a man's voice, right next to her ear.

She appeared to be stuck to this person. Her sheer mesh top on something of his. She wriggled, but it was no good. 'We're attached,' she said.

'Wonderful,' he said, and his voice was rounded, smooth. There was the intense smell of aftershave, lavender and citrus.

'Argh,' she said. She twisted round one way, then the other, and caught a flash of a neon stripe on his face. It was the guy Lydia had pointed out before. 'Can you help me, please? I'm literally stuck to you.'

He seemed to take a moment too long before gently

pushing himself off the wall. ''Course I can.' This time he sounded warmer, more cordial.

His fingers were light, hardly touching her. CARPE DIEM was tattooed on his hand. He carefully held the back of her top. 'It's my jacket,' he said. 'Hang on.'

He shifted, eased off the jacket, keeping the weight of it in his hand, and worked the zip gently until it released itself from her top.

'There,' he said, and leant back against the wall, the offending item dangling from his hand. 'Hello again.' He rolled his head to the side, and cast a lazily appraising look at her.

The music thudded through the floorboards, the cheer of the crowd strangely dampened. It was so dark up here, red tissue paper over the few lights. The smell of sweat and perfume. Everything had dulled, become muted and pulsing. Everything except him, who seemed hazy and sharp at the same time. He had short, dishevelled dark hair, tanned skin and ridiculously bee-stung lips.

'Hello,' said Charlie, feeling somehow still fixed on the spot.

He was gazing at her as if half-dreaming. 'You're completely divine.'

No one had ever called her that before. Not exactly that. 'That sort of talk isn't getting you anywhere,' she said, bolstering herself.

'Who says I'm trying to get anywhere?' he said, still in his odd reverie. He was really very, very high on something. 'I'm just stating a fact. I take aesthetics very seriously, and you're definitely a very serious aesthetic.'

He was wearing a floral shirt, slightly too big for him, three – no, four – buttons undone, and a slick, completely hairless chest. The hollow at his neck shone like it had been brass-rubbed. Definitely a bit younger than her. Younger and, it had to be said, ridiculously attractive. And for some reason seemingly utterly fascinated by her.

He was currently perusing her shoulder with extreme intensity. Goosebumps rose up on her skin, even though it was about forty degrees in here. 'Stop it,' she said, but she couldn't help smiling.

He was smiling. 'Stop what?'

'What you're doing.' No one had looked at her like that since Alex – since *before* Alex. Since ever.

'I'm only looking,' he said. 'That's allowed. It's demanded, when the sight before me is so impeccable.'

'Not if I say it's not,' she said, feeling alarmingly disarmed. '*Shh*.'

He smiled again, more widely. Her every word seemed to delight and encourage him further. 'You're on another level,' he said. 'You don't belong with us down here. You should be painted on a frieze. On a fresco. Michelangelo would have had a fucking field day. Where d'you live?'

'Yeah, I'm not falling for that one.' Definitely the first rule of dealing with fey, lustful boys. God, he smelt good. The ground underneath her seemed to be undulating slightly.

'Where do you work, then?' He suddenly put a finger very close to her lips, and then on his own. 'No. Let me guess.'

She crossed her arms, unable to resist being drawn in. 'You'll never guess.'

He grinned, a gleaming, wicked thing. 'Fashion house. Designer.'

'Way off.'

'Primary school. Teaching the littlest mites. Reading them stories.'

She couldn't help a half-smile. 'No.'

He gazed at her for a long time, so long that she could feel a single droplet of sweat trickle from her neck all the way down her spine to the waistband of her skirt. His eyes were the most preposterous shade of emerald.

'Vegan chef,' he said.

She made the sound of a quiz show buzzer for a wrong answer. '*Uh-uhh*.' Though she knew someone who was, if vegan chef mostly entailed making oven chips.

He gave her another enraptured grin that showed off his perfectly white, perfectly aligned teeth, apart from a slight chip to one that only made him look sexier. 'You really are completely exquisite,' he said, more thoughtfully.

'You really are completely off your face,' she said, thinking *exquisite* right back.

He put his hand on his chest, fingers splayed, and assumed a look of beautifully refined horror. 'My heart,' he said. 'I give you my word that if you saw me tomorrow, utterly sober, I would say exactly the same thing.'

'Thankfully, I'm not going to see you tomorrow,' she said.

'Go on.' He put out his bottom lip. She had a deep desire to touch it. Bite it.

'Gotta get back to my mate,' she said, and walked very quickly away, her heart doing double-time in her throat.

Charlie lay awake that night, listening to the tiny whine in her ears from the excessively loud speakers, her heart accompanying it. Her skin was tacky. She should have showered. She swore she could still smell him on her.

THIRTEEN

A Surprise Visitor – A Daring Adventure

O n Monday, Charlie was just returning from a lunchtime walk around the park, blasting dubsteppy house from her headphones, when she saw someone strolling next to Walt, holding a spade for him as he made his way to the allotments, chatting exuberantly. Someone with a carefree swagger and short, artfully disarranged hair.

'Oh, my God,' she said aloud.

Lydia was in the second hen-coop, swiping at the sawdust with a dustpan and brush.

Charlie dashed up to the wire-mesh fence. 'Lydia. That guy is here.'

Lydia's cheeks were blotched red with the effort and heat. 'Who?'

'That guy.'

'Guy?' She looked blank.

Charlie curled her fingers round the wire. 'The *guy*. From Saturday.' She had told Lydia of their encounter on the first night bus home and how insanely attractive she found him (the mojitos had helped). Lydia had waggled her eyebrows and confessed that he'd found her when Charlie had gone to the loo again, asked how they knew each other and where they worked, and that she'd not only told him but helpfully pinned it on the map app on his phone and given him three transport options.

Lydia wiped the side of her forehead, leaving a smudge of dirt and a single flake of sawdust there. 'Oh, my days. You are so. In. There.'

'I didn't think he'd actually *come*.' Though, if she admitted it to herself, she'd spent all of Sunday daydreaming about him turning up, giving her that devilishly handsome expression.

'You deserve it, mate. I would totally give him my last Rolo.'

Maybe she *did* deserve it, she thought, and went to the office to get her scarlet lippy.

She found him leaning oddly over the fence to the goat-pen, wielding a large camera, one foot up on a post and shoulders hunched.

'No leaning on the fence,' she said, with what she hoped were sexy managerial vibes.

He turned, the camera in his hands, and took her in with a languidly charmed grin. 'Hello, you.'

Eyebrows, cheeks, lips, she thought, in quick succession. He was wearing a worn, faded purple T-shirt with a tiny hole at the hem of one shoulder. Jeans, rolled up at the ankle, and loafers with no socks; a fine golden chain visible around his neck as well as the camera strap, and a beaten-up leather satchel at his feet.

'It's very quaint down here, isn't it?' he said, with a grin.

She glanced around. A goose was currently flapping

dramatically by the tiny pond and a toddler in wellies jumped up and down in a puddle. 'It's not quaint,' she said, suddenly defensive, though in truth she'd probably thought the same when she first arrived. 'Cute, maybe.'

'Not the farm.' He waved his hand, almost regally. 'South of the river. It's all very... villagey.' He raised an perfectly arched amused eyebrow.

Ridiculous. They were next to a massive hospital and the other side of the park was one of the most deprived areas in the whole capital. 'It's not villagey in the slightest. Loughborough Junction's round the corner.'

'Well, I think it's adorable,' he said, scrutinising her with an artistic appreciation, and definitely noticing the lipstick. 'You look even better in daylight.'

Annoyingly, he'd spoken the truth the other night. Today he was very sober, and just as flatteringly articulate. Charlie couldn't think of a single thing to say in response.

'I'm Franco,' he said, unhesitatingly. 'And you're Charlie B Hughes.' The neckline of his T-shirt was frayed, enough to see his smooth collarbone.

'How do you know?'

'I saw it on the noticeboard. What does the 'B' stand for?'

'None of your business,' she said, feeling contrary.

'Bashful.'

'Really not.'

'Beguiling.'

'Likewise.'

'I beg to differ.' He put his hand on his heart, seeming to feign a subtle shiver. 'Bewitching. Sorry, no – too obvious,' he said, putting a curled forefinger to his lips, and rubbing them thoughtfully. 'Blithesome. It means full of lightness—'

'I know what it means.' She hadn't entirely. 'You're pretty brazen, aren't you?'

'Just being honest.' Another dreamily analytical look. 'You don't mind, do you? You can take it. I sense a lightness of spirit.' There was a dash of something alternative about him, like he enjoyed aerial yoga or practised reiki. The way his ridiculously sparkling eyes – more aquamarine than emerald – fell on her neck made it burn.

Charlie clamped a hand on her throat and wrapped her other arm around herself. 'I should really get back to work.' She went past him on the woodchip path back towards the office, and felt him moving behind her, rather close. 'Stop following me,' she said, laughing, not looking back.

'I'm a paying customer.' A guileless voice.

She turned. 'The farm is free, as you well know.'

'Well, I'm a legitimate visitor, then,' he said, and flicked his finger at the nearest enclosure. 'I'm looking at the llamas.'

'They're alpacas.'

'Alpacas. That one's got eyelashes almost as long as yours. God, you're divine.'

She couldn't help laughing again. 'You're outrageous,' she said, but she felt something beginning to loosen in her. She'd never had someone be so open, or quite so flattering. He was totally unashamed to speak his mind. Maybe she was allowed some appreciation, after what Benji had said.

Franco was still behind her, full of lightly choreographed movement, trailing his fingers along the rail by the chickens, swapping hands, overtaking her until she had to stop to avoid bumping into him. 'Can I take your photograph?'

She turned to see that he hadn't lifted up his big camera but had brought a retro, analogue model out of his satchel. 'Wait. Are you an actual photographer?'

'Partly,' he said, taking off the lens cap. 'I'd like to do more. I've got an exhibition in Dalston next month. In a Spanish bookshop.'

'Oh,' she said, taken aback. 'That's cool.' She had always enjoyed drifting through galleries, and was especially drawn to photography – she checked out the Deutsche Börse prize every year, liked documentary-style images that focused on people rather than landscapes.

Before she could think to hold herself in any sort of proper pose, he'd snapped her and brought the camera down again, a glint of satisfaction on his face, as if she'd just given him the perfect shot.

She resisted the urge to make sure her hair had been in place. 'What else do you do, then?'

He leant back against the rail and positioned his face up to the sky, and the summer light fell on him like a lover. 'A number of things,' he said, eyes shut. 'Acting, mostly. Theatre. And I'm a tattoo artist.'

'You're not,' she said. None of that sounded the slightest bit credible.

He faced her. 'I am,' he said, with a smile that turned from lazy to penetrating, as if she were a fiendish maths equation he'd just about solved. 'Come and get a tattoo.'

She couldn't help laughing. 'No. Thank you very much.'

'D'you have any?' His eyes drifted lightly over her.

She suddenly imagined herself naked in front of him, and felt the heat rise to her neck. 'That's a very personal question.'

'You don't,' he said, as if seeing straight through her. 'Why not?'

'It's hard to choose, isn't it? I mean, what if you go for something you end up hating in ten years' time? Bit awkward when it's not wipe-clean.'

Even his shrug was artful. 'You can overthink these things. The risk and spontaneity's half the point.' He put a hand on his chest and gave a deferential half-bow. 'In my humble opinion.'

'If you say so,' she said.

He gave a watchful hyena-smile. 'I'll give you a tattoo. A free one.'

'No,' she said, but was still grinning. 'That's obviously insane.'

'Really,' he said, and suddenly seemed more intimate, sincere, just as he'd changed moods at The Fir Tree. 'On the house. It would be my pleasure.'

'No, thank you. I'm going to my office now because I have stuff to do, unlike someone.'

'Come and watch me, then,' he said, undeterred. 'Swing by, hang out.'

Charlie was suddenly aware of Gábriel carrying two big brooms towards the barn, glancing over at them. She really should be working right now. 'Where is it?'

'Holloway. The other side of the river.' He leaned his elbows on the fence, his back to the donkeys.

'I'm not going to get a tattoo.'

'No, 'course not.' He leaned slightly sideways towards her so that his arm touched hers. 'We can have a drink, though.'

She watched the hairs rise up on her own skin.

'Eight o'clock tonight,' he said.

Charlie got off the tube at Archway and walked down the hill along the main road. It was still light, just. The sky was a mottled mauve and navy. She barely knew this part of north London; it wasn't central enough to be visited much. A little more Turkish, a little less Caribbean and Nigerian up here perhaps, though the evangelical churches were still out in force. There were organic vegan delis and Irish pubs, nail bars and proper caffs, kebab and chicken and furniture shops, and one of those lawyers' firms specialising in immigration visas; estate agents, displaying houses for sale at fantastical prices; a 1930s-painted sign for Brymay Safety Matches on the brick wall of a building was mostly concealed by a free-standing display digitally advertising 'Gather', a networking event for ambitious women.

Note to self, thought Charlie, as she counted down the street numbers. On arriving home from work, she'd resolved to stay in with a pasta dinner and several episodes of a new series featuring two badass international spy women, not thinking about Franco for a single second. Not long after that, she was lying on her bed staring at the clusters of hard, mid-sized apples on the tree outside, feeling the same tacky sweatiness she had felt after The Fir Tree; then she found herself unsuccessfully searching for any Francos on social media; this transformed into her trying on several outfits, each more sensual and revealing than the last; which became a bowl of stuffed ricotta tortellini and half an episode of the new show; followed by rushing back upstairs to put on one of the outfits, which was now too tight after the pasta, and ending up with something a little more modest (and more forgiving).

Practically everyone had tattoos these days. Jan's arms were more ink than bare skin. Gábriel had the tree on his back, glimpsed that one time. Lydia had a heart on her upper arm with 'GRAN' emblazoned within it, and Joe had his date of birth on the back of his neck in florid numerals, given to him by an obviously disreputable tattooist, seeing as he was under eighteen.

There. Number 533, between a bakery and a Thai nail and beauty place. The shop front was painted purple, the blinds down, and SCARLET AND BLACK TATTOO PARLOUR stencilled on the glass in a gothic font. It was as if a thread had been gently coaxing her all the way from the cottage's front door to this one.

Charlie hovered. She watched the bus wheezing past, and scuffed the pavement with her silver trainers. He probably wasn't even in there. He hadn't asked for her number.

A sweetly clamorous bell sounded as Franco opened the door, not looking the slightest bit surprised. 'There you are,' he said, in a rather sweet, dark voice, and let her in.

A large, ginger-bearded white man, naked from the waist up, was lying on his front on a black leather reclining chair, his beefy arms wrapped around it. Franco had ushered Charlie over to a beaten-up leather sofa, a hand gently on her back, and said he would be done in fifteen minutes.

The tattoo parlour had a plush Moroccan-style carpet and smelt of cinnamon, a single incense burner smoking in the corner. Music was playing, a hypnotically droning guitar riff, handclaps and men and women's voices in unison in an unrecognisable language. Franco and his client were talking about it, discussing nomadic tribes and the Islamic groups denouncing popular music in Mali.

Franco, completely absorbed in his work, didn't look over once. They conversed in relaxed murmurs, and the buzz of the tattoo gun hummed intermittently amongst the strange, bluesy desert-guitars. He was wearing a deep-red vest that displayed lots of tattoos that Charlie hadn't yet seen. His arms were slim and perfectly muscled. He looked – to use his word – divine.

The music, the murmuring, the incense: it was enough for her to want to blissfully doze off. But then Franco was finishing up, showing the client his shoulder blade in a mirror, and calling Charlie over to have a look. The tattoo was of a starkly ornate wolf, wrapped around a man whose arm was in its mouth; the big guy explained in a sonorous voice that it was the Norse god Týr sacrificing his arm to the wolf Fenrir. Franco said, as he taped cling film carefully over the top, that it had taken three sessions. The client towered over him when standing, paid him in cash before embracing him as if they were old friends, gave a courteous wink and a nod to Charlie, and was gone.

'Right,' said Franco, and it was as if his intense focus now shifted to her, his gaze lively and deep. 'Now I'm all yours.'

He said he'd get her a drink, coming back out from the beaded curtain with two heavy-bottomed tumblers and a bottle of something dark red, before sitting down next to her on the sofa.

'He seemed happy,' she said.

'I'm good at it,' he said, with a winning lack of self-deprecation.

'Someone's happy to blow their own trumpet.'

'Someone has a very fine, highly polished trumpet to blow.' He looked deadly serious for a moment, before grinning.

She raised her eyebrows. 'OK.'

He laughed through his nose, handed her a glass and pulled the cork out of the bottle with his teeth.

'What are we drinking?'

'Vista Alegre,' he said, in a convincing and disconcertingly alluring accent, as he poured. 'Vintage ruby port.'

'Check you out.'

'I like the finer things.' A deliberately assessing look. 'Obviously.'

She took a breath, and no words followed. Part of him brought out her sass, and part of him made her melt into arousal. 'Go on, then,' she said. 'What other finer things do you like?'

He slung an arm over the back of the sofa and let out a deeply pleasurable hum, as if sinking into a hot bath. 'Oh, you know. Art, music, sex. What was it Oscar Wilde said? "I threw the pearl of my soul into a cup of wine. I went down the primrose path to the sound of flutes. I lived on honeycomb."'

'Wow,' she said. 'Get you.'

He told her he lived with some other artists in Haggerston, and painted a hedonistic picture of riotous parties by night and the smell of turpentine and coffee by day. It made Charlie feel like she really hadn't been living her fullest life of late, though she tried to make the farm and her cottage sound as fun as possible.

'So, Franco,' she said. 'Is that… Italian?'

He shrugged. 'I was christened Frank.' He screwed up his nose and grinned, unabashed. 'I prefer Franco.'

Of course you do, she thought.

He stretched his neck with artful elegance. 'So, what d'you think?'

She cast her eyes about the room again. 'Really not what I expected,' she said.

'What did you expect?'

'Bikers, beers, cartoon bluebirds.'

He laughed, a small, genuine amusement. 'It can be. The owner is a bit more alternative but you still get the same old requests: dolphins, roses'—he upturned his palm graciously towards her—'bluebirds. Anyway, that's not what I meant.'

She raised an eyebrow. 'Hmm?'

'What d'you think about a tattoo?'

Her other eyebrow rose to join the first. 'You're really gunning for this, aren't you?'

He scrunched up his nose again. Oh God, he was so handsome. So *pretty*. 'Go on.'

'What, choose something, like it's not going to live on me forever?'

His gaze was keen, amused. 'Live in the moment. Dare you.'

She gave a wavering hum of both indecision and excitement. She couldn't help it – his easy manner was infectious. Wasn't that why she had come here, to at least think about it? She sat forward and propped her head on her hand, looking over towards the laminated display boards concertinad on the wall.

'Forget that,' he said, briefly putting his hand over her eyes, his palm brushing her skin for the merest moment. 'Something personal. I want to dig deep.'

Charlie bit her lip, hoped she looked coquettish, *felt* coquettish. There was something mesmeric about the echoing guitars still playing, the incense, the glisten of sweat on his collarbone. 'I don't know,' she said. 'It's hard.'

He very lightly touched her shoulder. 'Think of someone you love. Really love. And something of them, or a connection to them. Could be from your childhood.'

As he spoke, Charlie felt her heart automatically harden, a protective instinct that kicked in once in a while.

'Take your time,' he said. 'You'll know when you've got something that feels right. It'll just click.' He laid his head back, shutting his eyes with a small, deeply sexy hum, as if inviting sleep to adoringly drape itself over him.

She regarded her glass of port, suddenly felt that it was her own blood she was staring at. She let her mind float, far, far back, to the years she usually tried very hard to forget, to before that, when things were sweet, safe, when it felt like nothing would ever break. She thought of her grandmother in County Cork, of the mountains in neighbouring County Kerry. How she had been upset not to be old enough to go for a hike up there. Something gently unlocked deep in her chest.

She glanced at Franco. The line of his arched neck, the gentle swell of his Adam's apple. He looked like a sleeping prince.

After a moment, he rolled his head over towards her, lashes blinking open. Suddenly sharply awake.

'Yeah, I've got something actually,' she said.

'Come and sit here,' Franco said, a little while later. He'd found some images on his phone, sketched her idea on a leather-bound pad, before drawing something more detailed, intricate. It *did* feel right. She knew she wouldn't regret it.

She rested her head on the back of the chair. There was different music playing now, a man accompanying his soulful, eerily high voice on an electric guitar that seemed to glow.

'Will it hurt?' she said, her voice rather more fragile than intended. The air seemed to have changed, become sultry.

He shook his head. 'No.' A smile. There was an inscription on his inner upper arm, bold black type. MILITAT OMNIS AMANS. 'Gonna tell me the significance?'

The tiny prickle of discomfort in her chest, the memory of a feeling from long ago. 'It's for my sister.'

He grinned. 'Is she going to like it? Or kill you?'

'She's dead.'

Instantly, his face transformed into seriousness. 'Oh,' he said, and there was something in the tender, drawn-out syllable that suggested he wasn't all swagger, but felt things deeply, properly. She liked how he didn't look uncomfortable about it either, as people sometimes did. He put his hand on her arm. 'I'm so sorry,' he said, and really seemed to mean it. He allowed the moment to linger, the slight suggestion of a priest's benediction, before removing his hand. 'It's going to be beautiful. You won't regret it.'

The blinds were down now, the tangerine of the streetlights striping the room, a single lamp casting its glow over both of them. Charlie felt a little hazy, not quite connected to reality.

'So.' He took her hand, turned it over and placed a single, very light kiss on the inside of her left wrist. 'Just here?'

He hadn't asked to kiss her wrist, and hadn't needed to. It was if he'd known that was exactly what she had come for, really. She shivered.

He'd drawn the silhouette on transfer paper and now she watched the impression of her tattoo appear on her skin.

'Now you must absolutely not flinch,' he said.

'OK.'

'And do something for me.' His voice was assured and oddly lulling.

'What?'

'Promise not to look until it's done. I'm going to do a good job.' There was something so persuasive about his eyes, the indigo depths in them. 'Trust me.'

On the speaker in the corner, the man's voice had become a sorrowful wail.

'Promise,' she said.

• • •

The pain was potent and deep, but not unbearable. While he worked, he told her about some of his own tattoos, and she concentrated on his voice. The Latin inscription was Ovid – every lover is a soldier – and he had a long, elegant sword on the inside of his other arm, to represent the military heritage on his mother's side. There were a couple of girls' names, one on each wrist, though he didn't talk about those and Charlie didn't ask. She forced herself not to look down at her own wrist, closing her eyes as the needle dug at her. When she did open them, it was to look at the carved wooden masks on the wall, the small glass cabinet of piercings, and the laminated racks of images for clients to choose from. His hand lightly gripped the upper part of her forearm, and his warm breath was on her skin. In spite of the pain, she felt hypnotised.

Less than an hour later, Franco leant back, twisting round to rest his tattoo gun on the counter. 'There,' he said, in the same enchanting, near-enchanted voice. 'All done.'

She blinked and looked down at her upturned wrist. There it was. A small, undeniably beautiful fern, the stem subtly curling, its fronds ending just before her palm. The skin was raw and reddish, the ink black-blue.

'You said it wouldn't hurt,' she said, quietly dazed.

'Of course it hurt,' he said. 'I was piercing your skin with a needle. But I was very careful. And you were very brave.' He stretched, an easy, feline movement. 'That guy I just did cried like a baby the first time – women are always braver than men in here. And perhaps elsewhere.' He leant over to the counter, and passed her the unfinished glass of port – he'd insisted she didn't drink too much before getting it done. 'There. You can finish that now.'

Charlie gazed at her wrist, at the fern that meant Jools. Part of her wanted to break open, to sob.

'You like it,' he said. Not a question.

She nodded. Drank deeply from her glass.

'I knew you would.' He curled his forefinger underneath the fingers of her other hand, easy as anything. 'Do you think your sister would have?'

'I hope so. Thank you.' She put her glass down and let out a long breath. 'Can we talk about something else now?'

He nodded, still sympathetic. But when he blinked, his eyes had a new sliver of flirtatious danger. 'We don't have to talk at all.'

'Oh, my God.'

Charlie was lying back on the tattooist's chair. Franco, still in his vest, was on top of her, and inside her, and he felt wonderful. The music had stopped, and there was only the squeak of the chair and the sounds of the street outside and Franco, kissing her neck and whispering a cocktail of beautiful and filthy things into her ear.

He'd pulled her up, held her hand delicately as if at a ball, before leading her to the galley kitchen behind the beaded curtain. He had pushed up her skirt and knelt down and she'd looked at the dirty mugs and coffee rings on the counter and wondered why no one had ever *quite* done what he was doing to her at that very moment.

Now they were back on the chair. She'd always had a second date rule. Never before that. Was this a date? a small part of her brain wondered. Maybe his farm visit had been the first. It didn't matter. It was absolutely happening and she hoped desperately that no one would think to peek through the blinds.

A police car went past, the siren throbbing. Everything was throbbing.

Charlie walked the longer way back to a different tube station, past the drinkers outside the pubs, past the shops with their shutters down, a tart, sweet pain in her wrist, which was now wrapped in cling film, and a sweeter pain just about everywhere else.

FOURTEEN

Franco And Charlie

'Well, it's all very adorable down here. *Recherché*.'

'You're doing it on purpose.'

'I'm not.'

'You are. Dissing my ends.'

Franco sat back, a sinuous pose that seemed to embody fox as much as it did human. 'You're the one who brought me here.'

Charlie and Franco had eaten lunch at one of her favourite places, up on Brixton Hill. The Cameroonian owner – who greeted her, as always, with *hello sista* and a beam – had turned it from a secondhand fridge shop into a sunny café selling veggie and vegan Caribbean food. They'd eaten galettes stuffed with jerk aubergine, plantain and green beans, and then walked down to Brixton Village, because if Franco kept insisting on South London being a village, she would bring him to one.

In some parts of Brixton, the march of gentrification was comically offensive – cocktail bars and small plate restaurants filled only with rich white people opposite the neo-brutalist Barrier Block flats, with its black old-timers shooting the breeze by the car wash. This area was her community; the mix of people gave it its soul, and always had. Brixton Village had been a run-down 1930s arcade-style shopping centre that began offering rent-free space a few years ago. But whilst Charlie had liked seeing the shops filled and the live music on Thursday nights, things were starting to change, with more expensive places moving in, the rents rising. It was currently a strange mix of hipster and local: expensive artisanal meats and vintage clothing alongside the Sierra Leone grocery store, and Jamaican shops selling super-sized bags of rice and red lentils, African hot pepper and stockfish cod; there was a cheap party shop and a long-standing wig bazaar, with plastic busts sporting luridly-coloured wigs. It was usually packed at the weekends, when people nursing hangovers crammed in to eat Mexican brunches, Thai noodle bowls and Taiwanese steamed buns.

Charlie and Franco had sauntered around the market with his arm slung over her shoulder as if they'd known each other for more than just a few hours in total. He'd only occasionally removed it to slide over to a window and point out a necklace or a bar of ginger soap, or to pick up a particularly glossy aubergine until the shopkeeper came out and scolded him, saying to buy it or put it back.

Now, they had left the market and gone further up Atlantic Road to another of Charlie's recent favourites, Brixton Pound, named after the area's own currency. The community café was pay-what-you-can, used surplus food from local shops on its menu and gave work experience to people with learning disabilities. Charlie realised that it had a similar feel to the farm, cheerfully raw and unaffected.

Now, she was telling Franco about Brixton having its own currency.

'Yeah, yeah, Brixton is the best, South London rules, I get it,' Franco said, grinning. 'Show us, then. Have you got some?'

She fished out her purse. 'Sure have.'

'Lovely.' Franco had caught the attention of the multi-pierced waitress and gave the most precise drinks order that Charlie had ever heard. 'So just a ristretto. The Ethiopian blend, definitely. If you could then add just the slightest dash more hot water, but literally the slightest. And then this much'—he held up his horizontally-straightened little finger to her, the other fingers tightly curled—'steamed single cream.' He sat back, an intoxicating smile taking over from the earnestness. 'That would be absolutely stellar.'

Charlie shook her head at him as the waitress left them. 'You are unbelievable.'

'I really am,' he said, self-deprecatingly but with a dash of cool astonishment, before he shrugged, more genuinely. 'I just like everything to be perfect. As well you know.'

She felt her cheeks flush. She couldn't help it. No one had ever spent the first two dates telling her that Botticelli and Delacroix would have killed to paint her; or had dressed her in their own shirts, fiddled with cuffs and collars, and bid them stand by the window where the light was better before taking an hour's worth of portrait photographs; or stopped dead in the middle of a sentence to unapologetically gaze at her. She kept reminding herself that it was OK to be a bad feminist, *à la* Roxane Gay.

The waitress came back with their order, and Franco gave her another charming beam. 'You're fabulous. Thank you. I love your nose-piercing, by the way.'

Though she seemed the sort of super-tough woman that

might play roller derby in her spare time, the waitress seemed perfectly happy to discuss body modification for a few minutes, until somebody called her from the kitchen.

Charlie watched Franco as he put his lips to his espresso cup. He had a way with people. He seemed to adapt at will, reflecting something of the person he was talking to; he'd become street and pally in the secondhand clothes and art place in Brixton Village, discussed 1970s dub reggae with surprising assurance in the record shop, and was all cut-glass charm in the ethical homeware store. He displayed a profound interest in everything and everyone, especially Charlie, from whom he'd already drawn out her childhood fears (crossing the road, jellyfish), favourite animals (tigers, cats), favourite artist (Frida Kahlo), recurring dreams (floating up and over the city), political beliefs (Labour-ish/Green-ish), and choice London haunts (the curry places on Tooting Bec Road, the South London Gallery, some of the boutiques around Brick Lane). Maybe it was the actor in him.

Over coffee, Franco told her of some of the jobs he'd had, from work as an extra on studio films to fringe theatre productions, including a play he'd written and taken to Edinburgh when a student. He made the work – even the endless rounds of auditions – sound grand, a noble calling. Charlie watched his hands as he talked, how they shape-shifted into characters and places, his short, bitten nails and the little inked rose at the base of his thumb.

'This is healing rather well,' he said, picking up her wrist and perusing it as if it were a classical sculpture in a gallery.

'It itches like crazy.'

'No scratching.' Franco looked authoritative and seductive all at once. 'Or else.'

'Or else what?'

'Or else I'll come and get you,' he said, and leant over the table so that his face was very close, voice lower and gossamer-soft. 'And do very bad things to you.' The inside of his lips was the colour of plums. 'I am *very* good at doing *very* bad things.'

'I bet you are,' Charlie said, feeling his inescapable, magnetising pull. She put her finger in the jar of brown sugar and placed the grains on her tongue. 'You are totally bad.'

'And yet here you are,' he said in nothing more than a murmur.

She kissed him. Even after the roll-up cigarette he'd just smoked, he tasted lovelier than the sugar.

They spent almost the entire rest of the day in Charlie's bed, variously under or over or entangled in the duvet, and during the quieter moments, she sleepily regarded him.

He was younger than her by three and a half years. He'd studied Anthropology and Art at Goldsmith's and had seemed to spend his time there forming short-lived bands with long names and getting epically wasted. For the six months after his degree he'd stayed at a friend's house on the Andalusian coast, swimming naked in the sea every morning, before smoking on the balcony and pretending to write a post-modernist novel featuring a version of himself swimming and smoking in Andalusia.

Charlie didn't care about his pretensions. She was bedazzled, and enjoyably so. He talked enthusiastically about Islamic art, jumping up to grab his phone to illustrate the first addition of the colour red in seventeenth-century Moroccan *zellige* tilework, and did it in a way that made Charlie daydream about doing an art history course. He kept calling her the names of goddesses, and made her feel attractive again after the nine months of schlepping about in jeans and wellies. He had a wealth of stories about people's choices of tattoos, from ghastly to tragic, and acted out his interchanges with them in an expert range of accents, yet never sounded condescending towards his clients. He made himself utterly at home in the kitchen, using all the ingredients in the fridge to make a vegan stew, fragrant and delicious, enthralling Lydia further by asking about Dorset and her course and offering breezy advice on her love life. He recited a Lorca poem off by heart. In Spanish. Naked.

It wasn't just the compliments, the boundless effervescence. Franco did have a thoughtful, emotional side. He gently asked her more about Jools, without prying. He readily told her about his own family – his apathy towards his dad, who lived in Australia and had done a distinct lack of fathering, contrasting with his obviously fierce love of his mum, who had her own nanny service and crèche in Hastings. She thought again – not a little guiltily – of Will, and how initially tentative he'd been to reveal anything of his true nature. Franco practically thrust his hand behind his own ribs and gave Charlie his bloody pumping heart.

Still, it didn't hurt that Franco was truly the handsomest man she had ever seen. His eyebrows rose up in the middle in a tortured 1950s movie star way; his hair looked incredible whether messed-up on the pillow or slicked back after their shower together; he was not tall, but lean and lightly muscled; and all of his tattoos seemed perfectly placed, from the panther prowling on his right hip to the Egyptian falcon on his ankle. He also smelt exceptionally wonderful, a mixture of that same cologne he'd been wearing in the Fir Tree, mixed with coffee and, more mutedly, cigarettes.

And he was, it had to be said, undeniably good at doing bad things.

'This place is an absolute fucking gem,' he said, tucking a pillow behind his head in Charlie's room. 'It's like I've woken up in Narnia.' It was the next night, and Franco hadn't left. There'd been no suggestion of him leaving from either of them. Lydia hadn't seemed to mind, probably because most of the time Franco was wandering around bare-footed and bare-chested in those shockingly low-slung jeans, occasionally serenading her with Prince songs, causing her to genuinely blush during a sweetly sexy bump and grind whilst he sang 'Little Red Corvette'.

'Mmm,' said Charlie, who was trying to bring herself back to reality following his head being at various positions between her legs for forty-five very soggy minutes.

'You alright, Juno?' he said. A wicked grin. He kissed her and she tasted herself.

A failed attempt at sounding detached. 'Mmm-hmm.'

He lay down next to her and shrugged his arm underneath her neck. For a halcyon moment, there was nothing but the two of them. Then he let out a breathy, fizzing sigh and shifted. 'Let's go out.'

'In a bit.' She could do with some sleep. She'd only had about five hours in the last forty-eight.

He gently kicked her foot with his own. 'Let's go get fucked up.' He'd already magicked a teeny joint when they were sitting outside the house by the firepit.

'Not right now.'

Franco crossed his arms, then his ankles, and lay still for

about five seconds before dramatically turning and leaning over her. 'Dinner, then. Let's eat until we're sick.'

'Too tired.'

'I'm not.' He was still hovering above her, his scent mixed with a new addition of recent spearmint gum. Even his sweat could have been bottled. His small gold crucifix necklace lay lightly on her sternum as he touched the mole on her jaw.

Charlie gave another hum.

'Fine.' He suddenly leapt up, a great cool absence of him next to her. 'I get the message.'

She opened her eyes and rolled over. He was putting on his T-shirt. 'You're going.' She didn't want him to go.

'I'd better get back anyway.' Watching him dress was almost as sexy as watching him take everything off, an unselfconscious slinging on of pants, jeans, shoes (and a still-defiant lack of socks). He put his keys and his wallet in his pocket before squatting and gently sucking on her big toe. Charlie had never hummed as much as she had in the last hour, ever.

A final stretch, before he raked a hand through his hair. There was something utterly boyish in him, a lithe energy and unpredictability. An alluring Peter Pan. 'Right. Goodnighty, Aphrodite.' He turned, lifted up the sash window further.

'What're you doing?'

'Leaving,' he said, as if it were obvious, and began to climb out of the window.

Charlie shot up, staggered to the window half-tangled in the sheet, and tugged at his arm. '*Franco*.'

He was partly perched on the apple tree branch, which bent a little, and managed a faux-innocent, pageboy-face. 'What? You wanted me to go.'

'You'll fall.'

'I'm very athletic. Limber.'

'Please come back inside and leave the normal way like a normal person.'

'Fuck that,' he said, and leant precariously back to her for a kiss. 'Catch you later, goddess.'

He shimmied further away from her, clambered down branch by branch and hopped onto the gravel. He looked up, gave a wide-armed, regal bow, and disappeared round the corner. She could hear him singing 'Kiss', *sotto voce*.

Work. The farm. All the things that Charlie had been getting better at since last September. She attempted to concentrate for the next few days, whilst occasionally staring into space, hay, woodchip or at the bright print fabrics of small children's summer wear. Franco hadn't messaged her – in fact, he still hadn't asked for her number and she hadn't asked for his. She'd finally found him on social media – over-exposed photos of parties, his tongue out, and several professional shots, exquisitely lit portraits that made him look like a piece of religious art, a beatified saint – but it seemed needy and crass to message him on there. She would give it a few more days.

The current objects of her staring power were the slim bare-root starter fruit trees that were being planted as part of the new orchard, which Gábriel was overseeing. The beehives had been introduced last month, motley-coloured wood boxes perched at wonky angles, with wildflowers and grasses planted around them. The London Beekeepers' Association had brought in the bees, and two of their volunteers made regular visits to induct some of the farm's workers. The blonde sisters, Charity and Faith, were particularly keen, as was Jami, although that may have been due more to the sisters than the bees, given the amount of eyerolling his sister Badiha did in their presence.

Apple, quince, pear, plum. Even the trees made her feel sensual. They were being placed at a decent distance from each other, and she tried to imagine them in a few years' time, broad and heavy with bulbous, ripe fruit. Tallboy was bringing over the final tree to Gábriel, its roots dripping after being soaked for several hours. They placed it in a hole in the ground and, with Tallboy still holding the wrist-slim trunk, Gábriel moved the tree up an inch and down again, before handing the shovel to another volunteer. He watched them for a moment before coming over to join Charlie. He was wearing a pink and grey-striped T-shirt and a pair of shorts with lots of pockets.

'It's going to be good,' he said.

'It is. Well done, you,' she said. 'Tree expert now, too.'

He shrugged. 'I read a lot of websites.' He gave her a quick half-smile, before glancing at the tattoo on her wrist. 'You just got that, right?'

She looked down at it. 'Oh. Yeah. Bit spur of the moment.' Though Franco had been right, she thought. She couldn't ever imagine regretting this. He'd deftly worked his way into that usually locked part of her, helped her express something that she'd kept hidden for so long.

Two of the hens began a squabbling match somewhere behind them, an outraged interchange.

'You like them?' Gábriel said.

'Like what?'

'The plant. I forget what you call it.'

'Oh. Ferns.' There was the pain, that indelible crush on her heart. 'Yeah, but... not me.' She looked at her nails. 'Not exactly. They're for someone else.' My sister, she wanted to tell him. For my big sister.

He bent down to swipe soil off his bare calf. 'It's nice,' he said, quietly, offhandedly.

'Yo, Charls,' said Lydia, who'd come from the steps to the side of them, putting a hand on Charlie's back. 'Your *loverrrr* is here.'

Charlie glanced over the brick wall to see Franco chatting to Marianne, and the old sadness was replaced by a flush of pleasure, followed swiftly by a small dash of shame at Lydia exposing her so. Gábriel straightened to follow her gaze. Marianne was laughing and swatting playfully at Franco's arm as he turned, caught Charlie's eye, and held up a hand while still continuing his conversation.

Oh, God. Just the mere sight of him made Charlie's knees turn to marshmallow. He had the look and demeanour of a globally successful boy band member in his rebellious solo career phase, and whatever he was saying seemed to be rapturously entertaining.

'Can't keep away, can he?' Lydia shifted the large plastic bag of feed onto her other hip and left them, singing in an over-breathless fashion, '*Cream. Get on top.*'

Moments later, Franco was bounding over to them with lissom grace.

'Hello, you,' he said to Charlie, as silken as always. He looked up at Gábriel. 'All right, mate?' A little cooler, perhaps, before a single blink returned his smooth, warm charm, and he addressed Charlie again. 'Your girl, Marianne, is an absolute queen. She was telling me about naming all the goats after black feminist theorists.'

'Feminist theorists, movie stars, football players, we've got them all here,' said Charlie, trying to sound aloof and wishing she didn't feel so uncomfortable standing between the two of them. Franco was smiling at her and back up at Gábriel, seemingly waiting for an introduction. Gábriel seemed to be holding himself rather stiffly.

'Oh,' said Charlie. 'Um, Franco, this is Gábriel.'

Gábriel nodded at him, before glancing at Charlie and moving past them. 'I have some stuff to do.'

Franco gave him a laddish nod of his own, patting him on the back as he passed. 'Safe, bro.' He watched as Gábriel collected the remaining plastic from the new trees, wrapping it up in a bundle and leaving the new orchard. Franco leant confidingly towards her, sticking a thumb back, and spoke in a stagey whisper. 'He's a bit clichéd, isn't he? He looks like he should be onstage in *Oklahoma!* "Oh, what a beautiful morrrr-ning",' he began half singing.

It smarted. It was the first time he'd been anything but gracious to anyone. 'Don't be mean,' she said.

He slid behind her and wrapped his arms around her waist. 'I'm sorry. Naughty Franco,' he said in a more velvety voice. 'Hello.' He placed a single gentle kiss on her earlobe.

'Hello.' The touch of his lips sent a shiver of electricity down her spine. 'What are you doing here, anyway?' she said. 'Shouldn't you be wielding your tattoo gun right about now?'

'The power's out at the shop. Thought I'd shuffle on down to *these coun'ry parts*'—an impressive imitation of Lydia's broad accent—'and get to know your nearest and dearest better. Feed them a few biscuits.' He sniffed with deliberately arch timing. 'I don't mean the big oaf.'

'They don't eat biscuits,' Charlie said, remaining in his embrace. He smelt of spearmint again. 'Don't feed them biscuits.' *And don't call him an oaf,* she thought, but didn't say.

FIFTEEN

Someone Speaks Their Mind

Franco continued to come to the farm. She'd find him holding court with the volunteers, whether talking football with Joe and Tallboy, politics with Marianne, or math rock with Moonie, who already knew his (very specific) coffee order. He would always look round at Charlie as if her arrival was an unexpected pleasure and not the reason he'd come at all, though it was never long before he was giving her his undivided attention.

'I swear you must have something better to do with your time,' she said, on his third visit in four days.

'Impossible. You're more addictive than heroin.'

'Tell me you haven't done heroin,' she said. Frankly, she wouldn't have put it past him, what with his ethereal tortured poet vibe, and he'd regaled her with a few tales of week-long benders fuelled by a colourful range of stimulants. She really hoped he hadn't done heroin.

'Of course not,' he said, and flashed her a wide-eyed grin, followed by a double-take, and a geisha girl-like giggle, before finally settling into a more genuine face. 'No. Obviously.'

'I've got work to do, you know.'

He followed her. 'You're different here, aren't you? The boss.'

'Not the boss.'

Franco made a short scoffing sound. ''Course you are. It's very sexy, you know.' He caught her hand, pulled her back to him and leant close to her ear. 'Come for a walk.'

'You're a very naughty person,' she said.

'And very tempting.'

She couldn't deny it. 'I can't. I have work.' Unlike him, who never seemed to have anything overly pressing to do.

'Take an early lunch.'

She felt her resistance weakening. 'It's only half past eleven.'

'You're hungry.' A light nibble on her earlobe, as his voice darkened. 'And so am I.'

'Oh Charlie, I just met a girl named Charlie, and suddenly that name, will never be the same to me…'

She had assented to a quick walk – convincing herself it was by way of a tea break, and so they ambled up to the park's flower garden and through the pergola that dripped with lilac wisteria. Franco went ahead of her, jumping onto and down from the low brick walls, bastardising a musical theatre song complete with flagrant hand gestures. It was a warm day, the leaves plushly green, and fat pigeons flopping between the trees.

'And suddenly I found how wonderful a sound can be…' He fluttered back to her, placing a perfect kiss on her lips. His voice, naturally, was a flawless tenor.

'Where d'you get your energy from?' she said.

'From you,' he said. 'You inspire me. Because you are glorious.' He took her hand and pulled her gently over to a copse between two paths, in the shadow of a cedar tree, a sycamore, birch and beech, with silver-veined ivy on the floor. He began kissing her in earnest, his hands making their way slowly down her sides, one sliding under the waistband of her skirt.

She felt herself begin to slip, soporific, her nerve-endings glowing, before realising that they might be visible to anyone passing close by them. 'Franco, I really should get back.'

'Fine. Then I won't do...' He whispered several things in her ear. 'Or...'

Charlie felt a deep bruising pain in her stomach, and rather lower down, and the heaviness swept over her again. How did he do that? Hypnotise her so? 'I've never had sex outside before,' she said, a little meekly.

An incredulous grin. 'You've never had sex outside? How old are you again?' He eyed her, amused, thoughtful. 'Look,' he said, in an explanatory fashion. 'There are crocuses.' He pointed to a cluster of pale lavender flowers – that may or may not have been crocuses – as if it were reason enough, before he stepped very close, pressed himself against her. 'I can be quick.' He kissed that place on her neck he already knew she loved. 'As well as slow.'

He *was* quick, and it was awkward and daring and outrageous, and her back scraped against a tree, and she swore she could faintly hear one of the sheep further down the park baa-ing.

Muggy, oppressive days. The sky is smudged colours and everything droops. The buses, trains and tubes are unbearable, travellers fanning themselves with the free papers, nobly perspiring in conditions not fit for cattle transportation. Some families escape the humidity, head to Broadstairs, Brighton, Southend. In the park, students sit in circles drinking beer and playing music from their phones; dogs rest on their haunches, tongues lolling. Two homeless men pack their tents down early each morning and sit under the eighteenth-century portico shelter to wait out the day. Gábriel begins a habit of bringing them each a flask of tea and a sandwich, picking up the flask again each evening. He encourages them to come over to the farm, and makes sure to pop by the office to tell Charlie. He lingers for the slightest moment longer than necessary, to observe the way the light shimmers on her cheekbone, the freckles emerging across her nose, though she does not notice, her attention already back on her computer. As he walks away, he shakes his head at himself, sighs so gently that it is lost on the heavy breeze that continues through the farm, ruffling the feathers of a hen, stirring the fringe of a donkey. By the classroom, the volunteers roll up their T-shirt sleeves over their shoulders and swig lukewarm cans of sugary drinks as they chat.

'He is *so* fit. I would give everything up for him. No lie.'

'You have a boyfriend.'

'I'd ditch him for Franco. Oh, my days.'

'You've gotta have more quality control.'

'Yeah, he's a player, you just know to look at him. Fuckboi.'

'He's a don. He knows people. Got connections.'

'What kind of connections?'

'That's for me to know. Under wraps.'

'Riiight.'

'That boy is gay. Definitely.'

'He is not gay. What are you like? Look how he is with Charlie. All over her like a rash.'

'He's definitely some sort of ting. I feel it.'

'Where do you feel it? About here?'

'Yeah, yeah, very funny, watch me laughing. I've got gaydar, you know. Man knows when man's a man's man.'

A month filled with Franco. Charlie had done nothing but work for almost a year; she deserved the attention, she told herself. There was something utterly luminous about him and his interest in her, how he would sit up, cross-legged, as she talked about everything and nothing, watch her face as if he had to memorise her lines, his own reactions beautifully exaggerated. She helped him with some actual lines for an audition, watched him transform into a depressed Midwestern man, his shoulders turning in, one foot dragging behind him. He got the part, took her out for a lavish Chinese meal, paid for on one of several credit cards. He had a fascination with the tiniest things: stopping dead on the pavement to crouch down at a daisy growing valiantly through the cracks; drawn by the way the colour of a discarded Post-it note blazed against a brick wall; putting a finger on Charlie's lips to make sure she heard the singular squeak of a train on its rail. They went to the opening of his month-long photography exhibition in the little Spanish bookshop, a night of prosecco and some very high-art people standing in front of his portraits and angular shots of London. Franco was utterly in his element, warm, loquacious, and always finding time to grin at Charlie.

· · ·

'Earth to Charlie Hughes,' said Lydia one night, after Franco had left.

Charlie was standing in the kitchen, her back to the sink, clutching a tea towel and gazing into the distance. 'Say what?' she said, still in her reverie.

'Wow. You've got it bad.'

'Super bad.' She'd never known anything like it. Her blood pulsed, her heart felt weightier and more plangent, her throat dried up. Seeing Franco was rather worryingly like an illness. 'I really need to get my act together.'

'Why? Just enjoy it,' said Lydia, merrily. 'What's that thing people say? Don't look a gift horse in the mouth.' She winked. 'If you know what I mean.'

A number of vivid and inappropriate images passed fleetingly through Charlie's brain. She heaved a massive sigh. She had really meant to treat Franco as a visit to a very sexy spa, but she could feel the pull, subtly fuelled by panic, of wanting more. Because he might get hit by a car at any moment.

'You don't mind him being round, do you?' She knew it wasn't fair, but she also knew that she did not want to spend any more nights at his place, which had turned out to be a squat with damp floorboards and occasional sightings of rats.

Lydia let out a wide-eyed snort. 'Are you kidding me? Those little dances he does... just *looking* at him is better than sex with another man.' She screwed up her nose and looked at Charlie in a frank, sisterly sort of way. 'Is he good? Tell me he is. A boy can't move around the way he does and not be total killer in the sack.'

'He really is,' Charlie said, feeling her throat dry up again.

At work, the talk was of a break-in over at Mudchute Farm – Jan was now working there part-time, with Gábriel deputising at Ruskin Park Farm when she was off-site. Nothing had been taken, but there was serious damage to the main gates and several of the perimeter fences. Ade was concerned, and asked Charlie to look into heftier security.

She was showing out a visitor from a central London security firm, who'd detailed the possibilities of taller fences, alarms and cameras, all of which sounded draconian and against the vibe of the farm, when she found Franco standing with Joe, Jami and Charity in front of the long brick wall by the entrance, graffiti cans scattered around their feet. Franco was in the middle of spraying a long swoop of white along the wall.

Franco had sat up one night, just after Charlie had begun to drift to sleep, and turned on the light. He'd said that he wanted to do something for her. She'd woozily hummed as he'd pulled over a magazine and started scribbling on it, and woken her up again to show her a drawing of cows, sheep and hens bordering the letters *RPF*. 'A mural,' he'd said. 'For the entrance. It's a bit drab when you come in. Needs some colour, man.'

From her post-coital half-sleep, Charlie had tried not to be offended and instead taken the gesture as it was meant.

'On the house, obviously,' he'd said. 'Leave it to me.'

Now, by the entrance wall, Franco finished his arc of colour and turned round, removing his mask and giving her an irrepressible beam. 'Hello.'

She hadn't left it to him, but it had given her pleasure to see him enlist volunteers to help – with his charm, it hadn't taken much – and Ade had approved, especially as it was free.

'Check it, Charlie,' said Joe. 'This wall is gonna be peak.'

'Awesome,' she said, and hovered momentarily as Franco supervised Jami in spraying a tall sunflower stem.

Back in the office, she brought up her emails and methodically worked through the first few of them.

The door opened and Gábriel put his head in. There was the slightest hesitation before he spoke. 'You know that the wall is having graffiti put on it right now?'

'Yep,' said Charlie, quite aware that he hadn't mentioned Franco's name.

'OK,' he said. 'I didn't hear about that.'

'Sorry,' she said. 'I thought I told you.' She knew full well that was a lie, though hadn't confronted exactly why she'd not updated him. But she was growing in confidence at making her own decisions – she didn't have to tell him everything. She made several small movements that conveyed that she was terribly busy and could do with getting on with her work. When he didn't budge from the doorway, she looked up at him.

Gábriel came in properly, shut the door and leant on it, his hands tucked behind him. 'He's no good.'

'It's going to be great. It needs a bit of freshening up out there, and he's doing it for free.'

'I mean he's no good for you.'

'Says who?' she said, half-laughing, not quite believing his gall.

He gave her an obtuse look, that slight hint of challenge that she remembered from their argument in the barn. 'He's perfectly good,' she said. Clever, quick, handsome as fuck, created colourful murals free of charge, made all the blood rush to her crotch.

Gábriel's nod had a bitterly amused quality. 'I'm sure he is.'

Charlie had an urgent image of Gábriel and Franco with

very little on pacing around each other, and swiftly tried to dispel it. She folded her arms. 'What, then? What's your problem with him?'

'You can't trust him.' He spoke so simply, as if it were obvious. He still hadn't mentioned his name.

'Gábriel.' Her amusement was beginning to be replaced with an astonished outrage. 'It's not really any of your business.'

He opened his mouth as if to retort very quickly, and closed it again. A small tilt of his head. 'You let him give you a tattoo,' he said, with quiet disapproval. As if she was a child who had done something wrong.

Lydia had clearly announced Charlie's spontaneity through a loudspeaker. He'd said before that he liked it. 'I wanted a tattoo. *You* have one,' she said, forgetting that he probably hadn't known that she'd seen him changing one day, and now sounded like a peeping Charlie.

A small, puzzled frown. 'I thought about it for quite a lot longer,' he said.

That hurt. He didn't know how much her fern meant to her.

He shoved his hands deep into the pockets of his jeans. 'William Boadu is a good man. Why don't you go out with him if you want to go out with someone?'

She wanted to laugh. 'And that's what you approve of, is it?'

'Better than him. I know you don't think of— I know there's no point in—' He stopped and shook his head.

In what? she thought, and didn't ask. He'd said before, extremely lucidly, that he didn't think of her that way anymore. Hadn't he?

Gábriel sighed and shook his head again. 'But I will still tell you what I think. And what I think is that he's a bad guy.'

He was unbelievable. 'Gábriel.' She took a deep, careful breath, not wanting this to turn into their bust-up in the barn, him stalking off saying he'd quit. 'It's really unfair of you to speak to me like that.'

He didn't apologise, only gazed rather deeply at the floor.

It hurt. They'd been getting on really well; with Jan at Mudchute half the time, she depended on him, his patience and unfussy practicality. They were beginning to anticipate each other's needs before needing to ask. 'Look,' she said, calmly, trying to understand where he was coming from. 'I don't—'

He cut her off. 'I see him talking to Joe a lot,' he said.

She was taken aback, but only for a moment. 'So? Joe likes him. They all do.' Everyone but *you*, she thought.

'It looks kind of like a secret.'

She shook her head, utterly bemused. 'What sort of secret?'

He shrugged. 'I don't know. Just like, between them both.'

There was the sound of a child running past outside, wailing, and their mother running after them.

Gábriel was still watching her. 'I'm just telling you what I think.' That soulful blink, just for a second, cutting through the stubbornness. 'You can do what you want.' He pushed himself off the door, and left.

Charlie threw herself into emailing five security companies and searching for cameras, bashing at her keyboard more violently than usual, before going back out to the entrance.

The mural was almost complete, Jami and Charity beginning to tidy up the cans and cloth. Charlie watched Franco coach Joe through the final edging of some leaves in darker green, saw how much Joe was trying to impress him. Franco shapeshifted to suit everyone's manner, and thus it was here: he was pally, jokey, just his bro. Gábriel had misinterpreted it. He simply didn't like him. He must be jealous – she hated to think it, but it seemed the only explanation.

Franco caught sight of Charlie and stepped over to her. He had a dash of electric blue on his cheekbone that only made him more swoonworthy. 'What d'you reckon, goddess?'

It was lovely, a vibrant, more nuanced version of his sketches, filled not just with animals but pumpkins, courgettes, sunflowers and a cockerel with his head tipped back.

'It's gorgeous,' she said, feeling her heart soften. 'Thank you.'

He pulled her to him as if to kiss her, but drew back, his mouth achingly close, making her wait that extra moment to increase her need. 'My pleasure,' he said, and finally kissed her, before pulling away, and giving his phone to her. 'Come on. Socials.'

She watched him corral Joe, Jami and Charity in front of the mural, and coax a few small children to come and join them. He leant down, getting them all to give thumbs-ups whilst he pulled an exaggeratedly surprised face, children's presenter-style, though genuinely looked very proud. It was adorable.

Gábriel is wrong, Charlie thought, as she snapped away. He's just wrong.

SIXTEEN

An Impetuous Decision

The next morning, Joe came into the office with his forearm in a cast and a plucky gold-toothed grin. 'Check it out, Charlie.'

'Oh my God, Joe. What did you do?'

'Skateboard. Comes with the territory. Took one of the Brixton Bowls, din't I? Bam. Ambulance came and everything. Proper scenes.' He waved it in the air. 'Will you sign it?'

'Of course I will.' Charlie swivelled round in her chair to pick up a board pen. 'Are you sure you should be in? Shouldn't you be resting or something?'

'Nah. I'd do my nut in at home,' Joe said, quite mutedly.

Charlie remembered their conversation of months beforehand, and supposed it hadn't got much better. 'Well, just take it easy,' she said, writing SKATEBOARD HERO and her name on his plaster cast.

'Is Franco coming in?' Joe said. 'Thought he could draw something sick.'

'I don't think so,' said Charlie. 'You get on with him, don't you?' She should make totally sure that Gábriel was misguided in his assumption, however preposterous it had seemed.

'Yeah, he's cool, he's cool,' he said, nodding.

'What do you guys chat about?'

Joe's face was as vacantly angelic as a spotty sixteen-year-old's could be. 'Huh? Nothing much. Just, I dunno, football and tunes and shit.'

'Yeah? Just that?' She remembered about his brother in prison; perhaps Franco provided something of a reassuring masculine presence missing in his own home.

'Yeah.' Joe's eyes remained blank with a slight hint of confusion, or embarrassment. 'Is it cool to go? Gotta sort the ferret.'

Charlie followed him to the petting shed, where Marianne was introducing the chinchillas to a small group of school children with different learning abilities. It was a good environment for those with sensory sensitivities, calm and dimly-lit. She gave herself a moment to appreciate the way they connected with the animals, touching them with careful outstretched fingers; and to appreciate that she was part of making it happen.

Three of the children turned wide-eyed towards Joe, who was lifting Slick out of the wood and wire mesh cage with his good hand, speaking softly as the ferret wriggled. 'Nah, nah, you're not getting out today, fam. No prison break for you.' He gently asked one of the children to stand on a stool and place a bowl of water into the cage, before showing Slick to the other two, holding him firmly. It was lovely to see him interacting with such maturity. Charlie wondered if he had potential to eventually take some of Marianne's classes in a couple of years. The kids seemed to love him.

'Aphrodite, Poppy, Limenia, Nymphaea.'

One Sunday afternoon, Charlie and Franco were in the Hayward Gallery, escaping the humidity amongst the cool concrete walls. Modern and contemporary painting ticked her boxes as well as photography, but she didn't know Cy Twombly, the subject of this retrospective, very well.

Franco, on the other hand, was a huge fan. He was currently reading a pencilled list of names from a column on a large canvas, with 'Venus' scrawled in bright red in the middle. 'It's like he wrote it just for you,' he said. 'Dude's giving me loads of good ideas. Oh, look, even better. There's us.' He turned Charlie round to look at the opposite wall.

This canvas had smudged images that looked unavoidably like buttocks and breasts, with the words 'Venus' and 'Adonis' in the artist's distinctive, child-like scrawl.

'So humble,' she said.

'I'm just saying it like I see it,' he said, grinning. 'Look, we're everywhere.' He glided to the far corner, to more Venuses and Adonises amongst other classical names.

She loved how absorbed he was in every moment, gazing rapt at every painting before his attention was captured by the next. She loved how his arse looked in those jeans, the way they sat so perfectly on his hips, the sparkle of his gold chain at the base of his neck. She loved— God, she loved— *Stop it*, she told herself. You have been seeing him for five weeks. Almost everything made her think of summer and sex; the huge canvases seemed loaded with virility and fertility, suggestions of overripe fruits here, the curve of his lower back, the crocuses they had flattened in the park that time.

They rejoined in front of a large canvas, the lower half a

sludgy brown and green, with words scratched in crayon above it.

'The Wilder Shores of Love,' read Franco, quixotically, and looked at Charlie.

She shivered and walked over to the next one, a load of dark, abstract scribblings that represented the seduction of Leda by Zeus in the form of a swan. Hearts, an anguished mouth, and possibly genitalia.

He caught up. 'I bloody love this place.' He put his arm over her shoulder. 'I bloody love you, too.'

Her blood fizzed. 'What?'

'You heard,' he said, grinning, and gifted her each word again one at a time, as if they were jewels. 'I. Love. You.' He raised his eyebrows, two perfect cutlasses, and looked as wickedly amused as ever. 'And you love me.'

A momentary dizziness. She wasn't supposed to be rushing headlong into things, like the old Charlie. But right now her heart was tugging her forwards. She took a deep breath. 'I—'

He lightly pressed a finger to her lips. 'No need. I know it.'

They sat down on a blonde-wood bench in front of four massive canvases that represented each of the seasons.

'I need to ask you something,' she said.

'Anything.' He plucked a stray hair off her jacket and blew it deftly from his fingers. He turned to face her, an arm on the back of the bench.

'How do you get on with Joe?'

'Joe who?' He looked perfectly impassive for a moment. 'The kid on the farm?' His brow furrowed. 'How d'you mean?'

'Just...' She looked at the huge summer painting, the

dripping yolky yellow, the spine-like red lines. 'I just want to check that it's cool between you. Nothing untoward.'

'Untoward?'

'Yeah.' It already sounded absurd. 'I heard that you were quite cosy.'

He looked intrigued, archly quizzical. 'He's a good lad. A bit try-hard, maybe.' He cupped his hands in a bowl and deftly assumed a doe-eyed expression. 'Please sir, can I have some more?' His face dropped; became honest. 'No, sounds like he's got a pretty rough home life in there. Poor wee tyke.'

'So, he hasn't, I don't know, asked you for anything? Or you from him?'

He looked baffled. 'Like what?' He shut one eye and assumed a camper version of the accent of many London estate teenagers. 'Who's been grassing on me?'

'Franco, please. I'm serious.' Somehow, she didn't want to tell him that it was Gábriel who'd cast doubt on him.

'It's all above board.' He shrugged. 'He's just some kid. I rib him about Chelsea, he ribs me about Arsenal. He bangs on about South London MCs, I pretend to know who he's talking about.' A self-deprecating grin. He clearly had no idea what he was being accused of.

Of course Joe hung on his every word. Franco was magnetic, and not just to her. She felt deeply relieved. 'Yeah, that's what I thought. Forget it.' She did love him, she thought.

They continued to gaze at the quartet of paintings. A woman moved slowly, standing still in front of each one, and an elderly gentleman held his audio guide to his ear and leant a little to the left.

'Hey. Let's go away,' Franco said.

'Away where?'

'Berlin.'

'Why Berlin?'

'Why not? Because it is beautiful and singular. Just like you. Let's go next week. We can look at as much art as you like.'

'I can't go next week. My holiday's not 'til the end of the month.'

'We'll go then,' said Franco, as if it was all decided. 'You graft your arse off on your little farmstead. Come away with me.'

'You could sell butter to cows, couldn't you?' Her dad's expression.

'I already have.'

He winked, before leaning over and kissing her neck, and she let her eyes sink into the autumnal painting in front of her, into its puddles of colour, dark green and black and blood-red.

Berlin, Charlie thought, sitting on her bed that night, moisturising her hands. She'd never been; hadn't done a city break of any kind for a while. Franco had an audition so she would have to slightly rearrange her holiday time and miss a board meeting to make it work.

But she deserved it, she thought. She definitely deserved it.

———

'Told you it was cool,' said Franco, coming back with two chilled bottles of Weißbier.

Charlie was currently reclining on a deckchair, her toes digging into the sand, soaking up the German sun, which was far fiercer than the English version. They were at a ramshackle graffitied beach club by the Spree, with Afro-Caribbean-centred street art and food stalls everywhere. The sand was imported, and reggae thumped from various ragged speakers. It was very cool.

Franco leant over her, put one chilled beer bottle on the sliver of exposed skin at her belly, before kissing her, a slow, sweet summer taste. He pulled back. 'Look at you,' he said, astonished, delighted. 'God. You look delectable.'

'Thank you very much,' she said, taking the beer from him and putting her shades back down, unable to help the satisfied smug-cat beam that spread across her face. Sun-kissed and Franco-kissed, she thought, and couldn't decide which was better.

Berlin dazzled. They were staying in Neukölln, a hotel with massive concrete pillars in the foyer and a painted bear up on its hind legs. Their room had exposed brickwork, several lightbulbs in mismatched jars hanging from the ceiling, and handcrafted espresso coffee soaps. Franco had asked Charlie to cover it for now, as his credit cards had reached their limits; truthfully, if she'd known she was paying for it all, she probably would have gone for something more budget. But, on the other hand, she hadn't had a holiday in so long, what with trying to claw back her debts. She was allowed to treat herself.

They did the touristy things, Franco graciously leading the tour of the Wall, the Holocaust Museum, the Brandenburg Gate, even though he'd seen it all several times. He bought Charlie pretzels and made her try ten different types of sausage. They looked at galleries old and new, and visited a vintage movie and theatre props shop, trying on wigs and army jackets and Regency skirts. There was the novelty of smoking bars, their favourite being a candlelit gin bar with battered brown leather sofas, East German film posters and a jazz trombonist crooning mournfully in the corner. She'd never had so much fun. Alex had always been going on about 360-degrees virtual reality videos or the benefits of online education, but it had never enthused her. Franco brought things to life, and he brought a part of *her* to life that had been lying dormant; he made her feel zingy, made her look at things with extra attention and enchantment. A constant head-rush.

She tried not to feel too guilty about the farm, and the three days when staff would be short due to her shifting her holiday time. She had given Lydia lots of her extra duties, though organisational and administrative skills were not her housemate's strong point. 'I mean, I'll do it,' Lydia had said, 'because I'm your wingman and everything, but I won't be as good. No one's as good as you.' Charlie had promised to give Lydia some cash on the sly, and had also persuaded Marianne to fill in a little bit. Her phone call to Ade in re-arranging her holiday time so last-minute had included the palest of white lies about an ill friend (Franco had an old mate in Kreuzberg recovering from leukaemia). Gábriel, whom she'd asked to represent her at the board meeting, had said it was fine, but the slightly incredulous look he'd given her just before he'd nodded stayed with her, like a small, precise bruise under the skin.

'Hey, you.' Franco was gently nudging her.

'Hey,' Charlie croaked, under the duvet in the hotel. They'd been out until 4am, having queued for three hours outside Berghain, before giving up and going to a scuzzy electro club instead. It felt far too early to be awake.

Franco was leaning over her, his face very close, looking irritatingly unlike someone who'd only had four hours' sleep.

Charlie prodded the skin of his cheek, which didn't seem to make a mark, before putting the duvet over her head. He had given her half a pill and all she could remember was jumping up and down a lot. Her ears were ringing.

Franco flung himself onto his back, putting the duvet over his head, too, and raising his legs so that it made a tent shape above them. 'You're the best thing ever.'

'*You* are,' she said. 'Except when I'm trying to get my beauty sleep. Then you are very annoying.'

'You don't need any.' He rolled his head towards her. 'Hey. Let's get engaged.'

'Very funny.'

'I'm not joking.'

'You're always joking.'

'Not about this.'

'I've known you eight whole weeks.'

'They used to get married at the drop of a hat back in the day.' His smile had an incredible knack of being part angelic, part utter devil.

Charlie watched him, waiting for the joke to finally rise to the surface. 'You're a very eccentric human being,' she said, wishing her heart wasn't fluttering around in her throat.

'I'm romantic,' he said, with another fiendishly dreamy smile. 'You've made me that way.'

They lay together underneath the duvet, a soft, muffled world. The only world. She could feel the calm, measured Charlie she'd been working so hard to find tussling with the excited, throw-caution-to-the-wind Charlie. *Wrestling*.

'Just enjoy it. Us, here, together,' she said, shutting her eyes. 'It's lovely.'

'I am. It is. But I'm always looking for the next thing. And the next thing is…' He started humming a slow version of the

'Wedding March' through closed lips and puffed cheeks, as if emanating from a very wheezy wind-up organ.

She couldn't help melting into giggles. 'I'm ignoring you now,' she said, and put her hand over her eyes, feigning snores.

'Pah,' said Franco, before suddenly moving, straddling her on all fours, the duvet settling around them in a new way. 'Now, lie still. I'm going to make you come four times.'

Charlie took her hand away from her eyes and gazed into his. 'That I can say yes to,' she said, and let him do just that.

A gentler day. They walked by the river, hand in hand, and Charlie thought about divided spaces, older and newer ones, and how her body seemed to be split into two clear halves right now. Heart. Head. Except even her head was getting in on the preposterous act of contemplating being married to Franco, a thought starting in one moderate place before spiralling out into a fantasy of cosy nights in followed by fabulous sex, him making her dinner, fabulous sex again, her working at the farm, him treading the boards in the West End or opening a proper photography show at the White Cube (celebrated with fabulous sex). A glamorous, handsome, unpredictable duo. Today, Franco was more tender, spoke softly, bought her lunch. They looked at a market, stopped in front of a jewellery stall that was selling stainless steel silver rings. He picked one up and placed it on the fourth finger of Charlie's left hand, whilst the silversmith looked between them both, smiling. 'Fits perfectly,' Franco said, before returning it. Grinning.

Later that evening, they went out to an exhibition opening at a gallery in Wedding – perfect, Charlie thought, though it was pronounced with a 'V'. Franco had received a message about it with two hours' notice, which apparently was the fashionable thing for Berlin galleries. The space was a former brothel, an unreconstructed square room with cracked walls and lurid pink lighting. A topless man had performed a contorted dance, LED lights stuffed into his mouth, and now the band – two girls with synths, shouting, with a sign saying BASIC WITCH hung haphazardly. Franco was of course making friends with everyone around him, though always making sure that Charlie was involved in the conversation. Right now, their company was a Japanese woman with a shaved head who wore an asymmetric structured black dress and huge metal earrings that looked like weapons, and whose deadpan humour made them both fall about laughing. Tired as she was, Charlie still felt vivacious and alive; she was clearly hanging out with the coolest people on the planet. She'd missed this; it was the complete opposite of the farm, with its quiet, cute, ramshackle nature. Then she felt a tiny flush of guilt, and made a mental note to check in with Lydia again.

On their final day, Franco and Charlie took the U-Bahn out northwest of the city to Flughafensee, one of Berlin's many peripheral swimming lakes. It was a beautiful tree-lined expanse of water with sandy coves, and was busy on this hot summer's day. Children tugged their inflatable rings and dinghies to and from the shore, and people spread out their picnics under parasols, the calm sporadically interrupted by the huge roar of the planes taking off from the nearby airport. Charlie, unused to outdoor swimming, had taken a little bit of coaxing to get into the cool, opaque water; Franco, on the other hand, moved through water with a supple agility, submerged and blew bubbles, did handstands, and pulled her to him for several very public aquatic embraces.

Now, he lay next to her on his back, face rapturously lifted to the sun, and she watched the droplets dry on his torso, pearl by pearl diminishing, disappearing. It was unsurprising that he had drawn looks as he'd emerged from the water: his slicked-back hair and slim, muscled figure, festooned in tattoos, made him look like some sort of naughty water god. But there was more to him than the obvious, visible attractions.

They'd talked half the night, more deeply than they ever had. He spoke of how confused he had been as a kid when his mum brought the odd man home, thinking each one was his dad and being heartbroken each time it didn't work out. How he'd helped his mum with the nannying in the early days, and how reading stories to kids only a few years younger than himself had given him a taste for acting. She talked about her mum's depression after Jools, how she would sit staring out of the window into the garden without really seeing. How hard it was for Charlie not to resent Casey for replacing her big sister. Franco had kissed the beads of her friendship bracelet and held her while she sobbed, and she'd felt achingly raw afterwards.

'This,' he said now, his eyes still closed. 'There is nothing better.'

'Agreed,' she said, still taking him in.

He stretched, lean and lazy, and clasped his hands behind his head. 'Seriously,' he said. 'You and me, here right now. It's a peach of a moment.' He opened his eyes, looked at her with a long, penetrative gaze, as if considering something philosophical. 'Wanna know a story about this lake?' he said.

'OK,' she said, a little flummoxed. 'Story me.'

He pushed up onto his elbows, and a thin rivulet of water

ran from his clavicle to his stomach. 'There's a drowned prince in there,' he said, nodding towards the lake which shimmered in the late afternoon sun.

'Uh-huh, sure there is,' she said, but he had a lovely storytelling manner, and she couldn't help being drawn in.

'It's true. Prince... Wolfgang.' He nodded an assent to himself. 'He was the only child of two very moody parents, who wanted him to marry some fat heifer of a bird from Bavaria.'

'Charming,' said Charlie. 'Body shaming much.'

He grinned. 'But Prince Wolfgang was fucking madly in love with a sweet country lass with nothing to her name but a worsted smock and a flock of sheep. They would meet here by the lake – before it was next to an airport, obviously – and he would declare his love and promise that one day he'd marry her. They decided to elope and he got her a lovely shiny wedding ring. Screw the fat heifer from Bavaria! But'—he gave a dramatic gasp—'tragedy struck. She went swimming in here one day, full of beans at the thought of marrying her hench German princeling, and also to wash herself because being poor meant zero baths, mate. Stinky lady. But she went out too far, and drowned. Choked on her own sick and everything. When the prince heard, he came to the lake, put the wedding ring he was going to give her on a chain around his neck and flung himself in too, because life wasn't worth living without her. The. End.'

'What a lovely, cheerful tale,' said Charlie. 'CBeebies Bedtime Story are beating your door down at home right now.'

He grinned and peered out towards the lake. 'And now,' he said, getting up again, for as much as he had revelled in the peach of the moment, it was over and he was on to the next one, 'I'm going to find him.' He rifled through his leather satchel, bringing out goggles, and without even looking back, jogged down to the shoreline.

'He is insane,' Charlie said to herself, but she couldn't help it. He was funny, affectionate, unpredictable, and so, so beautiful.

She watched him glide straight into the water, leaving a ribboning ripple in his wake, a broad, graceful front crawl that took him beyond all the kids and the other swimmers. She sat up, shading her eyes as he swam right out into the centre of the lake, and then... a flip of his legs and he had disappeared beneath the surface. There was no sign of him for several seconds.

'Yes, yes, Franco,' she said to herself. 'Very amusing.'

The several seconds became ten; of course, he knew she'd be watching him, and wanted to keep his ruse going. But ten seconds stretched out to half a minute, then a minute or more – she wasn't timing it, but surely it had been a minute by now? – and the water out there remained glossily flat. 'Oh my God,' she said, and put her hand to her chest, heart suddenly rollercoastering. With a lurching panic, she rose and ran down to the shore. She didn't know the German for *please help, my super-hot boyfriend is drowning*. He had got caught in some weeds, or was seized by cramp, or his heart had stopped, as hers seemed to have and she couldn't lose him and—

There. A head, two arms, and he was visible again, waving at her. What was that poem she'd studied at school? *Not waving but drowning?* She was about to call to the large man standing with a kayak and wearing only a very revealing thong, but Franco did seem to be swimming again, back towards her. He occasionally stopped and waved again, shouting something, but she didn't really take it in, flooded with relief that he wasn't dying or dead but thoroughly alive and just a total drama queen. She waited with her feet in the warm shallows as he passed the kids and finally stood, hip-deep, wading towards her like a more excitable Daniel Craig.

'You gave me a heart attack,' she shouted to him, but he was saying something back and didn't hear her.

'I found it,' he said as he reached her, looking oddly jubilant. 'I only fucking found it.'

'Found what?' she said.

He had his hand at the base of his neck, was holding his chain, pulling it out a little. 'I fucking found it, Charlie!'

'What are you talking about?' she said. People were starting to look over.

He waded to her, still holding his chain, and she saw something glint there that wasn't just his little gold cross but something larger, and silver. A glint of turquoise. 'The prince's ring,' he said, grinning. 'I bloody well found it.'

The kids in the shallows were watching. The barely clad kayak man was watching.

She was caught in a mixture of relief and bafflement. 'But you just made that story up.'

'Nope,' he said, and his smile was as glittering as the sun on the water. He was reaching out behind his neck, and unclasping his chain, holding his palm out to catch whatever was on it. He pinched it between two fingers and knelt down, dripping, in the sand, holding it out to her. A ring.

'Oh, my gosh,' she said, in a voice that was somewhere outside herself. 'What are you doing?'

'Fulfilling a fairy tale,' he said. 'Following my heart.'

The ring was the one he'd picked up and shown to her at the market yesterday, a turquoise stone on a silver band. He must have stolen back and bought it when he'd gone out for their coffees this morning.

'Franco,' she said, laughing, utterly self-conscious of the gentle murmurs of the bathers who had all begun to take note. 'You're mad. You've got sunstroke.'

'I've got Charlie-stroke,' he said. 'I'm fucking raging with it.' He held the ring out to her. 'Charlie Hughes,' he said, and his voice was decidedly unquiet. 'I would very much like you to marry me.'

There were some understated cheers around them. One little kid screamed something excitable in German. Two or three people clapped, and someone was filming it on their phone.

Charlie put her hands at the back of her neck, then on her cheeks. 'Franco,' she said, in barely more than a whisper. Was he actually doing this? Proposing to his extremely recent girlfriend, on a German beach, with a large (almost nude) man watching them?

'*Ja!*' shouted a woman. '*Sag ja!*'

Franco was grinning up at her, nothing but easy charm and confidence. 'Go on,' he said. And winked.

SEVENTEEN

An Announcement – New Arrivals

The summer stretches out into September, the days still delightfully warm and golden amongst the plane trees around South London. The mornings, however, are brisker, and today's wind causes the first autumn leaves to skitter in circles on the pavements. On the farm, the cries of goats and children are almost indistinguishable. A toddler eats straw picked up from the ground. The two sows are ready to burst, their pregnancies visible to all in these last weeks, and a family gathers at the fence. A girl with a giraffe rucksack makes oinking snoring noises at the slumbering Ethel. 'She's snoring like your brother,' says her dad. 'More like your father,' says her mother, giggling. Blackberries cluster in the brambles by the railway line, and are picked by adult members of the green gym club, to be made into plentiful crumbles and fools by Leila. By the café entrance, several farm staff are currently clustered round Charlie, who is reluctantly showing them her engagement ring.

• • •

Everyone on the beach had been watching. Franco had gone to a lot of trouble, sneaking the ring into his hand when he'd picked up his goggles, holding his breath and threading it onto his chain underwater, in the centre of the lake. Of course she'd said yes. She would give the ring back when they were on their own somewhere quiet, and tell him that his crazy, theatrical gesture was the loveliest thing ever, but it was far too early in their relationship. She would do it when they were at their hotel, she'd told herself on the U-Bahn back from the lake. She would do it when they were on the plane back to London, she told herself in the hotel room, as they were packing. She would do it when they landed, she told herself on the plane, rubbing the ring with her thumb. She would do it when they were back at the cottage, she told herself as they landed, hands clasped. Sometime soon, she told herself, more faintly, when they were having sex in her bedroom.

'It's lovely, Charlie,' Marianne said, delicately holding Charlie's hand, examining the thin-beaten silver band and small turquoise stone. 'Turquoise is a very positive stone.'

Charlie's intention to make a quiet entrance after her week away had been wishful thinking. When she came down to the kitchen on Sunday morning, Franco having left early, she found herself continuing her experimental wearing of the ring as she made her coffee. Lydia had come down, and had – clearly possessing some sort of engagement ring radar – seen it immediately; after several ear-splitting shrieks, she spent the rest of the morning singing an atonal version of Beyoncé's 'Single Ladies' in a breathy voice while gyrating and flinging her fingers in the air. Charlie hadn't corrected her, but in fact spent all of Sunday curled up on the sofa, looking at her hand. Engaged. She appeared to be engaged.

Now Lydia had blabbed to everyone working on the farm today, including Gábriel, whom Charlie had hoped to avoid for a little longer.

'It brings good fortune if given by the right person,' Marianne was saying.

'Thanks,' she said, and glanced at Gábriel, who was standing there, saying nothing in a very loud sort of way.

His eyes flickered to hers. 'Congratulations,' he said, and it was absolutely impossible to know what he thought about it. He was wearing gardening gloves rolled up at the wrist and holding a pair of large secateurs by his leg. He seemed to have started growing a beard.

'Very healing, too, Charlie,' said Marianne. 'Lots of self-realisation and balance. Right. I've got to sort out bamboo poles for those pesky broad beans.' She ambled off.

'So fucking romantic, man,' said Lydia. 'When is someone going to propose to me literally just after meeting me? Come on, Gábriel, now's your chance.' She puckered her lips in a cartoonish fashion.

Gábriel, still looking at Charlie in the same impassive way, only registered Lydia when she hit him lightly on the arm, before blinking and giving her a reluctant smile. 'You're too good for me,' he said.

'Yeah, *right*,' Lydia said. 'Number ten to number two more like. I know it and I'm fine with it!' She yelled over to Joe, who was shunting RiRi out of the way of the gate so he could leave the pen. 'Oi, Joe! Marry me!'

Joe glanced up and made a sound of some disgust. 'Nah, man, no way in hell. I'd go gay first.'

Lydia was already bounding up to him, singing 'Here

Comes the Bride' whilst Joe shoved his body against the gate to stop her getting in, shouting 'I'm gay' over and over again.

Gábriel and Charlie stood side by side, watching the madness. He took his gloves off, one at a time, his forearms lightly scratched from the holly he'd been cutting. The summer had turned his skin the lightest bronze.

Neither of them said anything. She thought she heard him take a breath as if he would, before he gave her a nod and said he had work to do.

Several days later, Franco messaged while she was at the farm to say he would come by. He'd been slowly packing up his stuff from the squat and had persuaded a friend with a mid-sized van to drive it all down to South London. In truth, it would be a bit of a squeeze with three of them in the cottage, but Lydia had been perfectly gracious – possibly even grateful. Charlie promised that they would get their own place soon enough, though she would have to start saving up again after Berlin.

She came out to say hello to the new young offenders' group on its trial run. Two of the boys were looking warily at the alpacas with squared shoulders and jutting chins, though in truth they were no match for the woolly trio and soon got on with their work.

Marianne was shadowing their specialist community worker, and wandered over after a few minutes. 'Well, they're a lovely bunch,' she said to Charlie. 'Everyone's equal when they're mucking out the beasts.'

'Definitely,' said Charlie. 'Hey, thanks again for covering for me. That was really good of you.' She'd heard from several people that Lydia had ended up delegating rather a lot of the admin work to her, after getting in a hysterical tangle over spreadsheets that she had been under strict instructions not to fiddle with, only making Charlie feel more guilty.

'Oh, it's no problem,' said Marianne unfussily. 'Takes me back to the world of work; reminds me why I retired.' A soft, weathered smile. 'And I know how someone can sweep you off your feet. I think it's rather lovely.'

Yes, thought Charlie. Why wait for two and a half years to pass, until they'd amassed shared experiences and enough joint houseplants for it to be deemed socially appropriate? Why be sensible when each breath might be her – or his – last? She loved him. That was enough.

'Far too much disunity in this country at the moment,' Marianne was saying. 'I much prefer unity. Isn't that your betrothed with Will Boadu over there?'

Charlie turned sharply to see Franco talking to Will by the entrance to the herb garden and allotments. Franco was in his deep-burgundy vest, those many tattoos on show, leaning on the gate proprietarily and with a broad smile on his face. Will had his back to Charlie, and it was impossible to see his expression.

She walked over, a strange feeling of dread in the pit of her stomach.

'Here she is,' said Franco, raising his eyebrows. 'My fiancée.'

Will turned. 'I gather congratulations are in order,' he said unreadably.

'Hi,' said Charlie. 'Um. Yes.' She gave an awkward laugh. 'Whirlwind romance and all that.'

'She couldn't resist me,' said Franco, hooking his little finger around hers. 'Could you, babe?'

Charlie gently disentangled it. 'Um. No. What can I do for you, Will?'

'Oh. I'm here to see Ade, actually. Our monthly lunchtime pint.' He looked rather drawn and distracted.

'How are you, Will?'

'Oh, I've been better,' Will said. 'My father's health is—' He cleared his throat, and glanced uncomfortably at Franco. 'Not great.'

'Oh, I'm so sorry. Can I do anything?'

'No, no,' said Will, glancing between them again. 'I shall leave you to your—' He glanced at Franco again, who was watching them with something of a bantam cock in his stance. 'Yes. Congratulations.'

They watched him go.

'Well, he's got a thing for you,' said Franco.

'No, he hasn't,' said Charlie. He really hadn't, not after everything.

'He definitely has.' His eyes narrowed, and for a moment, he looked like someone you wouldn't want to meet in a dark alley. 'Do you need me to fuck him up?'

'*No*, Franco.'

'What? I'd be defending my wife-to-be's honour. I'll do it, you know. Pistols at dawn.' He twirled an imaginary gun with one forefinger before his hand deftly transformed into the weapon itself. The countenance of a dandyish sergeant.

'Franco, leave him be. He's a good person.'

'Hmm,' said Franco. 'We'll see.' He leant in for a kiss, and she let him, all forgiven. Just.

'All set then, mate?' Lydia said.

'Yep,' said Charlie, wrapping her tiger-print scarf around her neck.

'Because, and literally no offence or anything, but you look as sick as a parakeet.'

'Parrot.'

Lydia sniffed. 'I'm keeping the references local. Don't at me.' She nodded down at Charlie's hand. 'It's properly happening, then.'

Charlie glanced at the ring that was still very much on her left hand. She really meant to have sorted this by now, but she couldn't help it. She *liked* the feeling of being engaged. Instead, Franco was coming over to Spenser Road for Sunday lunch and they were going to announce it.

'Reckon he can win over the famalam?'

She felt a little faint. 'I really have no idea.'

He did, of course. He was half an hour late, but full of light apologies about South London train confusion, and bearing an expensive bottle of chianti and a sizeable bouquet of flowers. He showered compliments on the house, its décor, Nellie's headscarf, and the smell of roast lamb emanating from the kitchen.

Whilst Charlie felt horribly nervous, a lump lodged in her throat, Franco was full of breezy confidence, as if meeting the parents of his fiancée was something he did quite regularly. Over lunch, he sympathised with Aidan over the increasing amount of exams in primary schools, and with Nellie on the decreasing resources in hospitals. He delivered a succession of witty anecdotes about his attempts to meet various famous actors during his bit-parts, and the fan video he once made and sent to Tom Cruise asking for a role in the next *Mission*

Impossible film. All the while, he kept a hand on top of Charlie's, a sense of casual ownership.

Only one of the company remained impervious.

'Charlie's told me all about you,' Franco said to Casey. 'You're a space genius!'

'Bit more complicated than that,' her sister said, stuffing half a Yorkshire pudding in her mouth.

'I'm sure,' said Franco, blissfully undeterred. 'I'd love to know more.'

Casey rolled her eyes. 'Have you got three years?'

Franco flashed Casey a thoroughly un-insulted grin, before looking at Charlie. 'I'm sure I've got tons of time.'

Casey took another Yorkshire pudding.

'That all went well,' said Franco, at the front door, shrugging on his leather jacket. He was going to a drinks meeting with the director of his upcoming play.

Charlie felt knackered, stupefied, though some of that might have been down to Aidan's sticky toffee pudding with whisky-laced custard. 'Yeah. I guess.' ('Right,' Aidan had said when they made their announcement. Nellie had initially looked between them with her mouth open, and Casey had almost choked on a pickled walnut.)

'See you back at ours later, then,' Franco said.

Ours. The word slipped off his tongue so easily. But it sounded good. Safe. 'Sure.'

'Beautiful,' said Franco, and leaned in for a kiss. He hovered after he pulled away, very close, the balm of his breath on her cheek. 'Beautiful,' he said again, practically a purr.

• • •

After watching him sashay down the road – he knew full well she was watching – Charlie went back to the living room, where her dad was sitting on the sofa and clutching a glass of port. Nellie was loading the dishwasher, and she decided that one parent was probably enough for the initial debrief. He put his newspaper on the side table when she sat next to him.

'Well, Charlie.' He folded his hands on his substantial belly. 'I'm glad you're happy, you know me, but…'

'But what?'

'Is it not quite sudden, this? Of course, Mum and I will trumpet marriage to the bleedin' heavens, and believe you me, I only want the best for my girls—'

'What, Dad? Just say it.'

Aidan put his chin to his chest and gave a great, bearish exhalation behind closed lips. When he spoke, his voice was gentle, with the slightest hint of admonishment. 'Charlie, we all have our ways of muddling through.'

Charlie felt the stirrings of a familiar prickle of nausea in her chest, because she knew where this was going.

'Casey looks up to the stars for meaning,' continued Aidan. 'Your mum puts so much of herself into all her patients. I look out for my little ones at school. And you'—he reached over and touched her nose, very lightly—'my YOLO girl. You fly into things with such enthusiasm, and I'm not trying to stop you, no good father would. But…' His expression softened, gracefully, into a well-worn grief that was almost comfortable. 'Just because your sister had such a precious, short life doesn't mean yours is going to be cut off in its prime. You can take your sweet time about it.'

By now, the prickling nausea had reached her throat; the feeling she always had when she remembered being told by him, after he'd come back from the hospital, that Jools was truly gone. Her dad saw right through her, to blood and bone.

'I try, Dad,' she said, rather quietly. 'But I can't help it.'

Aidan nodded, and sighed as he put his arms over his broad chest. 'I understand. I just mean that some things like to brew, marinate, *percolate*. You don't have to get married straightaway.' He wagged a playful finger. 'No shotgun wedding in Gretna Green or Las Vegas, please. You can be low-key about it. Chillax.'

Charlie smiled. She could absolutely see Franco in Vegas, dressed up as a sexier Elvis, throwing a handful of hundred dollar bills that he'd just won at the roulette table into the air. 'You know no one says that anymore.'

'I do and I say you can chillax. You two have plenty more to discover about each other.'

Charlie sank back into the sofa. It was impossible to chillax about Franco. He left her breathless. But being engaged was definitely enough for now. 'I promise, Dad.'

Aidan watched her for a while. 'If you're happy, then I'm happy,' he said, rather pragmatically, and put a palm on Charlie's knee. 'Now. Let's watch some telly. There's a documentary on grime on BBC4.'

Casey was less generous. 'Why you marrying him?' she said, leaning against the wall in the hallway, pulling chewing gum out of her mouth in a long string as Charlie put her boots on.

'Because I love him.'

Her sister made a scoffing sound. 'Seriously, marriage. It's so over. Institutionalised bullshit.'

Charlie straightened. 'Some time, Casey, it's going to hit

you, you know. One day you're going to look across the room and see someone—'

Another noisy, disgusted exhalation. 'Oh, my life. Seriously.'

'You will. You'll see someone, and your legs will go and your heart will feel massive and you'll know you'd do anything for them.'

Casey chewed her gum with stoicism. 'You've gone mad in the head.'

Charlie couldn't exactly disagree.

Phone. Buzzing. Charlie rolled over, and Franco made a small, distant moan. She picked it up. A message from Gábriel.

Morning
Can you come in
Something's happened

She sat up immediately, pulling some of the duvet with her. 6.45am.

Franco made a muffled protest. 'Literally middle of the night,' he mumbled, his hair awry, eyes still closed.

'I've got to go to work.' She slid out of bed.

'Way too early. Evil.'

'I think there's an emergency,' she said, and leant over, kissing him on the ear. 'Good luck in your rehearsal.'

. . .

She caught the bus, sending Gábriel several messages on the way, none of which he replied to. Even when she called him, he didn't pick up. It must be really bad.

By the time she reached the farm, several calamitous scenarios had presented themselves, though for once, she didn't automatically blame herself. The barn had burned down this time, for real. Sheep had escaped. An alpaca had turned cannibal and eaten the others. But when she closed the gate behind her, the farm seemed serene. No smoke. No anguished baa-ing.

She checked every building and pen. Gábriel was waiting for her outside the pig pen.

'What is it?' she said, out of breath. 'What's happened?'

He looked solemn. 'It's in here,' he said, and turned to the shed.

She followed.

Inside the pig shed there was the thick smothering smell of straw and faeces, and she was aware of a strange, otherworldly burbling. Of movement, and pinkness.

Charlie made a small, soft sound, and her heart exploded. Piglets had arrived.

The shed was divided by brick into two halves, with a sow lying in each. Annie, still pregnant, slumbered in one, and in the other, Ethel was surrounded by countless piglets.

Adult pigs might be said to have singular charms, but they were wide, bristly beasts. The piglets, on the other hand, were the most adorable creatures she had seen in her entire life. Better than the lambs and the goat kids put together. They were tiny, far smaller than the piglets she'd seen last year, a tawny ginger – the skin pink underneath the hair – and variously black-spotted. Amongst generous heaps of straw, they tottered on quivering legs before tumbling onto their sides or bottoms. There was a gentle high-pitched babble emanating from most of them, utterly unlike the guttural snorts of adult pigs.

Gábriel was watching her, his expression having lost its solemnity.

'You know you gave me a coronary,' Charlie said. 'I thought the farm had burnt down.'

A small smile. 'Thought you would like to see them before everyone else.'

One popped its head out from a pile of straw, before emerging and shoving another, which fell over. Every piglet looked different.

'How many are there?'

'Ten.'

'Were you here?'

'No. Ethel just got on with it overnight.'

'Slaying it,' said Charlie, under her breath. Ethel was heaving herself onto her feet, nosing one of the piglets. 'Oh, *look*.' This one was perhaps her favourite, more black than gingery pink, big patches on its body and a whole black ear. Gábriel leant over the brick wall, scooped it up in one hand, and passed it to Charlie.

She hardly dared breathe. The little piglet in her arms was so light, its hair far more silken than the wiriness of its mother's; elfish ears and wet, glossy black eyes. 'You're a proper little plum pudding, aren't you?' she said. 'Living up to your breed.' It emitted a tiny squeak. 'I think I'm going to die of the cuteness,' she whispered, and suddenly felt exceptionally broody.

There was a quiet laugh from Gábriel, who was sitting on

the wall, watching the others. There were whisper-thin lines at the sides of his eyes, and dark blotches underneath them.

'How come you were here so early?'

He looked over. 'Couldn't sleep,' he said.

For half an hour, the two of them sat with a piglet each, swapping for another occasionally and watching the rest as they explored their new world. They moved floppily, or slept, all screwed-up eyes and perfect candy-pink snouts. Gábriel's was propped in the crook of his elbow and he was gently scratching between its ears. Charlie stroked the black spots on her own piglet with the back of her forefinger. She placed it back in the pen and watched it rejoin two of its siblings, head-butting one and nuzzling the belly of another. A little trio.

This was what had begun to make her feel truly good – the rhythms of the farm, the surety of breeding and births, sowing and growing; tasks that always had to be done to keep everything rolling along smoothly; workmates relying on each other.

She put her hand on her lap, her left hand in the well of the right, the ring heavily present on her finger. It felt too tight. Perhaps she would need to get it re-sized. She rubbed the pad of her thumb over the silver, and remembered what Aidan had said. As she looked again at the trio of piglets, she thought of Casey's derision towards her and felt a small wave of melancholy, one that brought her hand reflexively to her chest.

'Are you OK?' Gábriel said.

She hummed a rather non-committal response, and rested her head against the brick. Her head hurt. Her *heart* hurt.

She felt his gaze rest on her for a moment longer, before he shifted, letting down one piglet and picking up another. It wriggled a little before settling in his arms. He must have begun growing his beard while she was away. The sandy glints at his jaw were not far off the colour of the piglets' hair. 'I like pigs,' he said. 'They listen good. I mean, well.'

'Yeah? You talk to them?'

'They know all my secrets.' He briefly touched its nose to his, and rubbed its head.

'Like what?' she said, trying to bring herself into the present. 'What are you keeping from me?' It was meant as a teasing comment, but it didn't quite come out that way, somehow.

He was looking at his piglet. 'Nothing. Nothing important.'

'Gábriel,' she said. She could still hear Aidan's words in her mind. *You fly into things.* 'It was a bit spontaneous, the engagement thing.'

He continued scratching his piglet's head and didn't say anything.

'It just...' One moment, she'd been sunbathing on a beach towel under a flight path, the next she was being proposed to. '...Kinda happened.' She put the index finger and thumb of her right hand over the top of her ring. She'd realised yesterday that Franco must have had some spare cash after all, or a credit card he'd not admitted to, to buy it. 'And now look. *Ta da.*' She tried to sound frivolous. She'd let herself get caught up in the theatre of it, the gleam of the lake and the ring and Franco's eyes.

Gábriel put the piglet he was holding back down into the straw and she waited for him to tell her that she'd made a mistake.

He straightened, and his look was inscrutable. 'Well, you've done it now,' he said.

That dusk, after Jan has locked up the farm, a dog-fox that is all the colours of autumn steps out from his earth by the garages and crosses the road. He slinks past the ankles of one of the Ruskin Park Farm volunteers, who stands just inside the park gate, hood up; a swift glance back and there is another figure there, no taller, their exchange brief and not unfriendly. A sleight of hands, a pat on the shoulder. Then the second figure is gone, and the fox disappears too, slipping amongst the trees into its shadow-self.

EIGHTEEN

Harvest Festival – A Party – A Terrible Thing

The piglets were a huge hit. Annie gave birth to nine more two days after Ethel, and visitors clustered around the pen to watch, take endless photos and coo. Even in a few days the nineteen offspring had grown, both in stature and in confidence. They were inquisitively playful, snuffling at the apples fed to their mothers, or rubbing their sides against the metal bucket, their kinked tails wagging madly. They would clamber on top of each other to feed, a row of tussling bodies butting at their mothers' teats, the sows indomitable. Charlie updated the farm's social media daily with the best pictures, and rather wished that they wouldn't be adult size and sent to the slaughterhouse within the year, however much she liked bacon butties.

'Babe.' Franco was stroking her earlobe as they sat interlinked on the sofa in front of the TV.

'Yeah?'

'Can you do me a favour?'

Charlie felt like she had been doing rather a lot of those. They hadn't exactly discussed how or when he'd pay rent; when she'd told him how cheap it was, he'd just said *bargain!* and moved the conversation on. Once in a while he'd come back with something lavish, like champagne or a pair of thirty-two-day dry-aged fillet steaks, but never anything useful. She'd massage his shoulders after his day in rehearsals for his play, even though she was just as knackered. He hadn't unpacked any of his belongings, the boxes currently piled up along one wall in the bedroom. She tried to ignore the tiny itch of doubt – they were just getting used to each other. It would even out.

'What is it?' she said.

'Can you shout me a little bit of money?'

'What for?'

'For the party. I've got to pay up front for the venue.' He was turning twenty-five in a few days. *Twenty-five*.

She'd already bought him presents: a signed anthology of poems by Lorca from 1942 that she'd found, and a print of the Twombly painting he'd liked so much: *The Wilder Shores of Love*. 'How much?'

'Two hundred quid?' He pulled a consciously wary face, lips pulled back over his teeth, as if she might hit him.

She felt like it. 'Franco. That's a lot. I haven't got much myself, you know.'

He moved up to her, his voice sleek. 'I know.' He rubbed his smooth chin against her cheek. 'I'll pay you back.'

'Berlin kind of cleaned me out.'

'I know. Sorry. I wanted to save my last pennies for you-know-what.' He touched the turquoise stone of her ring.

'But... your job,' she said. 'Haven't you got anything coming in soon?'

He sat forward, stretching artfully. 'Yeah. About that.' He pulled out his tiny bag of weed – he always seemed to have enough for that – and a rolling paper and began pinching some out onto it.

'What do you mean?'

'There was a disagreement.'

'What sort of disagreement?'

'Creative differences. The director and I didn't see eye to eye.' He seemed uninterested, leaning forward to get out his rolling tobacco from his back pocket. 'She wanted me to be more vulnerable, and I didn't.'

'So what happened?'

He shrugged. 'Got sacked.'

She sat back. 'Franco.'

'Fuck it. I've got to stick to my principles.' He shot her a tortured, pleading look, the inner edge of those eyebrows drawing up. 'I only want everyone to have a good time on my birthday.' He let out a small sigh, before he gazed at the bookshelves opposite them. 'People are coming from all over. Johnno's flying in from Lisbon.' He leant towards her, a gentle side-nudge. 'I mean, I did do the farm mural for free.'

Charlie felt her own sigh fizzle in her chest, to be replaced with a whisper of hurt. That seemed very unfair. It had been his idea.

'Sometimes it's like this,' he said, unaware of the impact of his previous words. 'Jobbing artist's lot, you know. I'm often minted. It's just a little bad patch.'

She looked at his slim, graceful fingers, coaxing the rolling paper round. 'Will you absolutely promise to pay me back? Forget about Berlin, but just this.'

He looked over again, suddenly boyish and animated. 'Yes. Of course. I'll get back on the roster at the shop.' He'd taken some leave from the tattoo parlour in order to meet the demands of the play's rehearsal schedule. 'And I'll hassle my shitty agent for some more auditions. Honest. Nose to the grindstone.'

'OK,' she said lightly, wondering what she'd have to cut back on. 'On one condition.'

'Anything.'

'You come and help during the day for the Harvest Festival.' Mid-September was one of the key days in the calendar.

For a moment, she swore that a fleeting annoyance ghosted over his face, but if so, it was swiftly chased by a beam. He plucked up her hand, kissing her knuckles. 'Of course. I was coming anyway.' He closed one eye. 'So can you...?'

'Only because it's your birthday.'

A faux-sheepish smile. 'And you're my almost-wife?'

'Yes.'

He tucked his joint behind his ear and became lupine, unfurling himself to lean over her and dash his hair in her eyes. 'Your almost-husband thinks you're awesome. And sexy. And seductive.' He continued adding words beginning with 's', drawing them out into a snake-hiss.

She let herself be drawn into his arms again, into that lazy, lullaby feeling. Except tonight there was a niggling sensation, a tiny pebble lodged behind her breastbone, that didn't seem to go away, no matter how much he kissed her neck.

———————

'Hot farm goss,' said Lydia, coming into the kitchen the next evening. 'Actually, two bits of hot farm goss. Which do you want first?'

'No idea,' said Charlie, stirring her pasta sauce, which featured the farm's own tomatoes and two wonky mini-courgettes. She hardly ate takeaways anymore.

Lydia passed her phone over. 'Seen this? Mr B being a total badass.'

Charlie looked at the news headline on her screen.

MEP SPEAKS HIS MIND IN CLIMATE OUTBURST

'Good on him, really,' Lydia said. 'Fighting for the planet and everything.'

The report seemed to say that Will had erupted in a meeting in Strasbourg to do with directives on renewable energy sources. A small part had been captured on video, and she watched as Will banged both palms on his desk and jabbed a finger at the chairman.

'Yeah,' she said. 'Good on him.'

'So weird to see him shouting,' said Lydia. 'He's normally like a little lamb.' She nodded at the hob. 'Your sauce is burning.'

Charlie passed the phone back to her and picked up the wooden spoon again, stirring half-heartedly.

'Don't you want to know the other bit of goss?'

'Sure,' said Charlie, still picturing Will shouting about energy consumption directives. She really hoped he was OK.

'G-Man's got a girlfriend.'

Charlie looked sharply over. 'Has he?'

Lydia nodded authoritatively. 'Totes he has. She came and met him for lunch.'

'Cool,' said Charlie, wondering why her stomach had wound itself into a tiny sailor's knot. Somehow, she'd never imagined him with a girlfriend. 'Verdict?'

Lydia had opened a bumper packet of salt and vinegar crisps and was beginning to scoff them. 'Bit hard to tell. Didn't get a properly close look. Tall. Blonde. Sort of like a Viking.'

She wasn't far off. There were indeed Norse vibes to Gábriel's girlfriend, who turned up again at closing time a few days later. She was almost as tall as him, willowy and rather fierce-looking, with arctic blonde hair, ash-white skin and cheekbones you could probably peel an apple on. Charlie saw her wave at Gábriel from the side of the sheep pen, and he came over and kissed her, a small, demure gesture. They bent down in front of the glass of the pig shed, before he took her in. *Visitors not allowed past the gate*, Charlie thought childishly.

Charlie brought her up at the end of the next day, joining Gábriel as he supervised the moving of massive amounts of manure over to the grab lorry. The whole site hummed with the smell, and adults from the green gym were wearing their oldest clothes and making valiant jokes about pegs on noses. There would have been a time when it would have impelled Charlie to run very far in the other direction, but here she was, stomaching it just fine.

'So, a little bird tells me you're seeing someone,' she said. It had meant to sound perky, humorous, but came out far more acidly than she'd intended.

'Yeah,' said Gábriel, leaning on his shovel. His beard had grown rather longer than artful stubble now.

'She looks nice,' Charlie said, and he glanced over. 'I saw you guys yesterday. She looks like she could have most people in a fight.' Another failed attempt at levity.

He didn't contradict her. 'She's a firefighter.'

'Oh. Wow.' Of course she was. 'Have you been seeing her long?'

'A couple of weeks.'

When she was in Berlin, then. There was a space behind her ribs that felt very blank and spare. She shifted her bag further onto her shoulder. 'Franco's having a birthday party on Saturday. Up in East London. He said to invite everyone.' She couldn't quite look at him. 'You and your girlf—'

'I'm busy,' he said. 'Sorry.'

———

The Harvest Festival went smoothly. The farm was packed with visitors, and Charlie had enlisted some of her younger volunteers to help set up first thing. She was beginning to know more instinctively how to get the best out of everyone. There was hot cider, Moonie's latest impressive cakes using root vegetables (and some of them, confusingly, modelled to look like vegetables, too), beeswax soap and candles for sale, and a small bouncy castle. Visitors could pay extra to meet the animals, and Jan and Gábriel were sporting tweed waistcoats. Gábriel was currently crouched down next to two very small children who looked quite terrified of Ida the goat.

'Bonzer,' said Lydia, who'd been manning the bowling alley alongside Walt, with butternut squashes as skittles and pumpkins as bowling balls. She slapped a hand on Charlie's shoulder. 'Nice one, Charls. It's proper good.'

Charlie gave an instinctively sunny beam. It was, and she had done it.

'Where's loverboy, then? Wasn't he supposed to be doing face paints?'

He was. Charlie had left Franco in bed, though originally he had said he'd come with her in the morning. Marianne was currently on the stall, decorating everyone in florid butterflies, whether they wanted them or not.

'Not sure,' said Charlie, trying to seem blasé, though her sunniness faded a little.

'Shame,' said Lydia. 'You'd have had all the slummy mummies paying loads extra to have him staring into their eyes for fifteen minutes.'

Charlie got out her phone. She'd texted him twice already.

Where u at? Xx

'Oh well,' said Lydia. 'I guess Mumsnet can keep themselves occupied with Gábbo. He looks well fit in that waistcoat. Give that man a job modelling for *Country Living*, the porn edition.'

Gábriel was still with the two little children, who looked much less frightened now, one holding out their hand to feed Ida, their mother smiling.

'Mmm.' Charlie glanced back down at her phone. She could see that Franco was receiving the messages.

'And it's deffo OK to come laters?' said Lydia. 'I mean, won't his lot be mad coke-snorting hipsters? I'm going to stick out like a sore bloody thumb.'

'You are definitely coming.'

'Wicked. I'll be in my best medieval slut-dress.' She winked and made a clicking noise at the same time, and Charlie wondered what on earth she was going to wear.

Franco had called the night an Autumn Equinox party; the Wicker Man themed invitations featured his over-anguished face superimposed on Edward Woodward's from the last moments of the film, and advertised the fancy dress code as 'sexy pagan'

The pub in Hackney Wick was down an unlit street close to the canals and surrounded by small industrial buildings, the huge Olympic complex not far away. Charlie turned on her phone's torch and wondered again why she was turning up to this alone. Franco had finally messaged her late in the afternoon with loads of apologies and flower emojis to say he was already in East London. Lydia wasn't with her, promising to come after a few pre-drinks with her uni mates. The air felt leaden, wind making a loose sign rattle loudly against a lamppost. A pressure headache. She followed the fizzing sound of music and people, turning into a yard, past graffiti-covered walls and a couple of skips until she saw the venue.

Inside, what had probably once been a large garage had been converted into a bar. It had a high corrugated iron roof and exposed pipes, and was filled with a cacophony of beats and shouting. There were perhaps a hundred people, many of them masked – devils, wolves, goats, bears and fish. Others had gone for impressively-constructed wicker necklaces or flower garlands, and there was a creepy-looking jester in the corner. Charlie had asked Marianne to festoon the sides of her face with luminous vines and leaves, which she'd impassively worn on the train up, topped with a pair of rabbit ears on a headband.

'Babe,' Franco said, coming towards her with a skull and antlers propped up on his head, his face a picture of contrition.

'I'm so sorry. I lost track of time. Sorting the party and everything. Look at your complete cuteness.' He went to kiss her and she moved so that he ended up kissing her cheek. He took her hands and looked at her coaxingly. 'Don't be like that. Not on my birthday.'

Your birthday's next Tuesday, she thought, and wondered what preparations he had been hard at work on all day. The decorations consisted of bunting and a terrifying-looking straw effigy propped up on the bar with candles in its mouth.

Franco stuck his bottom lip out, his eyes dewy, trying to absorb her attention.

'Fine,' said Charlie. 'Can I have a drink, please?'

'You can have one of mine,' he said, leading her towards the bar. 'Everyone's been buying me loads. Birthday win.'

Charlie just didn't feel like a party. She was exhausted after her early start and being at the farm all day. She hovered by the bar, drinking some of Franco's champagne and occasionally turning herself onto social mode with a too-bright smile and some conversation, or rather yelling in someone's ear over the raucous speakers. A few of his mates, whom she'd only met a couple of times, came over to congratulate her on the engagement. She watched Franco DJ, hunched over his laptop, nodding earnestly to his massive basslines and queasy synths.

After a few tunes, he took the mic. 'Ladies, gentlemen, and everyone in between,' he said in a velvety tone, and everyone whooped. 'So listen, it's my birthday'—more whoops, and whistles—'but it's also more than that. If you didn't know already, I recently met a total goddess, and she bewitched me.' A few people turned round to where Charlie was sitting. She shrank a little further back towards the bar. 'She bewitched me so hard and so fast that... we're *only totally fucking getting married*!' The end of the sentence was loud and distorted by the mic. During the applause that followed, he shouted her name, putting his hand over his eyes to block out the lights and find her.

Nothing for it. She got off her stool and went to the DJ booth, where Franco took her hand and twirled her around before putting his arms around her and giving her a deep kiss. He picked up the mic again. 'And to show you how much I appreciate you all coming out tonight, I've got a little something for you.' He waggled his finger at his friends. 'I know what you like, you massive load of dirty bastards.' More whistles, the wolfish kind. 'Please put your hands together, and welcome...' His voice became smooth caramel, Barry White-ish. '...Miss. Kitty. Vacant.'

A pale, voluptuous woman came out from behind a black curtain and into the centre of the room, the crowd widening a circle around her. She was wearing a corset and cloak, flower garlands in her hair and her face was painted half blue and half white. In her hand, she held a dragon mask with a grotesque tongue, and stuck out her own as some weird drone-folk was played. Charlie's heart sank – not because she hated burlesque, but because she was fairly sure that Franco had probably spent her money on the performance rather than the venue hire, as she'd assumed. It was just unnecessary.

She drifted to the back of the crowd, and watched Franco absorbed in the routine, his eyes sparking. One of his mates came up to him and whispered in his ear, and he nodded, his fist coming up to his mouth as if to hide a smile, before slapping him on the shoulder and following him to the toilets.

The droney folk music had turned into beats, and the burlesque dancer was moving to one of the ribbon-festooned pillars in the middle of the room. She picked up a ribbon and circled the pillar, pulling off her cloak to general delight, before twirling more ribbons and losing more of her clothes.

'Do you like her?' Franco was next to Charlie again, lightly rubbing his thumb and forefinger over his nostrils.

'Please tell me you didn't spend my money on her,' she said. 'Or on that.'

'On what?' He knew she wasn't into coke.

'You're not fooling anyone, Franco.'

He made a breathy sound through his lips, and briefly draped his arms around her, gently singing 'girls just wanna have fun' in her ear, before pulling away to give the loudest wolf-whistle of the night as the dancer revealed tiny fox nipple tassels.

Charlie watched Franco drift away again towards his friends, feeling despondent. This was not how an engagement was supposed to feel. She fished out her phone to see where Lydia had got to, and was surprised to see three missed calls from Gábriel. Perhaps he'd decided to come after all, him and his firefighting Viking girlfriend, who was Swedish and called Agnes – divined by Lydia, of course – and had got lost in the mean streets of post-industrial East London.

She messaged him.

What up. You nearby?

No. Heading to farm. Emergency.

He was still typing.

More piglets been born by some amazing miracle?

she wrote, and added a pig emoji and some heart-eyes.

No. Break-in. Police are there. I'm going over now.

'Oh, no,' said Charlie, suddenly incredibly sober. She dashed outside and phoned him. The wind had grown portentous and seemed to fill the yard, and it was hard to hear. Gábriel was on the bus; he didn't know any more than she did yet, only that someone had reported some people by the gates, and some possible damage. She was about to tell him she'd be there soon when an arm was slung onto her shoulder.

'Who are you talking to?' said Franco.

'It's Gábriel. There's been a break-in at the farm. I've got to go.'

'No, no, you're not going. No way. It's my birthday, babe. Give me that.' He took the phone from her and tucked it between his ear and his shoulder, whilst rolling a cigarette. 'Hello, mate, how're you doing? Listen, Charlie's staying here. You've got it under control, haven't you? She's always going on about how great you are. Yeah? You've got it? Nice one. Lovely. *Ciao*.' He hung up and gave the phone back to her, smiling sweetly. It was beginning to drizzle. 'Nothing's going to take my Venus away from me tonight.'

She stared at him. 'Seriously?'

'What?' he said.

She shook her head. The farm. *Her* farm. 'I'm going, and I'm going right now,' she said. 'Happy birthday.'

By the time she reached Ruskin Park, the rain was torrential, the roads slick with it. Two police cars were stationed by the traffic lights next to the gate. There were torches flickering, and several shadows by the pigpen, right at the end. She could make out Gábriel's slightly rounded shoulders, even with his hood up. He turned as she raced up, and she could see from his body language that it wasn't good.

'Tell me it's OK,' she said, blinking up at him through the rain.

He shook his head. 'The piglets have been stolen.'

NINETEEN

A Search - A Recovery - Market Day

'Making a pig's ear of it.'

Charlie had hardly slept, jittery with worry. Franco had woken her at 6am, his face very close, asking where the hell she'd gone. Now he was standing in the kitchen, waiting for his stovetop espresso maker to start fizzling. He hadn't come to bed, and was probably still high.

'Oink and you'll miss them,' he said, with a hint of an astringent grin.

'It's not funny.' She was pouring milk into a bowl of granola. Her head hurt.

After the initial shock last night, Charlie and Gábriel had walked round the site with the police officers. The piglets had definitely gone. There was damage to the fencing on the inner edge of the farm, meaning the thieves had come through the longer side of the park. Eventually, Jan had arrived too, fuming. 'Those fuckers,' she'd said. 'Those absolute fuckers.'

'Por-cine of the times,' Franco said.

She whipped round, pushing him in the shoulder. 'I mean it.'

He saw how furious she was and finally lost the grin, putting his hands up in surrender. 'OK. I'm sorry. It's just pretty outlandish, isn't it? Lifting a load of pigs. You've got to admire their chutzpah. Their gumption.'

Last night the police had asked about extra security – the one CCTV camera they did have hadn't picked anything up – and Gábriel and Jan had glanced at Charlie, who'd stuttered something about currently working on it. Extra security had been on her list, but she'd needed to get approval for funding; in fact, that had been on the agenda at the last board meeting she'd missed. Now she wondered why on earth it hadn't been her top priority.

'I haven't got to admire anything,' Charlie said. 'They're criminals. Thieves.'

Worse than thieves. Gábriel had said as soon as Charlie had arrived that the piglets needed their mother's milk to survive. Nothing else would do.

Franco lifted the espresso maker off the hob. 'Of course they are. What can I do?' He cleared his throat, an unpleasantly phlegmy post-party sound.

'Nothing.' She picked up her bowl and walked towards the living room, not looking at him. 'I don't want your help.'

The farm remained closed to visitors for the day, though some of the volunteers came in, variously upset and appalled at the news. Charlie mostly stayed glued to her desk; she had never been more focused. She put out a plea for help on the news page of the website, spread the word on social media via the other farms and the local council, and talked to reporters on the phone. A London news crew came over and filmed Gábriel and Jan with the dejected-looking sows, Jan just about managing not to swear on camera.

'What sort of total stupid fucking wankstain bastard would steal piglets?' said Lydia, tearfully angry. It was clearly someone who had no idea about farm animals; the police had two days, three at an absolute push, to find the piglets before they died. It was an utterly pointless crime.

Will phoned from France, consolatory and businesslike, and asked how he could help. Charlie told him wearily that making as many people aware of it as possible was all that could be done. An hour later, he'd put a short video on Twitter, which was widely shared.

Ade spent the day accompanying the police as they interviewed all staff members. Charlie phoned all the volunteers she could, and most came in, including some from the young offenders group. There was the risk of it being an inside job, the police had said, on evidence from previous city farm incidents. But Charlie couldn't believe it. *Wouldn't* believe that anyone working here would be involved. Anyone who really knew this place would never jeopardise it.

The next day, Charlie kept at it. The story had gained some national interest, and she talked to more reporters and got the Social Farms and Gardens network to put the word out. She fielded hundreds of messages of support and made a leaflet for a neighbourhood watch group to distribute. The community gathered together, but as yet there'd been no leads. No one, it seemed, had spotted what must have been at least two people clambering over the park's perimeter fence, or heard the squeals of nineteen confused, hungry infants. Until this moment, she had not realised quite how much she loved the farm, and all the creatures it housed. Every time she shut her eyes, she saw the piglets trapped in a dark cupboard or basement, being force-fed milk or water that made them sick. She saw her favourite piglet, its big black patches and sleepy eyes growing tired. Cold. The sows were milked, and the milk stored, just in case.

'It will be OK,' said Gábriel, standing in the porch outside the office with her at the end of the afternoon, watching the rain descend in columns from the awning. It was another stormy day, the clouds darkly swollen.

'No, it won't,' she said.

He sipped from his mug. 'There are a few more hours,' he said. 'Let's have a real drink.'

They ran to The Sun and sat on stools by the fire to dry off, consuming bottled ale, packets of crisps and nuts, and both constantly checking their phones. Charlie stared into the flames and bit her thumbnails down to nothing. She didn't know where Franco was tonight and she didn't care. He hadn't entirely forgiven her for bailing out on his party, and their interactions had mostly been curt messages.

'I feel so useless,' she said.

Gábriel leant his forearms on the table. 'We just have to wait. I'm sure the police are doing their job.'

The police had been very kind, but Charlie was well aware that they'd been junior officers and that most of them had far more important things to do. She sighed and gazed into the fire again, felt the heat spread onto her cheeks, the melancholy deepen in her bones. There was a flash of lightning outside, the rain more determined.

Gábriel went to the bar for more beers. As he returned, a hip hop song came on with a familiar spitty flute sample and laconic rapping.

'I love this tune,' Charlie said, rather forlornly. She had memories of bopping with her dad as a teenager whilst Casey sat with her arms folded and her headphones on, listening to science programmes on Radio 4. She tugged distractedly at the cotton thread of her friendship bracelet. It was getting thin; she'd need to re-thread the beads again soon.

'I used to play the flute,' said Gábriel as he sat down, and looked amused at her astonishment. 'When I was a kid.'

'I totally cannot imagine that.'

He'd pushed his wet locks back off his forehead. His hair was getting longer, as well as his beard.

'What else did you do? When you were young?'

He told her about trying to fix his bike to be more like a BMX; about a cartoon featuring a fisherman and a worm; of cadging cigarettes from the temporary workers on his family's farm and listening to a lot of Black Sabbath. Charlie, at least for a few minutes, let herself be distracted; tried not to think about the piglets, and saw only them, siblings lying closely packed, going quiet, going still.

'How about you?'

'Mmm?'

'When you were a kid. What kind of things did you do?' It was obvious he was trying to cheer her up.

'Oh. Um—' As she tried to think of something, she pulled again at the thread of her bracelet, harder than she intended, and in a single moment the thread had snapped and the little beads were scattering over the table and onto the floor, as percussive as hail. 'Oh, my God,' she said, horrified tears

257

spiking her eyes, as she jumped up and began to try and collect them. 'For fuck's sake.'

Gábriel crouched down next to her, picking some up. 'Hey, it's OK. I'll get them. Sit down.'

'No,' she said, and didn't care how overwrought she sounded. 'I can't miss any out.' There were gaps in some of the floorboards. They might fall down them, be irretrievable.

'I won't miss any.'

His calmness made her stop, take a shuddering breath and drop her shoulders. She returned to her stool, gathering the beads that had managed to stay on the table.

When he sat back down, he let the beads fall into her cupped palm.

'Thanks.'

'It's no problem,' he said, and the words were open, as if giving her the option to talk, if she wanted to, without any pressure at all.

She shook her head self-admonishingly. 'You must think I'm weird.'

'I don't think that.'

She looked at the beads again, their faded colours of peach, pink and lavender. She found a tissue in her bag and folded them up in it. 'I was sad. When I was a kid.' She pulled her beer bottle over.

'OK,' he said, frowning gently at the table.

She touched the condensation on the neck of the bottle, blotting a drop, watching it fall again. She shrugged, the action absolutely the opposite of the words that came next. 'My sister was killed when I was six. She was nine.' She let out a sigh, a puff through pursed lips. 'Not killed. Not exactly. She got run over. It wasn't anyone's fault.'

'Oh. I'm sorry.' The words were spoken with restraint, the

way he so often did, not trying to pretend he knew anything about it, or how it might feel.

'Yeah.' She gave a small, unhappy smile.

'You don't have to talk about it.'

But suddenly, she felt that she wanted to. She told him about the visit to the friend, Jools not looking; the court case, Nellie's pre- and post-natal depression.

'It's hard to process when you didn't see it,' she said quietly. 'You know, if she'd got a terminal illness or something, you'd have a chance to understand what was going on, and where it was headed. Drips, and hospital beds. To get used to the idea. But one minute she was there, and then she wasn't.' She opened one palm. 'Jools.' Then closed it into a gentle fist. 'No Jools.'

They sat there, listening to the crackling of the fire and the relaxed beats coming from the jukebox. She was aware that Gábriel was still watching her, as if waiting for more.

'When you're six... it's too small to have any kind of capacity, emotional or otherwise, to deal with that. I was just this bewildered little kid, in a house with a mum who couldn't get out of bed for a while, trying to understand why this new baby wasn't anything like Jools.' Her voice winnowed. 'I don't think I've ever got over it.' She looked at him. 'Did you ever lose anyone close to you?'

He shook his head. 'Only my grandma. She was sick for a while.'

'I'm sorry.' She began methodically peeling away the moist label of the bottle. 'Maybe you don't ever stop grieving. It just takes different forms, you know? If I think about it, if I concentrate, there's this dull ache'—she rested her hand on her stomach—'so deep down it's almost unreachable. It's always going to be there. I've been trying so hard lately to honour her, to do better, *be* better – with the farm, with everything. And now the piglets have been stolen.'

'That's not your fault,' he said.

'It's all my fault.' She could have got cameras up already, if she'd moved really, really fast. They would have surely been a deterrent.

He knew what she was thinking. 'Might not have stopped them.'

The beer bottle label was in shreds. She felt the old anger at herself for being ill that day, because if she'd gone with Jools to see the pet rabbit, she would have remembered the Green Cross Code. She would have saved her. She took another sip.

'I'm really sorry,' Gábriel said. 'About your sister. That's so shit.'

She couldn't help smiling. Somehow swearwords sounded sweetly formal in his accent, and not sweary at all. 'Yep. Very shit.' She looked at him, dragging herself back into the present. 'That's why when you got hit by the car door—'

A look of alarm, or shame, passed swiftly over his face. 'Oh, no. I'm sorry.'

'No, don't be. It wasn't your fault. I just had to make sure you were OK, you know?'

They looked at each other for a moment. On the pub's speakers, the tune had changed to Massive Attack's 'Protection', the emphatic echoing snare drum hollowing Charlie out.

'That's what this is for.' She turned over her hand to expose her fern tattoo.

'Yeah?' he said, rather gently.

'Yeah. In County Kerry – in Ireland, where my dad's family's from – there are these amazing mountains. Really beautiful. The last time we went there, I mean when Jools was alive, she was allowed to walk up the first part of this hiking trail with my mum, and I wasn't allowed to go. I was too small. I was so jealous. And Jools came back with this fern that she picked from the path, and pressed it into a book for me. So that I had some of the mountain all for myself. They always make me think of her.'

'That's really nice. Really...' His sigh was short, frustrated. 'Sometimes I wish I had better words. My English.'

'What are you talking about?' She hit him lightly on the forearm. 'Your English is better than mine.'

He gave a small, slow smile. '*Megható*,' he said. 'That's the word I want.'

'What does it mean?'

'Kind of like sad, but sweet and'—he put his palm on his chest—'giving you emotion.'

The gesture was so similar to her own frequent action that she just gazed at him for a moment. Hand on heart. She was always promising things, as if to seal people's commitment to her, and make sure they didn't go anywhere.

He put his hand down. 'I'm sorry I was mean about your tattoo before,' he said. 'That was bad.'

'Oh,' she said, offhandedly, feigning that she'd forgotten it. 'Don't worry about it.'

'No, I...' He was looking rather deeply at her, as if to make sure that she really took him in. 'I'm really sorry.'

'Thank you.'

Everything seemed to have shrunk down, suddenly, to the liquid female vocal on the track, their table, the golden glints in his beard teased out by the fire. There was a strange, molten pause that she wasn't sure how to fill.

His phone suddenly juddered across the little table by his

knees, and he looked at it. She watched for his reaction. He glanced up at her. 'It's not them.'

'Is it Agnes?'

'Yeah.' He put one hand in the pocket of his hoodie, and seemed to be blushing, though it might have been the fire.

She tried to shake off her grief. 'How's it going? With her?'

He put his phone away. 'It's nice.' His voice was distant.

They both looked at the fire. Drank their beers. Perhaps the piglets were all dead now.

'I should go,' she said, not wanting to.

He stood up with her. 'I'll see you tomorrow.'

Early the next morning, Franco woke her up. 'Phone.'

She took it from him to hear Jan on the line. 'Morning, mate. Good news.'

Charlie gave herself a head-rush as she sat up. 'Yeah?'

'Yeah. Thank fuck.' A heavy sigh. 'The little babs have been found.'

By the time she got to the farm, the piglets were already being given their first feed, having been whisked back by police escort. They were very weak, each held and fed with a bottle, with Jan, Gábriel and Lydia, along with Tallboy and Walt, all kneeling in the straw. The warming boxes were ready and waiting.

'Is it all right?' she said, out of breath from having hared up the path, and trying to count them. 'Are they all here?'

Gábriel looked up. 'Three have died. The rest should be OK, hopefully.'

. . .

The papers – some national, as well as the local press – reported that a man in South Croydon had heard unusual, high-pitched sounds coming from a shed in a neighbouring back garden, and subsequently noticed two young men creeping in and out of it. He'd sat down with his cup of tea to watch the local evening news, seen their follow-up report, and had picked up the phone to the police.

Charlie took screenshots of the best headlines, for the farm's publicity:

AN AWFULLY PIG ADVENTURE

THE TROTTERS CLUB!

RETURNED SAFE AND SOUND

HAM-FISTED CRIMINALS MAKE A PIG'S EAR OF IT

LONG PORK TO FREEDOM

'Mine were better,' sniffed Franco, later.

Tallboy said he thought he recognised the two guys from the photo as recent visitors. They didn't seem to have any links to the farm, thankfully.

The pig-shed remained off-limits for a week while the piglets recovered. Charlie made visits every day to see the sixteen survivors and scratch the black ear of her favourite, whom she had privately named Splodge. 'You're my bae, aren't you?' she said once. 'No one's taking you away from me. I'll karate-pork-chop anyone who comes near you.'

A small, private mirth. She wondered if she'd tell Franco that one later, but somehow, she knew she wouldn't.

October. The summer seems long ago. In Camberwell, one of the banks shuts and re-opens as a charity shop. Chips are scattered on the pavement, and plastic traffic barriers clog up the junctions. Neon-yellow cranes tower over the hospital, the new helipad surrounded by scaffolding. The dark green of the trees in Ruskin Park has become lime, golden, rose-blush; conkers and hard berries fall. There seem to be more squirrels than people, using the trees as an assault course, and parakeets bomb between the trees, their sound obliterating the smaller birds' calls. Some afternoons, a man plays free improvisations on his tenor sax in the bandstand, and the unpredictable, soaring lines can be heard half a mile away.

Franco is working at the tattoo parlour again, and comes back at erratic hours. When home, he slouches on the sofa, smokes weed in the garden, or spends hours with his headphones on in front of his laptop's DJ software. He did not sell many photos at his exhibition, and has been trying to persuade the tattoo shop to display them. He wants to ink Charlie some more, but she has fended him off as yet. Occasionally he visits the farm and baa-s at the sheep, who remained unmoved. He is here today, loitering outside the hen coop, watching some volunteers collect eggs.

'Hey,' said Charlie. 'What are you doing here?'

'Seeing my girl,' Franco said. 'If that's all right.'

'Of course it's all right.' Just a few words in, and they'd already become defensive. Ever since his birthday party, things hadn't been right between them. 'How was the audition?'

'Shit.' He scowled at the cages. Jami and Faith were

giggling together, Jami pretending to drop the basket of eggs he was holding. 'Can I borrow some money?' He hadn't even turned towards her.

A tiny, dull throb of sadness. 'What for?'

'Surprise.'

'What?'

'Wouldn't be a surprise if I told you, would it? Something for you and me.'

She took in a long breath and let it out gradually. He was supposed to have a meeting with the bank for a loan. She wondered if he'd gone at all. 'I've got twenty quid in my wallet. That's literally all I've got.'

'That's perfect.' He looked faintly impatient. 'The tattoo shop will pay me next week. I'll be sorted from then.'

She took a deep breath. This would be the last time she gave him money, she told herself. 'Can you make dinner tonight?' He hadn't in ages; he simply squatted down in front of the fridge and pillaged.

'Yes. No. Can't. Got a mate's gig to go to.' His gaze was cool, enigmatic. 'You know, Barney. At the Garage.' A blink, and a disarming smile. 'Tomorrow, though. Promise.' He drew her into his arms and kissed her forehead. She rested it against his lips, wondering why he wasn't asking her to come, and at the same time very glad he wasn't.

At the weekend, they went to Broadway Market, by the canal in Hackney – Franco missed his East London hangouts, complaining that south of the river didn't do it for him. They walked down the street, taking samples of cheese, square centimetres of salted caramel brownie, and spelt bread with local honey. Franco spotted an actor, recognisable from film and TV, and sulked for ten minutes about being less successful than him, before saying he was going to get them both coffees. *With my money*, Charlie thought. She stood by the Jewish deli stall, watching cream cheese being expertly swiped onto bagels, feeling miserable.

She put her forefinger and thumb around her engagement ring, which she hadn't had re-sized yet, twisted it and watched the skin corkscrew. She should have given it back to him on the U-Bahn back from the lake. She hadn't meant for it to turn out like this. But she couldn't give up. Not yet. There was her pride to think of, if nothing else. How would it look, to say it was over, after a month? She had to remember why she'd fallen so deeply for him. He was just in a rough patch, job-wise, as he'd said, and it had made him snarky and low. Perhaps it would be better when he got a good acting job or two, to get the ball rolling – it seemed to be what he wanted to do most. She imagined him top of the bill in an off-West End play (slightly more realistic than the West End), the reviews coming in, him doing a humble version of his flourishing bow; it made her smile, and she turned round to look for him.

He was by the coffee truck, but not in the queue. Rather, he was standing to the side of it, and talking to someone, bending down, his hand on their shoulder. A young black woman, who didn't look more than a teenager, cornrows dyed a deep gold. Charlie took a step forward to get a better look and at the same time, Franco glanced round at her, straightened and seemed to almost push the girl, who vanished out of sight behind the truck.

He was coming back over, coffee-less, hands in his back pockets.

'Who was that?' she said.

An untroubled look, faintly bored. 'No one.'

She'd looked really young. 'Did you know her?'

'She came into the shop once. Wanted a tattoo. I didn't give her one. Responsible, you know. Happens all the time.' He shrugged. 'You getting us bagels, then?'

TWENTY

Apple Day – A Shock

pple Day might have sounded like an ancient custom, but it was founded in 1990 by a charity to celebrate the nation's countless varieties largely ignored by supermarkets. The other city farms had annual events and, like everything else, Charlie dutifully put it in the diary for this year and hauled herself over early in order to supervise the set-up. Everything felt better here – reliable and comforting. She knew she could do this; she trusted herself enough. Today featured apples in many forms; though the farm's own fledgling trees would not bear fruit for a while, she had arranged for orchards in the neighbouring counties to bring their wares.

At various stalls, fruit was displayed in rustic bowls and boxes, with names reminiscent of a grandmother's perfume: Winter Gem, Sweet Society, D'Arcy Spice. There were mellow dessert varieties, tart apples best for cooking, or with hints of aniseed, nuts, honey. Some were scotched green and red, others blushing golden. A woman was demonstrating apple-identification tastings every hour.

Franco had promised to come and help again, though

Charlie didn't hold out much hope. Things had not improved. He would say one thing and do quite another: a vow to clean the kitchen of his mess had turned into him disappearing to a party with his tattooist colleagues; agreeing to come out for drinks with one of her university friends had become a succession of texted excuses; and there hadn't been any sign of a present for the both of them from the twenty quid she'd given him. She now kept her contactless card in a safe place, just in case. Although she knew that she needed to not just give the ring back but also break up with him, a small part of her kept holding out hope that any moment now things would come good for him, his mood would change and only lovely, pre-engagement times would follow. She couldn't have made this bad a judgement.

'This tastes better than sex feels,' said Lydia, chomping on a Hoary Morning and continuing to speak with her mouth full. 'Well, maybe not better than all sex. Depends on who you've been having sex with, I suppose.' She nudged Charlie. 'You having one? Apple, not sex. Though I don't think you've had that for a few days.' She caught Charlie's befuddled look. 'I can usually hear you through the wall.'

'Oh, God,' she said. 'Sorry.'

'No bother,' said Lydia, cheerily. 'I get my kicks where I can.' She held out another apple. 'Get your gnashers round that.'

Charlie shook her head. 'I've had two already,' she said (a Beauty of Bath, and a Discovery). 'I'm appled out.'

'You can't be,' said Lydia. 'We've got tons of apple-tivities yet. Apple bobbing, apple treasure hunt, longest peel competition. No way are you bailing. Have some cider.'

'Not while I'm on duty.' Drinking on the job was definitely a thing of the past.

They walked along the main path. There was an indie-folk band, mandolins and a cello amongst them, setting up by the café. Performance poetry to be read, later on. Leila had outdone herself in the kitchen with a special menu of Persian apple-themed foods and iced apple rosewater, and Moonie had made perfectly-glazed tarts. Over in the barn, pumpkins were being carved, too – Charlie was tying the day in with Halloween. Gábriel was here, though he'd finished what was officially a half-day for him; she'd seen him strolling around hand in hand with his girlfriend, drinking hot cider.

Right now, though, he was talking to someone else. A figure that looked familiar. Charlie stopped dead and loitered by the fence. She could see Agnes a little way off, smiling at a small pair of siblings as they knelt in front of the goat pen. Gábriel was standing with his back to Charlie, scratching his temple. He lifted his shoulders. He towered over the young woman, who seemed very much like the one Franco had been talking to in Broadway Market last weekend. The same deep gold braids. Gábriel nodded and put his hands in his pockets, and the young woman moved, pushing something. She had a child's buggy with her.

Charlie followed Gábriel, and got to him before he reached Agnes. 'Hey.'

He turned around, and his expression was a peculiar one, for him. As if he'd been caught doing something he shouldn't.

'Who were you talking to?' she said. 'Was she OK?'

'Yeah. She was, um…' He rubbed at his forehead. 'She was looking for Franco.'

'For Franco?' She felt a knot of confusion between her eyebrows. 'Really?'

'Yeah.' He looked odd. Almost shifty.

'What? What, Gábriel?'

He swallowed. 'I think maybe you should go and talk to her.'

Charlie found her leaning over the buggy and speaking in an incredibly soft, musical voice.

'Hi,' she said. 'Can I help you?'

The young woman turned around, and Charlie saw that her pushchair was a rickety, old-school one. There was a tiny, light-skinned baby inside, wearing a furry hood, eyes two perfect little lines in sleep.

'Oh, wow. This one's gorgeous.' Charlie bent over. 'Hello, honey.'

'Yeah. She is.'

Charlie straightened. She didn't seem old enough to be her mother. Sister, maybe. Au pair. She was doll-like, with false lashes and very plucked eyebrows. Underneath it all, though, she looked exhausted. 'How old is she?'

'Five weeks.' She rolled the pushchair forward, back, forward, back. She looked up at Charlie. 'Do you know Franco? I think he, like, comes here?'

'He's my fiancé,' she said, with a slight flash of defensiveness. 'How do you know him?'

The young woman smiled, a strange look that seemed part sheepish and part defiant; bright, intelligent eyes. 'How do you think?'

Charlie looked down at the pushchair.

'There you are,' said Lydia. Her face was wet. 'No one's beaten me at apple-bobbing yet. I've told Franco he's next. That boy is going to get got.'

'He's here?' said Charlie.

'Yeah. Pumpkin carving.' Lydia wiped her cheek with the sleeve of her fleece. 'You all right, Charls? You look like you've seen a ghost or five. Halloween's not for another week yet.'

Charlie was already moving away. She *felt* like a ghost; fragile, made of something diaphanous. As if someone could put their hands right through her.

He was in the barn, with a pumpkin between his thighs and a large knife in his hand, holding court to three boys aged ten or so. 'You've got to go for something original. None of this boring old eyes and teeth nonsense.' He leant forward, bringing them into his confidence. 'You've got to think, "what would the modernists do?" Babe,' he said, seeing Charlie. 'Told you I'd be here.' He tossed the knife in the air to the side of him, caught it perfectly by the handle, and winked at the boys.

'There's someone here to see you,' she said.

'Yeah?' He looked puzzled, then pleased. 'Is it Scorsese, come to his senses at last?' He assumed a thick New York accent. '*You talkin' to me?*'

She shook her head. She felt queasy, as if the world was swaying. 'In my office.'

Gábriel was a few feet away, an unobtrusive presence. Franco looked at Charlie, and back at Gábriel. 'The strong silent type's a bit passé, isn't it, mate?' He addressed Charlie. 'What am I missing, babe?'

There was so much she wanted to say, and yet the words were clogged in her throat. 'Just come, will you?'

. . .

There was hardly enough space in the office for all of them, and yet she still shut the door behind her. Franco immediately lost his swagger when he saw who was there.

'Hi, Franco.' The girl was standing in the middle of the room, one hand clutched in the other. Her wrists were very thin.

It was a small moment in which the air seemed to disappear.

When Franco spoke, it was in a voice that Charlie had never heard before. Small, simple, without ostentation. 'Funmi,' he said. 'What are you doing here?' He turned to Charlie, and beneath that guileless expression, she saw him consider repeating the same lie from the other day – about her being too young for a tattoo – and realise that it was too late.

'Looking for you, obviously,' Funmi said. 'Been trying. One of your tattoo boys said you might be down here. There's someone you should meet.'

She turned to the pushchair and Franco went a very pale shade, paler than his worst hangover. Funmi bent down, brought the tiny bundle into her arms, and Charlie saw how well the baby fit into the crook of her elbow, how quickly she'd become a mother.

'I was trying to tell you the other day.'

Franco was staring in a mixture of wonder and horror at the baby.

'Say hello to Mia,' Funmi said in a feathery voice. There was something ethereal about the pair of them, the slight teenager and her tiny child in its leopard print babygro. As if they glowed. 'Say hello to Daddy, Mia.' A glance up. 'You've been hard to find.'

Daddy. Even though Charlie already knew it to be true,

hearing that word made everything tilt. She fumbled for the back of her office chair and sat down. Her knees shook.

After a moment, Franco spoke. 'Charlie.' There was the sound of him swallowing. 'I didn't know. I didn't know about this.'

She'd never seen him so shorn of frippery, of artifice. 'She's *seventeen*,' she said, the words only half-there. And she'd been sixteen when they were together, Funmi had already explained. Just the right side of being legal, Charlie thought. But the very wrong side of everything else.

Franco closed his eyes for a moment; didn't deny that he had known it.

'You knew she was pregnant,' Charlie said. Funmi had told her that they'd split up just after she had found out.

'She was going to have an abortion.' He leant round, sinking onto his knees in front of Funmi, his hands on her hips, his voice pleading. 'You said you were going to get an abortion.'

'Couldn't though, could I?' Funmi shifted the bundle in her arms, and there was a faint mewling noise as the baby began to wake up. 'Mum said she'd help, so…'

'Why didn't you tell me?'

Her attention was on her daughter, stroking her cheek, shushing her. 'Because we'd split up. I knew you wanted to do your own thing.' A little look at him. 'I didn't want to ruin your life.'

Franco often posed like he was in a painting or a prize-winning portrait photo. This was a new one, him kneeling on the rough office carpet, his perfect chin tipped upwards, looking at the mother of his child, and the child herself.

. . .

Franco and Charlie sat on the wall by the winter vegetable beds.

'That's it, then,' she said.

He picked at a chard leaf, pulling it away. 'I'll have to make a go of it.' It was a new Franco. As if he'd been stripped. Sobered.

'Yeah, you will.' Her throat felt acrid.

'Don't look at me like that.'

'Like what?' All those late-night heart-to-hearts and he'd conveniently missed this part out. 'Like I've been engaged to someone who had a teenage girlfriend? To someone who ducked out on her when she was pregnant?'

'She said she was getting ri— Getting an abortion.' He gave a ragged sigh and shuddered, as if shaking something from himself. He dug his thumb into the red stalk of the chard and drew it down until it split. 'I'm not lying.'

'You're not lying about *that*. You've lied all the time. You've taken my money, made me look... made me *feel* like a total—' She couldn't finish.

'You know something else I won't lie about?' For the blink of an eye, he looked almost feral, like he might attack her. 'I split up with Funmi *because* she was so young. I knew it was stupid. But she is far more beautiful, and far more perfect than you could ever be.' He stood up, tossing the remnants of the leaf away. 'Fuck you, Charlie.'

She didn't watch him go. She sat still; looked at the intense purple of the kale behind her, the pendulous squashes, and put her fingers in the soil. Her breaths came at intervals, with a dark, silent space in between each one.

'Charlie?' Behind her, Gábriel's voice was careful.

She didn't turn round.

'Are you all right?'

Charlie went to say yes. Instead she lowered her head into her muddy hands. After a moment, she heard his footsteps, padding lightly away.

'*Mate*,' said Lydia, the word drawn-out and heavy with sympathy. 'Hey, it's OK.' She sat next to Charlie, very close. There was a smell of cider. 'Gábriel just told me. Is it for real?'

Charlie nodded, not lifting her head.

Lydia let out a long breath through her teeth. 'Shitting hell.' She didn't say another word for two minutes, simply sitting there with her arm round Charlie's shoulders. There was the sound of the little folk band starting up again, and a smattering of applause. 'I reckon you should go home.'

'Apple Day,' said Charlie stupidly, her voice muffled.

'Don't you worry about that. I'll sort it.' She let the words settle. 'All right, Marianne and Gábs will sort it and I'll supervise-slash-delegate-slash-eat-my-weight-in-cobbler.'

Charlie lifted her head.

'Jesus, look at you. You've got mud everywhere.' Lydia licked her thumb and wiped at one cheek, before giving a gentle slap to the side of Charlie's thigh. 'Go on. Off with you.'

The cottage was cold. The boiler, which had been playing up occasionally, wouldn't restart. Charlie sat in the dark, wrapped in her duvet on the sofa, eating stale corn chips, fresh tears occasionally falling over the not-yet-dried ones.

TWENTY-ONE

A Crime – A Confession – Worry

A quiet day. Everything has been made spongy and soft by the rain, the woodchip paths soggy underfoot, and strings of raindrops hang from the mesh fences. The animals all find shelter, apart from Gaga, who is steadily cropping the grass, seemingly oblivious. The hens huddle under the small triangular roofs of their feeding sheds, their feathers sodden. Small children seem to mind less, clad in bright wellies and raincoats with their hoods up, standing by the fences wondering where the goats are. Tallboy and Badiha sweep the rainwater into the drains with big brooms, wearing their RPF cagouls, and elsewhere, the volunteers' talk is muted.

'I knew it.'

'You didn't know nothing. You were making big eyes at him just like everyone else.'

'I knew he was a player. Sowing his seeds.'

'Oats. You sow *oats*.'

'Speak for yourself.'

'I'm just saying he was always going to have a babymama.

Man like that. Probably got them all over town. Baby in every borough.'

'Why do the fit ones have to be so bad?'

'Nature, innit.'

'Straight up.'

Charlie sat in the half-darkness of the petting shed, with Snowflake the chinchilla in her lap, taking a break from emails. Her companion made tiny chirrups, and she imagined it to be advice. *Move on. It's right that he look after them both. More fish in the sea. You needed a way out.* Easier said than done. Her heart hurt. Her *pride* was unutterably hurt. Of course everyone on the farm knew, but she hadn't yet broken the news to her family that the engagement was off. She looked at her wrist, at the tattooed fern that would be there forever, to remind her of her mistake, however much it was for Jools.

Snowflake wriggled, chirped, and Charlie held his soft body between her palms. However appalled and ashamed she felt, at least she had this place: a warm hug in the form of fur and wool and feathers. *My YOLO girl*, her dad had said. Well, she wasn't going to do that anymore. Head, not heart. A trot, not a gallop.

A light, unobtrusive tap sounded on the door. Gábriel was there, the rain running off his cagoul. 'Have you got a minute?'

'Of course.'

He came and sat down next to her, pulling his hood away, and watched her stroke the top of Snowflake's nose. 'I was speaking with Will Boadu.'

'Is he back in town?'

'Yeah. I had a drink with him.'

'Really?' They seemed unlikely boozing buddies, the pair of them getting solemnly plastered together.

'He was telling me about some business plans. He wants to open a butcher's in Battersea for his farm. All ethical meat. Asked me about working there.'

'Oh. OK.' Of course. That would be perfect. Franco taking off, Gábriel resigning. Everyone deserting her. 'You should do it.'

He didn't say anything for a moment. There was just the small tick of the heat lamp above the snakes' cages, and the rustle of straw as the rabbits lolloped about. 'I'm not going to.'

'Why not?'

'I'm needed here.' She looked at him. 'With Jan going and everything.' Jan was making the move to Mudchute, a full-time job finally available. It was a good move for her, a much bigger farm with many more animals. Gábriel gave a slender smile. 'Unless you have someone else in mind to be Farm Yard Manager.'

'No,' she said. 'You know the job's yours. Ade's already said. No one would do it better.' Cradled in her lap, the chinchilla erupted into a flurry of tiny cheeping sounds. 'And Snowflake insists.'

A quiet laugh. 'All right.' He stood up and wiped his cagoul down. 'I'll tell Will.'

'Gábriel,' she said, and he looked back over. 'How did he seem?'

He gazed at the ferret cage for a moment. 'He seems kind of sad. I think his dad is sick.'

'Yeah, I think he is.' A dull pang, something indefinable. 'Did you mention...?'

Since Apple Day, Charlie had seen Franco twice. He'd come to pick up some of his stuff from the cottage, though had left loads of boxes still piled up in her room, saying he'd come and get them later, once he knew what he was doing. It was almost laughable, how quickly it had all been over. She hated that somehow he'd still managed to get the upper hand, and break up with her before she could break up with him.

Gábriel glanced at her. Not once had he said *I told you so.* He'd just made her an occasional cup of tea and left it on her desk. 'No. It's none of my business.'

'Do you ever imagine what it would be like with her here, Mum?'

Charlie had bit the bullet and gone over to Spenser Road. Nellie, ever the pragmatist – being a nurse meant that very little shocked her – had only given Charlie the longest of hugs when she'd told her about Franco and poured her a very liberal glass of red wine. Charlie didn't talk to her about Jools very often because of the fear of triggering that blanket of depression, though Nellie hadn't been ill with it for almost twenty years. But now, she felt very much that she needed to.

'All the time, sweetheart,' Nellie said. They were sitting on the sofa, very full of the shepherd's pie that Aidan had made at Charlie's request, while he washed up in the kitchen. 'I imagine how she'd look, what haircut she'd have, what she'd say in an argument, or about the world. I imagine the three of you altogether, at a dinner or a party or a wedding.'

The three of you. That was the problem. Charlie envisioned that big empty space to the right of her, with Casey stroppily folding her arms on her left – a shimmering void where her big sis should be. Jools would have told her what to do, whether to go for the farm job or not, whether Franco was a dickhead or not. She would have balanced Charlie out, countered Casey's stroppiness. She just felt it. 'I used to talk to her so much,' she said. 'After she'd gone. I mean.'

'I know. I remember.' Nellie smiled. She was in her cream silk pyjamas, which she often changed into right after getting home from the hospital. 'I used to hear you in your bedroom, chatting away.'

'Oh, God. I hope that didn't… make you more ill.'

'No, sweetheart. Anything but, actually.'

'I don't remember when I stopped doing that. Whether I was ten, or twelve… just that I did. I miss talking to her. No offence, Mum, but Casey's not the same.'

Nellie's laugh was soft, forgiving. 'She's her own person. Going her own way.'

Charlie gave a tight half-groan from behind closed lips, one that didn't convey the well of sadness that sat deep in her, and tilted herself until she was laying her head in her mum's lap.

Nellie stroked Charlie's hair with light fingers. 'You don't have to make up for the lack of Jools, my love,' she said, gently. 'You don't have to be anyone but yourself.'

'Come on, Charls,' said Lydia. 'You know you want to.'

Though Charlie and Casey had very little in common these days, Halloween was one tradition they'd always stuck with. Perhaps surprisingly, the only other thing Casey had any interest in was the supernatural, albeit in a morose way ('the zombie apocalypse is coming any day now, I'm telling you'). So on the Saturday nearest Halloween they would head down the road to a neighbour's house party dressed as evil clowns or wearing Day of the Dead masks (Charlie) or with unnervingly accurate facial wounds (Casey). But Charlie didn't feel like it. Instead of comfort-shopping her way down Brick Lane as in years past, she'd found some solace by walking in Sydenham Woods, with the odd Spiderman, Ghostbuster or Elsa flitting through the oak trees to either side of her. Now Casey had come over with some sickly alcopops, having agreed that they could have a gentler night, though Lydia was doing her best to suggest otherwise.

'Really don't feel like it,' said Charlie. She had put the engagement ring in a little box at the back of her tights and socks drawer, where she rather hoped it might dissolve into thin air.

'You've kicked that boy to the kerb,' said Lydia, who was wearing elaborate vampire make-up, albeit a vampire eating a chocolate spread and banana bagel.

'Urgh,' said Charlie resolutely, on the sofa, taking another swig of punch.

'You've got to get back on the horse!' Lydia had already attempted to cheer her up by singing Whitney Houston (dangerously out of tune), doing Britney Spears dance routines (highly uncoordinated), and forcing a wealth of cute kitten and puppy videos in her face. 'Or at least come to my party. I know it's students, but they're bang up for a good time.'

'No horses,' said Charlie. 'Except for Elle.'

'Never thought I'd see you on a horse,' said Casey. 'Like you're a member of the royal family. Next up, polo.'

'I feel very much not like a royal,' sighed Charlie. 'But I do like riding Elle.'

'What about Will, though?' said Lydia, a little more carefully.

'What about him?'

'He likes you,' said Lydia.

'Mmm. Maybe he did for about three seconds.' Before she made him look like an idiot.

'I mean, he *is* nice. Trustworthy. And he'd happily let you sit on his face for as long as you liked, no questions asked.'

This time, Charlie's hum was a groan. 'I've literally just broken up with my fiancé. No face-sitting. Only horse-sitting. Please.'

Naturally, Casey had no interest in boy-talk. She looked at the time on her phone. 'We've gotta go,' she said. '*Beetlejuice* calls.' Charlie, never a fan of scary movies at the best of times, had vetoed anything remotely more frightening. She felt perfectly rattled on her own.

'And party after?' said Lydia, hopefully.

'PeckhamPlex and then bed,' said Charlie firmly. She'd been to the much-loved indie multiplex every week when she was a kid; she and Jools would watch *Jurassic Park* and *The Lion King*, kicking each other's trainers and sharing sweet and salted popcorn. It had never been the same with Casey, but it was what she needed tonight.

'Your loss,' said Lydia, putting her day-glo plastic fangs back in. 'Thee you on the other thide.'

Halloween proper was celebrated lightly at the farm. Volunteers wrapped the tops of the fences in fake spider webs and strung a few skeletons around. A man came to do a presentation on the Ruskin Park bats, and in the classroom the kids made ghost-sheep masks with cotton wool. Tallboy was wearing little devil horns and Joe was a zombie, hood up and elaborate face-paint, so that every time he turned around he made a child cry, and would crouch down to reassure them, which only made it worse.

Charlie was looking at her online bank statement, and the flashing alert around it. Franco had never paid her back anything – for Berlin, his birthday party, all the other money she'd lent him. He didn't reply to her messages and was absent from social media, apart from a single photo of a tightly-curled baby's fist, and the word 'Daughter' followed by countless messages of astonishment and congratulations. Now she couldn't ask him, because he had to support a teenage girl and their child. She hadn't paid Lydia for the month's rent yet. She took a deep breath and was about to click on 'LOANS' when she heard raised voices outside. A woman's voice, and Marianne's smoother, calmer one. She got up.

There was a woman with babies in a twin buggy outside, and she gave a curt glance to Charlie as she emerged from the office. 'Are you the manager?'

Was she? For the purposes of this, she thought it best to say so. 'Yes. Hi. What can I do for you?'

Marianne had taken a step away, but looked worried.

'I'd like to make a complaint,' the woman said. 'Urgently.'

'OK. I'm sorry to hear that. Sure.' Charlie tried to snap out of it and bring herself back into her assertive farm administrator self.

'That boy—' The woman turned around.

'Which one?'

'Him.' She jabbed a finger towards the sheep pen, where Joe was high-fiving Lydia. 'The zombie one. I saw him take a small packet of something from a man, by the barn.'

'A small...?' Charlie's momentary confusion gave way within a second to a strange, teetering sensation. She called to him, and Joe jogged towards them, slowing as he realised something was wrong. He put his hands in his pockets, gave a jerking nod, chin up. He removed his hood.

'Joe,' said Charlie, as his eyes darted to the woman and her children. 'This lady says that she thought she saw you—'

'Not *thought* I saw,' the woman interjected. 'I *did* see. You've got it in your pocket now. Drugs.'

Even behind the make-up, Charlie could see Joe's eyes cloud, his jaw tighten. 'What? No, I never. That's lies, man.'

'You absolutely did.'

'Joe—' said Charlie.

'She's chatting shit,' he said, and made a talking motion with his hand, fingers and thumb moving together like castanets.

Charlie could see how easily his wall came up if attacked. She softened her voice and put her arm on his elbow, leading him slightly away from the woman.

'She don't know what she's talking about,' said Joe, shrugging her off.

'Unbelievable,' said the woman, and pulled her buggy a little away, rummaging in her bag.

'Tell me honestly,' Charlie said, and moved several times, Joe turning his shoulder to her, until he finally made eye contact. 'Can you show me what's in your pockets?'

'No, man. I know my rights.'

Behind them, the woman had her back to them and was speaking on the phone.

'Joe, it's OK,' Charlie said. 'We'll sort it out, but I need to know what happened. You're working here, Joe.'

He looked away again, shaking his head. The world against him.

'Who were you with?'

'No one.'

'Was it Franco?' The teetering sensation was still there. The memory of Gábriel, voicing his suspicions.

He gave a dark scowl, making his zombie-face look even more terrifying. 'No. Why would he be here? He's bounced, hasn't he.' Joe turned away from Charlie again and gave a jagged huff. 'Liberty, man.'

'This is a community farm. Nothing like that can happen here. If it's something innocent, then just say. But if anything has—'

'It hasn't,' he said, the words stabbed out, before muttering sour curses under his breath. This was a different Joe, the one she never saw here on the farm. She could see the bones of his knuckles protruding through the pockets of his hoodie.

The woman behind them was speaking. 'I've called the police. If you're not going to do anything, then they will. It's not acceptable – this is a place for families.'

As she spoke, Joe's eyes, fixed on Charlie, became vulnerable. He stared at her for a long, still moment, before suddenly bolting, a blur of navy blue and a last flash of his zombie face.

'Well, that says it all,' said the woman.

The farm closed for the second time in six weeks. This time, police officers with more seniority came, and took statements from the woman who'd called them, from Charlie, and from the volunteers. They viewed the CCTV footage – one of the extra cameras covered the barn. She watched, her heart sinking, as the black and white footage showed Joe covertly taking something from the hand of a youngish man she didn't recognise. It was obviously something illegal. Gábriel, who had a day off, said he would come in after receiving her message, but she told him not to.

'You didn't know anything, did you?' Charlie said to Tallboy, who'd always seemed closest to Joe.

He shook his head, his dreamy eyes wide. 'I didn't, Charlie. Swear down. I thought he was past all that.'

Joe couldn't be found. She gave the police the address that she had for him – an estate in Loughborough Junction – and Tallboy reluctantly offered a couple of other suggestions, but nothing was successful. She left several messages on his phone, gentle ones, trying to persuade him to come to the farm, to no response.

'I don't know what to think,' said Charlie to Gábriel the next day.

There was a deep moment's silence, in which she knew that they were both thinking about his warning to her. Franco and Joe.

'We'll see,' Gábriel said.

She was locking up the next evening when a figure slipped from the side of the fence and almost bumped into her.

A pale face glowed from under a hood. 'Didn't have anywhere to go.'

'Joe,' she said. 'You can't be hiding. It will make everything worse. You just have to talk to them, that's all.'

He looked down, scuffed at the pavement, and looked up again. 'Just... can I see Slick before I do?'

They sat in the petting shed, Joe feeding the ferret's lithe, ribboning body through his hands, his arm now out of its cast, though still limp. He was finally getting stubble on that smooth jaw of his. 'I'm gonna go down,' he said eventually.

'Not necessarily,' she said, though she didn't know for certain. She had no idea how severe the penalties were. 'Just tell them the truth.'

Joe held Slick up in front of him, put his forefinger in the animal's mouth and let it nibble.

'What was it? That you took?'

He spoke to the ferret. 'Just weed, innit. Nothing serious.'

Just. She took a long, deep breath. 'But on the *farm*, Joe.' She couldn't understand how he could be so stupid.

'I know. Man was supposed to meet me after but he just showed up early. I didn't arks him to come on the farm. They'll say it was intent to supply. But I don't do that no more.' He looked up. 'It was just for me. Things are dead at home, man. Just makes me feel better.'

'Who was it?' At the very least, they could get the man who supplied it.

'Just a friend of his. Not, like, a dealer. Your mans said he'd sort me out. Like, as a favour. Bargain price.'

'My man?'

Now Joe was eyeing her like she was the stupid one. 'Yeah. Franco.'

Charlie went cold.

'He said not to tell you. He said it would be OK.' He sucked his teeth.

She stared at him.

He lifted the mesh at the top of the ferret's cage and put Slick back in. 'Do you think I'll go young offenders this time? Because it's a second offence? I don't wanna go.' His voice cracked, and he sounded very young and very old all at once. 'I love this place, man. Best thing to ever happen to me.'

U lying bastard

she texted.

U lowdown piece of scum

She hadn't contacted him since he'd gone. Until now.

Franco. *Franco* had done this. She wanted to scream; rage. It was worse than she'd imagined. Franco had been giving him weed on the sly and Joe – young, impressionable, wanting to seem a big man – had taken it. Franco had sent his *friends* to him. And now this sixteen-year-old boy was at the police station, having been accompanied by Charlie and Jan, and released on bail. He asked several times not to go home, to go to a foster place, but his request had not been granted.

Franco was texting back.

Calm down. You'll get over it. We both agreed.

She wanted to tear him to pieces. Jabbed at her phone.

Not ME, you fuck

He sent back a single question mark.

JOE

she texted.
There was no reply.

—————

Ade came at the end of the next day. She hadn't seen him for ages. He'd basically left her to it, apart from their monthly session and the board meetings. 'Charlie. We need to speak.'

They sat in the office.

Ade sighed and pulled the skin of his forehead together. 'If we're not careful, there's going to be a report on this, at least in the London papers.'

Charlie could picture it: DRUG DEALERS ON CITY FARM. She nodded, mute.

'And it's an inescapable fact that someone you know was involved in this. Possibly – that is to say, probably – set it up. Someone you were intimately involved with.'

'Ade, you have to believe me,' she said. 'I had no idea.' Not quite true. Gábriel had told her something was going on, and she hadn't done enough. 'I made a…' She swallowed, and the words emerged in a croak. 'A really bad choice.'

He nodded, several times. 'I do believe you. I understand your commitment to this place.' He gave an uncomfortable cough. 'Nonetheless. Questions are going to be asked about your position here.'

She felt her mind go numb. 'Yes. Of course.'

Ade gazed at his brogues. 'Come in tomorrow and finish off the week, but after that…' He looked up at her. 'I think it's best if you take a few days off.'

She walked towards home, and continued walking past the turning to the cottage, along the main road, through Streatham, Balham, and past her favourite of Tooting's South Indian restaurants. She thought she'd perhaps go and see her mum, on the later shift at St George's, but she walked on for miles, eventually finding herself outside Deen City Farm. A small, perfect farm on which no drugs were dealt. Her feet hurt. She sat on the ground by a tiny river next to the site, her coat not quite long enough to stop the dank vegetation seeping in. She listened to the cackling laugh of a duck somewhere in the dark. She sat for a long time, shivering, her stomach grumbling. Perhaps she would stay there all night.

When she finally looked at her phone, there was a flurry of messages from Lydia, in response to her single one, which had said: *Ade's gonna fire me.*

no
fuck
4 real tho?
ur not gettin fired
not on my watch
that dickface Franco
im gonna get him
that boy is dead meat
where ru?
u ok?
CHARILE
just tell me ur ok & ill stop buggin u
maybe

The next morning, there was a firm knock on the office door, far firmer than Ade's usual one, and Charlie's heart plummeted. This was it, then. She was going to be fired.

But instead of Ade's head, Will Boadu's face appeared. 'Might I...?' he said.

'Oh. Hi, Will,' she said, her voice not her own. 'Yeah. Sure.'

He shut the door quietly. He was wearing a dark-blue suit

and a hunter-green shirt with an EU pin on his lapel. 'Forgive the intrusion. I heard about what happened.'

She looked at her knees; felt nothing but a profound shame.

His voice was warm, dependable. 'I'm here to help.'

'I don't deserve it,' she said.

'That's untrue.'

She stood up and pushed the office chair back away from her, feeling like she needed to escape, run out of the farm, out of the park, out of everyone's way. All this time, she'd been working so diligently on the farm, and she'd ruined it all by letting her pride get in the way again. By not listening to Gábriel. 'I've let everybody down. I've been irresponsible.' She burst into tears.

There was a deeply awkward moment – she, horrified at her own weeping and unable to stop it; Will, watching her a little astonished – before he took a step forward and put his arms around her.

She found herself with her head against his broad expensively-shirted chest, her uncontrollable tears soaking it. She was crying for the loss of Franco, for her idiocy at having been attached to him, at the idea of not being able to work here, on the farm. Her farm.

'It's quite all right,' he said in a smooth murmur. 'You've been fantastic for this place. It's perfectly obvious. Let me see what I can do.'

TWENTY-TWO

Dinner – A Disappearance

O ver the next week, Charlie stayed at home. She made endless cups of tea, did another cross-stitch pattern (a floral one for her mum), watched seasons four to seven of Buffy, and painted her nails midnight purple. None of it worked. For the first time in her life, she had been doing a job that she loved. She didn't wince when the alarm went off and didn't count down the minutes until she could leave; she didn't mind the office windows fogging with condensation; getting mud on her shoes or jeans. The farm had made a space for her, shaped her, made her see that she could be valuable. She cared about all the people who worked and volunteered there, and about all the animals from the chinchillas to the donkeys.

She kept googling the farm for any news reports, praying that no journalist would get hold of the story. Lydia said that Joe, who wasn't allowed on site, kept messaging Tallboy for updates on the animals, with requests for photos. He would have to go to the youth court in a fortnight's time. She felt sadness and shame twist in her gut. However indirectly she had caused this, it was still her fault.

Will was true to his word. He'd privately convened with Ade, and there was going to be a meeting with the board next week to discuss her position.

'You didn't have to do all this,' she said to him, in Brixton Pound.

Will blew into the froth of his coffee. 'I very much wanted to. The farm can't do without you.' He gave her the briefest look, before sitting back in his seat.

It was hard to make him out. Gábriel had said he seemed sad, and it was true that he appeared tired. There was a prickle of stubble at his jawline. It didn't help that the news from America was the worst it could be: a misogynist racist would be in the White House from the beginning of next year. 'I'll grab *his* fucking pussy,' Lydia had said. But there was that no-nonsense, businesslike politician, in his stiff shoulders and his clipped sentences; and the sense of his deep generosity in all he was doing for her.

'Have you been riding?' he asked.

'Yeah. On and off.'

'Do keep going. Elle will always be pleased to see you, I'm sure.'

Charlie gave him a clumsy half-smile. He was still gazing at her. There was a small vein pulsing in his temple. 'How are you, Will?'

'I'm… it's been a little tumultuous. I think I mentioned about my father.'

She nodded.

'Well, we've heard this week that it's terminal.'

'Oh, man.' She was suddenly outside herself, concerned. 'I'm so sorry. That's awful.'

'Thank you. Yes, it's not been easy.' He managed a smile, the politician in him overriding the authentic emotion. 'So we've both had a bit of a time. I understand – or, rather, I heard that—' He glanced down at her left hand, at the absence of a ring.

Hers seemed rather less significant now. She put her hand to the back of her neck. 'Yeah. That is definitely over.'

The coffee machine behind them made its shuddering, guttural noise, as if to echo her embarrassment.

'What do you say to some dinner?' Will said, and seemed discomfited by the suddenness of the words. 'Nothing fancy. Just to take your mind off things. Just as friends.'

She regarded him. He was the opposite of Franco: grounded, dependable, capable. Doing everything he could to salvage her job, her *career*. He needed cheering up as much as she did. Rather more so. She looked at the froth in the bottom of her mug, the bubbles popping one by one.

'Yes. Thank you,' she said. 'That sounds good.'

At the weekend, there were drinks in The Sun for Jan's leaving do. Charlie hadn't wanted to go, but Jan had called her and used her most menacingly friendly tone.

'Are you all right?' said Gábriel, joining her. She had been sitting a little forlornly at the edge of a conversation – not because she hadn't been made welcome, but because she felt awful.

'Oh, you know,' said Charlie, and of course he did know, because he always seemed to.

He was giving her the sort of calmly assessing look a paramedic might give a patient. 'It's gonna be OK,' he said.

'I don't know,' she said, cupping her hands round her rum and Coke. 'Aren't you going to say it now?'

'Say what?'

She shook her head, hopelessly. 'That if I'd listened to you, none of this would have happened?'

'No,' he said, and though his tone was kind, it was as if she'd suggested something distasteful. 'Why would I do that?' He seemed about to say something else when Jan stood up, tapping on her pint glass with a fork, to make her leaving speech. Or, as Jan called it, the passing of the Ruskin Park Farm torch.

'I am leaving you in the capable hands of this young man,' she said. 'The Hungarian dreamboat, the man all sheep follow, the man who would win Farm Yard X Factor in a heartbeat: Gábriel Büki.'

There was a round of applause, and an acute wolf-whistle from Lydia, making Gábriel smile into his beer.

'Seriously though,' said Jan. 'I wouldn't leave if I didn't know it was in good hands. I really fucking love that farm.' She wiped away a fierce tear to more applause, and sat down next to Charlie with a big, passionate sigh. Her wife, sitting opposite them, put a comforting hand over Jan's.

'The farm's going to miss you,' Charlie said, and her voice broke a little on the last two words.

'Thanks, missus,' Jan said, clapping her free hand on Charlie's thigh and throwing her an uncompromising look. 'Me and Beth are off to swing dancing tomorrow night, aren't we, love? You want in? You'll have a right laugh. Good distraction.'

'Oh,' Charlie said. 'I can't.'

'Oh, yeah?' She narrowed her eyes. 'Give me one good reason why not.' She addressed Gábriel, on the other side of her. 'You're gonna come, mate, aren't you? You were like fucking Fred Astaire last time.'

He shrugged and awkwardly scratched the back of his neck. 'I was thinking about it. Maybe.'

'I'm off out with Will.' Charlie said.

Jan raised her eyebrows. 'Aye, aye.'

'As friends. He's trying to save my arse. Save my bacon.' Gábriel glanced over again, and didn't acknowledge the pun. 'I want to.'

Will's idea of nothing fancy was Charlie's idea of everything fancy, she thought, as the waiter poured them an extremely expensive glass of red wine that apparently had hints of cherries and lavender with an aspect of roasted wild Provençal herbs. The restaurant specialised in nose-to-tail dining, and a neighbouring table was having an entire suckling pig. Lydia would roar protest chants and throw water bombs if she were here.

Instead, Charlie was sitting opposite Will at an intimate corner table, a candle melting in a gothic fashion between them as their first courses were served. He was in jeans, but the smartest kind – ironed – and shiny, light-brown leather shoes. He'd had his hair clippered into a perfect line across the top of his forehead. He'd definitely made an effort, but she found she couldn't begrudge him for it.

As well as asking Charlie about hers, Will told her about his earlier life – he'd been a speed chess champion as a kid, getting carted around town halls in the UK by his devoted mum. He'd played a lot of rugby, until he broke his collarbone. He talked about his couple of years in Washington DC after university, where he'd intended to get into American politics but had mostly spent his time playing, in his words, 'extremely mediocre jazz trumpet.' He was very into theatre and talked about the acoustic merits of various auditoriums, and his enthusiasm for new writers. It was nice to see these different aspects of him.

He spoke of his worries over how his mother was coping with his dad's diagnosis; of his farm in North Yorkshire and the livestock there; of the difficulties in overseeing it from a distance; the changeable weather, the winter snows, his plans to expand to the organic butcher's shop in London and even a chain. 'I mentioned it to Gábriel,' he said, between mouthfuls of bone marrow and salad. 'I'm not sure if you heard.'

'I did.'

'I wasn't trying to poach him exactly. I can see he's a capable man, with ambition, that's all. And a butcher previously, of course. But I understand how loyal he is to you.'

She looked up. 'To the farm.'

He gave her an odd, benign sort of look. The candle made his cheekbones glow. 'Indeed.' He seemed to be growing in confidence again. 'And how are you feeling? About the end of your... the engagement?'

She determinedly sliced up her duck leg. 'I don't want to talk about it.'

'Of course. Apologies.'

There was a moment of awkward silence, in which she wished a waiter would come with more wine. 'How's everything with work?' she said.

He glanced at her. 'It's fine. I suppose you saw what happened in Strasbourg.'

Many papers had been quite respectful of his outburst, in

the end. *Eco-Warrior Will*, said some papers. *Hothead MEP Boadu*, said others, however. He received all sorts of vile abuse on Twitter and managed to respond with impressive civility. 'Sometimes I just lose patience,' he said. 'It's not like we have all the time in the world on this. Politics moves so damned slowly when you need it to move quickly, and vice versa.'

'I hear that,' she said. 'Well, we all thought you were awesome.'

He looked rather charmed.

'Especially Lydia.'

'Ah.' He smiled, though she wondered if there was something rueful in his eyes. 'Well, that's the main thing.'

They stood outside the restaurant, full of various lurid cuts of meat and far too much wine, at least in Charlie's case. She wondered if he might ask her to go for a last drink somewhere, and wondered what she would say. Mostly, she still felt like curling up into a ball in her bed, burning some of Lydia's great-gran's ancient essential oils and listening to a playlist called Melancholy Electro. But there was a part of her that would have been interested to see where it went.

But instead, he said, 'I'll get you a cab,' and stepped up to the kerb.

'Oh, I'll get the tube.'

'No, no, here's one,' he said, holding up his arm as a black cab passed with its light on. 'It's on me.'

She felt a twang of guilt as she got in, Will discreetly giving the driver some money. He was so kind to her. 'I'm really grateful,' she said, looking back at him, the car's door still open. 'Honestly. I don't know what I'd do without this job. It's meant a lot to me. I really appreciate—' There she was, about to cry again. She drew in a fortifying breath. 'Thank you for dinner. And this.'

Will nodded – warm, gracious. 'Goodnight, Charlie. I'll see you soon.'

She turned as they drove away to see him still standing there, watching the cab disappear.

'Hey, Charls.' A couple of days later, Lydia called her.

'Hey,' said Charlie, who had been lying on the sofa, watching a daytime cookery programme with a distinct lack of focus. The board were meeting this afternoon to discuss her future and she could think of little else. 'What's up? Can it wait 'til later?' Lydia had been giving her daily updates from the farm, which only made her feel worse.

'There's someone here asking for you. Um, don't freak out, but I think it might be Franco's girlfriend? Gold braids, baby in tow.'

Charlie's stomach lurched. 'OK,' she said. 'You mean... is there any sign of Franco?'

'No. Just those two. Are you able to come over?'

Funmi was outside Denmark Hill station's pub, The Phoenix, just as arranged, crouching down by her buggy and adjusting the baby's gloves. When she saw Charlie, she straightened. 'Oh. Hi.' She was wearing a thin-looking parka, its fur-lined hood half-up. 'Sorry to bother you. I thought you'd be at the farm.'

'That's OK.' Charlie didn't feel like explaining why she wasn't. She looked down at the baby, trying to glean a hint of

Franco's puckish countenance in her face. She took a deep breath and folded her arms. 'What can I do for you?'

'Um, I just wondered if Franco was around?'

Charlie's mind flattened and went blank. 'No, he's not. He's not allowed to be on the farm. He's banned.' *As am I*, she thought.

A hint of confusion ghosted over Funmi's face.

'He—' Charlie was about to say what had happened with Joe, but something in Funmi's countenance stopped her. 'Why do you think he'd be round here?'

'I didn't know if you guys hooked up again or something.'

'Oh my God, no. Absolutely no way. Why would you think that?'

Her shrug was minimal. 'Oh. He's kinda disappeared on me.'

'Disappeared?' Charlie was beginning to regret her earlier thought. There was something in the way Funmi held herself, elegant and vulnerable at once. 'How do you mean? I promise he's not been over this way, and I'm three hundred per cent not seeing him.'

Funmi swallowed, and there was the subtlest shine of a tear in her eye.

'Come on,' said Charlie. 'Let's get you a cuppa.'

They sat outside the pub, and Funmi – having drunk most of her hot chocolate in one – recounted how she, Franco and the baby had gone to Brighton for the day. They'd walked along the front and onto the West Pier; Funmi said it was only the second time she'd seen the sea. She'd wanted to sit on a bench to watch it, and Franco had grown impatient and gone for a stroll. She'd sat on a bench with Mia, and the few minutes she assumed he'd be gone stretched to ten. She'd fancied he was getting them drinks, or buying Mia a toy. But it became thirty minutes, then an hour, and when she'd tried phoning him, he didn't pick up.

'I started asking people if they'd seen him, but no one was any help. It was starting to do my head in. I thought he must have, like, fallen off and drowned or something. So I found the police station, and they took my details, but they didn't seem that bothered. Like they didn't believe me. I didn't know what to do. I stayed by the pier for the whole day. Poor Mia was frozen, weren't you?' She leant down to her baby, who blinked back up at her with dewy brown eyes. 'We had to get the train back on our own.'

Charlie felt a strange, spare sadness. 'And... you haven't heard anything from him?'

Funmi shook her head. 'No. I've called him about five hundred times. He's not been to the tattoo shop – they said they'd fire him if he didn't come soon. His mum said she hasn't heard from him.'

'How had he seemed? Beforehand?'

'I dunno.' She gave a sheepish smile. 'He's Franco, isn't he? You never know what you're going to get with that boy.' But the tear that had threatened earlier finally made itself known, and another, and she dabbed at them with the cuff of her parka. 'But he wouldn't have just taken off. We were going to get a studio flat together.'

Later, Charlie scoured social media for any sign of him – she'd deleted him and all his messages from her phone already, and didn't have his number anymore. There was nothing since the picture of Mia's hand on Instagram, and no sign or mention of him on the pages of the couple of his friends she'd connected with. It was easy for Charlie to think the worst of him, but would he really go to such lengths to ghost the mother of his child, and the child herself? He had seemed like he genuinely loved her, been clear-headed, determined even. Funmi had phoned Brighton's A&E and the local police again, to no avail. Maybe something really *had* happened.

While she was endlessly scrolling, Will's name came up on her phone.

Charlie. I've some news. May we meet?

'Oh, God,' she said.

'I hope you don't mind,' said Will. 'I wanted to tell you myself.'

Charlie felt sure that he'd suggested the café at Battersea Arts Centre because he had bad news to deliver, and wanted to do it in a public place where she wouldn't wail and cry too embarrassingly.

'OK,' she said. She looked at the curved grain of the wooden table between them and felt empty.

'All's well,' he said.

She looked up. 'All's...?'

His face was plain, kind. 'Well.'

She swallowed. 'Really?' The word was feather-light.

He gave a deep, solid nod, and she listened, allowing his words to sink in. He said that the board had agreed that Charlie should carry on working on the farm. It sounded like Will had vouched for her utterly, and though there was some debate in the meeting, the vote had been strongly in her favour.

It had been assisted by a collection of statements from co-workers and volunteers, some in handwritten scrawls, all testaments as to why Charlie should stay.

'Ade will call you later today,' he said. She'd be getting a first written warning from him, but Will had dismissed it as a formality.

Charlie exhaled a long breath that she felt she must have been holding for days. She'd thrown her long winter coat and beret over her un-showered self and was suddenly aware that she wasn't at her best. 'I can't believe you did this for me. You're amazing.'

Did Charlie imagine the briefest flash of delight in his eyes? If so, it was gone in an instant, replaced with something more graceful. 'Not just me,' he said, leaning back in his vintage armchair. 'I'd love to take all the credit, but it was Gábriel who got the staff and volunteers to write statements of support. He went round to a few people's houses, too, I understand – those that weren't working on the farm that week.'

'He did?' She felt her eyes begin to line with tears.

Will sat forward and put down his mug. 'You are cared for, Charlie. The farm is a place that looks after its own.'

She gazed at her feet, the tears coming properly now. She was an unwashed, sobbing mess. 'Oh, man.'

She pressed her lips together, swallowed, and put her knuckles to the side of one eye. She felt as if she'd just come off a tightrope between two very high buildings. 'Thank you, Will. I can't even—'

'My pleasure,' he said, rather gently, and reached into the inside pocket of his suit jacket to bring out a tissue.

December brings air with an edge to it. In the park, a man hand-feeds squirrels nuts from a plastic bag. Only the dark pines keep their foliage now, the branches of the other trees stark against a bitter winter sky. Tinsel is wrapped around the fence posts and Christmas trees are placed in the barn, donkey pen and café, each with a growing number of decorations made by visiting primary school classes. Charity, Faith and Walt decide it is not too early to wear Santa hats – Walt is often mistaken for the real thing by hysterical children – and Moonie curates an uncompromising selection of seasonal music, from Slayer to The Fall. Charlie is welcomed back to work in a restrained fashion, as if she has never been away. She keeps her head down, applies herself quietly and humbly, knowing that she will never put a foot wrong again.

'Look at this, man.'

'*The Argus*. What's that?'

'Brighton's local paper.'

'Newsflash: killer seagull on the loose.'

'Jokes.'

'Nah, look at the photo—'

'Make your screen bigger—'

'It's Franco, innit.'

'Oh my God, for real? He's missing?'

'MIA.'

'"His partner, Funmi Rose, is appealing for witnesses."'

'Mad ting.'

'Maybe he's dead.'

'No way. Mr Fuckboi just fucked off. Believe.'

Charlie stood at the fence of the sheep pen at the beginning of the day, watching the animals methodically crop the grass. Life seemed so simple for them. Grass. Hay. Defecate. Sleep.

Pink gave an outraged, drunken blurt.

'Yep,' said Charlie. 'Same.'

She'd been working on a template to entice corporate businesses to invest when Lydia had told her about the news report. Franco was now officially missing. She had thought the very worst of him, had imagined fights, long articulate outpourings, revenge, and now this. Not even *he* would have done this to Funmi and Mia. She searched for more news reports and on his Instagram, where there were now a few comments along with praying hands emojis. Four of Franco's boxes were still stacked in the corner of her bedroom, marked with things like *Franco's shit* and *Franco's other shit*. She'd taken Funmi's number, in case she could do anything else to help.

'Hey.' Gábriel had soundlessly come to join her, leaning on the fence. He was in tracksuit bottoms, trainers.

She looked behind her at the small stream of people coming out of the yoga class. 'I didn't know you did yoga.'

'Yeah, sometimes.'

'When am I taking you out for curry?' She'd wanted to do it as thanks for getting the statements of support.

'You don't have to do that,' he said. He looked at the sheep.

'I want to. I owe you. Big time.'

There was a pause in which he didn't suggest any dates. She guessed that he preferred spending time with Agnes than with his unreliable co-worker. Fair enough.

'You would do the same for me.' He looked at her and raised his eyebrows, the semblance of an amused challenge.

'Of course I would,' she said, and his face subtly altered in surprise at her vehemence. She sighed. 'But you'd never have been so stupid. Or so proud. I should have listened to you.'

The shake of his head was so slight that she barely registered it. 'I understand.'

'I'm just...' The words tripped out very lightly, but the weight underneath them was obvious enough. 'Very, very grateful.'

He clasped his hands together over the fence. 'You being back here is good enough for me.' He spoke so unassumingly that she wasn't quite sure if he meant it, or if he was just being kind, like he always was.

Bey-Bey was looking at them, her jaw working stolidly. Charlie stole another glance at him, but his face was unreadable. *I'm not going to mess up again*, she wanted to tell him. *Not ever.*

'You should do it,' he said. 'Yoga.'

She blinked herself back into reality. 'Yeah, I should.'

'It's good for taking your mind off things.'

She realised that she was stroking the fern tattoo on her wrist, an action she'd found herself doing repeatedly, and that Gábriel was watching her do it. She couldn't help it. She was worried about Franco, and about Funmi and Mia.

'There's always stuff to do here,' he said. 'The animals always need you. And there's Joe tomorrow.'

Joe's hearing, where Charlie, Gábriel and Jan went to give character testimonials, was in a bland building in a blander room. He looked very young in his old school shirt and he jiggled his knee constantly as the three of them spoke, but by the time Charlie had finished, his leg had stopped moving and he'd given her a doleful grin.

Following discussions between the presiding official and

the borough's Youth Offending Service, the youth court agreed on a sentence of community service and strict regular supervision; he was told very plainly, however, that on the occasion of a third misdemeanour, he would go to an institution. Charlie immediately got in touch with the service and offered Joe an internship at the farm. Ade had taken a lot of persuading, but Charlie was determined; she had been given a second chance, and therefore so should he. It was agreed that Joe would sign in every day that he wasn't at college, and that he would have his weekly meetings with his probation officer on site after hours.

When he arrived for his first day as an intern, Charlie took him into the office and gave him a new RPF jumper.

'Cheers, Charlie,' he said, rather mutedly.

'It was my fault, Joe. What happened.'

'What? No way, man. How was it your fault?'

'Because if I hadn't met Franco – if he hadn't been coming here—' She briefly looked at her nails, and back up at him. 'It was on me.'

'Nah,' said Joe. 'Don't be blaming yourself. You're a G. I'm just… My head's not always in a good place.'

'I understand,' she said. 'Hey. One more pressie.' She handed him a mug that she'd had personalised, saying FARMER JOE IS A DON.

He took it from her and stood there hanging his head, and she wondered for a moment whether he might cry. 'I won't let you down, Charlie,' he said. 'Swear.'

'I know you won't,' she said, and determined that she, too, would work her arse off to be the best she could be, not let her pride come first, and never let the farm down again.

TWENTY-THREE

A Diversion – A Shock – Breakfast

'Penny for your thoughts?'

Will had taken Charlie to the theatre. It was the second time they'd been out together since their dinner and he'd made no move beyond buying her drinks. She'd readily agreed to his invitations – she found herself increasingly liking his company, and could do with the distraction from wondering about Franco, who still hadn't turned up anywhere. Funmi had said she'd let her know.

In the inside theatre of the Globe, she watched as candles were lit by the actors in the otherwise dark space, watched them banter and carouse to the delight of the audience, iambic pentameter dancing off their tongues.

When Charlie had told Will that she hadn't seen a Shakespeare play, or film version, since the one time they'd had to go for secondary school, he'd laughed and talked about some adaptations he'd really loved over the years. She hadn't corrected his assumption that she thought Shakespeare dry or baffling; kept it to herself that it was the name of the road where Jools had died. But when Will invited her, Charlie had taken a deep breath, and told herself that it was time to move on, that it was hardly Shakespeare's fault, and accepted.

Towards the end of the first half, she'd stiffened and sat bolt upright as an actor appeared from behind the audience on the opposite side, face heavy with stage make-up and wearing a ludicrous wig. He looked like Franco.

Of course, it wasn't him. Now, in the interval, she was staring at the cast list in the play's programme, just to make sure. She kept wondering about Funmi's thought of him falling off the pier; wondered if there could have been the slightest possibility of him jumping, the pressure of fatherhood becoming too much; kept seeing his skin, a waxen, ethereal blue, seaweed wrapping itself gently around him. But more than anything, Franco had been full of life, grabbing it by handfuls. It didn't make sense.

'Charlie?'

'Sorry,' she said, and handed the programme back to Will. It was perfectly enjoyable being out with him. Not Franco-levels of excitement, but she knew now that she had to look beyond such things. He was attentive, courteous, respectful. 'It's nothing.' She smiled at him.

'I'll get you a drink,' Will said, and moved to the bar.

Afterwards, they walked along the river towards Waterloo. The German Christmas market was in full force, small stalls festooned with fairy lights, iced gingerbread houses and pretzels on display alongside the tat. It only made her think more of Franco, of their trip to Berlin.

She said goodbye to Will at the back of the Royal Festival Hall, saying she'd get the bus, and took the underpass. It was starkly lit and quiet, the sort of place she could be with her thoughts. She imagined Franco coming towards her, his face mostly wiped free from the theatre make-up, apart from perhaps a smudge underneath one eye wearing one of his beautifully devilish grins. *Babe. Did you see me? Treading the boards at last. Just where I should be.* Then she shook her head, trying to rid herself of it.

Someone bumped against her shoulder, making her stagger, and before she could say anything, the person turned around and stood in front of her.

Not Franco.

A white man, very skinny, in a matching tracksuit that looked dirty. Perhaps he needed money. She could get him a sandwich from—

'Bag,' he said, in nothing more than a mutter, beckoning with his fingers. He was looking past her.

'Sorry?'

'Bag,' he said again, and she noticed the bony knuckles of his left hand, and how his fist was clenched around the handle of a small knife, held close to his hip. There was a sudden, throbbing pain in her throat and in her stomach.

'You deaf? Or blind?' His eyes darted down towards his hand, the tip of the blade angled towards her. '*Bag.*'

'Sorry,' she said. Part of her wasn't inside her body; had floated up to the flat concrete ceiling. 'Please don't—' She took her bag off her shoulder and he grabbed at it, tugging her forward slightly, and dashed past her, back the way she had come. The whole encounter had lasted a moment.

Charlie stood very still, the sensation of several heartbeats and pulses all firing at once, her head buzzing. She heard herself finally take a huge breath and emit a garbled cry, before she ran faster than she'd run in her life, the opposite way through the underpass and up the steps, suddenly back in

London by the roundabout and the IMAX cinema. Lights. Cars. People. Her breath was heaving now, the cold air in her throat, tears spiking her eyes. She leant against the wall, folded over, waiting for her heart to calm. Everything was spinning.

'You all right, love?' someone said, but didn't stop.

She could hear herself making small, scraping whimpers. Phone. Her phone was in her coat pocket. She fumbled for it, and brought up Will's number.

He was there in what seemed like seconds, stepping out of a black cab, taking her hand and drawing her into a hug. There she was, sobbing in his arms again, and this time she was nothing but exceedingly grateful.

He drew back, hands on her arms. 'Are you hurt?'

She shook her head. Her nose was running copiously.

'All right. Good. Let's get you to the police station.'

Charlie gave a brief statement to a police officer in a small, striplit room, watching her hand tremble and starting to feel a bit silly. It could have been so much worse. The policewoman took it all down, asked clear, pertinent questions about the man's description. She expressed her sympathy, told Charlie she'd done the right thing, and let her finish her cup of very sweet tea.

'I apologised to him,' Charlie said to Will in the foyer, still holding the mug. He looked at her. 'I literally said sorry and gave him my bag.'

'Of course you did. Anyone would. Very British,' he said with a hint of a smile. He watched her drain her tea. 'Shall we take you home?'

'No one's there. Lydia's away. Not back until tomorrow.' She was at a national business management conference in Sheffield with fellow students, and if there was one thing that Charlie could not imagine, it was Lydia at a national business management conference in Sheffield. 'And no keys now, obviously.'

'Ah,' he said, and there was a deep pause.

She dug her thumb into her palm and watched the skin pucker.

'To mine, then.' He spoke lightly. 'I've three bedrooms. Plenty of space.'

She looked at him. She could be calling her mum and dad; sleeping on the camp bed in Casey's room; listening to her snore.

'Here you go.' Will set down a decaf coffee on the black chrome table in front of her, and straightened. 'Everything sorted?'

Will lived in a third floor flat in a red and white brick mansion block in Battersea, with an entrance of ornate white stone and very high ceilings. There was a fireplace at either end of the long living room – the sort of apartment she could never, ever afford.

She'd phoned the bank and gone through a series of security questions in order to have her cards cancelled. 'Yeah. I guess so.' She had her legs folded underneath her on Will's artfully battered leather sofa, a cushion on her lap for extra comfort.

He sat down next to her, a little distance between them. 'I'm so sorry you had to go through that. I wish I'd been there.'

'Why? Would you have decked him?' She still felt jittery with adrenaline.

'Probably not,' he said. 'I suppose a knife is a knife.'

'Don't know why he bothered, anyway.'

'With what?'

'With mugging me. They won't find anything on my cards. I swear the bank person on the phone laughed when she looked at my accounts.' She looked at him. 'I'm so broke.' She let out a tiny, hopeless laugh. 'Um, I don't suppose I could have a proper drink, could I?'

By the time he came back with her brandy – a thumb's-width rolling in a fat-bottomed glass – she had opened the double doors and stepped out onto the balcony. 'Needed some air.'

They stood together as cars passed below them, their breath fogging in two separate clouds. She became aware of the murmur of music – a plucked bass, a piano – from the living room behind them.

'I'm sorry to hear about your money troubles,' he said.

'Thanks.' She looked at him. 'I was cleaned out a little bit.' She hardly had to say by whom. She looked at her palms. 'I owe Lydia two months' rent. She's a diamond, but… I don't deserve her.'

'I'm sure that's not true. He leant his elbows on the balcony, cradling his own brandy.

'You have a very nice place,' she said, looking behind her again.

'Thank you,' he said, with the briefest pause. 'I rattle around in it a bit.'

. . .

She slept in the guest room under a quilted duvet. Everything was impossibly tasteful: the small walnut bed-stand, scented tissues, a rose candle. A painting – seeming to mix Picasso with an African traditional style – of a queenly woman in a headwrap. Charlie spoke to her mum and dad, and reassured them that she was fine. Lydia texted back to say she'd get home first thing in the morning to let her in, following a series of messages that included various threats of avenging comic-book-style violence against the mugger. She heard Will padding about in the hallway. He'd left her a new toothbrush by the sink, and a small, packaged soap; he seemed very prepared for guests.

She lay awake, her head still buzzing. She found herself imagining tiptoeing over to his room, knocking on his door, sliding into his bed. How he'd happily take her in his arms and not push for anything more, because he knew she was shaken up, and she'd feel protected, and safe.

She heard his door click shut.

In the morning, Charlie found the dining table neatly laid, teak-coloured tea in a clear glass teapot, triangles of brown toast in a metal stand, and Will serving up scrambled eggs. He was dressed for work, impeccably as always.

'Good morning,' he said, as if her being here was a regular occurrence. 'How did you sleep?'

'Well, eventually. Thank you.' After she'd exhausted herself by replaying the mugging repeatedly in her head.

He set a plate of sunshine-yellow eggs and smoked salmon in front of her, and sprinkled fresh chives on top.

'Wow,' she said. 'Check you out.'

'I like to look after my guests,' he said, with a smile that could be read as tentative.

She took Will in, spruced-up, straight-backed. He'd been patient, unlike her, falling for Franco without seeing the full picture. Going out with someone older could be good for her – someone sorted, his life neatly alphabetised. 'Well, I feel very looked after. You're very nice to me.'

'You're very nice,' Will said. There was a sliver of vulnerability amongst the warmth, and she saw then how much he liked her. 'I...' He tucked his chin into his chest for a moment. 'Charlie, I'd hate to make you feel beholden or anything like that. And I am more than aware of the age difference. But I'm really enjoying your company and I'd love it if we could spend more time together.'

Head, not heart. She pictured jazz gigs and dinners; joining him in Brussels for the weekend. 'Yeah,' she said. 'I think we could.'

His face lifted with an expression she'd not quite seen before.

'It needs to be baby steps,' she said firmly. She was going to be in charge. 'Tiny, newborn baby steps. I'm not rushing things anymore.'

'Of course,' he said. 'Absolutely.'

'I'll call you, then.'

'Wonderful,' he said. 'But perhaps... if you could do me one thing.'

'What's that?'

'I'm having a fundraiser. In a week and a half. A Christmas party, of sorts. It's for the stables, and various other community-minded charities in my constituency. It would be an honour if you'd join me. To represent the farm. I've mentioned it to Gábriel as well. There are plenty of people I'd love to introduce you to. Influential people.'

'OK,' she said. 'Let's do it.'

'Excellent,' he said, and seemed re-energised. 'I must go. Just let yourself out – there's no rush. I've left a little bit of cash by the door and a spare Oyster card should you need one.' He held up his hands to stop her protesting. 'You can pay me back if you like. You'll let me know if you need anything? Anything at all?'

She nodded and stood up. 'Thank you, Will. Thank you for looking after me.'

He gazed at her for a moment, then stepped forward and kissed her on the cheek. 'Always,' he said.

She ate her breakfast, all of which was delicious if now lukewarm, and slowly got her act together. As she left, she saw the five twenty pound notes laid on top of one another, and a small note:

Just to tide you over. Will x

Charlie sat with Gábriel in the barn, having brought him a flat white, his preferred coffee. He was sawing logs at a workbench, fulfilling a long-standing promise to Kaden that he could add to the goats' climbing structure; his young charge kept showing him elaborate and increasingly ambitious designs. She had just filled him in on the events of yesterday night. He'd looked very concerned after she recounted the mugging, but turned back to his work once she found herself telling him about Will.

'Am I ridiculous, Gábriel?'

'About what?'

'Going into another relationship so soon. Possibly. Probably.' She thought back to the money Will had left her. He'd meant well, but it was far too much. She'd taken twenty quid, and she'd return it to him.

He didn't look round. 'Whatever you think.'

'What do *you* think?' Gábriel always knew what was best; could see far more than she could. It was about time she started listening to him.

He put the crosscut saw down, pushing the goggles onto his forehead. He leant against the workbench and took up his mug. 'He's a good guy. It was nice of him to look after you last night.'

Charlie took in a breath, and held it for a long time. 'He is,' she said. 'And it was.'

He sipped his coffee. 'Do you like him?'

She sighed. 'Yeah. I do.' He was a striking, clever, considerate man who wanted nothing more than to make her happy. Who would never abandon her for the teenage mother of his child, or take her money. 'I've decided that slow and steady wins the race. Love at first sight is total bollocks.' Outside, she could hear one of the donkeys bray, a comically squeaky sound.

Gábriel took off his gloves, one by one, and wiped some flakes of wood from his wrist. 'I don't think so,' he said.

As if from a far distance, she felt her heart delicately slump. He'd fallen in love with Agnes straightaway, then, and it had worked out. She wondered why she was so envious of another person's happiness.

'Why do you want to know what I think?' he said.

'I just want an objective opinion.'

If Charlie had been listening very carefully, she might have heard the small, very subtle exhalation from Gábriel – not quite a laugh. He glanced over at Charlie, and didn't say anything else.

TWENTY-FOUR

A Christmas Party – An Appearance

No expense had been spared for Will's fundraiser. The Merchant Taylors' Hall dated back to the fourteenth century, and the building was a mish-mash of medieval to post-war styles. The lit fountain in the courtyard had a jade-green marble statue, and the grand stone entrance was heavy with dark foliage and glittering fairy lights.

Charlie arrived from the tube in the black off-the-shoulder dress that she and Lydia had agreed on. ('Literally smokin',' Lydia had said, incorrectly.) It had been ages since she'd dolled up so much – these days she just rotated three RPF jumpers on the farm. Tonight, she had pinned up her hair, with a smooth scalp on one side of her head and a tumble of curls on the other; oversized gold hoop earrings, lots of black eyeliner and the reddest of red lipstick.

A man in a burgundy jacket took her coat and she moved towards the sound of the people. The room was large, with an opulent floral carpet and massive chandeliers as well as mahogany-panelled walls. A jazz quintet was playing in the corner, and a girl at a grand piano was singing an offbeat, gentle version of 'Have Yourself a Merry Little Christmas.'

Will was standing with a small group of expensively-dressed guests and, catching sight of her, excused himself. He was in a black velvet tux, black shirt and bow tie and did, she had to admit, scrub up very well.

'You look absolutely radiant,' he said, and leant down to kiss her cheek.

'Thank you. You look sharp.' She smiled and looked past him. 'This is all amazing.'

He glanced around, as if he'd forgotten it all. 'Yes. Good. The glitzier everything looks, the more money people might cough up. I'm pleased you like it,' he said, looking rather deeply at her again and Charlie saw that she had left a glossy stain of red lipstick on his cheek, just visible.

'Oh,' she said, and fumbled in her clutch bag for a tissue. He looked puzzled. 'It's just…' She pointed to his cheek and his expression remained.

It was quicker and easier to just do it; she reached up and wiped the side of his face with a deft, delicate movement that to an outsider might have looked very tender indeed, and certainly did to the two press photographers, who instantly snapped it.

Will was an impeccable host, and a generous one. He introduced her to several people who worked in large charities, as well as some potential donors, and with each introduction made her sound far more important than she was. Sometimes he stood next to her, and at other times he would drift away to a different group. When she wasn't doing her damndest to suggest that the farm was badass but could definitely benefit from more money, she'd glance over to find him gazing back rather adoringly.

Gábriel arrived, looking incredibly out of place, wearing a shirt, a skinny wool tie and a grey jacket. He scanned the room and seemed surprised when a waiter came up to him with a tray of champagne.

'You're allowed it,' Charlie said, as she joined him. She saw him blink at her and take her in, realising he'd never really seen her at her most glam either – at least not since last Christmas. She gave him a champagne flute and took one for herself. 'Where's Agnes?'

'She had to work.'

'Ah, Gábriel,' Will said, arriving next to them. 'Fantastic that you could make it.' He laid a hand on his shoulder. The two men were the same height, though Will was bulkier and dressed much more smartly. 'Have I said, Charlie? I've been talking to Gábriel about doing something on the consultancy side of things. So I wouldn't be taking him away from you.'

'Oh. That's great.'

Gábriel was looking at the floor.

'Charlie.' Will put his hand on her upper back, between her bare shoulder blades. 'If I could steal you away for a moment.'

She thought he wanted to introduce her to someone else, but instead he took her to a quiet stairwell.

'I bought you something,' he said. 'I hope you don't mind.'

He reached into the inside pocket of his jacket, bringing out a fine gold necklace. It was a teardrop style, jet-black stone with three tiny crystals embedded in the small ball above it.

'Oh. Wow. That's—' *Too much*, she thought. Way too much. 'That's really sweet, Will, but—'

'It's just a little thing,' he said. 'I saw it and thought of you.'

'Oh. Thank you, but, um—'

'I was thinking,' he said. 'Do you fancy going away somewhere? Madrid? Barcelona? Get away from everything?'

'Will,' she said, looking at him squarely. 'Baby steps, remember?'

He looked rather crestfallen. 'Yes. Of course. I'm sorry.' He shook his head and self-consciously cleared his throat. 'Perhaps…' There was a faint tinge of hope in his expression. 'Just for tonight? It would go so well with your dress.'

He looked so sweetly beseeching that she relented. 'OK. Just for tonight.' She turned, allowing him to fasten it behind her neck, the stone settling above her breastbone.

Behind them, the quintet were playing an extremely quirky version of 'All I Want For Christmas Is You.'

'There,' he said. He put his hand on her elbow. 'There's something about you, Charlie, that—' He stopped suddenly, as if he didn't dare continue. He smiled, seemingly at himself, and then at her. 'I've got a speech to make shortly. But afterwards, we can spend some time together. Just you and me.' He leant down, lightly kissed the skin of her neck, and disappeared.

She remained in the stairwell, then drifted to the large foyer, where a few latecomers were still arriving, their coats being taken. Suddenly, it all seemed to be spinning out of control. Perhaps this wasn't going to work out after all. There'd been something a little desperate in his eyes just now.

She was about to turn back to the main room, to find Gábriel and at least make this evening work for her by talking to some more rich potential benefactors, when she caught sight of someone stepping into the foyer – a slim figure that moved with a cocky sway.

It couldn't be.

'Franco…?' she said, her voice rather far away.

The figure looked over. 'Hello, darling,' he said, and he was not an apparition, not a sea-ghost draped in seaweed, but *there*, in front of her. He was wearing jeans and a flowered shirt, topped off with some sort of military jacket, Adam and the Ants style, and an untied bow tie slung around his collar. 'Thought I'd dress up for the occasion. This is fucking swanky, isn't it?'

'But…' she said, feeling the floor undulate beneath her. 'What the hell are you doing here?'

His pupils were massively dilated. 'I've come to see my fiancée,' he said, with a glittering smile.

'Franco,' she said, the word more tangible this time. Naming him again made him real. 'What the fuck? You've got to leave.' She numbly tried to push him towards the exit.

'Where are we going?' He looked over her shoulder towards the main room. 'I want to go that way. That's where the action is. And the money. Jesus, this place fucking *reeks* of money.'

People were starting to notice, looking over, conversation hushing.

'Funmi thought you were *dead*,' she said, the anger beginning to rise in her. There was a strange rushing noise in her ears. She had made him a tragi-romantic figure, and now here he was, distinctly unromantic. 'Even *I* half thought you were dead, because why the fuck else—'

'Nonsense. Nothing shall kill me.' He raised his voice and threw his hand out. 'I shall live forever.'

'But…'

'But – but,' he mimicked.

'You just disappeared. You left your girlfriend and your *child*. There was a fucking news report about you.'

'Oh. Yeah. Fame at last. Well,' he said, putting an arm around Charlie's shoulder, his hot breath on her ear. 'Turns out fathering is…' He gazed into the distance and pursed his lips as she shrugged him off her. 'Not what it says on the tin. It is, in fact, a total pain in the arse. I just needed to have a breather from all the nappies and shit and piss and wailing and zero sleep. Thought I'd go quiet for a bit; spend time with the mermen. By which I mean two video installation artists in Kemptown. Then I remembered that I had no money and wondered who would give me some if I asked nicely.' He blinked his long lashes at her, several times. 'Can I have some money, please?'

He was so high, and his breath smelt dank; vegetal. 'What about Funmi?' she said, unable to help her own voice rising. 'What about your baby?'

He shrugged. 'Oh. She'll deal, in time. Probably better without me anyway. I'm not very responsible. You, on the other hand. You'll put with all sorts of crap.'

'You almost got me fired.'

He raised his eyebrows. 'Oh, yeah. Sorry about that whole…' He fluttered his fingers. 'Little shenanigan. *Did* you get fired?'

'No. Because—'

'There you go, then,' he said. 'Worked out fine. Let's go get some fizz. I definitely spy fizz.' He took her hand.

She stayed rooted to the spot, wresting her hand from his. 'Franco. Please don't embarrass me like this. People are looking.' She was supposed to be impressing people here, not drawing attention to herself.

'Oh, of course,' he said, and did a flouncy half-bow. 'Mustn't embarrass you. Definitely not. Not in front of the poshos.'

'Please,' she said. She would calm him down; make him phone Funmi.

A waitress passed with a tray of champagne glasses. 'Oooh,' he said, and took two. 'The fizz has come to us. Perfect.' He drained one and put it back on the waitress' tray. 'Thank you very much, darling.' He cast a narrowing eye at Charlie's chest. 'That's not very you,' he said. 'Is it real?' He plucked up the pendant, pulling Charlie a little towards him, the chain digging into the back of her neck.

'Don't.' She put her hand around his wrist. 'What's wrong with you?"

There was a deep, firm cough, and they both looked round to see Will standing there, his hands behind his back. 'Take your hands off her, please.' She'd never seen him look so impenetrably fierce. She dropped her hand from Franco's wrist.

'Or what?' Franco said.

'It's time for you to go,' Will said. There were people gathering behind him, a small, subtle movement, curiosity getting the better of them.

'I've only just got here, mate,' said Franco, with a challenging beam. He was still holding on to the stone of her necklace, rubbing it absent-mindedly.

'It is invitation only. Would you please take your hands off my— Charlie.'

There was a long moment. Franco looked between Charlie and Will, before pretending to spit out champagne and letting her go, the necklace forgotten. 'Seriously?' He waved his glass towards Will's face and looked over at Charlie. 'This cunt? I always thought you liked that East European one, you know, the gloomy fucker with hay in his hair. This guy is the same age as my *dad*,' he said, impossibly tickled.

'Enough,' Will said.

'Mate,' Franco said, putting an arm around him – or attempting to as Will was rather a lot taller – and his voice grew soft, intimate. 'Charlie and me are going to get married. Like we intended.'

'Oh, my God,' said Charlie, putting her hand to her forehead, but somehow the scene had begun exclude her.

'I just had a little wobbly,' continued Franco. 'Had to have a think about things, but I'm back now. Our honeymoon —' He stopped abruptly and put his fingers and his champagne glass to his lips as if in a private joke, before leaning confidingly up to Will. 'Do you know how much she likes my cock? Our honeymoon is going to be me banging her so hard all day and night that she'll end up as limp as a rag doll.'

The next few moments happened so quickly that Charlie barely took them in. Will took one of the epaulettes of that ostentatious jacket as if to haul Franco towards the exit.

'How dare you!' said Will, not quite under his breath.

Franco lithely slid out of his reach with a fiendish grin. 'Because I *am* daring, you fuck.'

Will grabbed the jacket again, lifting it partially away from Franco's shoulder. 'She's not yours, do you hear me?' he said, through a tight jaw. 'She's not yours. She's with me now—'

As he spoke, Franco resisted, pressing one hand over Will's chin, neck, mouth, while – gallingly – still holding his champagne glass in the other. Will grasped his wrist, trying to push him away, and for a few seconds, it became an awful, pathetic scuffle, the two of them shoving ineffectually at each other with palms and splayed fingers, Will trying to resist,

Franco pushing further. She couldn't bear the sound of their tight-lipped effort and a shout of pure glee from Franco. People had begun to draw closer.

Charlie, who had been too horror-struck to move, began to step towards them. '*Stop!* Both of you. What are you—'

Too late. As she spoke, Franco finally chose a moment to put down his champagne glass and forcefully push his rival by the chest with both hands. Will lurched back against a marble bust, and Franco followed through, swinging his fist and catching Will soundly in the temple.

In a single, appalling second, Will spun, colliding with a waitress holding a tray of drinks, and crumpled to the floor, taking her with him. The sound of glasses shattering mixed with the shrieks and gasps of a few guests.

And the there was a great hush, broken only by the sound of the two photographers, clicking once, twice, three times.

WILL BOADU MEP TAKES A BEATING

BAM! MEP BOADU PUNCHED AT PARTY

LIB DEM MAN IN FIGHT OVER STUNNER

VICTIM OF LIB DEM MEP ASSAULT TELLS ALL

Everyone loved a good scandal. Though Will had done nothing wrong, the headlines were mirthful, most papers united in this matter, if no others. They'd focused on the scuffle, which had lasted mere seconds, and not the punch. There were photos of Charlie, dabbing at Will's face. Of Franco, giving a thumbs-up, his tongue out. He'd sold a pack of horrible lies to the lowliest of tabloids, including details of him and Charlie, and she'd hid for days at her family's house. There had been column inches speculating about Will Boadu's 'mystery woman', though she wasn't a mystery for long; photos were used from very old social media posts of her in a bikini holding a massive cocktail, her friends cut out of the shot. Awful things were posted online. Paparazzi had hung around at the farm for three days, but Lydia said that Gábriel had eventually threatened to call the police, due to cameras being near children.

'I heard the big man got properly decked.'

'Franco must have vexed him *hard*, blud, to get into that.'

'He was proper into Charlie, though. Other day, he asked me what her favourite cities were. Like, how am I supposed to know that? I don't even know what *my* favourite cities are.'

'That's because you've never stepped outside SE5.'

'Shut up, man.'

'Yeah, I saw him once outside by his car, talking to himself, like he was practising something. One of those times he was picking her up. I thought he was on his phone with an earpiece, but he saw me and looked all shifty.'

'Cheez. I ain't never going near love, fam. Keeping things strictly platonic. Farm squad all the way.'

'Like you have a choice.'

Will chose not to press charges against Franco. He'd made a dignified statement apologising for the distress caused, and calling it a 'misunderstanding that got out of hand.'

He wrote to Charlie – not an email, but a letter, handwritten in fountain pen and addressed to the farm.

Charlie,

*I am deeply sorry. I shouldn't have got involved in the way
that I did.*

*I think it's best we don't see each other. The papers do love this
sort of thing, and I'd rather not put either of us through it.
My work is deeply important to me, and I must put that first.
I'm heading up to Yorkshire for a few days, to spend time on
the farm and with my family.*

*Please do not feel that you have to respond, but know that I
take full responsibility for everything that has occurred. I
shall not embarrass you further.*

I wish you joy.

Will.

———————

'Hey, sis.'

Nunhead Cemetery was one of the Magnificent Seven – great Victorian cemeteries built in a ring around central London. This particular example was an atmospheric mix of Gothic arches, woodland paths and broken-winged angels amongst the ivy and lime trees.

Jools's grave was in a modern section, a small, polished black headstone that Nellie regularly cleaned of bird shit and dried leaves. Charlie had always found it numbing, the engraved letters meaningless.

A BELOVED DAUGHTER AND SISTER,
GONE TOO SOON.

The dates. Charlie had once seen a documentary with some modern Slovakian graves that bore colourful mosaics featuring a scene from the deceased's life. She often imagined something similar when she visited – tiny tiles depicting Jools jumping off the biggest diving board in Crystal Palace National Sports Centre or having chips with Slush Puppies afterwards.

'So I've had a fun time,' she said.

The family always came on Jools's birthday, but Charlie used to visit on her own birthday, too. Jools had always loved her younger sister's big day, and would give her handfuls of sweets all individually wrapped and blow party whistles in her face, the paper uncurling like an elephant's trunk.

'Sorry it's been a while.'

The last three years, though, Charlie had told herself that she'd do it later in the day, and the hours had passed swiftly as she got ready for whatever celebration she was having, the guilt fading with each drink.

'What have I been up to...?' She looked up at the horse chestnut tree. 'Let's think. Got broken up with, chucked out, fired. Got the best job in the world – not that I realised that then. You'd love it, Jools. It's so up your street. I took it for you, really, but I kept at it just for me.'

She picked up her little can of gin and tonic.

'What else? Oh, yeah. Got engaged. Slight error of judgement there.'

I'll say, she heard, as clear as a bell. An amused, throatier version of the voice in her memory.

'Yeah,' she said, and sighed. 'I wish you'd been around to

tell me that. Casey and relationship advice don't really mesh well.'

I get it, sis. He was stupid hot. East-London-hipster-artwanker-hot, but I get it. As a zero-strings thing, though, not as lifelong partner material.

'Yeah,' she said. 'Well, I know that *now*. And I messed it up with another guy, too.' She lay down, propping herself on an elbow, not caring about the mud, and it was as easy as anything to talk to her again.

He was kinda nice, she heard. *Bit old. Bit serious. You want someone solid. Someone who says what's what.*

'I guess,' said Charlie. 'But to be honest, I've decided I prefer sheep. You know where you are with a sheep. And I've got six of them.'

Mmm-hmm, she heard, in a strangely challenging tone. *If you say so.*

'I missed you,' Charlie said, touching the cool side of the headstone. 'I *miss* you.'

There was a silence then, in the wood, in her head. A wren, tail tipped up towards the sky, briefly alighted on the nearest overhanging branch and vanished again.

Not going anywhere, sis, she heard.

TWENTY-FIVE

Summer – A Country Show – An Announcement

The year turns. On the farm, the rhythms are reassuring. There are fresh volunteers, and others leave. In late February, the lambs come. The goat kids in April. Animals are sent to slaughter, and return as produce for the shop. In the beds, the soil is dug over, and new seeds planted: aubergine in January, beetroot and tomatoes in March. Aamiina, the Somalian lady who has now moved to temporary housing, takes special pleasure in the sweet potatoes that emerge in the greenhouse. It is a long winter and in May, spring finally dashes colour into the park. The hospital's helipad opens; the animals are thankfully unfazed by the roar of blades above their heads.

There is a new wildlife garden. It has a small reedy pond and grassland-loving flowers in pastel colours: greater knapweed, ragged robin, ox-eye daisy. It is June now, and Charlie and Gábriel sit on one of the benches carved into the trunk of a great fallen oak.

'Pig.'

'*Malac*.'

'*Malac*. Donkey.'

'*Szamár*.'

'*Szamár*. Goat.'

'*Kecske*.'

'*Kecske*. Sheep.'

'*Bárány*.'

Joe was taking a group of nursery school children – the same nursery Charlie had been to herself as a kid – round the garden on his first workshop, with Marianne supporting him and the teacher and assistants looking on. He was currently crouched down, pointing to something in the pond.

'*Bárány*,' said Charlie, passably flicking the '*r*' sound.

Six months of hard work. After emerging from the sanctuary of her parents' house, she had gone back to the farm, and ignored the looks and the comments. She had gone to a dinner with Ade, in which he had tried to talk lightly about it never raining but pouring.

She had taken a deep breath and picked up the phone to two people she'd met at Will's fundraiser, hoping they remembered her for more than just causing the awful fight. It had worked. She secured funding for the solar panels now stacked along the roof of the barn, and for an official partnership with the SW9 Stables. Every Wednesday after work, she would ride Elle around the yard at the stables and groom her. On the farm, there were new training projects for adults with learning disabilities, and lucrative corporate away days that brought the occasional sight of city bankers bemusedly sweeping up animal pellets. One morning, Ade had told her he'd just be doing half a day a week from home now, and gave her the new title of Farm Manager. She delegated some of her admin to Faith, who rather surprisingly proved to be better at spreadsheets than she could ever be.

Gábriel and Charlie would meet for coffee most mornings, before it opened for visitors, to discuss anything pressing; they often didn't have to say anything at all, the other knowing what was needed. As the only full-time staff, apart from Leila in the kitchen, they very much ran the place together.

In the wildlife garden, Joe was now showing the class a frog. This was what she felt proud of these days: not the new title but the flourishing sedge-grass and buttercups, the new platform by the pond, and all the children gathered around Joe, rapt. Giving back to her community. She would always work for charities now, she knew; places that encouraged her to look outside herself.

'How's Agnes's Hungarian these days?' Charlie asked. She hadn't heard any mention of her for a while.

'I don't know,' said Gábriel, throwing a blade of dry grass into the pond. 'We're not together now.'

'Oh,' she said. 'I'm sorry.'

He didn't say anything.

'What happened there, then?' she said, gently.

'I told her we weren't right for each other,' he said, almost looking over, but not quite.

Joe led the nursery children out of the garden and towards the classroom in single file, all of them hopping and making ribbit noises. Somewhere behind them, a blackbird belted out its florid song.

'I was thinking,' said Charlie. She nudged his calf with her trainer.

He turned his head towards her.

'We should go in for Lambeth Country Show.'

A pause. 'Yeah?'

'Yep. It's time.'

He smiled as he gazed out at the pond. Nodded. 'Let's do it.'

On the third weekend of every July, Brockwell Park in South London was taken over by a much-loved, two-day community event that mixed the feel of a large agricultural show with a music festival. Alongside cake competitions, birds of prey displays and medieval jousting, there were local activist and charity stalls, and stages thumping with reggae, Afrobeat and ska. You could buy plants and flowers, kente-print dresses, local crafts and enough jerk chicken and vegan junk food to make you feel sick, or indeed *be* sick if you went on the fairground's pendulum ride afterwards. You could marvel at the legendary vegetable-animal contest, which this year included Moonie's own controversial entry, featuring politicians and pigs in rather uncompromising positions using only swede, beetroot and celeriac.

One end of the park was given over to agriculture, and farms from all over London and the South-East brought their smaller livestock, the great vans lined up at the edge of the site. Inside a large white tent, pens for the sheep were filled with hay and buckets of water, the farms' various banners behind them. It was a muggy day, and the air even heavier in here. Punters filed by, taking selfies and scratching the animals' noses. In their corner, Charlie had made a display about the farm, with leaflets and photos alongside a small amount of produce by which Jami and Charity were loitering, looking far more focused on each other than on their wares. Gábriel was unfussily explaining to two teenagers how thick the Oxford Down's wool could grow.

'Here they are,' said Jan, coming over, her Mudchute cap on. 'The upstarts.'

'We are going to slay you alive,' said Lydia, who, like Charlie, had glitter on her cheeks. 'We are totally going to have you.'

'Not a chance, mate,' said Jan, grinning. 'Don't get me wrong, I want you to do well, but there's no way.'

'Everyone loves an underdog. An undersheep.'

'Whoever loses Best Rare Breed Sheep is buying all the pints.'

'Bring it,' said Lydia, with an alarmingly aggressive fighting stance.

'You two are ridiculous,' said Charlie. 'I'm going outside to watch. Don't hurt each other.'

The sheep show – essentially Crufts, but for sheep – was held in a large enclosure by the livestock tents. Plenty of people were gathered round, hanging over the metal gates with pints in their hands.

'Hey, Charlie.'

Funmi was there, in a bright-red maxi-dress and sunglasses that took over her whole face, holding on to the handle of Mia's buggy.

'Hey, hon.' Charlie gave Funmi a hug and lightly touched Mia's nose. 'Hey, little cutester. It's so nice that you both came.'

Funmi had appeared on the farm again in February, Mia already much bigger. They were still living with her mum in Bethnal Green, Funmi juggling her studies – A-levels in Politics, Philosophy and Economics – with childcare. She continued to visit every month or so, and Charlie had bought Mia a small toy lamb, embroidered with her name on the belly, for her christening. There had been no sign of Franco at the ceremony.

'Good luck with your sheep,' Funmi said. 'We'll be cheering for you, won't we, Mi-mi?'

Mia gave a garbled, musical response and threw her plastic rattle to the ground.

There were several individual sheep breed classes over the weekend; Charlie and Gábriel had decided to come down on the Sunday only, and to enter just two. A previous competition was winding up, the sheep being led back to the white tent. The MC had a T-shirt that said 'SAN DIEGO SUMMERTIME' stretched over his beer belly, and introduced the next round with the laid-back patter of a working men's club compère.

'It was nice of you to give the handling to Lydia,' Charlie said to Gábriel, who'd come to join her. 'I am actually feeling weirdly nervous.'

'Me too. Why did you think I let Lydia do it?' he said, and it was the first time he'd smiled all afternoon. He'd seemed a little strange in the last few days. Subdued.

They watched as the sheep were brought out by handlers in white coats, including Jan, and Lydia with Ruskin Park Farm's newest Oxford Down ewe, Rey, her cream wool plush and unsheared.

The MC was rattling through the breeds as the judge, a stout white lady with bleached-blonde hair, walked by each sheep, looking at teeth, the shape of the heads and the length of the body. 'Now, the Wensleydale is a lovely sheep,' he said, as the judge came to a boy, surely only eleven or so, and his ovine competitor. 'A longwool breed, distinctively tall, very alert. Some have a lovely tight crimped wool like this one, and others have a softer, looser look. Very in demand, this wool.'

'Mate,' said a man next to them. 'He needs to go down the barber's.' His female companion burst out laughing.

'And it's nice to see the youngsters doing it,' the MC said. Lydia rolled her eyes at Charlie, then straightened as the judge came towards her, as if being inspected herself. 'And here's the Oxford Down, crossbred in the 1830s between Cotswold rams and South Down or Hampshire ewes.' The judge gave Rey a long scrutiny before moving on, and Lydia sent over a sneaky thumbs-up.

The winners were announced swiftly, a man in dark-green cords and tinted aviator shades coming over with rosettes. Neither Jan's nor Lydia's were pointed to.

'Dunno why we bother,' said Lydia, back in the tent. 'Bloody load of old rubbish.'

'There's still our girls,' said Charlie, as a crackling tannoy announcement invited exhibitors to bring their pairs. 'Keep the faith.'

There was myriad hilarious baa-ing during the best pair class, including one ewe that sounded like a very upset old man with bronchitis.

'This one's still hungover,' said the man next to Charlie.

'Not as much as me,' said his companion.

Lydia stood with RiRi and Bey-Bey, her face as stoic as her sheep, as the MC waxed lyrical about Shetlands.

'Come *on*,' said Charlie, and tucked her hand into Gábriel's arm as the judge took a final, sweeping look at the competitors. 'You can do this. Come on, RPF.'

She was entering into the spirit of it all, but really, she

didn't care. She felt, with a gin-clear realisation, that it wouldn't matter if the farm won anything or not; that it *had* won, by simply surviving, and that she had, too. She had stuck at this job and it had blossomed into something she adored; something she felt dedicated to. *Yay me*, she thought, and handed herself a mental rosette.

Suddenly, swiftly, the judge pointed at their Shetlands, and Lydia's face went from determinedly stern to incredulously delighted as she took the rosette from the judge.

Charlie whooped and threw her arms around Gábriel with a sudden rush of adrenaline. '*Yes*, Gábriel! I knew it,' she said, pulling back to look at him, her hands still on his elbows. 'We have the ultimate best sheep.'

Lydia waved the rosette at them before turning to Jan and making the best and most graphic *up-yours* sign she could muster with two sheep-leads in her hand, before performing an extremely unselfconscious dance that was all hips and pointed forefingers, as if on stage at the O2 and not an area of fenced grass that currently smelt of animal shit.

Charlie let go of Gábriel, wondering when the last time she'd hugged him had been. Why didn't he seem very happy. 'Aren't you pleased?'

His smile was small, distracted. 'Yeah. Of course I am.'

'What's up, then?'

He watched the MC introduce the rare breed rams. 'Nothing. I've got to go do my singing now.'

'Singing?'

'Yeah. It's a local thing I do. A choir. In Peckham.'

He hadn't ever mentioned it before. 'Such a dark horse,' she said, grinning. 'Or some farm animal, anyway.'

. . .

After a brief break – a pint of Essex-brewed cider, watching kids on the inflatable tractor slide, she and Lydia pulling cross-eyed gurning faces at Gábriel in the back row of his choir on the community stage, while he tried his very best to ignore them – it was back to the enclosure for Best in Show.

Seniors and yearlings, rams and ewes, long and short-haired. Horned or polled. Some of the sheep seemed to resemble their owners: the tall, long-haired man with his Cotswold ewe, the Roman nose of both the blue-faced Leicester and its handler. Jan was back out with a big White-faced Woodland ram, both of them standing squarely as if bracing for a fight outside a pub. The sheep shuffled distractedly and were moved back.

'Brap, brap,' called Joe, from the other side of the enclosure, as the judge examined RiRi and Bey-Bey again. 'Winners! Look at them! Gold medals!' he shouted, before pissing himself laughing with Tallboy.

Lydia looked more focused than ever, as if she were standing for Parliament.

'I have a very good feeling about this,' said Aidan. Charlie's dad had come to join them after corralling some of his Year 6 girls into dancing on the community stage. 'I feel it in my gut.'

'You feel *sausage* in your gut,' Charlie said, looking down at his hot dog. 'Didn't you eat one of those already today?'

'The diet always starts after the Lambeth Country Show,' he said, gesturing with his frankfurter towards the judge. 'She's finished, I think.'

'Come on, come on, come on,' said Charlie under her breath, her head light from the cider. Gábriel, who'd been persuaded by Lydia to have a dab of glitter on each cheek, was next to her.

The judge said some words about the standard being very

high, before pointing at two sheep that were not theirs for third and second place, and Jan's for Best in Show. The Mudchute crew erupted into high-fives.

'Winning isn't everything,' said Charlie, back in the tent.

'Don't say it's the taking part that counts,' Lydia said, with a threatening finger. 'Or you will be ended.' She gave a huge sigh, something she'd been doing a lot recently – she'd had her graduation ceremony this week and had spent the last month trawling the internet for jobs and rewriting her CV. 'I'm going to hold a barn owl,' she said. 'It's literally the only consolation.' She took off her white coat and stomped out.

Gábriel picked up her coat and rolled it into a neat ball. He still seemed quiet.

Whatever it was, he needed cheering up. 'I'm buying you lunch,' Charlie said, and he looked at her. 'You haven't done Lambeth Country Show until you've had goat curry.'

'Told you,' she said, watching Gábriel polish off the last of his curry. 'Proper local now.'

They were sitting on their coats under the central circle of trees in the park, watching the bands on the main stage a little way down the hill, the speakers ear-piercingly harsh even from here. More clouds had come across, the air humid. She had lost the farm polo shirt in favour of a Choose Love T-shirt to go with her little denim shorts and wellies, defiant of the total lack of sunshine.

Gábriel didn't say anything, just put his tray down by his legs. He seemed to take a long time chewing his last mouthful. 'I have to tell you something.'

Charlie was watching a kid in sparkly wings and face-paint near them perform some cute, bouncy movements to the dub band onstage. 'Shoot.'

He watched the stage for a while and she wondered if he'd forgotten what he wanted to say. When he did speak, it was very simply. 'I'm going home,' he said.

'You can't. We've got to take the sheep back. You're the only one who can drive the van.'

'I didn't mean that.' He looked over, before leaning towards Charlie's ear to make sure she heard. 'I'm going to go home. To Hungary. First of all, anyway.'

His expression made it clear that he didn't just mean for a visit to his family. Home. To Hungary. The words swirled and caught up in the jagged beat until they repeated, with the same loping thud. 'But— You can't.'

He had a strange, melancholy smile. 'It's not the same anymore. This stuff in the news all the time. I still don't know if I'll be allowed to work here.'

The words were heavy. They throbbed in Charlie's chest. 'Yes, you are. You're safe. You're not going to be chucked out.'

'But it's not the same. I'm not wanted.'

'Of course you are. This is… this is *London*.' But even as she said it, a small part of her worried that it wasn't true anymore. Things felt like they were shifting, and nothing was certain.

He shrugged and put his arms on his knees as he watched the musicians grind about on stage.

Charlie felt a barren sort of desperation, as if something very fragile was floating away from her. 'But the farm, Gábriel.'

His smile was incredulous, and sad and slow at the same time. 'You don't need me on the farm.'

'Of course we do.' She registered the tiniest change of

expression in his face at her saying *we* instead of *I*, because she knew him so well after almost two years.

'There are other people who can do it,' he said, rather offhandedly. 'I want to move on in the world.'

'What about you working with Will?'

'We only ever talked about it. Nothing more. I want a better job, and—' He sighed. 'It feels harder to do that here now, to start my own business again. I wanted to go to America, once, but I don't think that's going to happen. I might go to Germany.'

Germany. Almost as far away as Hungary. 'But...' *I need you*, she thought suddenly, dramatically, the words louder in her head than the massive PA in front of them.

'Lydia can do my job. She'll be great.'

She could sense the stubbornness in him, as heavy and pressing as the air. It made hers swell up to meet it. 'If that's really what you want to do,' she said lightly. 'Of course I'll support you. I want you to be happy.'

'Great,' he said, the word blunt.

They watched the band, the singer announcing the final song, her arm flung upwards, shouting about togetherness. Charlie and Gábriel sat side by side, his elbow very near her knee. Gábriel, who'd always been there, early in the morning and late at night. All the times something went wrong on the farm. All the times something went wrong with *her*. Now, out of nowhere, he was leaving her, and she swore there was a subtle sense of satisfaction in his announcement. He wanted it to bruise, just a little, and it angered her.

'Don't feel you have to give formal notice,' she said, still facing the stage. She felt him turn his head and didn't look back at him for a while. When she eventually did, her face was more composed. 'I'll talk to Ade. We'll make it as easy as possible for you. I'll see you get your full month's pay whenever you go, obviously.'

He looked at her, and his eyes became more solid, his jaw stiffening. The electric blue glitter shone on his cheek. 'Fine. OK.'

TWENTY-SIX

Leaving – A Declaration

Summer rain comes with an entrance. The sky gathers itself, shudders, and tips three days of apocalyptic weather on London. By Herne Hill railway station, a man undoes his trousers and stands in his pants, arms outstretched as the water sluices him, and people take photos. There are jokes about rain dances and Noah. Umbrellas are broken by the wind, and people run from tube stops to their offices. Car alarms are set off. A few small children in wellies jump up and down in puddles whilst their parents call their names with exasperation.

None of the animals wanted to be out. Charlie watched it pour down from inside the office, and a small pool form underneath the door. Gábriel was an impassive presence, the rain making him into a simpler shape as he moved between enclosures. He didn't seem to care about it, his hair plastered to his forehead, his mac on. He never looked over at the office window, never came in for a coffee, never spoke to her unless he had to, and when he did, there was none of the old, easy rapport; it was as if they were strangers. She felt a quiet melancholy, much quieter than the rain that battered the concrete pens in the centre of the farm. But he hadn't said any more about leaving – perhaps he was going to wait for a bit longer, she thought, and didn't bring it up.

Halfway through the third week since his announcement, she was gazing at the accounts, the numbers merging into one, when he knocked. He hadn't felt the need to knock on her door before coming in for a long time.

He stood there, his hair as ruffled as hen feathers. 'I'm going on Friday,' he said. 'I have a flight booked for the weekend.'

'Oh.' Friday. This Friday. 'OK,' she said.

When he shut the door, she stared at her computer for twenty minutes, and didn't type a single thing.

'Wait, what? Where's he going to?' Lydia said that night, when Charlie broke the news.

'Back home.'

'That's a load of old arse. Why would he do that?'

Because he hates England, Charlie thought, *and because he hates me*. 'I guess he just wants a change,' she said.

Lydia made a sound like an old, angry bull. 'Aren't you going to try and make him stay?'

Charlie stared at the dregs of her wine, swilling them around so that sediment clung to the glass. 'Not if he doesn't want to.'

'Maybe he just needs a good reason,' said Lydia, waggling her eyebrows, and dropping her shoulders when Charlie didn't respond. 'Seriously, Charlie. Do you really not...?'

'Not what?'

Lydia gave an interrogatory frown, before shrugging. 'I always thought you two had a bit of a... you know.' She made a sound like a cockerel, followed by a whistle and a couple of explanatory hand-gestures.

'We're friends,' Charlie said to her wine. 'Nothing ever happened.'

'Because both of you are daft bloody muppets,' Lydia said, before shrugging. 'Your loss. Gonna be sorry to see him go, though. The man's a legend. Plus he's my Jenga partner at the pub. Who's going to take over from him? Don't you need to advertise pretty sharpish?'

'You are,' Charlie said, and watched Lydia's face drop in shock, begin to lift, and finally illuminate. 'We have to advertise it, for formality's sake, but Ade and I agreed that it's yours if you want it.'

Lydia stood up, her mouth open. 'For real, mate?'

Charlie nodded.

'Oh my days, that's amazing!' She jumped practically on top of Charlie and crushed her in a hug strongly scented with body spray and mildewed straw. 'Wait til I tell my mum! She'll be ugly *crying*! I'm phoning her right now.'

Charlie listened to Lydia's elated squeals to her mum in Dorset, and slumped back on the sofa, trying to remember what Gábriel had smelt like when she'd hugged him at the Country Show, and not being able to.

His last day. Charlie had an afternoon meeting off-site that had been scheduled in the diary for ages and when she looked for him after lunch, Marianne said he'd popped out. She sat in the office of the trust fund, trying to concentrate, speaking slightly louder than necessary. She was invited to coffee, and didn't feel that she could say no: not when more money for the farm was on offer. By the time she got back, it was almost five.

'He's gone already,' Marianne said, putting her cardigan on.

She felt a hollowing in her stomach. 'Did he say anything?'

'He said he'd stay in touch, bless him.' Charlie was checking her phone. No messages. 'Shame he didn't want a leaving do, isn't it?' Marianne said. 'But he's such a humble soul.'

She walked to the stables, her bones heavy. She brushed Elle and saddled her up. The horse seemed to sense her listlessness and returned it, fluttering breath through her nostrils, a tremor running through her.

She rode the slowest trot. He hadn't left her a note or anything. He hadn't bothered to say goodbye. After all the time they'd known each other.

Charlie leant down and hugged Elle's neck. She remained there as the horse kept circling the yard.

'Mate,' said Lydia, who was eating takeaway chips, her fingers slicked with grease, as Charlie shut the front door. 'Where have you been hiding? I called like, a hundred times.'

Charlie looked at her phone and saw the run of missed calls and texts. 'Stables.'

'You had a visitor.'

Her heart fell over. 'Who?'

'Who do you bloody think? Gábriel. Came round, didn't he?'

'How long ago?'

'A little while. He said he had to go home and finish packing. It sucks arse that he's leaving. I'm going to right miss him.'

Charlie lay on her bed, watching the late evening sky fade from lavender to deep blue to dusky grey. She listened back through Lydia's increasingly combative voicemails, hoping for a shorter one from Gábriel at the end, but there was nothing. Lydia had said he was going from Gatwick in the morning, and she'd checked the times: he must be getting the noon flight to Budapest.

The farm without Gábriel would be a bare, empty thing. She pictured him moving amongst the pens, the barn, the beehives, the orchard, walking with the lightest bounce, as if the ground beneath him was springy; how he commanded the respect and, in Kaden's case, devout adoration, of the volunteers, and how he tended to the animals. She'd taken him for granted, his advice, his friendship, his… everything.

A siren went distantly past, its long wail dissolving into the hum of traffic. The sky was now dark.

Somewhere, deep down in her brain, a small voice was getting louder. A voice that told her how idiotic she was being, how headstrong. She'd thought, last year, that a relationship with Will might be a slow-growing thing. And there *had* been something growing, just not in the places she'd been looking. Now this was her last chance. Wasn't it?

'Oh, God, I don't know,' she said aloud.

Are you kidding me right now, sis? she heard.

She sat up with a lurch and phoned Gábriel. No answer.

'Shit,' she said, and rolled off her bed.

. . .

Jan and Beth lived in the top two floors of a Victorian terrace on a quiet street round the corner from Peckham's Rye Lane. Charlie took two buses – a long wait for the first followed by an even longer wait for the second – and finally arrived outside their house. No lights were on. She checked her phone one more time before crouching down to pick up a piece of gravel from the path. The window on the left was his room, she was fairly sure, trying to remember from the one party that she'd been to ages ago.

She threw the gravel and it pocked very lightly against the glass. The window remained shut; opaque. She picked up another bit of gravel and tossed it up. This one missed, hitting the wall. She threw a third, and then a fourth with rather more force.

The sash window next to it was lifted up abruptly. 'I think you've chosen the wrong fucking window to hit.' Jan's voice. 'Do it one more time and I'm calling the police, you little shitbag.'

'Hi, Jan,' said Charlie, in a stage whisper. 'It's me. Charlie.'

There was a short pause and Jan leant further out. 'Charlie? What the hell are you doing here? It's bloody one in the morning.'

'Sorry,' said Charlie, in their hallway. 'Just wanted to... say goodbye to Gábriel.'

Jan was in a thick purple dressing gown, her stout calves on display. Her usually perfectly-coiffed hair was askew. 'Right,' she said. 'I don't think he's in.'

Charlie felt a little faint. 'He's gone already?'

Jan shook her head as she led Charlie up the stairs. 'Off in the morning. Heard the door a little while ago. Probably gone for a last walk. He liked this neighbourhood.' She gave an expansive sigh. 'I'm going to miss that bastard.' She gave a light knock on the wooden door, before looking over. 'He'd have to be pretty dead to the world not to hear the Raiders of the Lost Ark boulders being lobbed at his window.'

'Sorry,' said Charlie again.

Jan gave a wry grin and opened the door.

It was a small room, with a single bed, the duvet creased; a decorative fireplace with floral Victorian tiles, and several framed pictures on the wall. There were two large cases open on the floor, and clothes either rolled up in them or flung on top.

'Bit plain in here now, but he made it his,' said Jan.

There was a book on the small bedside table. *Allátfarm*.

'He said to give that to you.' Jan nodded at it.

Charlie went in properly and picked it up. On the inside cover, he'd written:

For Charlie. To improve your Hungarian. Gábriel x

Jan was leaning against the wall, her arms folded. 'He's not going to stay out all night. Just wait here. To say your goodbyes.' There was something of a challenging glint in her eye. 'I need some kip. Early start tomorrow.'

Charlie sat down on top of the duvet, looking at his handwriting, which was not something she'd seen very often. She noted the curl of his 'r's. She tried to phone him again and when he didn't pick up, she sent a message.

Where are u?

She lay down on his bed. She put her nose in the pillow and inhaled a warm, musty scent. She closed her eyes and felt a tear fight its way out.

Her phone buzzed.

Home

he typed.

No you're not
I'm in your room

There was a pause of several minutes.

I'll come back
I'm at the end of Rye Lane

his message eventually said.

Somehow, she didn't think she could wait a moment longer. And how could she say what she needed to with Jan and Beth on the other side of the wall? She got up, ran down the stairs, and accidentally slammed the door a little too hard. 'Sorry, Jan,' she said to herself as she legged it towards Rye Lane.

It was busy, clubbers starting to queue up outside the Bussey Building and for the bar on top of the car park, and clusters of people outside McDonald's. Litter rustled across the pavement. Charlie turned south towards the park, suddenly realising that there was more than one road for him to turn down and that she might miss him. She got out her phone again, and walked straight into him underneath the railway bridge. He caught her elbow to steady her and dropped it just as swiftly.

'Gábriel,' she said, a little out of breath, and unable to say anything else.

He was wearing slim tracksuit trousers and an olive-green T-shirt that almost matched his eyes. It was a little too cold to be out without a jacket. 'Hi,' he said, the word tipped up very slightly.

'Hi.' She gave a weak smile, and he returned it, guardedly. 'You didn't say goodbye.'

'I came round.'

'I wasn't there.'

'I know.' He bore a patient look.

Charlie opened her mouth, and no words came out, only a tiny, staggered breath.

'OK, then,' he said.

She swallowed. Her heart was still accelerated. 'OK.'

He didn't hug her. It was as if he knew it would be too painful. Instead, he looked at her one last time, with the spring-green hazel of his eyes, the grave reassurance of his gaze. 'Goodbye, Charlie,' he said, in a strange half-voice, and began to walk past her.

'Please don't go.'

He stopped abreast of her and looked at the pavement. 'I booked my flight already.' There was a small blink back up at her, a flicker of uncertainty.

Of *hope*, she dared think. 'Please, Gábriel.' It didn't matter that she was losing her cool, that she was sweating from having dashed down the road, that there was a deeply pungent smell of fish that had been sitting on ice all day coming from the shops behind them.

He looked over her head. 'You don't need me.' His voice was cloudy. 'You think you do, but you don't.'

'I do. I *do* need you.'

Gábriel was gazing at her, waiting for her to say something else, and the words inside her stuck. She didn't dare. There was a subtle loosening in his shoulders, as if something he'd been clutching onto for a long time had finally left him, and he began to step past her again.

Now. Now, or it wouldn't happen. '*I* need you, Gábriel. Me. Not for the farm, not if you don't want to. I've got the farm sorted.' She realised how much she meant that – she trusted herself enough now. 'I don't want you to leave me.'

He stared at his feet for a rather long moment, before bringing his eyes up to her. They were beginning to look bruised, vulnerable. 'Why not?'

She had to tell him. If she didn't, he would go away, to Hungary and beyond, over to the apparently more welcoming parts of Europe, and she would never see him again. It didn't mean she wasn't independent. It didn't mean she couldn't think for herself, and be capable, and run a farm.

She took a deep breath and looked right at him. 'You asked me out once. And I said no. Because it wasn't right for me, just then. But I didn't forget. Not deep down. I got… distracted, but I didn't ever forget.'

His mouth came open, just a little, as he took the most careful of breaths.

Goosebumps rose up on her arms. *Do it.* This wasn't impulse. It was a little seed that had patiently germinated within her, needing just the right amount of time, and now it was ready to head towards the air.

'Will you go out with me, Gábriel?' she said, with ridiculous delicacy. She shook her head. 'Not *out*. Be with me.'

She didn't care that this much-less-delicate command was strung with desperation. 'Be with me and don't ever go anywhere else.'

His expression was more watchful than it had ever been before. 'Do you mean it?' he said very quietly.

'Yes,' said Charlie, and put her palm on her chest. 'Hand on heart.' This was a promise she would keep because here was the person with whom she could follow her heart *and* her head. 'Don't go home. Come home with me.'

He raised his eyebrows with a muted, careful amusement.

'I want to take you home right now,' she said, trying to chew away her smile and failing.

She swore he blushed, just a little. He stepped towards her, and she put a hand on his arm, and their first kiss was careful, light, sweet. Their second and their third and the ones after that, rather less so, and for quite a while it seemed that all the marvellous rowdiness of Rye Lane – the cabs, the buses, the shutters coming down on the takeaway shops, the shouting outside McDonald's, the radio coming from the Afro Foods store, the boombox pumping out from one car – had disappeared, and there was only the two of them, Charlie leaning up on her tiptoes, Gábriel's arms round her waist.

'Get a room, bruv,' said one of a pair of boys as they walked past with boxes of fried chicken.

'Poonani time, innit,' said the other. 'Rah.'

Charlie and Gábriel laughed, then, and pulled back to look at each other.

'Come back to mine,' she said.

He was definitely still blushing. 'I'm closer.'

'I have a bigger bed,' she said.

· · ·

It had been easy. Easy to bring him home to the cottage, easy to take him straight upstairs, to remove his clothes and he to remove hers, and to slide straight together as if they'd been doing it for years. They'd put their hands over each other's mouths to stop the giggles when Lydia came crashing into the house halfway through the night, and then they'd started all over again.

In the morning, after far too little sleep, Charlie watched the curtain billow into the room, and the shadows made by the early sun on Gábriel's back, along the black-inked branches of the tree tattooed between his spine and over his shoulder blades. His presence in her bed felt natural; she felt an utter lack of surprise to find him there. She listened to the little click in his throat every time he inhaled, and how the grain of his breath seemed warm, content.

The sound of Lydia getting up an hour later woke him. He blinked at Charlie slowly, the edges of his eyes gummy. They lay, side by side and a little apart, as Lydia caused loud havoc in the bathroom, things dropping to the floor, shushing herself and swearing.

'Is she always like that?' Gábriel said, almost under his breath.

'Almost entirely,' Charlie said, just as quietly. 'You get used to it.'

There was a dull, bodily thump on the door. 'You all right, mate?' Lydia said, from the other side, in a horrifically croaky voice. 'Can I come in? Gotta tell you about last night. It was *legendary*.'

'No,' said Charlie, more loudly and urgently. 'You definitely can't.'

A long pause. 'You've totally got Gábs in there with you, haven't you?'

'None of your business,' Charlie said, still looking at him.

There was a swishing sound as Lydia pushed herself away from the door. 'About bloody time!' she shouted. 'I'm going to have a street party in celebration. But first I'm off to the caff to soak up this great big arse of a hangover. Laters, gators!' She thudded down the stairs, beginning to sing 'and Iii-ee-iiiiii… will always lo-ove youuuuuu,' with grotesquely elaborate melismas. Five minutes later, the door slammed.

The cottage began to right itself and become calm again. Now there was just the creak of the wood floors and the branch of the apple tree tapping against the pane. Charlie had never felt so peaceful as she did with him here, lying on his front, the muscles of his upper arms rounding as he put his hands underneath his pillow. Last night, she had discovered a spray of freckles on each of his shoulders and a pinkish birthmark on his inner thigh.

'Will you stay?' she said.

He didn't blink. It was a long moment, but one in which she didn't feel anxious. 'I'm going to take the flight. I should see my family. I miss my mum's kitchen – paprika in everything.' There was a hint of wistfulness in his smile. 'But I'll come back.'

'You'd better.'

The understated smile remained, and he gave enough of a nod for her to know that he would. 'I'll have to find a room, though. Jan and Beth have a new lodger coming next week.'

'Stay here,' she said.

He seemed a little more surprised. 'In the cottage?'

She nodded. She really didn't want to let him out of her sight ever again. Not now that she'd said everything. Now that she knew herself, and understood what she needed. 'I want you to.' It wasn't like the heart-rush of Franco, part-excitement and part-panic. It just felt right. 'I promise I'll get in lots of paprika.' She pronounced it the Hungarian way, with the emphasis on the first syllable.

'Smoked paprika.' He was still smiling.

'Smoked paprika.'

'Will Lydia be OK with it?'

'Are you kidding? She loves you just as much.' Charlie smiled, before realising exactly what she'd said, and what it implied.

He didn't move, though his expression changed; became watchful; carefully tender. He blinked, twice, enough for her to know that he didn't mind her saying that; that he thought it too.

'You know, if you're feeling rubbish about your EU status, then...' she said.

'Then what?'

She gazed at his mossy eyes and at his tattoo, before using a single fingernail to trace the sturdy tree stretching all the way up to his shoulder. *Woah, little sister*, she heard. *Someone's getting ahead of themselves again.* Yes, she thought, and knew that she could slow down, and no one would think any less of her. 'It's a bit too soon,' she said, and smiled at him.

TWENTY-SEVEN

A Gathering

I t is the beginning of the hottest summer on record, a summer in which the grass in the park will turn to straw and crunch underfoot by July. A summer in which everyone will get used to bikini tops as daywear and everyone will own a desktop fan. A summer in which Brockwell Lido will be as packed as the Costa del Sol, the water slick with suntan lotion. A summer in which Aidan – and Charlie, and many people like them – will lose faith in the government, the country that they had always known as home, for not being as welcoming as they once promised to be. A summer in which people wonder what the next years will bring, and cannot forecast it. But today, in the place where several of South London's neighbourhoods conjoin, it is beautiful, the sky clear but for two airplane trails crossing together. On the farm, there is a sense of expectation, and the smell of lavender, sweet marjoram and mint.

'This is never gonna work, man.'

'Isn't it illegal or something?'

'Nope. You helping or what?'

'Fam. This place is mad.'

'Oh my God,' said Lydia, in the farm's classroom. 'You look frigging beautiful.'

'Thank you,' said Charlie.

'You're totally going to get pig shit on your dress, you know.' Lydia was sucking on a gobstopper lolly and watching the hair stylist put the final pin into the one side of Charlie's hair that wasn't tumbling with curls. She'd already done her own make-up and her nails were drying.

'That's fine,' Charlie said. She hadn't gone for the massive meringue and train, but there was probably still a risk that her vintage 1920s lace dress might get grubby.

'You know you could be using a pub, don't you?' said Lydia, wearing a burgundy one-shoulder dress. 'A pub with a nice clean wooden floor.'

'It's a test.' Charlie waved her polished fingers in the air again. 'If this one goes well, then we can open it out for the public. The photos have to be really nice.'

'Can't believe you're already making sure that your wedding photos advertise the farm,' said Lydia. 'That is totally shameless.'

'I *am* shameless.'

'Badass is what you are.'

'Why are all the animals inside?' Charlie asked, distractedly.

Lydia glanced out of the window at the blue sky and sniffed. 'Looks like rain.' She walked out of the room whistling 'going to the chapel and I'm, gonna get ma-a-arried' with several wrong notes.

• • •

'Ah, Charlie,' said Aidan, his heft just about held in by a waistcoat in the same shade as his deep-burgundy shirt. 'You look absolutely savage.'

'No one says savage anymore, Dad.'

'I do.'

'Thanks, Dad.'

They were standing at the entrance to the café. Inside, the tables had been cleared away and rows of chairs draped with ribbons and straw. There was bunting around the upper edges of the walls and stands of wildflowers from the meadow. Charlie was carrying a small posy bouquet of farm herbs.

Gábriel was standing at the far end of the café, dressed more smartly than she'd ever seen him in the navy-blue tweed suit they'd picked together, and Jan next to him as Best Man (or Best Jan, as she preferred). He turned around and caught sight of her. Her knees went to jelly.

'Hot,' sang Lydia behind her, under her breath.

'Right, miss,' said Aidan. 'Time to become a Mrs.'

'I told you, Dad, I'm going to be a Ms,' said Charlie.

He kissed the side of her head. 'That's my girl. Well, I'm still giving my daughter away.'

'You've got another one,' Charlie said.

'I'm never getting married,' said Casey stoutly, from behind them. She'd been bribed into wearing her bridesmaid's dress with an all-expenses-paid weekend trip to a dark skies site in Northumberland.

'Yeah, yeah,' said Charlie. She took a deep breath and, in her head, listened for Jools again. She'd continued talking to her big sister, quietly and occasionally, and it never felt childish. But Jools was quiet right now. That was OK. She'd be there when she needed her.

She folded her arm into Aidan's. 'Right, Dad, let's do this.'

'Yes, sweetheart,' Aidan said, before turning his head to the bridesmaids. 'Off we go then, ladies.'

'Hey,' she said, at the other end of the café.

'Hello,' Gábriel said, and smiled.

These days, they weren't colleagues. At the end of last summer, Gábriel had got in touch with Will to ask if he might still work for him. Now, if you went to the corner of a road almost exactly equidistant between Clapham Junction and Battersea, you would find a butcher's shop selling meats from Will's expanded North York Moors farm and, underneath the Black Sheep Foods sign in smaller, grey-painted lettering, Gábriel's name.

In the café, words were said, and blurred together with the sound of a sheep or two, baa-ing.

'Charlene Badb Catha Hughes,' said the registrar, pronouncing the Irish incorrectly.

Aidan corrected her. 'It means "battle crow",' he announced proudly to the entire room.

Joe, Charity and Badiha snickered behind their hands.

'Shut it,' said Charlie serenely, not turning round. 'I can still fire all of you.'

The registrar didn't blink. 'Do you take Gábriel Büki to be your lawfully wedded husband?'

Charlie looked over at him. 'I do,' she said. 'I absolutely do.'

At the end of the short ceremony, Charlie and Gábriel walked out to Whitney Houston's 'My Love Is Your Love', remixed by Joe at his begging request. As Whitney's lines were broken up, the beats filling the spaces, Charlie and Gábriel reached the doorway to the café and stopped dead.

All the animals were out of their shelters, snuffling by the gates or chewing resolutely. Every single one had a large pink bow around its neck.

Two of the sheep were loitering outside the gate on the cobbles with pink love-hearts sprayed on their sides.

Gábriel was laughing quietly, his hand at the small of Charlie's back.

'Ta *daaaa*,' said Lydia, her arms outspread. There was a splodge of pink on her bridesmaid's dress.

'What have you done to them?' Charlie said.

'They're due for a shear soon anyway, seeing as it's so goddamned hot,' said Lydia. 'I'm in charge, so if I want to decorate my animals, then I bloody well will.'

Everyone cheered, and Lydia did a fabulously awful curtsey.

'Happy wedding day,' Charlie said to Gábriel.

He lifted her hand, and kissed it.

Author's Note

Ruskin Park Farm is fictional, though the park is real and the site perfect for it (I designed a map and everything)! It does have a beautiful community garden. There are, however, countless city farms over inner and outer London, as well as elsewhere in the UK, all doing vital community and educational work. I was particularly influenced by Surrey Docks Farm, Vauxhall City Farm and Stepping Stones Farm in Stepney.

Eleven piglets really were stolen one night from Surrey Docks Farm in September 2018, just a few days after I had seen them; extremely sadly, they were never recovered.

SW9 Stables is directly inspired by Ebony Horse Club in Loughborough Junction, South London.

The Lambeth Country Show is a legendary summer event in Brockwell Park. From the summer of 2018, Lambeth Council started, without consultation, controversially erecting two-metre-high perimeter fences, body searches and a ban on alcohol being brought in; this was seen by some community groups as a radical change to the spirit of the free family weekend.

The Brixton Pound is a real local currency, started in response to the 2008 global financial crisis. Its lovely pay-what-you-can café, using only surplus food, opened in the summer of 2016; naturally, it was scuppered by too-expensive rents and closed in 2019. Please think about supporting the places that work hard to give back to the community – they need your love to share the love!

You can also support your nearest city/community farm by visiting it, volunteering or making a donation. You might also like to donate to: Friends of Ruskin Park, Right2Roam, and Land In Our Names (a grassroots collective reconnecting black communities with land in Britain).

Acknowledgments

My thanks first and foremost go to Heidi S, for reading the first draft's chapters as they came, Dickens-style, and for her encouragement and many awesome thoughts as we went along. To Thomas Hardy, err, obviously, and to the AirBnB cottage in Scotland, which had a dog-eared 1960s Penguin copy of Far from The Madding Crowd; I devoured it while there and then, um, stole it clean away. Needless to say, the copy has completely fallen to pieces now. Hmm, I really owe them a new copy. I also really recommend the audiobook version of *FftMC* read by Jamie Parker, who does a stellar job of making all the characters live and breathe and stink of slightly-rotting hay. And to David Nicholls, for his subtly modernising treatment of the text for the 2015 film adaptation, which showed me a thing or two.

To Jessica, my agent, for belief and openness. One More Chapter's Jennie Rothwell, Charlotte Ledger, and Bethan Morgan for steering this book patiently away from Victorian social values and dodgy ideas about womens' fickleness! Helen Gould of Salt and Sage Books for a valuable and instructive sensitivity edit.

To Michelle Frank of Vauxhall City Farm, for kindly and expertly reading over this and responding with such warmth. Gábor, for all the Hungarian help, for pointing me towards amusingly long-haired sheepdogs and for an Animal Farm-related eureka moment. Daniella, for some vital comments on an earlier draft, and Simon for the same. To Ruth I, for Lydia and Charlie's cottage inspiration (this cottage really exists, FACT).

To South London!

To my husband, for being my sounding-board when needing cool things about Berlin, and sniggering appropriately when I read him the odd line, and for everything, always.

If you're not a ten on Sophie's spreadsheet, you're never getting her between the bedsheets…

No aspect of Sophie's life goes unrecorded in her Excel spreadsheets, so when she accidentally sends it to her entire contact list instead of just her best friend, Sophie has a lot of uncomfortable explaining to do.

First on the list? Dr Michael Adams. After a disastrous first date, Michael scored a '3' on Sophie's 'love life' tab, but when she shows up to apologise for sharing his result with the world, he issues an unexpected challenge: ten dates to prove that love can't be calculated by an equation or contained by boxes on a spreadsheet.

Available in paperback and ebook!

A laugh out loud witchy romcom!

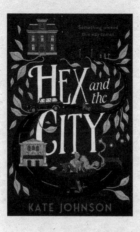

Things you should know about Poppy:

1. She's a witch

2. She has magical hair like Rapunzel from *Tangled*

3. She lives with Iris, the head of her coven, in a beautiful, ramshackle house next to Highgate cemetery

4. She works at Hubble Bubble, a magic shop in Covent Garden. Though none of it is real magic as that would be highly irresponsible. Until…

…Poppy accidentally sells gorgeous celebrity magician Axl Storm, all six-foot-four of him, a cursed pendant.

Available in paperback and ebook!

ONE MORE CHAPTER

The author and One More Chapter would like to thank everyone
who contributed to the publication of this story…

Analytics
Emma Harvey
Maria Osa

Audio
Fionnuala Barrett
Ciara Briggs

Contracts
Georgina Hoffman
Florence Shepherd

Design
Lucy Bennett
Fiona Greenway
Ana Hard
Holly Macdonald
Liane Payne
Dean Russell

Digital Sales
Laura Daley
Michael Davies
Georgina Ugen

Editorial
Laura Gerrard
Arsalan Isa
Charlotte Ledger
Lydia Mason
Jennie Rothwell
Salt & Sage Books
Kimberley Young

International Sales
Bethan Moore

Marketing & Publicity
Chloe Cummings
Emma Petfield

Operations
Melissa Okusanya
Hannah Stamp

Production
Emily Chan
Denis Manson
Francesca Tuzzeo

Rights
Lana Beckwith
Rachel McCarron
Agnes Rigou
Hany Sheikh
Mohamed
Zoe Shine
Aisling Smyth

**The HarperCollins
Distribution Team**

**The HarperCollins
Finance & Royalties
Team**

**The HarperCollins
Legal Team**

**The HarperCollins
Technology Team**

Trade Marketing
Ben Hurd

UK Sales
Yazmeen Akhtar
Laura Carpenter
Isabel Coburn
Jay Cochrane
Alice Gomer
Gemma Rayner
Erin White
Harriet Williams
Leah Woods

**And every other
essential link in the
chain from delivery
drivers to booksellers
to librarians and
beyond!**

YOUR NUMBER ONE STOP

ONE MORE CHAPTER

FOR PAGETURNING BOOKS

One More Chapter is an
award-winning global
division of HarperCollins.

Sign up to our newsletter to get our
latest eBook deals and stay up to date
with our weekly Book Club!
<u>Subscribe here.</u>

Meet the team at
<u>www.onemorechapter.com</u>

Follow us!
@OneMoreChapter_
@OneMoreChapter
@onemorechapterhc

Do you write unputdownable fiction?
We love to hear from new voices.
Find out how to submit your novel at
<u>www.onemorechapter.com/submissions</u>